Beyond Olympus

Gary L. Gibbs

AuthorHouse™
1663 Liberty Drive, Suite 200
Bloomington, IN 47403
www.authorhouse.com
Phone: 1-800-839-8640

© 2009 Gary L. Gibbs. All rights reserved.

No part of this book may be reproduced, stored in a retrieval system, or transmitted by any means without the written permission of the author.

First published by AuthorHouse   3/26/2009

ISBN: 978-1-4389-6162-0 (sc)
ISBN: 978-1-4389-6163-7 (hc)

Printed in the United States of America
Bloomington, Indiana

This book is printed on acid-free paper.

FOREWARD
THE CYPHER

He grasped the precious metal object that hung on the chain around his neck. He traced its odd shape with his thumb and forefinger and felt its warmth, warmth absorbed from his body as well as from that of the midday sun. He wasn't really sure of its true purpose or from whence it came. Nor did he know who had made it, or how it was made. There were only the tales, passed on by the old ones, Council Elders such as his grandmother, stories told and retold (and perhaps each time embellished) at the great council fires of his people.

    He did, however, know its name…the Cypher. Once, according to the legends, there had been twelve Cyphers, all of which had been possessed by his Clan. One by one, over the span of many years, the others had been lost; carried off the boldest and the bravest of his people, each on a quest, none to ever return. Now, he possessed the last Cypher; now he was the final hope. And now he too had embarked on the great quest, the quest to return the Cypher to its fabled home, in order to unlock the secret of his people's past, and in so doing, to perhaps return them their former greatness…

The Journey

The first hint of sunrise had just broken through an opening in the dense forest canopy; it was time for the young traveler to interrupt his journey once more. First, he found a good secluded spot to make camp. This day it would be under a huge old oak near a small stream. He dropped his cloak, belt and gear under one of the ancient tree's large low hanging limbs. He pulled a few meager provisions from his knapsack and placed them on his cloak. Next, he climbed high up into the oak and tied his knapsack to one of its upper branches, out of the reach of any predators. Finally, carrying only his lance for protection, he went to the stream to wash himself and refill his canteen.

    The weary youth intended to quickly clean up, eat his humble breakfast and curl up in his cloak. He hoped to sleep for most of the day, as he had trekked all through the night. (As dangerous as it was to travel through an unknown forest in the darkness, it was even more perilous to travel by day in the lands of the Zealots.)

    The morning appeared crisp and clear as more of the sun's first light began to penetrate the dense foliage. Planting the point of his lance down into the stream's sandy bank, he knelt down beside it. He looked at his reflection in a calm part of the stream. *You're looking just a bit worse for wear every day*, he thought to himself. It was the seventeenth dawn of the young man's journey.

The young man rinsed his face, and then caught a reflection of movement on the far side of the stream. He looked up into the clear blue eyes of an enormous gray she-wolf, who immediately showed her fangs and began to snarl. She had materialized on the other side of the stream, not five paces away. As the fur around her neck stood up, the young man felt the hair at the base of his neck stand up, as well. Instinctively, his hand reached for the lance. As he touched it, the beast's snarls instantly became even more ferocious.

Suddenly, one of his uncle's old lessons leapt into his mind, *"Wolves hunt in packs, lad, and they do it right well. Don't fear the wolves you see, near as much as the ones you don't."*

He turned his head just in time to see a blur springing at him from behind. In one quick motion, he rose, turned and spun his lance around. He thrust it into the chest of the dark gray wolf just as the animal leaped, pushing the young man into the stream. One yelp and the wolf collapsed on the bank. Without hesitation, he yanked the lance from the great beast's chest and spun again, as he heard the first wolf splash into the stream. He didn't have time to bring the lance around to stab the she-wolf, but he was just able to leap aside and slash her snout. She yelped and backed off, shaking her head violently and pawing her nose with a foreleg as if she were trying to scrape something off of it.

The young man now turned again to face three more growling wolves that had moved in behind the first dead beast, and were now threatening to surround him. He looked around desperately for a better position from which to defend himself. He knew that if all three attacked at the same time, he was finished. He also knew that if he tried to run, it would trigger just such an attack.

Ankle deep, the stream was much too shallow and narrow to afford any protection, but he noticed that just twenty or so paces downstream it was somewhat wider and deeper. Swinging his lance madly back and forth in front of the wolves, he began slowly moving backward downstream. He was now almost surrounded by the four wolves, as the first she wolf had recovered enough from her injury to resume the hunt.

With one of its members dead and another injured, the pack had become more wary of the business end of his lance. The three, one big male and two adolescents, followed him on one bank and the female trailed him on the other, but they didn't attempt to charge him. Gradually, too gradually, the stream widened and deepened. Finally, the stream was almost knee deep and perhaps ten paces across. He felt nervous, clumsily wading in such deep water surrounded by a wolf pack, but he knew that any wolf foolish enough to plunge in after him would be completely helpless. The predators seemed to realize the same thing, for although they growled at him and showed him their fangs, they stayed out of the water.

Presently, he noticed a large, rather flat boulder in the middle of the stream that jutted about a foot above the surface. At this spot, the water was almost waist deep. His teeth were chattering and he was shivering, from fear as much as the cold water. His heart was still pounding. The rock was large enough to sit on, almost large enough to spread out on. He pulled himself out of the water, keeping a wary eye on his stalkers.

As he curled up on the rock, the wolves seemed to take the cue and laid down panting on both banks. *Wonderful...* he thought to himself, *they are just going to wait me out.* Nonetheless, the young man was exhausted. He had been hiking all night and his fight with the wolf pack had just about used up all of his remaining reserves. He curled up on the rock, cradling his lance and laid his head down, with one wary eye on the wolves. Blessedly, the morning sun broke through between two pine trees and its bright light warmed him. *I'll just rest a few minutes,* he thought to himself...

* * *

With a start, the youth woke up and rose to a sitting position. *Stupid! Stupid!* He thought to himself as he looked all around. He didn't know if he had been asleep for a moment or an hour, but he did know that he had instantly fallen into a deep and very vulnerable sleep. There was no sign of the wolves, however. It was as if they had been part of a dream... or perhaps a nightmare.

So the question was...now what? Could he just backtrack and get his gear? Or were the wolves clever enough to be waiting in hiding to ambush him? His instincts told him that they were gone, but he wasn't sure if he was ready to bet his life on his instincts, just yet.

The young traveler decided to wade carefully back upstream for his gear, watching carefully for any signs of the pack. He would then quickly grab his knapsack, weapons and cloak and dash back to the stream. From there he could make his way a few miles downstream so that, hopefully, the wolves would lose his trail, if they were indeed still stalking him.

The plan worked, although after several more hours of wading downstream, he was even more exhausted. It would be mid-afternoon before the young man felt confident enough to stop and make camp again. Finally, exhausted, he was able to sleep....

* * *

Darkness was now falling, so it was almost time to rise once again to resume his journey. The young traveler's name was Valerian.

Valerian was a lean, fair-skinned young man, browned dark by the sun. He was clean-shaven, and wore his long light-brown hair in a loose knot tied at the back of his head by a leather thong, along with a wide leather strap tied across his forehead. He wore a simple gray-green tunic that fell to just above his knees and deerskin boots that were tied just above his calves. A wide leather band was fastened around his left forearm. The young traveler only wore one piece of jewelry, a silver chain around his neck from which hung a small intricately made device.

Now, after stretching for a moment and taking his bearings, he hesitated, deciding that he should wait just a little longer, until complete darkness had descended, before continuing his journey. For several minutes, he stood perfectly still and listened intently into the gathering darkness. He heard bird calls in the distance and off to his left, the sound of some small creature shuffling through the tall grass. But he heard nothing that could be construed as man-sounds...or wolf sounds, for that matter.

Satisfied that he was truly alone, he sat back down. He then reached into his knapsack and tore off a small piece of the precious dried venison he carried. He knew that tomorrow he needed to begin hunting small game so that he could save the dried meat for a time when game might become scarce. He chased the dried meat with a swallow of water from his leather flask. He then pulled out another one of the hardened corncakes that his grandmother had packed for him. As he nibbled on it, he reflected on how he had come to this place.

* * *

Three months earlier, in the dead of winter, Valerian had approached his grandmother in her small cottage with his proposal. They had both warmed themselves in front of the small stone fireplace as he had revealed his plan to her. And as the cold night wore on, the old woman's initial skepticism had gradually faded. She had always known that the young man sitting next to her was special, now she believed that she had a vision of what his true destiny might be. He just might be the one to solve the riddle of the Cypher. She would appeal to the other Elders for a special meeting of the Council in the next few days.

It was said that if a Cypher could be returned to Elympias, the legendary city of their ancestors, the secrets of their mighty forebears might be revealed. It was said that the ancient and long abandoned city held secrets that could give them unimaginable power and enlightenment. The city itself could give them knowledge of weapons to protect themselves from all danger, techniques for growing food so that they would never again know hunger, methods of preventing or curing all manner of illnesses. Legend had it that the city could provide his people with unlimited warmth and light; some stories even said that the city could teach them the secret of flight!

Valerian doubted the veracity of these old tales, as did most of the young men and women he had grown up with. Over untold generations the legends had been transmitted by word of mouth, by the Elders around the Council fires, or by countless mothers and fathers to their children at bedtime. Who could know now how much was true and how much was fantasy?

Certainly, there must be some truth to the legends, since so much evidence of an earlier civilization still remained: pieces of machinery whose purpose had been lost over time, wide roads largely overgrown and that now often went nowhere, the crumbling remains of towns and great cities that were said to now only harbor filth, disease and scavengers.

Then there were the books left behind by the Ancients. Every town had them. Most were in advanced states of decay; a precious few were still in fairly good condition. Some only contained mysterious writings that could no longer be deciphered, others also contained pictures. How much of what was pictured in these books was real and how much was the fanciful imaginings of the Ancient authors no one knew, although many scholars and Spiritual Elders loved to endlessly debate and speculate over these possibilities.

Certainly, however, all agreed that some great race of people had existed in the dim past and had fallen for reasons only hinted at in the legends. Perhaps it was greed, perhaps selfishness, perhaps arrogance. Who would ever know?

So, over the span of many years, his people had tried to return each one of the original twelve sacred Cyphers to its home. Over many generations, the Elympian Clan had sometimes dispatched small bands of warriors on their swiftest horses to try to outrun the enemies that surrounded them. Sometimes large and powerful war parties were gathered to attempt to fight their way through with brute force.

During Valerian's lifetime, only two Cyphers had been left. When Valerian was just a small boy, a charismatic leader named Tobias had taken up one of the two. From each of the Clan's six townships, Tobias had recruited what, it was said, was the most powerful war party ever assembled for a Cypher quest. Altogether, he would have over one thousand well-armed and well-provisioned men and women. Tobias was a great leader, and his followers were inspired; nothing would stop them. The feasts lasted for days as the preparations were made.

Then, on a fine spring day, with great fanfare, the war party mounted their horses and made leave. As they left Aurora, the Elympian capital and the Elympian's largest town, the children chased after them and the women sang one of the old farewell songs. They were never seen or heard from again.

That was the worst year in Valerian's memory. With the best hunters and warriors gone, food was scarce, and everyone was worried whether their Clan could protect itself in the event of a major attack from one or more of their enemies. To make matters worse, the year was dry and that season's corn crop was meager. But no serious attacks came, and in succeeding years, the boys who had been too young to hunt or fight grew to take the place of those who had vanished. But now there was only one Cypher left; one final chance remained.

* * *

It was almost totally dark now. There would only be a slim crescent moon and a sea of stars to guide him, so the young wayfarer would have to proceed with caution. A sprained ankle, or worse, a snakebite, could hamper or even ruin his plans. But he had excellent night vision, and the darkness would make him nearly invisible.

As Valerian rose again, he pulled his cloak back over his shoulders and tied it at his neck. He arranged the strap of his knapsack over his neck and left shoulder. Over his right shoulder, he slung his bow and quiver. Finally, he picked up his lance and sheathed the long hunting knife and hand axe on either side of his wide leather belt.

The air was getting a bit chilly, so the young woodsman pulled the hood of his cloak over his head. Setting off, he would follow the stream as long as it led him in generally the right direction.

Valerian followed the stream for most of the night, as it had accommodated him by keeping to a generally southeasterly direction. Towards dawn, however, the brook had taken a sharp turn to the right, almost due south by the young man's reckoning. So, grudgingly, the young man took a long last drink of its clear waters, refilled his canteen, and silently said goodbye to the pleasant murmuring that had kept him company through the night.

Striking out into the depths of the forest, he soon came across a deer trail that seemed to be going in the right direction. Another hour's hike along the trail and the darkness began to give way to the grayness of predawn. The forest had thinned into hilly meadows and copses of aspen and cottonwoods. It was time to find a place to make camp.

Selecting a thick stand of timber and brush to his left, Valerian made his way into it. Just as dawn broke, he laid his cloak and other gear in a secluded spot surrounded by underbrush. He hung his knapsack in a nearby cottonwood, out of sight. Returning to where his cloak lay, he took a long look around. The first rays of the rose morning light were just breaking above the distant mountains to the east. Seeing and hearing nothing of concern, he removed his belt. He took a last long drink of water from his flask and curled up between the layers of his cloak. As he waited for sleep to overtake him, he thought back to the events that had set him on this lonely course…

2

The Council of Elders

So it was that, shortly after his nineteenth birthday, Valerian, of the small township of Antares, had proposed to the Council of Elders that he should be the one to finally bring the last Cypher to its home. On that day he had stood in the great Assembly Hall before the thirteen citizens that made up the governing body of his people. The Elders were seated in their high-backed chairs arranged in a semi-circle around him. His grandmother, Elanor, one of the most senior of the Elders, was seated to his right. (Without her as a sponsor, he knew that it would have taken months to be granted such an audience.)

"And what in the name of our ancestors makes you think that you can accomplish such a feat?" asked Alera, the tall, graceful Council Tribune, who was first amongst equals on the Council. "You're not a noted warrior or leader; you're too young and inexperienced to be either. How do you propose to succeed where so many great men have failed?"

Before he could answer, his grandmother had spoken on his behalf, "It's true that he's not recognized as a great man, *as yet*. But I submit that he has the seeds of greatness in him." That brought smiles from some of the other Elders, the old woman had noticed. She pressed on, anyway.

"I know what you're thinking…maternal pride. It's true, I raised him and I couldn't be more proud of him. But he *is* special! Some of you may remember that Valerian passed the first trial of citizenship when he was only eight years old. Few children even attempt to take it before they are twelve!"

Several members nodded at this; Valerian had indeed been something of a prodigy. He had, in fact passed all three tests by the age of fifteen; no one in memory had ever accomplished such a feat. In fact, few passed the three Trials before their twenty-first year. Some never did, and could therefore not participate in the Clan as full citizens. They couldn't vote, or own property, or stand as Guardsmen, Leaders or Council Elders. So the Council heard the young man out.

"I propose to go alone and afoot. Stealth and guile, rather than strength or weapons will serve to protect me. I will live off of the land, travel at night, and avoid contact with any people. I will stay off of the roads, keeping to the forests and hills. I will give towns or villages that I may encounter a wide berth. I will not fight unless I'm cornered… and I don't intend to be cornered."

The young man continued, "It's true I'm not a proven warrior, but everyone knows that I'm one of the best woodsmen and hunters in the Clan. I know how to live off of the land, how to travel silently, how to make a fire with hardly a trace of smoke, how to navigate by either the sun or the stars. In the Challenges, I have won every long distance race that I have entered; I can trot all day with a mouthful of water, if need be."

"And how do you propose to actually find Elympias?" Duryn, a tall, distinguished Elder asked, with a faint air of skepticism. "Would you just keep heading southeast and hope for the best?"

"The tales give some clues where to look. Elympias is supposed to be located between two lakes in a large valley. This valley is supposed to be on the other side of a great mountain range with snow tipped mountains. It was said that our ancestors traveled northwest for some four months before they finally reached the Great Western Sea and safety," the young man explained, then continued with a smile, "So my plan is simple. I will head southeast for about two to three months, since I believe that I can travel much faster than a band of hungry and exhausted men, women and children. When I encounter a high range of mountains, I will cross it and look for a valley with twin lakes. If I find such a place, I will begin my search in earnest for the city."

"A simple plan, indeed, and hardly an original one...without a vast amount of luck, you might be searching for Elympias for years with such a plan," commented Julian, a small, wiry Elder with piercing blue eyes.

"I don't deny that I'll need luck, but what plan wouldn't?" replied Valerian. "And I'm young enough; I've got the years to spare." Some of the Council members chuckled at that.

"However, I'm also hoping that I will encounter Caravans in the east that can provide me with clues to the location of Elympias."

Caravans made up of members of the Trade Guild crisscrossed the known world. They were the only peoples who could cross the territories of the various warring Clans with impunity. The Trademaster's white tunic, marked with a red handprint on its chest, guaranteed not only safe passage, but also the protection of each and every Clan.

Such protection was assured because each Caravan brought two precious commodities that could be had in no other way: The first commodity was trade goods, cloth from some Clans who specialized in weaving, pottery or furniture from others who had expertise in those crafts. Then there were foods, canned goods, spices, dried fruit and sometimes even fresh fruit and vegetables. And always the tools and strange devices scavenged from the cities and towns of the Ancients.

The second commodity was news of the world. With direct commerce or communications cut off due to the constant state of warfare between the Clans, only the Tradesmen could provide a small window to the outside world. Granted that their view was often sketchy and unreliable, but it was still precious because it could be acquired in no other way.

So it was that the great wagons of a Caravan would pull into the outskirts of a town and set up camp. The townspeople would rush out to greet the Trademasters, anxious not only to see what the traders possessed, but also to hear what they knew. And so it was that within the circle of the Trademasters' wagons great bonfires would be lit. And around the bonfires there would be feasting, and bargaining, and the telling of tales.

"The territory of the Zealots is directly to our east and south. Do you really believe that you can cross right through their lands?" This time it was Vanya who spoke.

Vanya was the youngest of the Elders, a fair-skinned and diminutive woman who was noted for her compassion as well as her thoughtfulness. She gave a small shudder as she asked the question, because the Zealots were the most feared of all the Clans. They were a fanatical, brutal and filthy people, who in battle were absolutely relentless. The Zealots had attacked their people in force countless times and had almost overwhelmed them on more than one occasion. Only the Elympian Clan's superior military leadership and organization had saved them.

"I really wouldn't have a choice. If I tried to circle around them to the north I would have to go hundreds of miles out of the way. Worse than that, I would have to pass through the lands of the Northern Alliance, who are known to be far better woodsmen and trackers than the Zealots, so I'd stand a much greater chance of getting caught." Several Elders nodded at this.

The young man continued, "On the other hand, heading due south would take me through the wastelands. There are only small bands of scavengers in that direction, but the likelihood of getting lost and dying of hunger and thirst is almost certain."

More nods of agreement, now, Mathius spoke up. Mathius was a large, heavyset black man with a thick beard and a deep voice.

"I believe that what we have here is more a question of ability, destiny if you will, rather than simple strategy. It would take a truly exceptional individual to succeed where all others have failed. The question really comes down to this…could Valerian actually be the one?"

"Therefore, I propose that we fashion a challenge to determine just how capable of such a feat our young friend might be," he continued. "Does anyone have suggestions?"

At that point, the Tribune Alera broke in, "An intriguing proposal, Mathius. If you will excuse us Valerian, let us discuss this issue amongst ourselves for a few moments. Please wait for us in the anteroom, and we'll recall you shortly."

Valerian nodded, turned and exited through the huge carved wooden door that served as the entrance to the Great Hall. He sat down on one of the ornate chairs in the anteroom, and immediately began to speculate over what sort of test the Council could conceivably devise to determine whether he was "the one".

* * *

Alera spoke as soon as the young man had exited the Council chambers, "Mathius, even if we can fashion such a challenge, would it be either wise or prudent to consider entrusting the last Cypher to any single person, particularly to a young man largely untested by life or experience?"

"But Valerian has been tested, severely tested, in the Trials, and he excelled to a greater degree than anyone in living memory. And are not the Trials devised to mimic as closely as possible the actual trials and tribulations that one experiences in life?" Mathius responded.

The Elder continued, "Hear my thoughts, Council. Everyone here can still remember the disastrous aftermath of the quest led by Tobias. With Tobias, we lost the flower of an entire Elympian generation. Those of us left behind nearly starved, and for years to come, we were terribly vulnerable to the Zealots and their allies, after the loss of so many good men and women. Our people have had to endure these quests for generation after generation, quests that denude us of our greatest leaders and best young men and women. And what do we have to show for it?"

Alera looked thoughtful for a moment. "Yes, Mathius, and of late, it is said that the young men in the marketplace are already talking about organizing yet another quest, a quest even greater than the one that Tobias led."

Vanya now spoke, "But that would be a disastrous waste of our young people! We must not allow such a thing to happen!"

Elanor responded, "Yes, but how do we stop them? We are, after all, a democracy; all women and men are free to do as they wish...including my grandson."

Mathius now spoke again, "Precisely. That is why it just might make sense for the last Cypher to be taken up by just one of Elympias's finest citizens."

Or perhaps two of them, Elanor was thinking of Sebastian, her only remaining son and Valerian's uncle, but said nothing.

Alera now spoke, "Very well. Let us vote on Mathius's proposal. Those who wish to vote 'aye', please raise your hands."

The vote was unanimously in favor.

Alera smiled. "Perhaps it is a just and proper fate for our People that the last chance for us to rediscover our past is in the hands of a single youth, a young man who perhaps best personifies our hope for the future."

Mathis spoke once again, "Now that that's settled, I also have a proposal for Valerian's challenge..."

* * *

After what seemed like an interminable length of time, the large oaken door had creaked open. A ceremonial Guardsman motioned Valerian back into the Council Chamber. Council Tribune Alera motioned for Valerian to be seated.

"One week from now, Valerian, your test will begin. Pass it and the last Cypher will be entrusted to you. Failure will in no way mean dishonor, however, because passing the test will require unexcelled courage and skill."

Alera seemed to pause for dramatic effect and then continued, "The test is simple, really. All you must do is to make your way from Antares, your home village, and back to the town square at Aurora. Within thirty days, you must travel the twenty kilometers from your home to our town square and ring the Great Bell in the square three times."

Valerian looked at the Council in some confusion. Why this was no test at all! He could make it from Antares to the capital in one day, blindfolded! There must a catch.

That became apparent as the Tribune continued, "However, between the walls of your village and our city will be deployed our best Rangers. Our own Council Guardsmen will be stationed all around the city and around the bell itself for the entire thirty days. If they capture you before you ring the bell, you fail the test. There are really no other rules to the challenge.

"You may leave your town whenever you wish and take as much time as you wish, as long as it's no more than thirty days from next Monday. However, once the challenge begins and you've left the protection of your town's walls, you become fair game. Young Valerian...do you accept this challenge?"

Now he understood. This would indeed be the ultimate challenge. The Rangers were incredible woodsmen and trackers. The elite Guardsmen were selected for their intelligence, courage and martial skills. Getting past both groups would be close to impossible.

Valerian simply stood up at attention, bowed and replied, "Council, I accept the challenge. I'll do my absolute best."

"Then you are excused, young man. Best of luck to you..." Alera responded with a smile, laying a hand on his shoulder.

The young man bowed again, turned and left the way he had come in...

3

The Challenge

The youth was running through the dense, darkened forest as if he were running for his life. As he ran, he tried to shield his face with his hands from the tree limbs and shrubs that tore at his tunic and boots. He didn't mind the stings from the branches; he just didn't want to be blinded by them. His main concern, however, was the noise that the foliage made as he ripped through it. He tried to minimize the sound of his passage through the underbrush as he had been taught, but it was too dark and he was forced to move too quickly to eliminate the noise altogether.

Occasionally, he would stop for a few precious seconds to listen for the faint sounds of his pursuers. Inevitably, he would hear the footsteps and whispers that assured him that they were still on his trail. In spite of the fact that he was well aware of the tracking skills of the Rangers, he was still amazed (and distressed) by their ability to track him on the run in almost total darkness. If anything, they seemed to actually be gaining on him!

Valerian despaired as he ran. He had thought that he had prepared well for this challenge. He had waited for a moonless, windy night before leaving his home village. He had left well after midnight and struck out in a direction almost directly opposite that from his destination, Aurora, in the hope of circling around any possible scouts. He had moved silently and swiftly through the meadows and paddocks that bordered his town, using low-lying terrain and underbrush as cover wherever possible.

Yet within an hour of leaving Antares, he had run headlong into a mounted Ranger scouting party. He and the scouts had spotted each other simultaneously. They were perhaps a hundred paces to his right. His only good fortune was that the edge of the Northern Forest was just fifty paces to his left. He had broken and run for the forest just as the Rangers shouted and spurred their mounts for him. Swiftly as he ran, the young man managed to plunge into a thicket just thirty paces ahead of his pursuers. Fortunately, as the underbrush was too thick for the horses, the scouts were forced to dismount to continue their pursuit.

Valerian knew now that he was heading for a series of deep ravines and steep hills that he might be able to use to throw off his trackers. The good news was that he knew this area of the forest like the back of his hand. The bad news was that the Rangers probably knew it almost as well. The chase seemed interminable with the young man slowly but steadily losing ground.

Suddenly, just as he plunged through a stand of tall grass in a gully, he almost stumbled into the arms of a big man who seemed to be just standing there waiting for him. The man grabbed him with two powerful arms and dropped to his knees, pulling Valerian down with him.

The young man began to struggle when his captor whispered urgently in his ear, "Shush lad!"

"Uncle!!!" Valerian whispered back in the shock of recognition. It was his Uncle Sebastian, other than his grandmother, his only surviving relative.

"Follow me, Nephew," Sebastian whispered as he rose and took off at a run.

Valerian fell in behind his uncle and quickly found himself hard pressed to keep up, although the man ahead of him was his elder by over thirty winters. The older man seemed to be taking delight in taking the worst possible course, up and back down the steepest cliffs, through the densest thickets of brambles, back and forth again and again through a waist deep stream. Their path seemed maddeningly irrational. Over and over, they reversed course, many times covering the same ground. On and on they went until Valerian, totally exhausted, was completely lost and disoriented in a forest that he had played and hunted in since he was small boy.

Finally, after what had seemed like an eternity, the older man had stopped at the crest of a small hill and dropped behind the trunk of a fallen tree. Valerian had fallen in a heap beside his uncle, gasping to try to catch his breath.

"Quiet now, lad. Let's see if we've lost 'em," his uncle whispered under his breath.

For a long while, neither moved nor made a sound as they listened for any faint sounds of pursuit. None could be heard and after some time even his uncle seemed satisfied.

"We'll rest here 'til dawn," the man of the forest said, then simply rolled over behind the log, pulled his cloak over his legs, and fell asleep without another word. (Though Valerian knew well enough that the slightest noise would awaken the older man in an instant.)

Valerian was exhausted. He piled some dead leaves for a pillow, lay down and pulled his own cloak over himself. In a few moments, he too fell into a deep sleep. He did not wake until the first light of dawn. He sat up with a start, and then shivered in the morning chill. Looking around, he saw his uncle at the base of the hill, sitting next to a small stream. He had a small, nearly smokeless fire lit and was sipping tea from a small tin cup. Valerian walked down the hill to join his uncle.

"Wash yo'r face and rinse y'or mouth out, lad, and I'll give you some tea."

The young man did as he was told. The water from the mountain stream was clear and cold on his face. He rinsed his mouth and his uncle handed him the cup refilled with hot tea. The last dregs of sleep cleared away with the first swallow of the hot, slightly bitter liquid. He looked at his uncle.

"Thanks for your help, Uncle. I believe that they would have had me if you hadn't showed up when you did. How did you know…?"

"Here's a corncake and a bit of jerky for your breakfast. If you had learned better what I'd taught you of the forest, you wouldn't have needed my help," the older man observed with just a hint of a smile.

Valerian smiled back at his uncle. Sebastian looked even older and more fearsome than he had just six months ago when the young man had last seen him. The woodsman's face was brown and deeply lined, his beard dark and flecked now with gray, his hair long and tied at the back of his head. The big man's buckskin tunic was worn shiny and was as weathered as his own face and hands.

Uncle Sebastian had become something of a legend over the years. He had been one of the greatest of all Ranger leaders and a hero in the great Zealot War. But the war that had made his uncle a hero had also made him a widower; the same war had also left the infant Valerian an orphan. While the war leader was winning a great victory over a force of invading Zealots in the Northern Forest, the main Zealot army had overrun their town. Sebastian's young wife Marian, his brother, (and Valerian's father) Josef, and Valerian's mother Rachel were all lost in defense of their town. Only those townspeople who had fled the village had survived. His grandmother, taking the infant Valerian into the forest, had been one of those few survivors.

Eventually, the Zealot invaders were crushed and driven out by a great Elympian army, an army that was being raised even as Antares was being sacked. Valerian, now parentless, was left to be cared for by his grandmother. Sebastian had sought refuge and solace in his beloved forest, living alone, only returning now and again to winter awhile with his mother and his young pup of a nephew. Slowly Sebastian became something of a hermit, a rather mysterious figure, respected and perhaps a bit feared by most of the townspeople.

Nonetheless, over the years, Sebastian had become the young boy's mentor, eventually his father figure. A man of few words, he would appear unannounced at his mother's cottage, stay a few days, then take the boy for weeks, or sometimes months, to learn the ways of the forest.

Valerian had learned from his uncle how to hunt and fish, how to stalk large prey and how to snare small game. He had learned which plants could be eaten, which could heal and which were poisonous. The older man had taught him how to move through the forest without being seen or heard, by man or by beast. Valerian had learned how to make a camp, and then how to take it down without leaving a trace. The old Ranger had taught the young man how to use the lance, the knife and the bow, either as tools for hunting or weapons for self-defense.

Sebastian had taught with few words, demonstrating a skill, and then letting his nephew try to imitate him. He would allow Valerian to try and try again, and when he failed, he would show the youth where he had erred. Valerian, fatherless, worshiped his uncle and eagerly tried to please him by being an exceptional student. In this, he invariably succeeded, although a grunt of satisfaction was typically the highest praise that he could expect from the older man.

However, over the years, Valerian had learned far more than woodcraft from his uncle. He had learned the patience of a hunter, the self-confidence of a man who can survive on his own. He had learned of courage and endurance. He had learned that thinking before acting could mean the difference between surviving and losing one's life...and more, much more...

Now, he was the student again, although hopefully a somewhat more advanced student. The few rules of his challenge had not excluded his obtaining help from any quarter and it was obvious that he would need all of the help that he could get to succeed.

"So, Uncle, what's the plan?" the young man asked as they erased all traces of their little camp.

"Plan? I was wonderin' just what *yo'r* plan might be, lad. After all, it's yo'r test, not mine," the old fighter replied with a grin. "I'm just here to pull yo'r coals out of the fire when your plan, whatever it may be, goes awry."

"Well, then, I suggest we head north into the deep forest where we probably won't be followed. Then we can head east for a few days before we turn south for Aurora. I think that we should take our time, take perhaps three weeks to reach the outskirts of the capitol. Perhaps by then, some of the troops guarding the town will have become a bit bored, maybe a bit careless. What do you think?"

"A lad could have a worse plan, I reckon, though I can't wait to hear how you expect to get past the guards in the town square to ring the bell."

"I'm still working on that part, Uncle."

"Well, in any case, we might as well use the next few weeks to teach you a thing or two that you haven't yet learned; things that might just keep you alive if, the heavens forbid, you actually pass this test and go on this mad adventure you've proposed."

"I thought that you had already taught me all that you could, Uncle. And do you really think that I'm crazy for proposing to be one who takes the Cypher home?"

"You young whelps always think that you already know all there is to know," the older man sighed. "Valerian, there be lessons that you just weren't ready to learn, lessons that you must now be ready to learn if you are even to survive, let alone succeed on this quest. And yes, I think that your plan is mad. But who knows, perhaps it's just mad enough to succeed."

With that they set off into the deepest forest. So it was that for the two men, the days, then weeks passed in the forest. And with each passing day, Sebastian, always before a man of few words, opened up to his young charge. The knowledge that he now wished to pass on was no longer the sort that could be demonstrated, only explained. As they made their way quietly along the narrow game trails or next to a small stream, his uncle would talk in a steady low voice that would not carry more that a few yards.

"On your journey, as the months pass, you will come to yearn desperately for companionship. Resist the urge. Avoid all towns, farms and settlements by the widest margins possible, even those that seem safe or isolated. Stay off of all roads, particularly the wide roads of the Ancients. Always take the most difficult paths, for those will be the paths least traveled. Remember, lad, always remember, that everyone must be considered an enemy."

"There is just one exception. You can trust any Tradesmen that you may encounter. They are, without fail, people of unimpeachable integrity and fairness. They will welcome you, particularly once they recognize you as an Elympian. You may trade fresh game for necessities such as tea, medicines or salt. You may also barter with them for information that may help you complete your journey."

Mile after mile, day after day, as they trudged on, Valerian eagerly absorbed every tale, every lesson, and every scrap of advice that his uncle offered. Only a few times did they encounter others: hunters on a few occasions, and once a party of Ranger scouts, perhaps searching for Valerian. But each time the encounter was at a distance and each time the danger of discovery quickly passed.

At one point as they neared their destination, Valerian expressed to his uncle an idea that had gradually taken hold with him over the last few days. "Would you consider joining me on my mad quest, uncle? Perhaps no man alive would stand a greater chance of succeeding than you, yourself."

"Nephew, I'm far too old and set in my ways to be off adventuring. Quests are for the young and the foolish, not old graybeards that should know better. Perhaps I would have considered it in my younger days…"

Valerian had fully expected the answer that he had received. Nonetheless, he had felt compelled to ask. Perhaps what he was proposing to attempt was beginning to weigh on him just a bit.

Finally, one evening, they made camp in a small, secluded spot at the edge of the forest, just a few hours march from Aurora. Both men agreed that this same night would be as good as any for Valerian to make his attempt to enter the city. The weather favored the young man this night. The sky was overcast, the wind was gusting and the showers had continued throughout the day and into the evening. It would be a cold, wet night for guard duty; even the most diligent Guardsman might be thinking more about a warm, dry bed than about catching a young upstart like himself.

"If you're patient and take care, you should be able to scale the city wall easily enough without being detected."

A rough, stone wall only three meters in height extended for several kilometers around the central part of the capitol, but it was designed for defense in a siege, not to keep out a lone intruder. Better yet, the city had sprawled well beyond the wall over the years, so that at many points a skilled infiltrator could work his way down dark alleys to within a few feet of the wall. There would be guards, but not enough to sufficiently watch the extent of the wall at all the places where it could be scaled.

"That's not the problem, however," his uncle continued. "The problem is at the town square. There will be plenty of men stationed right by the Bell, with strict orders to stay put. All the Guardsmen have to do is have the discipline to stay right by the Bell, and you cannot possibly reach it."

"Right you are, uncle, but hear my plan," and the young man explained to the elder the scheme that he had been working out in his head the last few days.

The big man laughed aloud in spite of himself. "Well, young lad, with just a bit of luck, I reckon you'll be on your way on a grand adventure in just a few days," Sebastian slapped his nephew on his back, (which almost knocked the wind out of him!)

A short while after midnight, the rain began falling even harder. It was time. Valerian bade farewell to his uncle and headed for the city. The hike was wet and cold and making his way through wet meadows and swollen streams was frustratingly slow. However, the foul weather seemed to have indeed convinced most of the normally diligent Guardsmen to stay at home. The young man entered the city without encountering a single scouting party.

On making his way into the outskirts of the city, Valerian had veered to the East Side. Here a long row of inns, taverns, and market stalls came to within a few meters of the central wall. All was quiet. It was now just a few hours before dawn and the rain had slowed to a steady drizzle. Valerian picked a particularly dark spot behind a rain barrel in an alley and hunkered down. Pulling the hood of his cloak down, he listened and watched for awhile, as his uncle had taught him. *Patience.* He saw no sign of a guard. He heard no footsteps on either the near or the far side of the wall.

Finally, Valerian made his way silently to the wall and began to search for handholds. He found a promising spot where the gaps between the blocks seemed a bit wider and hoisted himself up. He moved slowly and deliberately, not wanting to slip on the wet stones. It was easier to scale the rough wall than he had expected. As his head cleared the top of the wall, he stopped again to watch and listen. Still, he heard nothing but the drip of water off of many rooftops. *Patience.* Still, he waited a bit longer.

Valerian's patience was rewarded this time. A guard with a torch came around a corner. Valerian ducked down a bit so that he could just see the guard, with his hooded cloak pulled close around him against the wet and cold. Valerian's fingers and toes began to ache as he clung to the wall. The young man began to consider whether he should climb back down when the guard rounded another bend and disappeared around the corner of a building.

Valerian quickly pulled himself up to the top of the wall and lay flat upon it for a few more moments. Hearing nothing, he quickly and silently dropped inside the wall, and in an instant, he was huddled in the shadows of a large stone building. *So far, so good.* Selecting a particularly dark and narrow alley, the young man began to carefully make his way towards the city center.

First, however, Valerian had a very important stop to make along the way...

Presently, Valerian found himself in the shadows of a small tavern at one corner of the town square. He could plainly see the four Guardsmen standing at the Bell at the center of the Square.

The men stood at attention with their backs to the object that they were guarding, each holding a torch aloft at the four points of the compass. And indeed, each of the men was cold, wet and tired. But their shifts were at just four-hour intervals, and theirs would be over at dawn. And dawn was less than an hour away. In fact, the Guardsmen could see the first lamps already being lit around the square, as bakers and shopkeepers began their daily routines.

Suddenly, a cloaked figure darted out of a dark alley just thirty paces from the guards. One of the Guardsmen shouted a warning and pointed with his torch. The other three turned as the runner burst out of the darkness straight at them. Just before the men could grab him, the young man veered away and disappeared quickly back into the darkness. The Guard leader shouted at his men to hold their position, although the temptation to give chase was almost overwhelming.

A few moments later, another shout, as out of the darkness from another direction the cloaked figure repeated his feint. This time the figure almost came too close, as one of the guards reached out to make a grab. Still, the men held their positions as the figure retreated. Now spectators began to appear as the odd game continued.

Now ten or twelve townspeople carrying lamps began to cross to the square to see what the commotion was all about. The Guard leader shouted at them to stay back and they obeyed, staying back perhaps ten paces. But more townspeople began to straggle in as excited youths spread the word. The challenge was on!

Suddenly, the young man burst from amongst the spectators and dove into a gap between the soldiers. He came within three paces of the Bell, but in a moment the Guardsmen had him wrestled to the ground. He fought back with vigor, but his struggle was futile; any one of the big guards could have easily restrained the slender youth. The crowd closed in with a hush to see the rather ignominious end of the great challenge. The big men, relieved that they had not failed in their duty, pulled the youth to his feet …

Then…

The Bell was ringing!!! What the…? All turned to see one of the youthful spectators ringing the Bell, right under the noses of the Guardsmen.

The Guard leader shouted at the youth, "Get away from there, boy!"

Suddenly, one of the townspeople held a lamp up to the face of the prisoner. "Hey, that's not Valerian. This is Micah…Mordechi's son!"

With that, the youthful prisoner laughed, "That's right, and that's Valerian over there ringing the Bell!"

Earlier, Micah had been awakened by his old childhood friend. A mischievous prankster in his own right, he had eagerly agreed to Valerian's plan. Over the years, many had commented that the two young comrades looked so much alike that they could pass for brothers...

All of the lamps, along with the torches of the guards, turned to the youth at the Bell. Valerian had to shield his eyes from the glare. In a moment, the murmuring of the crowd became a cheer. The challenge was won! Even the Guard leader, though deeply embarrassed, extended his hand to the young man.

In the darkness of a nearby alleyway, a big man smiled to himself with satisfaction and more than little pride. He then silently turned and melted away into the shadows...

4

Prelude
March 25th, 2084

Michael Edward Vincent Ph.D. waited patiently in the anteroom of the great man's office. To bide his time, Michael observed his opulent surroundings, attempting to do so as inconspicuously as possible. The young professor felt as if he had entered Xanadu. Exquisite Persian carpets were laid over floors of Italian marble. Striking Impressionist paintings were hung on beautifully paneled walls of polished oak. Grecian urns set on marble pedestals, huge indoor trees and ferns in great stone planters were tastefully arranged here and there. If the intent was to induce awe, the effort had been imminently successful, for Michael, at least.

After awhile, to distract himself from his nervousness, he donned a VR visor from the coffee table and toured a lunar mining operation. However, he soon became disappointed with the program. He had hoped to experience the exotic vistas of the moon, but was instead taken on a tour of an automated mine deep beneath the lunar surface. He soon disengaged from the virtual reality simulation and dropped the visor back on the coffee table. Instead, he let his thoughts drift back to speculation over just what he might be doing here in the first place...

* * *

Five days earlier, the summons had arrived on his personal Uplink as he sat listening to student essays in his small cluttered office at the university. The cyber-gram had included an attached letter, along with a first-class roundtrip plane ticket and a hotel reservation. The letter was both brief and cryptic. It congratulated him on his recently published book, **Storm Warning.** Then, incredibly, it invited him to a meeting in New York with one Jonathan H. Graham III, all expenses paid. It seemed that Mr. Graham wished to discuss some of the theories expressed in his book.

The letter hinted that the meeting might lead to certain interesting opportunities for the young professor. It closed with a rather emphatic request that the meeting be kept strictly confidential. The meeting was set for Friday; the c-gram had arrived on Monday. Michael had quite simply been dumfounded. He had listened to the letter again, eventually convincing himself that it was legitimate. Only then did he send a positive reply, his head still spinning.

Considering the indisputable fact that Jonathan H. Graham III was perhaps the richest and most powerful man on the planet, a suggestion of interesting opportunities could hardly be taken lightly. Besides, this looked like a real adventure, and Michael was ready for a little adventure. The excitement of actually getting a book published six months earlier had quickly waned as the book had failed to take off in the cybermarkets. That should have hardly been a surprise. Books that combine social theory with an analysis of historical trends rarely tore up the cybershelves. Well, at least his book had perhaps attracted one admirer and a very important admirer it was, indeed.

So Michael had quickly arranged with his department for a few days off. He'd asked Charlie Farris, fellow bachelor professor and pal, to look after his apartment and take care of his roommate, a Siamese cat named Chang. Then on Thursday afternoon, he'd packed his suit bag with a few essentials, including his one decent suit. He then bid farewell to Chang and headed for the airport. Boarding the sleek DeltaStar 979 hyperjet, he had settled into his luxurious first-class seat, (riding first-class really was a first for the young associate professor). He had then donned the seat's disposable VR visor and earphones and selected a first-run virtual movie. It all still felt just a bit unreal.

After arriving at Kennedy, Michael had caught an autocab, giving the New World Trade Center Sherilton as the destination to the cab's autopilot. Along the way, he tried to make conversation with the live cabby. However, the man apparently hailed from some indeterminable third world country and barely spoke English.

So Michael just relaxed and gazed through the cab's window at the nighttime skyline of New York City, something he had previously only seen in VR. The young traveler then checked into his room and considered exploring. However, it was late and he was tired, so he just keyed in room service and turned in early. He fell asleep wondering what the next day would bring.

Just this morning, Michael had arrived at the ultramodern Global Technology Center almost an hour and a half early. That was a good thing, since he had to pass through no less than three layers of security just to reach Graham's penthouse.

A half-hour earlier, Michael had introduced himself to a very attractive but rather demure receptionist seated at the front desk. The young lady had welcomed the professor and introduced herself as Olivia, Mr. Graham's personal assistant. She had then showed him to a seat and asked him if he would like a cup of coffee or tea. Michael had declined. Olivia had then assured him that Mr. Graham would be seeing him in a few minutes and returned to her desk.

* * *

Now Michael waited for his appointment with great anticipation, tempered with no small amount of trepidation. It had occurred to the young man that Graham was precisely the sort of modern day "Robber Baron" that Michael had warned of in his book, **Storm Warning**. Graham was one of the new breed of mega-tycoons that had actually attained the status of *trillionaires*, a level of wealth undreamed of in the twentieth century.

And Graham himself was, arguably, the first amongst equals in that rarified club. He had made his fortune in communications and high technology. Some said that the man now held a virtual economic stranglehold on the CyberNet, the fifth generation super high-speed worldwide network that had become the ubiquitous backbone for virtually all communications and commerce.

Michael's appointment was scheduled for 9AM, and at precisely 9AM the elegant grandfather clock on the opposite wall struck nine times. A few seconds later, he could hear the soft warble of the executive assistant's

Uplink. Olivia answered, nodded and responded, "Yes sir, Mr. Graham." She then gracefully rose, walked over to Michael and gave him a warm smile.

The young woman gestured toward the door and said, "This way, Dr. Vincent." She then ushered him in through the grand hand-carved, oak paneled, double doors.

"Good morning Dr. Vincent. I hope you had a pleasant trip." Jonathan Graham stood in front of his desk, and walked forward to greet Michael and shake his hand.

Graham gave the younger man a solid handshake, and Michael returned it in kind. Graham seemed a bit shorter than Michael had imagined, but no less imposing. His eyes were piercing gray-blue, eyes that instantly betrayed a keen mind and a forceful personality. Michael thought that they hinted at perhaps just faint twinkle of ironic humor, as well.

The tycoon looked to be in his early sixties, with a closely cropped head of gray hair and a well-trimmed salt and pepper beard. He was dressed in a dark turtleneck shirt, an elegant sport coat and set of slacks. Altogether, he could have passed for the chancellor at an Ivy League university, or perhaps the chief administrator at a prestigious medical institute.

The older man led his guest to a pair of leather high-backed chairs facing each other next to the floor-to-ceiling glass wall that afforded a grand view of the city. He gestured Michael to one of the chairs and eased into the other.

"Would you like a cup of coffee, professor?" This time Michael accepted. Graham poured a cup for Michael and himself from the silver decanter on the small table between them.

"Well, Dr. Vincent, no doubt you're quite curious about the reason for our meeting." Michael nodded and leaned forward in anticipation.

"I suppose that one of the possibilities that you might have considered was that I had taken exception to your rather crass denunciation of myself and my contemporaries in your book."

Michael held up his hand in protest and Graham chuckled, "Don't be concerned professor; I have been skewered by the press, lambasted by my competitors and harangued by my ex-wives for over thirty-five years. In comparison, your book was positively mild in its criticisms. More to the point, truth to tell, I found it to be exceedingly perceptive."

"I suppose, by the way, you also wondered why I didn't just invite you to a VR conference. Call me old-fashioned, but I prefer to meet a man or woman in the flesh, particularly for the first time. I find it's much more revealing to take stock of a real live human being, rather than a digital simulation. Besides, I thought that you might enjoy seeing our facilities, as well as our fair city, in person."

"Quite right on both counts, Mr. Graham. Thank you for inviting me," Michael responded, "but it's also true that I'm very curious about your purpose in inviting me."

"We'll get to that in due time, professor. But first, let me give you a bit of perspective. It's a little known fact that I am, in actual fact, semi-retired. As far as the day-to-day operations of my various corporations are concerned, I'm little more than a figurehead these days. That is, of course, by choice. In the last few years, I have developed other interests; interests that are rather more far-reaching."

"Excuse me, sir, but what on earth could be more far-reaching than running the largest corporate empire in history?"

Graham smiled and leaned back in his chair, "How about changing the course of history? But I'm getting ahead of myself. Do be patient with an old man; we occasionally take a little while to get to the point."

"Dr. Vincent, Just suppose for a moment that all of the acute observations and dire warnings that you laid out in your book are little more than the faintest glimpse through 'Alice's Looking Glass'. You predicted that mega-corporations such as Graham Enterprises might eventually subvert the economic and political systems of the developed nations to their advantage. Suppose I told you that this had long since been accomplished?"

"You warned that concentrating too much wealth and power in the hands of a very few might eventually lead to a worldwide collapse of our modern technological society...might even result in a new Dark Age. Suppose I told you that we already know that such an eventuality is not only imminent, but quite possibly unavoidable? What would you think, professor?"

Michael gave the older man a perplexed look, "Quite honestly, I wouldn't know what to think Mr. Graham."

"Call me Jonathan, Michael. Of course you would...you'd think that perhaps I might be a delusional megalomaniac, if I were making such wild assertions."

Michael started to respond, but Graham smiled and cut him off, "Don't bother denying it, Michael. You are obviously a rational man. Based on what you know now, you would have every reason to think that I am crazy at this point. But what if I showed you proof...hard data? What then?"

Graham stopped to calmly sip his coffee, and then warmed up his and Michael's cups with a little more from the decanter. Picking up the cup, Michael tried to keep his hand from shaking.

What am I dealing with here? He thought to himself, *Is this test? A trick? Could Graham be serious? Or was the old man indeed just plain crazy?*

"Michael, you were certainly on the right track with your book, but you really had no idea how extensive our power had already become. In actual fact, we, along with our major competitors, for all practical purposes, control the agenda and the governments of all of the developed nations. The governments themselves are a sham, a chimera to pacify the masses, so that they have the illusion that they are controlling their own fate, rather than we. The elected governments no longer make policy; they simply administer it at our bidding."

"Graham Enterprises, along with our contemporaries, can bring the world's stock markets up or down, as we see fit, to maximize profits. We can, and have, started wars, and then stopped them when it suited our purposes. We can, and regularly do, manipulate public opinion at will. We decide who will get elected and how they will behave when they are elected. You called us the new 'Robber Barons'... 'Puppet-masters' might be a more apt description."

Graham paused again, taking a sip of coffee and giving Michael a chance to assimilate what he had just heard. Michael was well aware that Graham Enterprises was a huge and powerful corporation. But Graham had just described an organization that already possessed power an order of magnitude greater than he or anyone else had ever suspected. Michael's mind raced ahead, trying to grasp the implications.

Graham continued, "However, we weren't alone. There were, and still are, four other mega-corporations, rival economic powers, none of which were quite as powerful as Graham Enterprises, but each of which have approached our power and influence worldwide. The cyber-media, as you know, have dubbed us collectively as the 'Great Powers'. Little do they suspect just how accurate that appellation actually is."

"You know, Michael, perhaps the greatest irony is that I never set out to rule the world...I just wanted to make more money! I think that this was much the case with my colleagues. But it seemed that that the more wealth we accumulated, the more political power we could wield. And, of course, the more political power we had, the more money we could make. It seemed to be an endless upward spiral, at least for a very long time."

"But, alas, all good things truly must come to an end. Some ten or twelve years ago, our organization began to discern troubling trends. Profits began falling off on our global enterprises for reasons we could not quite grasp. We began trying to see the bigger picture. To better do so, we established the Graham Research Institute, the GRI, during this period. We have spent literally hundreds of millions of dollars in that effort."

"Mr. Graham, Jonathan, might I be so bold as to anticipate the conclusion that those hundreds of millions eventually bought you?"

Graham smiled.

"Why certainly professor, be my guest."

"It was you, wasn't it? I mean, not you personally, but all of you...the new 'Robber Barons'. Your own influence had begun to work against you, was that not so?"

"Excellent, young man, excellent. That is why I invited you; you go right to the heart of the matter. Yes, indeed, we ourselves were the problem."

"For decades, we had prevented any serious efforts to control global warming, because we refused to allow any such efforts to cut into our profits. We stymied every serious political effort to address the issue. As a result we have massive crop failures caused by chronic drought conditions in North America, Asia and Europe. We have thousands of miles of valuable coastline awash and monster hurricanes making much of the Gulf coast uninhabitable."

"We set off little brushfire wars to keep arms sale up. Unfortunately, some of them, once started, refused to be put back out. Instead, some spread to the point of disrupting global commerce."

"We manipulated the global economy to funnel virtually all new wealth into the hands of a very few...such as yours truly, allowing the standard of living of the masses to gradually decline. And we used our control of the mass media to make them not only accept their fate, but embrace it! But as their wealth was reduced, so was their purchasing power..."

"So have you begun to try to reverse the process?" Michael asked.

"Yes Michael, a few years ago, we began to quietly take steps. You are familiar, of course, with the landmark Prague Accords on Global Warming, signed by over three hundred developed nations in 2082? That was our work. How about the International Trade Organization's Initiative for Economic Equality? In truth, it was a Graham Enterprises initiative."

"However, I presume that your efforts have been too little and too late?"

"Sadly so, professor. Shortly after my sixtieth year on this troubled planet, I received a rather unusual birthday present. It was a seminal report that I had commissioned from GRI a year earlier. It was dubbed, rather awkwardly I'm afraid, the 'Long Range Assessment of Global Trends'. I prefer to call it simply the GRI Report."

"And I presume this is the report that predicted worldwide collapse?"

'Yep, Armageddon, End of Times...whatever you want to call it. And I, Jonathan Graham, will go down in history, (if there is a history) as having played a leading role in bringing it about. How about that for a legacy, young man?"

The older man paused to let the young professor ponder what he had just heard. Both men gazed for a few moments out over the city skyline. The multitude of sleek glass and steel skyscrapers stood out in stark relief against the bright blue sky. Skybuses, aircabs and an occasional private craft skimmed purposefully back and forth between buildings, carrying commuters to work. Michael wondered randomly if it was really possible that those commuter craft could be a thing of the past in just one short generation.

Michael finally broke the silence. "I have just two questions. How confident are you of the report's conclusions? And can anything be done to avert the crisis?"

"Unfortunately, we are very confident in the report's conclusions. The collapse could happen in as little as ten years or as far out as thirty. However, we calculate the highest probability for the collapse to be in about twenty years."

"As to your second question...can we do something about it? I don't know. What do you think, professor?"

Michael was taken aback by the question. "Mr. Graham...Jonathan, I still really have no idea what to think at this point."

"Quite understandable, young man. Nonetheless, we would very much like to have your help in finding an answer to that momentous question. Can something be done? And if so, precisely what?"

"Professor, basically, I'm offering you a job," Graham continued. "For the last three years, we have been building a huge new GRI complex outside of Colorado Springs. You may have already read about it. It will soon become a self-contained community, initially staffed by GRI personnel. However, we have also recently begun quietly recruiting the best and the brightest from around the world, business leaders, academics such as yourself, political scientists, economists, scientists and researchers in practically every discipline. These people will mount an effort unique in the history of mankind. Our goal will be nothing less than the salvation, and ultimately, the renewal of civilization. To accomplish that goal, we intend to spare no effort or expense."

"But, Jonathan, what can I contribute, really? I'm an academic three years out of graduate school, with no practical experience in government or business. With my book, I may have anticipated to some small degree on what we may now be facing, but I have no idea how to go about actually finding practical solutions. I'm basically just a theoretician, after all." Michael leaned back in his chair.

"Don't sell yourself short, Michael. The first step to finding a solution is to properly understand the problem. You have accomplished much on your own, with minimal resources. Now, I want to harness that exceptional intellect of yours to help us find a way to avoid the abyss that we are fast approaching."

"How are you possibly going to keep such a massive effort secret?" Michael asked. "Surely, you wouldn't want the true purpose of this new facility to become public knowledge, would you?"

"Of course not, but the cover story is already in place. It is quite simple, and therefore should be rather effective… that the Graham Research Institute, to improve efficiency and security, is simply consolidating many of its far-flung facilities around the world into one huge complex. Wouldn't that story have far more credibility than some wild tale that we are trying to save civilization?"

"Yes, I suppose it would. But the U.S. government and the Great Powers will surely come to know what you are up to," Michael responded.

"Certainly, but we expect the federal government to remain relatively neutral unless they come to see us as a direct threat. They will, however, have as great an interest as we do in keeping any potential crisis under wraps. Widespread public panic will only serve to make matters worse for the both of us."

Michael harbored little doubt that Graham was right; the government would do little to interfere. Both the present Congress and the President were little more than weak, vacillating puppets of the special interests such as…Graham Enterprises. Indeed, many officials were doubtless on Graham's payroll.

"The other Great Powers, on the other hand, will certainly try to hinder us in every way imaginable. Although I eventually shared the findings of the GRI report with them, they unanimously rejected it. It appears that they believe that this is all a ploy for me and my organization to somehow attain hegemony over all of them."

"So what do you say, Michael? Will you join our effort?" Graham now leaned back in his chair, to give Michael a few moments to consider his response.

After a moment's hesitation, Michael said, "I'm going to have to have a little time to think this over, Mr. Graham." In reality, Michael hoped that before he committed himself, he could do a bit of hurried research back home to try to validate some of the more astonishing facts that Graham had just imparted on him.

"I'm sorry Michael, but I must have your answer now. If you leave today without accepting my offer, the offer will be withdrawn...permanently."

"Just out of curiosity, aren't you concerned that if I decline, I might compromise your plans? I could go to the authorities, or even the media."

"I'm not concerned with that at all. Michael, please don't take this as a threat, but if you decline my offer, you will be unable to prove that you even traveled to New York, much less that you met the renowned Jonathan H. Graham III. My office would issue denials that we had ever heard of you. Travel records would be eliminated. Even cybernet records would be altered. Our meeting would never have happened. The only result would that you would wind up looking more than a little delusional. That wouldn't necessarily be a good career move for a young professor."

Michael got the point. It wasn't a threat, but it was most certainly a polite warning.

"Would it possible to have just one night to think this over? I try to never make a major decision without sleeping on it, first."

"Request granted. In fact, I can do better than that." Graham touched his wrist Uplink "Olivia, could you come in for a moment, please?"

Olivia was through the door in a heartbeat. "Yes sir, Mr. Graham."

"Olivia, would you be so kind as to show our young guest a bit of the city this afternoon? Take him to dinner this evening, perhaps? You two could use my table at Antonio's, if you like."

"It would be my pleasure, Mr. Graham. I can get Alyssa to sit in for me up here for the rest of the day." Olivia gave Michael another of her warm smiles.

"What do you think, Michael? Or, would you perhaps prefer some time alone to contemplate your decision?" Graham added with just a hint of amusement.

Michael smiled back at the lovely young woman, "I'd say that it would be most impolite to decline such a gracious offer."

"Well said. Very well, Michael, I believe our business for today is completed. Enjoy yourself for the rest of the day, and leave a message for me in the morning by 9AM. A simple yes or no will do. I'm afraid we won't be able to talk again for a while; I'll be leaving in the morning on business."

The older man stood up and the younger man followed suit. The two men shook hands and Michael turned to follow Olivia out of the office.

Graham knew that he was leaving the young man in the best of good hands for the rest of his stay in New York. In addition to excellent administrative skills and a charming personality, Olivia Bertrand was an Olympic class marksman and an expert in a variety of martial arts. She was also well trained in both electronic and personal surveillance, skills she had acquired during a four-year stint with the Special Operations Group and another two years with the Secret Service.

As the door closed, Graham sat his desk, put on his VR visor and called up Michael's dossier. He selected script rather than audio. In this regard, he was a bit old-fashioned, as well. Sometimes the older man just preferred to mull over a written document, rather than simply have a digital simulation recite it to him. The report materialized before him:

Subject: Michael Edward Vincent:

Background/Personal:

Born in 2055 in Austin, Texas. Parents Madeline Scott Vincent and James Edward Vincent. Father an insurance adjuster, later owner of a small insurance agency. Mother a teacher, later an assistant principal. Reportedly, his parents' relationship was stormy; his father had a chronic drinking problem. Parents divorced when Michael was eleven. His father remarried and moved to Dallas; he now has little contact with Michael. His mother never remarried. After his parents divorced, Michael and his mother moved from a comfortable suburban home to a small apartment. Michael lived there until he graduated from high school; his mother still resides there.

By all accounts, Michael was an average student in high school, friendly but something of a loner. He rarely dated, and never had a steady girlfriend. He was not a member of any extracurricular activities, such as sports or clubs; most of his after-school time was spent on a variety of part-time jobs helping his Mother to make ends meet.

Nothing whatever appears exceptional about his record until his college entrance scores are recorded. Although he had been a 3.0 student through high school, his test scores are ranked in the 99th national percentile, across the board. A battery of achievement test yields similar results.

Based on his exceptional test scores as well as his low-income status, Michael is granted a Clinton scholarship to the University of the Southwest, all expenses paid. He passes a variety of advanced placement tests, helping him to graduate with a bachelor's degree in political science in just three years, (summa cum laude). Michael seems to have blossomed in college; his acquaintances there recall a much more outgoing individual than do those who remember him from high school. He dated more regularly, and had a wider circle of friends.

After receiving his BA, Michael's scholarship is extended for graduate work. He earns his MA and then Ph.D. after just three more years. His doctoral thesis becomes the basis for his cyberbook, **Storm Warning**, which is eventually published two years later. After receiving his Ph.D., Michael is offered, and accepts a teaching position in the school of political science at his alma mater. He is still currently teaching there.

Michael has had three serious romantic relationships, one in college, the other two after graduation. All three lasted about one year; the latest was with a graduate student, one Susan Marie Parker. Their affair broke off about six months ago; reportedly they are still friends.

With his friends, Michael frequents a local pub just off campus a few times a week. He is also an eclectic reader. Michael's other recreational activities are mostly of the outdoor variety, such as camping, mountain biking and backpacking, activities he partakes of regularly on weekends. He spends little time in recreational VR.

Finances:

The report went on to describe in detail Michael's finances (minimal debt, minimal assets), his health, (excellent, athletic), his criminal record (two speeding tickets), and the detailed (and highly confidential) psychometric profile he had taken in college. Attached were all of his national tax records, along with his banking, payroll and medical records.

Graham vaguely supposed that he should regret how completely that he had invaded the personal privacy of the young man, as he had of so many others over the years. However, he knew that far more ruthless methods would soon become necessary in the coming struggle, methods that he had in fact used without reservation throughout his career to relentlessly further his ambitions.

He wondered if Michael would perhaps be perceptive enough to see through the half-truths that Graham had shared with him, and to catch a glimpse of what really might be happening…

For Graham, life had always just been an enormous chess game, and at a rather tender young age he had become a world-class chess master. How strange that fate had decided to change all the rules this late in the game. In the end, it seemed that all Graham had really accomplished was to contribute to the end of modern civilization.

Graham was a man of few regrets, who nonetheless possessed a fine sense of irony. And just now, he smiled at the rich irony of his present situation. Over the next twenty years or so, he intended to sacrifice everything that he accomplished, all the wealth that he accumulated, in order to attempt to rewrite in some small way the history that he had helped so much to create, in the first place…

5

The Picnic

As Michael followed Olivia to the private elevator, he could hardly help but feel every inch the country bumpkin. Ph.D. or not, he knew he would be the proverbial fish-out-of-water in this city, particularly in contrast to the confident and sophisticated young woman who now walked a pace ahead of him. Thankfully, at least he could detect no trace of condescension in her demeanor as she entered the elevator first and turned toward him.

As the door closed, he was surprised that she told the elevator "Roof" rather than "Lobby". In a moment, the elevator door opened again, and Michael was greeted with a breathtaking view of the city from 180 stories above the street.

Twenty paces away, a black and gold luxury sky cruiser was perched on the building's launch pad, its three turbolift engines giving off a low whine at idle. With a shock, it dawned on Michael that the sleek craft was waiting for none other than Olivia and himself. He had ridden on the large public commuter skybuses and aircabs on occasion, but never on a private craft...those were those reserved for the very rich.

As they entered the cabin and settled into their leather seats, Olivia turned to Michael and asked, "So, Michael, just how would you like to spend your one day in the Big Apple?"

Michael hesitated, and then responded, "I really haven't had the chance to give it much thought. What would you suggest?"

She seemed to think it over for a moment then answered, "You don't seem too much like the tourist type, so how about just picking up some subs from one of our famous New York deli's, then having a picnic in Central Park? Maybe later in the afternoon we can take in the Metropolitan Museum. How does that sound?"

"That sounds absolutely wonderful," Michael answered sincerely, though he wondered about having a picnic in the business clothes that they were both wearing. Olivia seemed to read his mind.

"Good, then we'll swing by your hotel so that you can change into something more comfortable."

"What about you?" Michael asked.

Olivia smiled. "Don't worry about me. I'll be fine."

She then gave their destination to the autopilot, the pilot in front waved in acknowledgement, and a few minutes later, they were landing on the roof of his hotel. As they entered the rooftop elevator, Olivia told him that she would meet him in forty-five minutes down in the lobby. Michael then got off on his floor and proceeded to his room. In a few minutes, he had changed into a casual khaki jumpsuit and a pair of loafers. That gave him a little time to sit in the big chair in his room and ponder the events of the morning.

The young professor was sorely tempted to accept Graham's offer, but he wondered just how much more there was to the story than what he had been told. One thing that he was sure of…there was more. A man like Graham wouldn't tell someone like Michael the whole story, just on general principles, if for no other reason. Well, with a little time, perhaps Michael could piece together the whole story on his own, if need be.

Meanwhile, in one of the shops in the hotel lobby, Olivia had quickly found a simple, disposable white jumpsuit and a pair of sneakers. In the small dressing room, she changed and pulled back her dark shoulder length hair into a ponytail. Adding to her purchase a cheap pair of sunglasses and a tote bag for her business clothes, in less than thirty minutes she was transformed.

Since she had a few minutes to spare, the young woman decided it would be prudent to scan for traces on Michael's Uplink, even though she didn't really expect to find any. Over the years, personal Uplinks had become practically ubiquitous, from the simple voice-only units that could be worn on the wrist, as a pendant, or even within the ear itself, to the larger pocket-sized terminals that could be used for more sophisticated purposes.

However, the same technology that was used to find and call any Uplink in the world could be used for more devious purposes. Any organization with the proper degree of sophistication could not only monitor a given Uplink, but also lock in on its signal and locate it (and its owner) to within a few meters. Of course, this sort of activity was highly illegal and (supposedly) restricted to law enforcement agencies and a few intelligence services.

Criminals soon learned to avoid detection by using stolen or unregistered Uplinks. Agents often used units registered to false ID's. A very few, such as Olivia and her boss, possessed highly encrypted Uplinks that could essentially change their registration continuously and randomly, making them virtually impossible to locate. Everyone else had to hope that the laws against such abuses were sufficient to deter them.

However, the scan that Olivia was now preparing to run required a degree of sophistication a full order of magnitude higher than simply monitoring or locating a given Uplink. Using the cybernetic resources of GRI, she intended to actually detect and locate anyone tracking or monitoring Michael's Uplink. She could thus monitor and track the eavesdroppers themselves. This capability was super-secret, only GRI and a few intelligence agencies possessed it, and only a few Graham operatives were aware of its existence; Olivia was one of the few.

Pulling a compact hand terminal from her shoulder bag, she accessed the GRI Net. Pulling up Michael's Uplink code, she quickly located his unit. Bringing it up on a map of the city, she quickly zeroed in on his location, which appeared to be right on top of her own (triangulation of the unit could not determine altitude). Satisfied that she was locked onto the correct unit, she initiated a scan routine. Such a routine, having to monitor and analyze billions of messages per second, could take up to 15 minutes to complete. However, in less than five minutes, Olivia was shocked to see a bogey detected.

She hadn't really expected anything; a bogey meant that someone already knew who Michael was, and probably that Michael had met with the Boss. That was extremely bad news. It meant that either someone had a very highly placed "mole" within the Graham organization, or that they had developed some way to cybernetically intercept Graham's own communications. She would have to report this to the big guy as soon as possible. Olivia considered simply calling Graham, but decided that it might be safer to brief him in person since his communications might be compromised. Meanwhile, she could keep the scan running, and perhaps, with a little luck, spot the bad guy.

As Michael walked across the lobby looking for Olivia, he almost walked right past the attractive young woman sitting in the overstuffed chair.

As Olivia put away a pocket terminal, she looked up, smiled and said, "Looking for someone, fella?" With a start, he realized that it was none other than Olivia herself.

"How…where did you get the new clothes?"

"The Boss is pretty liberal with expenses, if they're in the line of duty. And you can find just about anything that you need in these hotel shops nowadays. Besides, I didn't want you to feel underdressed," she replied.

"So what do you think?" she asked as she executed a little mock modeling turn. (She could already see the answer in his eyes.)

"You look terrific," Michael answered, trying to maintain his composure. The young professor was still trying to figure out how he had come, on this beautiful spring day, to being flown around New York City in a limo, and escorted by a beautiful woman. It just didn't compute.

"Thank you, sir. Well then, let's be off." With that, she led the way back to the elevator, up to the roof and into their waiting skycraft. As they settled back into their seats, Olivia gave the new destination to the autopilot, and then pulled the pocket terminal out of her bag.

"I hope you don't mind Michael, but I'm going to have to be checking for messages periodically throughout the day. The Boss expects me to keep up even when I'm out of the office."

Olivia was careful to keep the screen tilted a bit away from Michael, as she watched the target on the map display. It hadn't moved appreciably yet; she could visualize some agent scrambling to hail a hovercab right at this moment.

A few minutes later, Michael found himself looking down through his window at the most famous municipal park in the world. A few minutes more, and the craft began circling toward a public landing tower on the edge of the park. As it settled down on the platform, Olivia unbuckled and turned towards Michael.

"Well, we're on foot from here on in. I hope you're in shape for a bit of a long walk," she teased. (Actually, she knew from his dossier that hiking was one of his favorite pastimes.)

"I'll try to keep up," the young professor replied, "but I'm not making any promises."

They exited the cabin and took the drop-tube down to the street level. Once on the sidewalk, Olivia pulled out her terminal, glanced at the screen for a moment, then turned to Michael and said, "How about scaring up some lunch? One of the best delicatessens in town is just up the street."

"Lead the way," Michael responded, as he felt the first faint stirrings of hunger.

With that Olivia put away the terminal, turned and headed at a brisk pace down a side street away from the park. Michael followed, catching up to walk beside her. They walked the next two blocks to the deli in silence. As they walked, Michael noticed that the young woman at his side seemed a bit distracted, scanning back and forth almost constantly, occasionally looking back.

Maybe she doesn't remember exactly where the delicatessen is, he thought to himself. He discovered that it gave him just a bit of comfort to see her somewhat unsure of herself. It made him feel a little less inferior.

Olivia wasn't lost at all; she was just trying to spot their tail. When she had checked her terminal at the landing tower, she had seen the target fast approaching their position. Obviously, whoever it was had obtained air transport; the bogey was moving too fast for ground transportation. Doubtless he (or she) had by now landed on the same tower and was now trying to close the rest of the distance to them on foot. Olivia was determined to spot him. What she would do then, she wasn't quite sure.

"Shenbaum's Deli–New York's Finest" the old-fashioned sign proclaimed. Looking through the front window, Michael knew this place from a hundred movies–the impatient line of lunchtime patrons waiting to give their orders; the harried employees behind the counter trying to keep the line moving, the glass case full of every manner of deli meat and cheese, bread, and roll and bagel. (It was a far cry from the automated cafes so much in fashion now.)

Opening the door, even the little bell sounded, just like in the movies. Inside, the wonderful aromas immediately assailed them; Michael's stomach instantly lurched into full rumble. They took their place in line.

As they waited, Olivia pulled out her pocket terminal one more time, gave it a quick glance, and put it away. The target was about thirty meters up the street in the direction from which they had come, and closing. The young woman casually turned to keep one eye on the front window. The line slowly moved forward. Presently, a large man appeared at the window, peered inside the deli, then pulled out his own compact terminal. He studied it a few moments, and then entered the establishment. *Gotcha!* she thought.

Olivia gave him an apparently casual glance, which in actual fact took in virtually every detail of his appearance…about six feet tall, roughly 220 pounds, eyes blue, hair thick and black, Slavic features, tough looking. Working class clothes. She was willing to bet he was ex-military, maybe Russian, maybe former *Spedsnatz*. Satisfied that she had him pegged, she turned her attention to the menu board. When their turn came, she ordered a turkey and swiss; Michael ordered pastrami on rye. They added a couple of bottles of root beer and a couple of slices of cheesecake. As the girl at the checkout register rang their purchase up and bagged it, Olivia asked Michael to wait while she used the restroom.

In the restroom, she quickly made her way to a stall and closed the door. Using her wrist Uplink, she placed a priority-encrypted call to Dan McCafferty, GRI chief of security, and nominally her boss. (She normally reported directly to Graham himself.) She got through to him immediately, and gave him a quick situation report.

"Damn. Play it cool for now, 'Liv', I'm going to send a fast response team to back you up. I don't think he'll make a move just yet, but we don't want to take any chances."

In actual fact McCafferty was worried. Two key experts that Graham himself had recruited for the new project, an economist and a systems analyst, had disappeared a few weeks ago, without a trace. A third, a meteorologist, had died in a fall down a flight of stairs shortly after accepting a position with the project just the week before. After that, the Boss had put his security apparatus on full alert.

"Okay, Mac, but I'm armed, and if I see him looking like he's about to pull anything, I'm going to take him out," she responded rather emphatically. (She too was aware of the three prior 'incidents'.)

Mac didn't argue; he had complete faith in Olivia's judgment…not to mention her reflexes. The security chief was glad that the old man had put the young professor in her care. She was one of their best.

McCafferty's first priority, of course, was to protect Dr. Vincent and his own agent. However, a very important secondary priority would be to catch this guy alive. Interrogating him just might give them clues about precisely just who or what they were up against. Of course, he probably wouldn't know much, but at least it might be a beginning. However, capturing him would probably be no easy task. He would undoubtedly be well trained, and would likely not go down easily. Another minor problem was that assault and kidnapping, even of enemy agents, was rather illegal for civilian organizations such as their own.

Mac quickly contacted Simmons and La Pierre, his two agents-on-call, briefed them, and told them to get moving. He knew that they would be in the air in a few minutes, and tailing the bogey inside of a half-hour. They were both good men, competent, reliable and discreet, if somewhat unimaginative. Until they reached the scene, Mac would just have to sit and wait, not one of his favorite pastimes.

After Michael and Olivia exited the deli, they turned left to head back toward Central Park. A few blocks down, they turned a corner, and there was the park, just across the street. They crossed the street, and soon they were in another world, a world of grass and trees, rather than concrete and steel. Midday joggers passed them on their path, young couples lay out on blankets picnicking, or reading, or just snuggling. Parents on park benches watched their children play. Altogether it was a lovely day.

"I know a really nice spot, deep in the park. Do you mind if we walk for awhile, Michael?" (She really did know such a spot, but she also wanted to keep moving until her backup team had had a chance to catch up and get into position.)

"That'll be fine. It's beautiful out here today."

Michael could hardly think of anything he'd rather be doing than walking through Central Park with this young lady at his side.

"So, how long have you worked for Graham," Michael finally asked.

They had been walking in silence for a while now. It seemed to Michael that Olivia had become rather distant, like she was thinking of something else.

"Oh, about three years," she replied.

Just then, the Uplink in her purse warbled. She pulled it out, flipped open the cover and quickly read the message on the screen. The message read:

> *Keep moving. You are now being followed by three hostiles at fifty meters. We are trailing them at approx thirty meters. Suspect hostile action imminent. Have sent for reinforcements, but will probably not arrive in time. Be alert.*

Oh shit! Olivia thought to herself as she methodically slowed her breathing and relaxed her muscles.

One tail would most likely have just meant simple surveillance; three meant definite trouble. They only needed three agents if they intended to either kidnap or kill the young professor whose life was now, unknowingly, in her hands. She wondered when they would make their move. Most likely, they were hoping that their "prey" would reach a more secluded spot. They would then casually catch up with the young couple, move in just behind them, and inform them, quietly, that guns were pointed at their backs. It would then be a simple matter to guide them to a waiting air-shuttle, and whisk them to an assuredly unpleasant fate.

They were approaching a bend in the trail. A plan came to her in that instant.

"Michael, I've got to reply to this message. Why don't you just keep walking, and I'll catch up to you in a few minutes?"

"That's okay, Olivia; there's no hurry. I'll just wait for you," he answered casually. (They were still walking.)

Damn...

"Michael," her voice was level, but it carried a definite air of urgency.

"It's very important that you do exactly as I say. I'm going to stop, but you are going to keep walking. Do not look back, and do not stop for any reason. I'll catch up to you in a few minutes. Will you do this for me, please?"

Michael turned and looked at her face. She looked back at him. Her face was outwardly calm, but something in her eyes told him that he had better just do as he was told.

That look made the hairs stand up on the back of his neck...literally.

"Yes, ma'am," he replied after a moment's hesitation.

"What in the world is going on?" he wondered, as he left her behind.

Olivia had to move fast now. She was still holding her pocket terminal. She stopped, and keeping her back to the bad guys, she quickly typed a response to the last message:

Close in. Now! Am about to make my move.

She keyed the send button and then quickly switched to the tracking display, thirty meters and closing. They would be intent on following Michael, as he was their primary target. Meanwhile, she would look harmless enough, just standing there with her back to them, apparently answering a message. When they had closed to within fifteen meters, she put her terminal into her handbag, and moved her hand to an equally familiar object. She hoped her backup had had enough time to get into position.

As she heard footsteps approaching, she whirled, both hands on her sidearm, and shouted, "Police! Freeze right there!"

They were clearly startled, but they moved like professionals. They began to separate, their hands moving to their weapons. They knew that she couldn't get all three of them.

Just then, they heard two male voices behind them shout, "Police! Put your hands in the air now or we will fire! Do it!"

That was it. They were surrounded. Three sets of hands moved up together. Simmons and La Pierre moved swiftly and efficiently from there. While Olivia and La Pierre kept weapons trained on the three men, Simmons disarmed them, then pulled each man's hands behind his back and bound them with e-cuffs, (which could either track a runaway or disable him with an electric shock.) They all breathed a little easier when that was done.

Next Simmons pulled out a pocket scanner, detecting and removing all of the men's Uplinks. Each man had the same three: an earpiece, a wrist unit, and a pocket terminal. He then put all of the Uplinks into a metallic bag designed to block all transmissions. As Simmons worked, the apparent leader (the original tail) asked politely, with just a trace of a Russian accent, if he could see some identification.

"Shut the fuck up," Simmons replied casually. Simmons, a big sandy-haired man with a ruddy complexion, happened to be an ex-New York cop, and he did have a false police department I.D, but he wasn't about to show it to this asshole. He just hoped that they could wrap this little operation up before any real cops arrived.

Mainly for the benefit of the spectators, after they had secured all three prisoners, Simmons quickly read the men their rights. Meanwhile, La Pierre, a tall, thin black ex-officer in the International Marine Force, politely asked the gathering crowd to disperse, telling them that the excitement was over. With that, and with only a nod to Olivia, they turned to take their prisoners to a waiting corporate air-shuttle. The whole operation had taken less than five minutes.

Olivia put away her sidearm, and quickly turned to catch up with Michael. She jogged a ways up the trail, but still didn't see him. Her heart rate went up a bit at the thought that something might have happened to him. What if there was another hostile team out here? She pulled out her terminal and put a trace on his Uplink. There he was, or at least his Uplink, about one hundred meters northwest of her position. She decided to risk a quick voice call to confirm that he was okay, and to tell him to stop and wait for her. She spoke his Uplink code into her wrist unit.

"Michael, can you hear me?"

"Yes, Olivia, where are you?"

She could plainly hear the consternation in his voice.

"I'm just a little ways behind you. Stop where you are and I'll be there in a couple of minutes," she replied as calmly and pleasantly as she could manage with the adrenaline in her system still draining off.

In actual fact, a wave of immense relief had washed over her as she realized that he was safe, after all. She trotted ahead at a pace that she hoped wouldn't attract much attention, and, as she came around another bend in the path, spotted Michael sitting on a park bench. He still cradled their picnic lunch in his lap, but the look on his face told her that a picnic wasn't the uppermost thing on his mind at this moment. She slowed to a walk to catch her breath.

"I'm really sorry about all of this Michael, but I'm afraid we'll have to have our picnic another time," Olivia said as she walked up to him.

"That's all right, but I would really appreciate it if you could explain to me just what in the devil is going on," Michael responded with more than a little frustration.

"We were being followed, but that's been taken care of. Right now though, to be careful, we need to take you back to headquarters, where we can give you a more complete explanation. Now then, you just have the wrist Uplink, correct?"

"I have a pocket terminal in my hotel room, but this is the only one I'm carrying."

"Would you give it to me please?"

Michael complied, undoing the clasp on the band and handed it over to the young woman. Olivia took the device, looked at it a moment, and tossed it in the trash receptacle next to the bench. Michael gave her a startled look. He was beginning to feel like Alice on the wrong side of the looking glass, and he wasn't at all comfortable with the feeling. He was getting pretty impatient to know just what the hell was going on.

"We'll explain that too, but later," Olivia said, pointing at the trash basket.

"Let's head back; our ride will be waiting for us at the edge of the park."

The young woman pulled out her terminal one last time, to let Mac know that she had rejoined Michael, and was bringing him in. She then turned and headed back the way they'd come, with Michael following close behind. They walked the rest of the way back to the landing tower in silence.

6

McCafferty

Olivia and Michael had continued to maintain an awkward silence on the ride back to the Global Technology Center. Olivia felt a jumble of mixed emotions. She had to admit to herself that she was rather pleased with the decisive way that she had handled the crisis in the park. At the same time, however, she felt at least partially responsible for putting the young professor in harm's way in the first place. Michael was a "civilian" who had had no idea what he might have been getting himself into. Well, like it or not, he was up to his neck in it now.

After landing on the rooftop pad, they took the elevator down to the basement. (Security was automated from the roof down. Only company skycraft could land on the roof and only a small number of high-level personnel could voice-activate the rooftop elevator, which was also continually scanned.) In the basement, as soon as they exited the elevator, they had to pass through another security checkpoint. Then Olivia guided Michael into a large office down the hall. The brass nameplate on the door stated:

Daniel Patrick McCafferty
Communications Director

Seated at the desk in the small anteroom was a clean-cut young man who appeared to be an executive assistant.

"Hi 'Liv. If you two will have a seat, I'll let Mac know you're here. Just as they seated themselves, however, the door to the office opened, and a tall, lean man with close-cropped blonde hair and steel gray eyes strode out.

"Dr. Vincent, I presume. I'm Dan McCafferty, chief of security for Graham Enterprises. But just call me 'Mac' like everybody else, doctor," he said as he extended his hand.

"And please, just call me Michael," the young professor responded, as he stood up and took Mac's hand. The young professor couldn't help but notice that Mac's hand was rock hard, not the typical hand of a middle-aged executive.

"I don't want to seem rude, but is this where I get to find out just what in the bloody hell is going on?"

"It is indeed," Mac smiled. "At least we can tell you some of the story. Let's go into my office, and you two can finally have your lunch while we talk."

With that, he turned and let the way into his office. Mac's office looked more like a command center than an executive's office. There was an assortment of display screens and electronic devices on his desk and on the shelves behind his desk. There were maps and charts of every variety on the walls.

To one side of the office was another door, which led into a small conference room. Mac led them through this door, and motioned them to two seats at the conference table. He moved around the table and took a seat at the opposite side. Michael noticed that the conference room was outfitted much like Mac's office, with display screens, maps and charts on the walls. Additionally, there was a holographic display unit, or HDU, on the center of the table, which was currently just displaying a static 3D image of the Graham Enterprises logo. Mac told the unit to switch off, so that the image wouldn't block their view of one another.

"Folks, why don't you have your lunch while we talk? I'll just have a cup of coffee while you eat," Mac said.

Michael had to admit to himself that, even with the excitement and confusion…he was still hungry. So with Mac's invitation, he wasted no time in pulling the packages out of the bag and laying them out for himself and Olivia. Meanwhile, Mac got up and asked the dispenser in the corner to pour him a cup of coffee. He then sat back down while Michael and Olivia started on their subs.

Mac took a sip of coffee, and then started, "Let me begin by letting you know that I have already briefed the Boss, that is, Mr. Graham, on everything that has occurred today. He wants you to know that he's relieved that you're safe, and that he regrets that you've already been caught up in all of this. Because of what has happened, he has cleared me to tell you a good deal of what we know. However, much of what I am about to tell you is highly classified, so we must insist that you keep it to yourself."

So he and Olivia had been in danger, after all. Michael had suspected as much, but he hadn't really been sure.

"As I believe Mr. Graham has already told you, the Olympus Project, (*so the project had a name!*), has been opposed, almost from the beginning, by the other corporate superpowers. At first, that opposition just amounted to increased espionage; it seems they just wanted to know exactly what we were up to. Then, regulatory hurdles began to be placed in our path. Agencies of both the state of Colorado and the federal government suddenly found reasons to delay the start of construction of the new facility. Next, a coalition of environmental groups filed several suits claiming that our construction would do irreparable harm to the environment. Eventually, we overcame all of those obstacles; construction actually began about three years ago."

"Construction was initially plagued with problems and delays. Contractors suddenly backed out, for no apparent reason. Important equipment was damaged in shipment. We had several major accidents at the site. Last year, a gas main exploded, killing four workers and injuring a number of others. Eventually, we began to suspect that someone was behind a good deal of this "bad luck", so we adapted. We formed our own construction company, so that we could control the project more directly. We also substantially increased security at the site, reducing mishaps. We prevailed, and the project moved forward."

"Then, about three weeks ago, there appeared to be a serious escalation by the opposition. Two key experts, who had just accepted positions with our project, disappeared within a few days of each other. We still have no idea what happened to them. Last week, another individual who had just accepted a senior position within our organization had a fatal fall down a flight of stairs. That incident might just have been a coincidence, but we tend not to believe too much in coincidences around here."

"So, I suppose that brings us to today," Michael said.

"Right. Today, we detected one or more operatives following you and Liv this afternoon, almost from the moment that you left this building. We believe that they were tracking your wrist Uplink. In the park, we picked up their trail; by then, there were three of them. Now all of this is very bad news, Michael. To begin with, we must have a very serious security breach for them to have picked you up so quickly, almost from the first moment that you met with Graham. Secondly, the fact that three agents were following you means that, almost without a doubt, they intended to abduct you. Lastly, the fact that they were prepared to act in broad daylight, with one of our own agents right at your side, meant that they have gotten very serious indeed. A real war, a covert war, may be beginning in earnest."

Agent? So Olivia was a lot more than she seemed, as well. With that last little revelation, it occurred to Michael that he was in far, far over his head. He had no way to know what was true and what was a fabrication. What if *these* were the bad guys? How would he know? What was real?

Olivia caught his look. "I'm very sorry Michael. I really am Mr. Graham's executive assistant; I just have a few particular skills that you don't ordinarily see in an EA. I also act as his personal bodyguard, and on occasion I take part in field operations. I'm certain that Mr. Graham just wanted to ensure your safety while you were in New York, even though we didn't suspect that you were in any real danger."

"How am I supposed to know for sure whether you guys are telling me the truth?" Michael asked in frustration.

McCafferty shot back, "You can't know for sure. But the boss tells me that you're a pretty bright guy, so you're just going to have to make your best judgment. I'll tell you this though. If you accept a position with our organization, we can take steps to ensure your safety. If you go back to your old job at the university, however, we won't be able to protect you; you'll be on your own. I'm sorry, but that's the harsh reality."

Michael pondered that one. Assuming that what these people were telling him was the truth, Mac's point was well taken. The only way for Michael to expect any protection from Graham's organization was to be a part of it. He felt like he was being carried away by events; things were just moving too quickly. What to do? He decided that he still wanted to sleep on his decision. They all three just looked at one another for a few moments.

"By the way," Michael finally said, "New York really does have world class pastrami." That broke the spell. Mac and Olivia chuckled as Michael downed the rest of his sub and emptied his bottle of root beer. He eyed the cheesecake...he'd save that for later. Olivia followed suit, finishing her sub as well.

"I need to have a little time to think all of this over. I'll still give Mr. Graham his answer in the morning," Michael said.

Mac now spoke again, "Very well, Michael. In any case, for your own safety, we would like for you to spend the night in this building. We have some suites normally used by our employees in transit. I will tell you now, if you accept a position with our organization, we will relocate you to Colorado under a new identity. Meanwhile, we will make it appear that the old Michael Vincent has accepted a position here in New York. Communications from your friends and family will be sent to New York, and then covertly forwarded to Colorado. Likewise, your transmissions will be made to appear to originate from here in the city, rather than from out West."

"Now then, Mr. Graham has also asked me to give you a glimpse of what we are building in Colorado," Mac continued.

The security chief asked the lights to dim, and then voice-activated the display on the table before them. "Holo on, display Olympus site, aerial view, altitude 500 meters."

Suddenly, the conference room tabletop transformed itself into a miniature city...and a city it was, not the campus of ten or fifteen buildings that Michael had expected. On the contrary, Michael was looking at a complex of hundreds of buildings situated along broad tree-lined boulevards that radiated out from the city center like the spokes of a wheel. A wall that Michael guessed to be about two stories high encircled the entire complex. At the exact center stood a truly monumental domed structure that dominated all of the other buildings. It looked like it might be a huge domed stadium or coliseum.

"That's the Alexandria Library." Mac had pulled a laser pointer from his jacket pocket and highlighted the huge building. "It's the focus of the entire project, and the old man's baby. Eventually, it will house the collected wisdom of the ages, on thousands of terabytes of permanent data store. In addition, there will be tens of thousands of old-fashioned bound volumes, everything from ancient texts to the rare first editions of the great works. The Library will include theaters, classrooms and meeting halls; it will also house a science museum and one of the world's great art museums. Additionally, it will be networked with the most advanced cybernetic intelligence system in the world. It will even have its own power source, an underground fusion reactor capable of supplying power, without maintenance for, literally, thousands of years."

Mac went on to describe the rest of the self-contained city: apartments, offices, schools (including a fully accredited university), a mall (of course), a medical center, a huge research complex, parks both inside and outside the city wall, recreational facilities. Aside from the reactor, solar arrays and small wind turbines situated on virtually every roof would provide power for most of the city. Transportation would generally be by foot or communal bicycles; for larger distances, automated people-movers radiated out from the city center.

For food, thousands of acres around the city would be set aside as automated farms for raising a variety of staples, such as soy, wheat and corn. Automated plants would convert some of the crops into several varieties of high protein synthmeats. Another huge, clear dome inside the city would be used to mass-produce hydroponically grown vegetables. Even many of the trees planted in the city park would be genetically customized to bear an optimal volume of fruit in the Colorado climate.

"We want to be able to continue to function effectively, even if there are severe economic and social disruptions around the rest of the world. Altogether, Olympus will be a fully self-contained community, which will cover about 64 square miles and will eventually house some 20,000 men, women and children. It will be populated by the best and the brightest from all around the world. And it will eventually cost more than all of the manned lunar and Mars missions, combined," Mac concluded.

Michael just sat transfixed for a few moments; he didn't know what to say. He was looking at something that was not only spectacular; it was noble; a city whose entire purpose was not just to preserve civilization, but to foster its rebirth. He still wanted to think things over, but in his heart, he knew that he wanted to be a part of this effort.

"So what happens next?" Michael finally asked.

"We'll have Marcus, my assistant, take you to your room. Your personal effects from the hotel should arrive shortly. Rest up awhile and we'll take you to dinner this evening," Mac replied.

Mac then summoned Marcus on his wrist Uplink, stood up and extended his hand to Michael, "Now then, if you'll excuse us, Michael, Olivia and I have some business to discuss."

Michael shook Mac's hand, then took Olivia's, and then turned to follow Marcus out of the conference room.

"Sit down, Liv, and let's talk about this afternoon," Mac said after the two men had left.

They both sat back down, and Mac became all business.

"That was some pretty drastic action that you took in the park. Do you think that it was justified?"

Olivia resisted the urge to become defensive.

"I think so, Mac. I felt that under the circumstances, it was much safer to act before they made a move, than to try to react after they already had. They could have closed in on us at any moment and drawn their weapons. At that point, it would have been practically impossible to deal with the situation without someone getting hurt."

"That's exactly what Simmons and La Pierre concluded… and I concur. As a matter of fact, I'd say that you did an excellent job of handling a potentially disastrous situation." With that, Mac relaxed back into his chair. Olivia relaxed a bit too.

"Thanks, Mac. So what happens to our three captives, now?" the young woman asked.

"They'll be interrogated, then hustled out of the country and released. Don't worry, they won't be harmed. They are undoubtedly mercenaries, and will spill their guts for the right incentives, like freedom and money. The problem is that they probably won't know much. But who knows, they may provide us with a few clues that may help us to eventually determine who is behind all of this."

"I hope so, it's going to be virtually impossible to defend ourselves against an enemy, when we don't even know who the enemy is," Olivia observed.

"You've got that right. That's why we have got to get to the bottom of this, and fast. Now then, what do you think of our young scholar?" Mac changed the subject.

"I really like him, Mac. He seems so boyish, so unsophisticated. Yet, I think underneath all of that, he is one very astute individual; I also get the feeling that he's someone you could count on in a crunch," the young woman replied.

"Yeah, well, let's just make sure that we keep our young friend alive and intact until we all get to Olympus," Mac added.

They were all already packed. Graham and all of his immediate staff were scheduled leave in the morning on Graham's personal jet to visit the Olympus site. With this latest security breach, however, Mac knew that his boss was seriously contemplating turning the visit to Colorado into a permanent move, even though the site was far from ready. New York was obviously becoming a dangerous place for Graham personnel.

"You're assuming that Michael will agree to join us," Olivia pointed out.

"Come on Olivia, you don't miss much, and I know that you didn't miss the way he was looking at you. When he finds out that you'll be escorting him to Colorado, there's no way that he's going to turn us down," Mac observed with a wicked grin.

"Damn you, Mac, I don't know what you're talking about," she was furious with Mac for making her blush. It was unprofessional...

7

The Dinner

Michael sat on the bed in his room, and tried to make sense of the day's events. He didn't have much luck. It all just swirled around in his head like a kaleidoscope. His meeting with the old man, his morning with Olivia, the hurried flight back to the center, the briefing by McCafferty. Could he trust these people enough to join them? Could he risk *not* trusting them? Even though it was only about four in the afternoon, he was exhausted. He lay back on the bed and dozed. Soon he was fast asleep. He awoke to a knock on the door.

"Who is it?" he mumbled.

"I've got your things from the hotel." It was Marcus again.

Michael opened the door. "Thanks. How did you get this without my voiceprint? Wait… never mind. I don't even want to know."

Marcus just smiled as he handed over the suit bag. He also handed over a garment bag that Michael didn't recognize. "This is a new suit, compliments of Mr. Graham. Olivia will be by to pick you up at seven for dinner. Good evening, Dr. Vincent."

It was six o'clock. That would just give enough time for Michael to shower, clean up and change before Olivia came by. He wondered if dinner would just include himself and Olivia; he had to admit to himself that he hoped so. After showering and shaving, he tried on his new suit; it was a perfect fit. The shoes included in the bag were also the correct size. These people were really scary; how much more did they know about him?

At precisely seven o'clock there was a knock on the door.

"Yes?"

"It's me, Michael," Olivia answered.

Michael opened the door. Olivia looked simply stunning. She had on a simple but elegant black evening dress, and wore her hair up. Michael tried to act casual…and failed. At least he didn't drool. He silently thanked Graham for the classy new suit; he feared that he would have looked pathetic next to this young woman in his old clothes.

"You look lovely."

"Thank you, Michael. You look pretty sharp, yourself," she answered honestly.

"If you're ready, let's go."

Michael nodded yes, and they both headed for the elevator. On the roof, they once again boarded the corporate craft and let the seat restrains conform to their bodies. Michael had to admit that cruising around in a luxury sky yacht could be something that would be pretty easy to get used to.

Olivia gave directions to the autopilot, and then turned to Michael, "Flying over New York at night is something that I never get enough of."

They both looked out the window as the craft rose off of the pad…and it was a magnificent sight…the constellation of lights from the skyscrapers, the moving lights of the traffic below and the blinking red and blue strobes of the other skycraft above and around them.

"We decided that Antonio's might not be a good idea. It's one of Mr. Graham's regular spots, so it might be under surveillance by the opposition. We're going to another place that's a little more out of the way, but just as nice. It's a place called Trevanian's. I just hope that you like Italian."

Michael liked Italian. Fifteen minutes later, they were landing on the restaurant's rooftop pad, ten minutes after that, they were seated at their table. Michael was as intimidated by the ambiance of the surroundings as he was by the elegance of the young lady that was seated across from him. It was a far cry from the pubs and cyber-cafes back home to which he was accustomed. Nonetheless, he was savoring the moment. He let Olivia order the wine; she ordered a good Chianti.

"So, is your job as always as exciting as it was today?" Michael asked after his first sip of wine.

"Not quite, but it's been quite an experience. When I first took the job, the site in Colorado was just getting under construction, and I had no real idea what was going on. After about six months Mac and the old man took me into his office, and told me the whole story. At first, to be honest, I didn't know what to believe. It was just so incredible. But over the last few years, I've seen enough. I believe that the future of civilization is actually in our hands."

"What did you do before you worked for Graham? Where did you grow up?"

"I'm sorry Michael, operations personnel aren't allowed to discuss their personal background. It's a security issue, you understand."

"That seems rather unfair. I'm not allowed to know anything about you, but you get to know everything in the world about me."

"What makes you think that, Michael?"

"Oh, come on now, Olivia. You guys know my shoe size, for crying out loud."

She knew he was right, but couldn't really say so. She looked away for a moment, embarrassed that she had been confronted over the depth of their intrusion into the young man's life.

Michael hadn't meant to embarrass her. "I'm sorry; I guess that drastic times really do call for drastic measures."

With that, she responded, "Well, I guess I can tell you a little bit about myself without doing too much damage to security. I grew up sort of everywhere. My father was in the military, so we moved around all over the world. When I was sixteen, we finally settled down in D.C.; my father had retired and taken a civil service job. By then, I had become something of a loner, not ever having stayed anywhere long enough to make any lasting friendships. I suppose I compensated by becoming 'miss everything': honor society, debate club, class president. I was on the high school swim team and gymnastics team, as well."

"I had also been a pretty rebellious teenager, but when I graduated, I found myself drawn to follow in my father's footsteps, almost in spite of myself. I attended a military academy, and found that I loved it. I craved the challenge, the discipline, the high expectations. The harder they pushed, the more I liked it. Then, after graduation, I served a tour in the military, and that, I really can't talk about."

"Right. I know, you could tell me, but then you'd have to kill me."

"Perhaps," she answered with a wry smile.

"Can you tell me how you came to work for Graham, or is that sensitive information, as well?"

"I don't suppose it is. I took a government job when I finished my tour in the military. After a couple of years in that position, I got a c-mail from Mr. Graham out of the blue, much as you did. I was intrigued, so I responded. In my case, though, before I met with Graham, I had to submit to a rather grueling psychometric evaluation that lasted a full day. I guess I passed, because I was invited to an interview with the old man himself a few days later. The rest, as they say, is history," she concluded.

The waiter had come back. They both ordered, and when the waiter left, they continued their conversation.

"Do you stay in touch with your mother and father? Do you have any brothers or sisters?" Michael was fascinated with this young woman, and found that he was hungry to know more about her.

"Nope, I'm an only child, but I'm in pretty regular touch with Mom and Dad. We visit in VR a few times a week, and I try to make it down to D.C. at least about one weekend every few months. It's funny, but the older I get, the closer I seem to come to my parents. They're really my best friends now."

"I wish that was the case with me," Michael responded. "My father pretty well wrote my mother and myself off after they were divorced. I've hardly spoken to him in the last few years, and to tell the truth, at this point I hardly care to."

"I stay in touch with Mom, of course, but it seems to get harder as time goes on. She has almost completely withdrawn into virtual reality, like so many others have these days, it seems. She works at the school, then comes home and escapes to VR. She's already put in for a VR teaching position, as well. She would just prefer to stay in her condo plugged-in twenty-four by seven, like the hardcore VR junkies. However, the waiting list for a VR position is so long, it may be years before she gets one."

"Maybe that's a good thing. It's just so hard for me to relate to escaping reality like that. The real world can be plenty exciting enough. I don't need to waste my free time pretending to be some warrior princess in a "swords-and-sorcery" epic, or a glamorous beauty queen in old Hollywood."

"Same with me. I used to plug-in pretty often while I was in high school, until I realized how seductive it had become for me. I was out of shape and out of touch. Before I began college I took up hiking and mountain biking...and girls. I pretty well swore off VR, except for work or research. But tell me more about yourself; what about friends?" Michael asked, as the salads were served.

"Most of my friends are the people that I work with. My job doesn't exactly lend itself to an active social life. I travel with the boss a lot, and we work all sorts of odd hours. Besides, I've got to admit that I'm still fundamentally a loner." Olivia took a few bites of her salad... it was delicious.

"If you mean romantic relationships, I've had my share over the years, but none have developed into anything lasting," she went on. "I guess I'm a pretty strong-willed, independent sort, and most of the men that I've gotten involved with seem to get intimidated by that, sooner or later...at least, that's my theory," she added.

"What a coincidence...the strong-willed, independent type is just the type I'm attracted to," Michael joked, and they both laughed. "Actually, I've been pretty hapless in the area of romance, myself...and I don't even have a theory for why. Sometimes I wish that they could just assign you a partner based on compatible psychometric profiles, and eliminate all of the confusion and frustration." With that said, Michael worked on his salad as well.

"Someone would have to understand what really makes us tick before they could write a program to manage that with any success. I, for one, doubt that that will ever happen. Besides, that would take all of the fun out of it, wouldn't it?"

"Who ever said that the battle of the sexes is fun?" Michael shot back.

"Point taken," she responded as the salads were cleared and the main course was served.

Michael had ordered some pasta dish with an unintelligible Italian name; he had decided to be adventurous. Olivia had ordered chicken marsala. Both dishes looked delicious...both were. They dug in.

When they came up for air, Olivia asked, "What got you so interested in social engineering, Michael?"

"Well, I had always been somewhat interested in social issues. Who knows, maybe it stemmed from my screwed-up family life. What is it that keeps people from behaving rationally? Why do so many people abuse so many others? You know, like we can land men on Mars, but we can't keep parents from abusing their children. It was all a great mystery to me. So I read and looked for answers, without a whole lot of success."

"Then, in my junior year in high school, I had a sociology teacher, Ms. Elizabeth Dupree. She was one of those rare and priceless teachers who really loves what she is teaching, and can inspire their students to love it as well. She recognized something in me, and took a special interest. She suggested books for me to read. She asked me to do research for extra credit. She picked on me in class, challenging me to see beyond my preconceived notions. In the end, because of her, I was hooked. After her class, I knew for sure what my college major would be."

"Then, in my sophomore year at UA, for a social psychology class, I had a professor, Dr. Luis Alvarez. He encourages the students to call him 'Louie', supposedly his street name from his younger years in Laredo. University lore has it that he was actually a gang member as a teenager. He's never confirmed or denied the story."

"In any case, he's a short, thin guy, soft spoken most of the time, but incredibly intense when he's lecturing or even just discussing his theories in a casual setting. He has a mind like a razor, and lectures, nonstop, at about a mile a minute. After the first course, I took him for every other class that he taught. He encouraged me to go to graduate school, and later pushed me to flesh out my doctoral thesis into a full length book and get it published."

"Professor Alvarez, Louie that is, has a vision of developing a sort of 'unified field theory' for social behavior. You know, Einstein dreamt of developing a unified field theory that could explain virtually everything in the physical universe. He died before he could realize that dream. Louie wanted me to help him develop the same sort of unifying theory for the human condition, a theoretical framework that would encompass genetics and evolution, psychology and sociology, religion and philosophy, economics and political science."

"Fascinating...ah, Michael, your pasta's getting a little cold," Olivia interrupted.

"Oh, sorry, when you get me going on this subject, I get a little carried away," Michael replied as he rather sheepishly went back to his dinner.

As soon as they had finished their entrées, the waiter cleared their table. They both decided to order cappuccinos to top off an excellent dinner. After the cappuccinos were delivered and the waiter had moved back to a discreet distance, Olivia leaned forward, "Michael, I have something important to tell you."

Michael leaned forward too.

"Tomorrow morning, Mr. Graham, several members of his senior staff, and a few of his security personnel, including myself, will be taking Graham's personal hyperjet to the Olympus site. The trip's been planned for a long time. It was supposed to be a visit for Graham and his top advisors to personally assess the progress of the project. However, the plan may be changing; we may not be coming back."

"I don't understand," Michael responded.

"Today showed us that it's becoming too difficult to control the situation in New York. The site in Colorado may be the only place where we can provide adequate security for our key personnel, especially for Mr. Graham himself. The old man will be making the final decision in the morning. In either case, we'd like you to come with us."

Michael tried his cappuccino...it was pretty good. Olivia took a sip too.

"I just can't believe all of this. Twenty-four hours ago, I hadn't even heard of you people or your project. Now, I'm being asked to uproot my life, abandon my career, move to a place I've never seen, all on the word of three people that I just met today," Michael shook his head.

"Oh, Michael, it's not really that bad. The boss hopes that you'll be convinced when you actually see the reality of the project. If you still want to decline our offer, of course, you'll be free to go home. You can still be back teaching your classes by Monday morning."

And maybe fall down a flight of stairs, Michael thought to himself.

"So, I take it that the deadline for my decision has been extended."

"Yes, after today's, um, extenuating circumstances, Mr. Graham thought that it was only fair that you be allowed to see a little more of our operation before giving us your decision."

"I appreciate that. Olivia, I suppose that it's obvious that I really want to be a part of all this. But it's all just happening too quickly. I'm not sure just how much of all this that I can believe."

"I understand, Michael. I really do. But like Mac said, you're a pretty bright guy. I think that you'll make the right decision."

"Well, I guess that it wouldn't hurt to spend the weekend in Colorado. I didn't really have anything else planned. After that, I'll guess I'll just play it by ear."

"Great. I'll let Mac and the boss know," Olivia smiled.

With that, she called for the check, and in a few minutes they were heading up to the roof pad. They both sat in silence on the flight back to headquarters, each lost in their own thoughts. For his part, Michael couldn't help fantasizing. Olivia would show him up to his room. He would say something clever, and invite her in for a nightcap. She would hesitate, and then relent; one thing would lead to another.

Olivia did show him up to his room, but at the door reality diverged from fantasy. Olivia bid Michael goodnight, and asked him if he would like to join her for breakfast at seven-thirty, before leaving for the airport. Michael, of course, agreed. He then took her hand, and thanked her for the most fascinating day of his life. Olivia looked up at him for a moment, smiled, and then kissed him on his cheek. Without another word, she turned and made her way down the hall. Michael entered his room and closed the door, still savoring the feel of her warm lips on his face...

8

The Flight

Olivia woke in the morning mildly irritated with herself. The impulsive little peck on the cheek that she had given Michael had been innocent enough, but Michael's reaction had instantly told her that it had been a mistake. Although she really did like the young man, she knew that this wasn't the time or place to be leading him on. Besides, she didn't really think that Michael was her type; she was generally more attracted to the strong, self-reliant variety of male, rather than the sensitive intellectual. In any case, she resolved to get back on track this day and reestablish a friendly, but businesslike relationship with the young professor, whose well being had largely been put in her hands. She quickly showered and dressed, then headed for Michael's room.

Michael woke up at about the same time as Olivia, but in a much more upbeat mood. The last twenty-four hours had held more excitement for him than his last twenty-four years. Tycoons, beautiful women, danger, and intrigue…what more could a young professor want? He quickly got dressed and ready, and then put on a VR visor to watch the morning news until Olivia arrived.

A global weather report was in progress. The Midwest drought was continuing with no apparent relief in sight. Widespread floods in India had claimed thousands of lives. Yet another monster hurricane was forming in the Southeastern Caribbean. Most of the rest of the news was equally depressing: food riots in Brazil and Ecuador, civil war in Indonesia and Kenya, another terrorist bombing in L.A. Just about the only positive note was from a report on the progress of the third manned mission to Mars. The report was interrupted by a knock on the door.

"Good morning, Olivia!" Michael greeted the young woman warmly.

"Good morning, Michael. Are you ready to go?"

Michael couldn't help but notice that Olivia was all business this morning. Maybe she just wasn't a morning person.

"Let's go grab a bit of breakfast. Just leave your luggage here and it will be taken to the shuttle."

With that, she turned and led Michael to the elevator. They took the elevator up a few floors to a small company canteen where they both had coffee, a roll and juice; neither was in the mood for a large breakfast after the last night's dinner.

"So what does the itinerary for today look like?" Michael tried to make a bit of conversation after finishing his roll.

"At eight, we'll be taking a shuttle to Kennedy International. We'll meet Mr. Graham and the rest of his party there. We're scheduled leave on the corporate plane at nine o'clock, and we'll be arriving at the Olympus site at about ten-thirty."

* * *

While Michael and Olivia were finishing their breakfast, Mac was already at the plane, scrambling to make last minute preparations. He was in a relatively foul mood. The old man had called him at three a.m. to tell him that he had made the decision to immediately relocate himself and his staff to Olympus. That was good news and bad news to the security chief. The good news was that Mac believed that his boss had made the correct decision; Mac could protect the key corporate personnel much more effectively at an isolated site such as Olympus. The bad news was that he only had a few hours to transform a weekend trip into a major personnel relocation. He would first have to round up additional security personnel and equipment, so he had contacted Marcus to get that moving.

Next Mac contacted Bill Atherton, the head of security at the Olympus site, and directed him to immediately make preparations to receive their new residents. Bill wasn't any happier about the lack of warning than Mac was, but he was a good man, and he had assured his boss that everything would be ready. Only then had Mac jumped into the shower, thrown on some clothes, and headed for the airport.

At the plane, Mac now continued making calls, one after another. He contacted the members of Graham's senior staff, to make sure that each one knew that this would now be a one-way trip. He was pleased that all but a few had already been contacted by the old man himself. He had also explained to each that their families or "significant others" could follow in a few days, if they so desired.

Mac didn't so mind so much being rushed…he was used to hustling from his years in the U.N. Special Forces. What worried him was the increased possibility of a major screw-up when the time couldn't be taken to consider all the angles. Sometimes, however, he knew that it just couldn't be helped. He and his people would just have to stay on their toes and do the best that they could under the circumstances.

Olivia and Michael arrived at the airport shortly before eight-thirty. Their craft landed at a pad just a few hundred feet from the corporate plane. Walking up to the sleek, black and gold Lockheed/Boeing SkyEagle, Michael was even more impressed than he had been by the corporate shuttle. He had seen pictures and read about these leading edge craft, but he had never seen one; now he was going to actually ride in one. He knew that these planes were equipped with engines that could transition from hover, to traditional subsonic jet flight, to ramjets for hypersonic speeds. Domestic flights only required a sub-orbital parabolic trajectory, although rocket boosters could take the vehicle into a lower earth orbit for transcontinental flights. The SkyEagle carried about forty passengers and required only a two-man crew.

Inside was a beehive of activity, with Mac at the center, giving commands and making calls. Most of the staff members were already in their seats, although Graham had not yet arrived. Olivia took the time to introduce Michael to some of the senior members before leading him to his seat. It was quite a prestigious group. First was Dr. Raymond Fitzpatrick, the ex-Surgeon General, who would now be the Chief Medical Officer of the Olympus Medical Center. The good doctor was a gracious and very patrician older gentleman with a shock of solid gray hair; he greeted Michael warmly with a firm handshake.

Next was Dr. Jacquelyn Ryder-Scott, who had served in a variety of senior posts in the Treasury Department and was now Graham Enterprises CFO. She was a trim, elderly lady, dressed in a conservative navy blue business suit, in contrast to the rest of the passengers, who mostly looked ready for a round of golf. She seemed a bit distracted and barely looked at Michael when she took his hand.

Then there was John Tanaka, Chief Technical Officer, a small, dapper looking man with a warm smile. Finally, there was Dr. Frederick Douglas Allen, a large, distinguished looking black man who served as the Chief Operating Officer for Graham Enterprises. Michael was also introduced to several of the two or three staff assistants that were accompanying each of the staff members.

As they took their seats toward the back of the cabin, Marcus, Mac's assistant, arrived with Graham and two additional security agents that he had rounded up at the last minute. Graham took a seat next to Dr. Allen, up front. Marcus took the seat next to Mac, across the aisle from Michael and Olivia, after directing the two agents to a pair of seats just behind Graham and Allen. Within a few minutes, the doors were pulled to, and the engines began to spin up.

Mac turned to Marcus and said, "Thanks for helping me to pull all of this together on short notice. By the way, who are the new guys? I don't think I've seen them before."

"The tall red-haired fellow is Brian Leahy, ex-SAS. The short, stocky guy is an ex-Interpol agent named Alain Gerard. They were both transferred from our Zurich branch around three months ago; I hear they're good men with excellent credentials," Marcus responded as the engines grew louder and the craft lifted off.

Almost immediately, the movement of the vehicle transitioned smoothly from vertical to forward and up. Soon they were pushed against their seats as the craft rapidly accelerated. Olivia explained to Michael that they would be reaching the stratosphere in about thirty minutes. Michael felt exhilarated; flying in a ramjet interceptor had to feel something like this.

In his seat, Mac was too preoccupied to feel exhilarated. Something was wrong, but he couldn't put his finger on just what it was. He looked around the cabin. Everything looked in order. He looked at Michael and

Olivia across the aisle; they were fine. He could just see Graham and Allen up front. They appeared deep in conversation; everything okay there.

Mac turned to Marcus, seated next to him. He was just leaning back in his seat, looking forward. Was that a bit of perspiration on his upper lip? Why would he be nervous? They had flown together many times; he knew Marcus had no fear of flying.

Maybe I'm just getting paranoid, he thought to himself. Then he reminded himself that paranoia was a job requirement for his position. So, he began to consider the basis for that itch at the back of his neck. He had handpicked Marcus Sternhagen as his executive assistant about nine months ago. Marcus had graduated from West Point with high marks eight years earlier, served a distinguished tour as a Ranger, and then another tour in the same unit of the UN Special Forces command that Mac had served in for years. He had aced the psychometric test he had been given as a candidate for his present position, scoring as an intelligent individual of strong moral character. He had also done an all around excellent job in his present position.

So what was the problem? Well, the security breaches *had* begun shortly after Marcus had arrived. And Marcus was one of the very few individuals with access to the information that would have made them possible. And why did Marcus just happen to select two agents for this trip who had recently been transferred from Europe, men whom Mac didn't know? Could they be *agent provocateurs* to be inserted at the Olympus site? Mac's reverie was interrupted by Marcus's hand on his arm.

"Mac, I have something very important to tell you," Marcus said in a calm, low voice.

"Brian has a gun pointed at Mr. Graham's head. We are going to divert to a new destination. If you or anyone else tries absolutely anything at all, Brian is under orders to pull the trigger, immediately and without question. If you all cooperate, no one will be harmed. My sponsors merely require a high level meeting with Mr. Graham. Do you understand?"

"Yes," Mac answered curtly, then looked forward. The big man did have his weapon at Graham's head; his other hand was holding the old man's collar. Gerard had gotten up, drawn his weapon, and was moving back their way. Leahy had then moved over to sit immediately behind Graham. Mac looked at Olivia across the aisle. She was looking back at him and seemed to be poised to go for her own weapon. Mac motioned her to be still.

Marcus got up and grabbed Mac's weapon from under his coat, while Gerard disarmed Olivia. The passengers were looking around in confusion.

Marcus then stood up and announced loudly, "We are in command of this plane. Everyone stay in your seats and remain absolutely silent. Do exactly as you are told and you will not be harmed."

He and Gerard then placed e-cuffs on Mac and Olivia and performed a brief but thorough body search on them both. Marcus then moved forward to the flight deck to give the crew their orders, while Gerard remained back to keep an eye on Mac and Olivia.

Mac could barely contain his fury, with the two agents, with Marcus, but most of all with himself. He had blown it, pure and simple. He was well compensated to prevent just this sort of eventuality, and he had allowed it to happen. And his own right-hand man had perpetrated it, no less!

But Mac knew that self-recrimination needed to be saved for later; right now he needed to consider his options. One option was to do nothing, which was the best option if Marcus was telling the truth. However, Mac almost immediately discounted that possibility; you don't hijack a planeload of VIP's just to have a conference. Almost certainly, they were all going to just disappear, and the threat that they had posed to the existing world order would disappear with them.

Mac did have one wild card. It was a birthday gift from a fellow commando, an old friend from years ago. At the time, Mac had joked that giving a knife for a present was bad luck...now he wondered. Its short handle and hilt, designed to be held between the first and second fingers, also functioned as a belt buckle. The short, razor-sharp blade slid into the end of the belt. Only the blade's edge was metal, the rest was made of composite material that wouldn't set off a metal detector. Mac had never expected to actually need the small but lethal weapon; he had worn it more as a memento of a bygone era.

But he knew that using the knife would take a very precise set of circumstances. He would have to patient, and hope that those circumstances would arise. Meantime, he carefully withdrew the weapon, and showed it to Olivia. She saw it. He then pointed to himself and held up two fingers, then pointed to her and held up one. She nodded slightly. Good...she understood. If he made a move, he would go for two of them; it would be up to her to handle the third.

Shortly, Marcus came back from the flight deck, and conferred briefly with Gerard, in whispers. He then went through the aft door back to

Graham's small private office in the back of the plane, doubtless to contact his superiors in private. Gerard remained at the back of the cabin, where he could keep an eye on everyone.

A few minutes later Marcus emerged, took a seat a row behind and across from Mac, and sent Gerard forward. They all needed to get strapped in. In a few minutes, the rocket boosters would fire and they would be shortly thereafter achieving low orbit; their destination was now to be considerably farther away than Colorado.

As Gerard moved forward, Mac unbuckled his seat belt carefully, so that Marcus couldn't see. He saw with his peripheral vision that Olivia instantly followed suite. Good. Mac pulled the knife, and at just the instant that Leahy's view would be blocked by Gerard, he bounded forward, his hands still cuffed. In one smooth motion, he plunged the knife into Gerard's lower back and shoved him hard between the seats and out of the way.

Just as Leahy sensed the commotion and began to turn, he felt a hand grab his collar and a sharp object press against the base of his skull.

"Hand me your weapon, butt first, *now*, or this goes in," Mac growled.

Mac meant it and Leahy knew that he meant it. The pistol came up, butt first. Mac heard a terrific struggle taking place in back—he knew that he didn't have much time. The sidearm was a standard issue S&W Colt pulse-charge weapon, which fired a low velocity soft round. The round wouldn't penetrate flesh; rather it acted as a high voltage capacitor that discharged a powerful jolt that could be either set to stun or kill. Mac quickly set the slide adjustment on the grip to a high stun setting, reached over and fired a round into Leahy's thigh. The big man convulsed.

Mac instantly whirled to help Olivia. His heart went into his throat as he saw Marcus on top of Olivia, pounding away at her. Her cuffed hands were still around his neck. Mac couldn't take a chance with the weapon; he dropped it and bounded toward them. Marcus just had a glimpse of a foot as he looked up. Then shooting stars exploded as the foot struck between his eyes. His head snapped back against Olivia's cuffed hands, and he was instantly knocked unconscious.

Mac pulled Olivia's arms from around Marcus, and roughly pulled him off of her. He quickly grabbed the unconscious man's wrist controller and deactivated both sets of e-cuffs. Just then, he saw Michael sprawled between the seats, unconscious.

Then he looked down at Olivia. Shit! Shit! Shit! Blood was spreading everywhere across her mid-section. A bloody knife was lying next to her. Now passengers were screaming; some were standing up.

Mac shouted, "It's all over. Everyone sit down and strap in, right now! We have wounded to attend to…"

Suddenly, the rocket boosters kicked in and Mac lost his balance. Several other passengers, who hadn't strapped back in, were thrown around as well. More screams.

The ship accelerated toward orbital velocity while Mac hung onto the injured young woman. Even as the boosters fired, he managed to pull up her blouse to look at the wounds. There appeared to be three deep stab wounds, bleeding freely. He applied direct pressure to try to partially stem the flow.

A few minutes later, though it seemed like hours, the boosters shut off. They were now weightless. Great. Michael and Marcus's bodies floated freely as did the corpse of Gerard. The unrestrained passengers struggled back into their seats with the help of their fellow passengers. Mac hung onto the base of a seat with one hand, while he tried to hold Olivia down and maintain pressure to her injuries with the other. This wasn't working.

"Dr. Fitzpatrick!" Mac shouted, "I need your help right now!"

The old man got up immediately, and began making his way awkwardly back towards them, using the built-in handholds on the seats. As Mac looked up, he noticed Graham struggling to make his way to the fight deck, using handholds placed for that purpose. Good. The boss was doubtlessly going to order the crew to get them back down as quickly as possible.

"Mac, I need an emergency medikit, right away, but first we've got to get her to Jonathan's office where I can have room to work on her. We can strap her to the sofa."

"Right doctor," the big man replied, though he was at a complete loss at how he could manage to maneuver the injured young woman in zero gee. Well, he would just have to get it done, somehow. Mac grabbed a seat handhold with one hand, and gently put an arm around her waist with another.

Olivia was very cold now, and that frightened him. It also filled him with determination. A fine mist of blood floated around them. He pushed with all his strength against the handhold up and back, propelling them both toward the rear cabin door. He missed badly, and they bounced off of the ceiling. He pushed again, and managed to grab the top edge of the door with his one free hand. That gave him purchase to push off toward the sofa.

This was like a bad dream. They floated past the sofa, but he managed to grab the leg of a small conference table bolted down just a few feet past. His heart was racing. One more push and he grabbed a handhold on the sofa, rolling her as gently as he could onto it. He quickly pulled one of the sofa's shoulder harnesses across her chest and the other across her legs. He was drenched from sweat from the effort; Olivia looked absolutely white.

Mac was about to shout for the doctor, when the old man came sailing through the door, and bless him, he had one of the large medikits under his arm. Mac watched in wonder, as the old man now seemed to negotiate his way effortlessly to the injured young woman's side. He held onto one of the sofa's harnesses.

"Help me get this kit open, Mac."

Mac opened the kit and the doctor quickly pulled out a small oxygen tank and mask. He fitted it over her face and turned on the valve. Then he pulled out three large combat-type dressings and taped them tightly over the wounds.

Mac didn't like the look on the doc's face; he seemed positively grim. However, he also looked very determined. It had been a lot of years since the old man had worked in an ER, but once upon a time he had been very good at it. Next, he pulled out a bag of plasma. He quickly inserted the needle into a vein, and taped it to her arm. Then he attached the bag to the top of the sofa above her.

Suddenly, the physician gave Mac a bewildered look, and told him, "Well, a gravity feed won't work. Mac, gently squeeze the bag so she gets a steady supply of plasma."

Mac needed three hands…one to hold himself down, one to hold the kit and one to squeeze the bag. He looped an arm through the harness and managed. The doctor then pulled out a bio-scanner from the kit and took her vital signs. He frowned.

Just then, Mac's wrist Uplink warbled. Well, what a fine time for a friggin' phone call! He almost laughed in frustration. The doc continued working as Mac answered the phone. It was Graham.

"Retros are firing in about three minutes, Mac. You fellows had better hang on. Alan tells me that you'll have gravity in about twelve minutes. But we're going to have a rough ride; I've told him to break every law but the laws of physics to get us down as fast as possible. We're going straight to the Olympus trauma center. Alan tells me that we can get there about as fast as anywhere else and we can have every possible medical asset standing by. How is Olivia doing, Raymond?"

"Not good, but we're doing all that we can. Jonathan, every minute counts. I can't do much until we get her down. She's bleeding internally. Her pulse is rapid and weak and her blood pressure is low. Please have doctor's Schmidt and Rosen standing by with a full trauma team."

"Alan tells me that we'll be touching down in thirty-five minutes flat. I'll take care of everything else. By the way Mac, Michael's going to be okay, and we've secured Marcus and his friend."

"Good, thanks boss," Mac responded.

He would take care of those guys later...really take care of them...

Mac had seen the doctor wince when Graham had told him thirty-five minutes. Mac knew that it would take some kind of miracle to get them on the ground from orbit that quickly. He also knew that thirty-five minutes could be an eternity to a trauma patient bleeding internally.

Just then, the retros fired and both men strained to hang on as they were thrown forward. All they could do until the retros finished firing was try to hold themselves and Olivia steady. Mac focused on holding the young woman and squeezing the plasma bag as steadily as possible.

As the retros continued to fire, Mac looked at Olivia's face, which was just a few inches from his own. He was just a bit encouraged by a hint of color in her cheeks. Perhaps, he thought, the oxygen and plasma were doing some good. *Hang on, young lady,* he whispered.

As soon as the retros shut down, the doctor asked Mac to open the medikit again. The ride was still rough, and they still only had partial gravity, but the old man seemed intent on continuing his work. Mac watched him pull out a hypo-injector, insert a vial and press the injector against her arm. She flinched a bit when he triggered it, and Mac took that a good sign too; at least she was still responsive. Mac didn't bother asking what drug the doc had given her, but he couldn't restrain himself when the old man took her signs again.

"How does it look, doc?"

"Fifty-fifty, Mac," the older man responded, "I wouldn't give her even those odds if she weren't in such superb physical condition. And I think she's a fighter."

"That she is," he muttered.

They were both thrown sideways as the craft executed a long, hard bank to port. He and the doc continued to hang onto the sofa's shoulder straps for dear life. Olivia let out a soft moan. Mac glanced out a porthole; all he could see was a rosy glow from the heat built up during reentry. He rather hoped that they weren't burning up.

In the cockpit, Alan Michener, ex-RAF Captain, ex-Eurospace shuttle pilot, with the expert assistance of his copilot, Akiro Watanabe, struggled to bring his bird down as rapidly as humanly possible. On initial reentry, they'd had no choice but to let the auto-guidance systems handle maneuvers that were simply too complex for any human hands. As soon as he could, however, he overrode the ship's guidance computers so that he could bring her down faster than the onboard programs would allow. The old man had ordered them to push the envelope; they were pushing the envelope.

As Alan handled the controls, Akiro monitored the critical systems, while simultaneously contacting the Air/Space ground controllers to declare a medical emergency. They would be coming in far steeper and faster than regulations allowed. In fact, they planned on remaining supersonic until just before they touched down. Now, heat was their primary enemy.

Normally, the guidance systems would automatically execute a series of gentle S-turns that would bleed off energy and gradually slow the craft during their descent from orbit. To save time, they would abbreviate these maneuvers so that would they be coming in, literally, "hot". It was a risk, but a manageable risk, due to the incredible heat and stress resistant properties of the SkyEagle's metalloid skin.

As the flight smoothed out and gravity returned, all Mac and the doctor had left to do was hold on to Olivia, watch over her, and wait. They had done everything that they could do for her with their limited resources. Time seemed to stand still for Mac.

At long last, gravity returned, and the flight had smoothed out somewhat. The fiery glow through the porthole was diminishing as well. Mac looked at his watch. About twenty minutes to touchdown–still an eternity. Just then, Dr. Ryder-Scott entered the rear cabin and approached the injured woman and the two men tending to her.

"Daniel, let me take over so you can clean yourself up before we land. I would have come sooner, but the ride was so rough that I was afraid that I couldn't make it back here without simply becoming another casualty."

"Thanks, Jacquelyn, but I'd just as soon stay here."

"Nonsense, just take a look at yourself. And don't worry about me. I served a tour as a Navy nurse before I went back to college and got my doctorate in economics. Now hand me that plasma bag," she ordered.

Mac looked down at himself; he did look like the victim of a low budget horror film. His hands were covered with blood, and his shirt was blood-soaked as well. He relented and handed Dr. Ryder-Scott the bag attached to Olivia's arm. He stood up with difficulty and stretched; he felt roughly twice his fifty-three years. The elderly lady knelt down to take his place next to Dr. Fitzpatrick. She took the plasma with one hand and gently placed her free hand on Olivia's forehead.

Mac headed for the main cabin. He decided to check on the two prisoners before cleaning up. To be safe, he pulled his bag down from an overhead bin and put an e-cuff on each man's ankles in addition to the cuffs that had already been put on their wrists. He then ordered the two staffers standing guard to stay alert.

Next he checked on Michael. The young professor didn't look too bad; he had a bump on his forehead, and it looked like both of his eyes were turning black. Then again, he didn't look too good either; he seemed as if he was still stunned. The young man did, however manage to ask Mac about Olivia.

"She'll be fine, Michael. In about fifteen minutes, you're both going to be getting the best medical care that can be had on the planet," Mac answered. He hoped that he wasn't lying about Olivia; he certainly wasn't exaggerating about the quality of medical care at Olympus. Its medical center had the very best in medical personnel and technology.

The security chief wondered just what had happened with Olivia and Michael in the struggle with Marcus during the few moments that Mac had been preoccupied with taking care of Gerard and Leahy. He decided that he should wait until later to ask the young man; Michael didn't look up to answering any questions just now.

Mac moved forward and briefly conferred with Graham and Allen. He then retired to the cabin's small restroom. He quickly stripped off his bloody shirt. He soaked a large handful of paper towels and cleaned himself up moderately well. He then grabbed a pullover from his bag and slipped it on. Finally, he ran his fingers through his hair a few times and looked at himself in the mirror. He looked almost human. Mac ducked back into the rear cabin to check on Olivia one more time. No change.

Just then, Alan announced on the intercom, "We'll be touching down in about five minutes, folks. Everyone please buckle up. We're going to land right outside the medical center, so please remain seated until our injured passengers are evacuated and our prisoners are removed."

Mac strapped into one of the rear seats in the main cabin. The volume and frequency of the engines changed, as the craft began to rapidly decelerate. The plane banked on final approach, and Mac caught sight of the Alexandria Library. He had seen the Holos of the structure, but this was the first time that he had actually seen the real thing. It was awesome, dwarfing all of the surrounding structures under construction around it. In a few more moments, the craft rapidly transitioned to a hover, and then smoothly dropped to ground level, touching down with a barely perceptible thud.

In a matter of seconds, the rear hatch opened automatically, and a four man medical team immediately burst through, carrying a collapsible litter. They made a beeline to the injured young woman in the rear cabin. While one medic took vital signs and conferred with Dr. Fitzpatrick, the other three quickly and efficiently transferred Olivia from the sofa to the litter. They had the young woman out of the plane and headed to the ER in just a few more moments.

While the medical team took care of Olivia, a three-man security team entered through the forward hatch. Mac got up and gave them a quick rundown of what had happened, and pointed them towards the two hijackers. He instructed them to keep the two secure and under wraps. They removed the e-cuffs from the men's ankles and quickly hustled the pair off of the plane.

Another medical team then entered the main cabin to take care of Michael, as well as several other passengers who had received an assortment of minor bumps and bruises during the wild ride. They put a neck brace around Michael's neck and escorted him to a waiting wheelchair just outside the plane. The rest of the passengers were then guided out the two hatches, with the injured in the lead.

Mac waited, and fell in behind Allen and Graham, who were the last to exit. Graham had taken a few moments to shake Alan and Akiro's hands and thank them for getting everyone down so swiftly, not to mention in one piece. As they passed through the hatch and down the ramp, Mac was surprised by a fine mist being sprayed on them from several emergency skycraft hovering around the big plane. Then he felt the intense heat radiating from the SkyEagle's exterior, and understood the need for the cooling spray. Bill Atherton, Mac's security chief at Olympus, and a small army of security and emergency personnel were waiting for them at the base of the ramp.

9

The Vigil

The passengers were all escorted to the lobby of the medical center. Bill then led Mac, Dr. Allen and Graham to a small waiting room near the ER. He also placed two heavily armed guards just outside the waiting room's door.

"We'll make sure that all of the members of your staff are well taken care of, Mr. Graham. We figured that you three might want to wait here while the trauma team looks after Olivia and the other young man. I can't tell you how sorry we are about all of this," Bill added.

"Thanks Bill. You were right, we'll want to wait here until we see how Olivia and Michael are doing," Graham responded.

"Well, then, if you gentlemen will excuse me, I've got some work to do. We have all of our security personnel on full alert. Mac, we're determined to prevent any more "incidents", at all costs."

"Good, Bill, later today, I'll want to meet with your senior security personnel. Like it or not, we're at war, and we're going to have to get properly prepared for it," Mac said.

"Right, boss, and if anyone needs anything, just give me a call."

As soon as Bill left, Mac moved into a corner to place a call that he dreaded to make. The call was to notify Olivia's parents in D.C. Her father was out; Mac told her mother calmly and briefly that her daughter had been seriously wounded in an "incident", and that the perpetrators were now in custody. He declined to elaborate, but offered to arrange emergency transportation to bring both parents to Colorado as quickly as possible. Olivia's mother took it well. She accepted the offer and Mac gave her a number to call to make arrangements. The three men then settled down to wait.

After a few moments, Graham spoke up, "Mac, that was a pretty bold action you took back in the plane. Where did you get the knife, anyway? And what do you suppose would have happened if you hadn't got to me in time?"

"You probably would have been killed," the security chief answered matter-of-factly. He went on to describe the knife hidden in his belt. "I'm sorry boss, but I figured that your odds were better if I acted than they would have been if we had all been taken to Siberia or someplace."

"Actually, Alan tells me that we were headed for Hong Kong. And I'm quite certain that you were right to act. I'm sure that if we had reached Hong Kong, none of us would ever have been heard from again."

"I quite agree," Dr. Allen added. "Mac, you did well. Thank you for all of us."

"Thanks aren't really warranted, Dr. Allen. Don't forget that it was my man that turned on us. However, after we find out how Olivia is doing, Mr. Sternhagen and I are going to have ourselves a little discussion. I can personally guarantee that the outcome of that discussion will be a complete and detailed disclosure of everything that our young friend knows."

A cloud had passed over McCafferty's visage at the mention of Marcus. It was an ominous look that made the other two men more than a little uncomfortable. They both knew Mac's history, as well as his reputation. Daniel Patrick McCafferty was just about the last man on the planet that you wanted to have as an enemy.

"Mac, don't do anything that you'll regret later," Graham cautioned.

"Mr. Graham, I can assure you that I will never regret anything in the future that transpires between Marcus and myself," Mac answered. The reply gave precious little comfort to the other two men.

Just then, Dr.'s Ryder-Scott, Fitzpatrick and Tanaka entered the room.

"We thought that you gentlemen could use a little company," Jacquelyn said. "We hope that you don't mind if we wait with you."

"Absolutely not," Graham answered as he stood back up.

"Please sit down."

They all sat down, and the vigil continued. In an examination room nearby, Michael lay patiently on a small gurney. A medical assistant had wheeled him in a short while earlier. The young lady had asked him to lie still, explaining that a doctor would be in to see him shortly. In the last hour or so he had been thoroughly examined by a team of medical personnel using an impressive array of high tech equipment.

It had seemed to Michael that the attention he was receiving was all out of proportion to his injuries, i.e., a bump on the head and a couple of black eyes. He had guessed that the level of care was more due to a mandate by Graham than to any real medical necessity. And all the while that he was being fussed over, he had wondered how Olivia was doing. He had tried to ask the medics about her, but they had gently turned his questions aside.

Now as he waited to see the doctor, his thoughts returned to Olivia. The grand adventure that he had anticipated had turned into a nightmare so quickly that he had scarcely had had a chance react to the turn of events. After a while, an attractive middle-aged woman in scrubs entered his room, smiled and offered her hand to Michael.

"It's okay to sit up now, Dr. Vincent, although we'd like for you to not move around too much just yet. My name is Dr. Anna Rosen. I'm sorry we've made you wait here, but we've been just a bit busy. I just finished assisting in surgery with your companion a short while ago, and I've just now reviewed the results of your cerebral multi-scan. You have a minor concussion, but a headache and perhaps some dizziness should be just about the only symptoms that you will experience. However, just to play it safe we're going to keep you here under observation for the rest of the afternoon."

"Now as to your companion…Olivia's surgery went very well. She had extensive internal injuries, but we've successfully patched her up and stabilized her. However, the bad news is that she suffered tremendous blood loss before we got to her, and her multi-scan does show some evidence of brain damage from oxygen deprivation. We are now running a molecular nerve scan to more accurately assess the extent of that damage. Of course, we will also have a better idea once she regains consciousness. Either way, it will probably be this evening before we have a better idea of just what we are dealing with. I'm sorry, but until then, we'll just have to wait."

"Dr. Rosen, isn't it true that you can regenerate lost nerve or brain cells?"

"Yes, Michael, we can generally use regenerative therapy to restore lost brain cells. However, we can't restore memory, and that includes muscle memory. For instance, we can restore a stroke victim's *ability* to speak, but then they must also relearn speech, like a child. Depending on the level of damage, therapy can take weeks, months or even years. But let's not get ahead of ourselves. For now, let's just wait and hope."

"Why does it take so long to run the nerve scan," Michael asked next.

Like most, the young man was used to all computer processes being pretty much instantaneous.

"The molecular nerve scan, or MNS, is an incredibly sophisticated process. Billions of neurons are scanned and the damaged ones are mapped against known brain functionality. A summary assessment of the injury is then output for analysis by specialists. Even this analysis is imperfect; no two brains function in exactly the same way, and the human brain has its own remarkable capacity to reprogram itself in order to work around damaged areas. Nonetheless, the MNS is an invaluable tool in making an accurate and detailed diagnosis."

"For now though, let's just get you into a nice room where you can get some rest, and we can keep an eye on you. I promise, we'll keep you fully updated on Olivia's progress."

The physician had quickly detected in Michael's voice and manner the level of his concern for the young woman. Dr. Rosen then shook Michael's hand once more and bade leave.

As Dr. Rosen was updating Michael on Olivia's status, Dr. Gregory Schmidt was reporting much the same to Graham and his party in the waiting room. He gave them an update on Michael, as well, suggesting that Michael be allowed to rest a bit before receiving any visitors.

Graham and Dr. Ryder-Scott determined to continue their vigil, but Graham suggested that the others move on to handle the many pressing issues at hand, promising to keep all of them updated on Olivia's progress. Dr. Fitzpatrick took his leave to confer with Olivia's medical team. Allen and Tanaka excused themselves to meet with their respective staffs.

Mac hesitated, then decided that he was duty-bound to start taking the immediate steps required to ensure everyone else's safety. Besides, he hated just sitting around and waiting; he just wanted to be sure to be there when Olivia woke up. Graham and Dr. Schmidt both assured him that he would be immediately notified when it appeared that Olivia might be regaining consciousness.

With that Mac took leave to meet Bill Atherton and start putting together a new game plan. He contacted the security director on his Uplink, and they agreed to meet in Bill's office. Five minutes later, Mac was in Atherton's outer office, introducing himself to the armed and uniformed guard at the desk. Mac was pleased that she took the effort to verify his voiceprint and to make a retinal scan even though McCafferty was well known as the head of the Graham security organization. After the security check, she ushered Mac into Bill's office; the director had not yet arrived. A few moments later, he rushed in, somewhat out of breath.

"Sorry about making you wait, Mac, but we're really scrambling around here. The attempted hijack was a rude awakening. As you well know, we've had some incidents of suspected sabotage, but we never expected anything like this. We've already begun taking steps to deal with the new reality."

"Good, Bill, give me a rundown of what you've done so far."

Mac held Atherton in high regard, even though Bill wasn't ex-military. The head of Olympus security was in his late-fifties, and rather looked it; he had thinning hair and a bit of a paunch. His background had been law enforcement and security. Bill Atherton had started out as a cop in a small mid-western town, then graduated to the Treasury department as a field agent and finally been promoted to head the presidential detail for the Secret Service. When Mac had first interviewed him for the job, the ex-military man had been less than impressed. Even with his sterling record, Bill looked every bit the government bureaucrat. Mac preferred warrior, or at least ex-warrior types, like himself. Although Mac had finally selected Bill to be the director of Olympus security, it had been with some reservation. That reservation had disappeared over the last three years, as Bill had proved to be a man of exceptional intelligence, competence and integrity.

"Well, Mac, we've got your two surviving hijackers secured in the basement of this building. We have removed all their electronic devices, and have had the medics check them out. We plan on interrogating them later this afternoon. We have called up all off-duty security personnel at this site, and plan on doubling our overall security staffing around the clock, for the foreseeable future. We've also put all Graham security operations around the world on full alert. We have also already begun thoroughly reviewing the background of all of our security personnel from the top down to try to spot any additional infiltrators. We're beginning with you," he added with a grin.

"Sounds good, Bill," Mac responded. "Just two additional things for now, I want to handle Marcus's initial interrogation myself, right away. I then want to meet with your senior security staff at 1800."

The two men discussed a variety of other security issues for another half-hour, and then Mac asked to be taken to see Marcus. Bill summoned a guard to escort Mac to the basement so that Bill could continue with his own responsibilities.

The guard took Mac down an express elevator, then down a long corridor. At the end of the corridor, in a small front office, sat yet another armed guard at a desk, who checked Mac's voiceprint and retinal patterns once more. The guard then ushered Mac through a metal door to a small adjoining room, actually a cell. The room had a small lavatory to one side, a small cot in one corner, and a metal table in the center of the room bolted to the floor. There was a chair on either side. Marcus sat on the cot, his hands as well as his ankles e-cuffed.

Mac couldn't help but feel a bit satisfied by the large, angry looking bruise on the center of the young man's forehead. Below the forehead, however, Marcus met Mac's eyes with a look of pure defiance. The guard took the prisoner by the elbow and sat him down on one of the chairs. He then attached his e-cuffs to a ring on the side of the table.

"You can't hold me like this, McCafferty. You have to turn me over to the authorities." Marcus had been determined to get in the first word.

"I'm afraid that if anyone checks, they will find that Marcus Sternhagen resigned a few days ago, and promptly dropped out of sight. Now then, Mr. Sternhagen, or whoever you are, you have exactly one chance to get out of this intact. That's by telling us everything that you know–nothing excluded, nothing inaccurate, nothing even slightly misleading. Once we have completely verified everything that you've told us, and are certain that it's honest and totally complete, we'll give you a plane ticket to anywhere you'd like to go outside of this country. The offer stands for exactly 24 hours. After that, there will be no deal, and you'll never be seen or heard from again."

With that Mac promptly got up and turned his back on Marcus to leave.

"You're bluffing, McCafferty! You can't...."

Mac slammed the door behind himself as he exited the cell. He then gave the guard explicit instructions.

"Unhook the prisoner from the table, and then leave him in the cell. Under no circumstances, except for a medical emergency, is he to see or speak to anyone else for the next 24 hours. I want him to have no food or light until I return. He can use the lavatory or get drinking water from his sink in the dark. Do you understand?"

The guard looked a bit nervous but nodded in the affirmative. With that, Mac flipped the light switch off for the cell. A moment later Marcus began pounding on the table and yelling at the top of his lungs.

"Ignore that completely. If the noise bothers you, move to the outer office. Do you understand your orders? Make sure that your relief understands them completely, as well. And contact me immediately if you have any questions," Mac concluded.

"Yes sir," the guard responded.

Mac turned to leave the way he'd come. Truth to tell, Marcus was right...Mac was bluffing. It was true that Mac had killed many times in combat, without hesitation. However, regardless of his ruthless reputation, he had never murdered or tortured anyone, nor had he allowed anyone else under his command to do so. Following those hard and fast rules throughout his career had allowed him to sleep well at night, even now.

However, McCafferty wasn't above a bit of psychological abuse if the results eventually saved lives. And abusing the man who had cold-bloodedly stabbed and nearly killed a young lady who, Mac had to admit to himself, felt more to him like the daughter he had never had than a subordinate, wouldn't make it all that difficult, either.

The problem, however, was what to do if the young man called his bluff? Well, he would just have to cross that bridge when, and if, he came to it. Meanwhile, by the time he met with Marcus again, he would know better how Olivia was faring, and that might just factor into the next step that he would take with Mr. Sternhagen.

* * *

A while later, as Graham and Jacqueline continued their vigil in the small waiting room, they were pleased to see Michael enter the room, accompanied by a nurse. The nurse showed Michael to the chair next to Graham, and asked him if he needed anything else. The young woman excused herself as soon as Michael assured her that he was okay. Graham had speculated during the wait as to what Michael's reaction might ultimately be to the madness of the last few days. Graham figured that Michael would either want to opt out and go home right away, or that the crisis would cement his commitment. He was betting on the latter.

"Mr. Graham, I just want to let you know that I want in on this project. I know that I'm probably jumping headlong into a world that I hardly have a clue about. Nonetheless, I think that I've seen enough to at least be pretty sure who the good guys are. And if even a small part of what you've told me is true, this project is without a doubt the most important effort that the world has seen in a long, long time…and I want to be a part of it."

"Michael, I assure you that you are right on both counts. We are certainly the good guys, and this is the most important effort that mankind has undertaken in a thousand years."

Graham rose and extended his hand to Michael, and the young man rose to take it. "Welcome aboard," the old man added.

Dr. Ryder-Scott also stood and shook Michael's hand. "Michael, I am certain that you'll never regret your decision."

Just then, Dr. Rosen entered the room.

"I thought that you might want to know that Olivia's neural activity has increased, indicating that she may soon be regaining consciousness. We have also just completed a preliminary analysis of her neural scan. If you will follow me up to my office, I will brief you on what we've determined so far. We'll also be just down the hall, so that we can all be nearby when she comes to."

Graham, Dr. Ryder Scott and Michael followed Dr. Rosen back up to the top floor of the five-story building, to a small conference room adjoining Dr. Rosen's office just down the hall from the ICU area where Olivia was being watched. Dr. Fitzpatrick was waiting for them. Dr. Rosen asked everyone to sit down, and then voice-activated the Holo situated at one end of the table.

"Holo on, patient: Olivia Bertrand, neural-scan, real-time."

Instantly, the 3D image of a human brain appeared about one foot above the projector. Most of the image was in gray-blue, however, several small areas were pink, and within a few pink areas were smaller red areas. The image also slowly rotated, so that everyone had a complete view.

Dr. Rosen pointed to some of the pink and red areas with a laser pointer. "The pink areas indicate mild neurological damage, the red, more severe. Luckily, as you can see, there are only a few small areas that are seriously damaged. These are areas of the cerebellum that effect speech and motor control. A preliminary analysis of these areas indicates that she will have slightly slurred speech and some coordination problems, particularly on her left side. In summary, her symptoms will be similar to someone who has suffered a mild stroke," the doctor concluded.

"And what is the prognosis for a full recovery, Anna?" Graham, ever the bottom-line man, asked immediately.

"They are excellent, Jonathan," the doctor replied. "She's fortunate; in the old days, months of physical therapy might have brought about some improvement, but she would likely have been left with permanently diminished capacity. However, with the techniques that we now possess for neural regeneration, ten to twelve weeks of therapy should bring her back to 100%."

"If I may, Anna," Dr. Fitzpatrick stood up. Dr. Rosen smiled and nodded to her colleague, handed him the pointer, and sat down.

"Holo, patient…Olivia Bertrand…Encephala-scan…T minus 60 minutes to real time," it was Dr. Fitzpatrick's turn to elaborate.

The image of Olivia's brain vanished and a series of graphs appeared in its place.

"As you can see, as we have reduced her level of sedation, her higher order brain activities have increased to the point where she should regain consciousness in fifteen or twenty minutes. All other brain wave activity appears normal, by the way," Dr. Fitzpatrick concluded.

Graham called Mac, who responded that he would join them immediately, so that he could be there when Olivia came to. Dr. Rosen suggested that they wait in the conference room until Mac joined them; by that time Olivia would be on the verge of consciousness.

When Mac arrived, Fitzpatrick took one more glance at the encephala-scan, "Good timing Mac, she should be just now regaining consciousness."

With that, the party moved down the hall to the young lady's room. As they walked down the hall, Dr. Rosen warned, "Let's keep it low key, and we're going to allow all of you in for just a few minutes. She'll be exhausted, and she needs rest and quiet more than anything else right now."

As they entered Olivia's room, Dr. Schmidt stood on one side of her bed, and a nurse was positioned on the other. Graham, Mac, Michael, Jacquelyn and Drs. Fitzpatrick and Rosen arranged themselves around Olivia's bed. A display above the head of the bed tracked the young woman's critical signs. Michael tried to interpret them with little success. He then focused on Olivia's face. She looked a bit pale and somewhat haggard, with her uncombed hair and a bruise under her left cheek. Nonetheless, she was still lovely, even with tubes and sensors attached to both arms.

Michael then noticed a slight movement of her eyelids, and a few moments later, the young woman's eyes fluttered open. At first, she appeared a bit drugged and somewhat disoriented. Gradually her eyes focused as everyone in the room muttered their hellos, mixed with words of encouragement.

Dr. Schmidt leaned over and spoke softly to his patient, "Hello, Olivia, I'm Dr. Gregory Schmidt, your surgeon. Do you remember what happened to you?"

Olivia nodded.

"Excellent, well we've patched you up quite thoroughly, and you're going to be just fine. However, you're going to exhibit some symptoms that are going to take a little longer to correct. Your speech may be a bit slurred and you may have some coordination problems on your left side. Don't be upset. With your cooperation, we'll have you as good as new in a matter of weeks."

"Hey kid, you did good in the plane. All the other passengers are fine, and the hijackers are in custody."

Mac struggled to sound upbeat and keep the emotion out of his voice. (And he didn't bother to mention the dead hijacker just yet.)

"Thhank goothness…"

Olivia winced as she spoke for the first time and the words came out muddled. The others struggled not to wince with her. It was difficult to see a young woman, so healthy and vital just a few hours ago, have difficulty uttering the simplest phrase now. An uncomfortable silence ensued for the next few moments. Graham broke it.

"Young lady, I think this situation warrants a substantial raise. However, it's not going to take effect until you're back on duty, so you'd better get with the program!"

Olivia smiled but refrained from her typical snappy reply.

After another uncomfortable moment of silence, Dr. Rosen spoke up, "That's it for now folks. The young lady needs her beauty sleep. No more visits for the next 24 hours. Let's go now."

One by one, each of the visitors took her hand and filed out. Michael had hung back so that he could be last, just behind Mac. As he took her hand he looked into her eyes, "I'm so sorry I couldn't have been more help in the plane..." He let his voice catch a bit with emotion as he spoke, in spite of himself. Olivia didn't say anything, but she held his hand a little longer and squeezed it a bit tighter. Her gaze told him it was all right, although he still didn't feel like it was all right. He felt that had failed her, pure and simple.

Mac hung back as the young professor left the room. "Don't be too hard on yourself, you weren't trained for a situation like what we saw on the plane."

Michael said nothing in reply. Graham had stopped and returned to talk to Michael, as well.

Graham put his hand on Michael's shoulder, "I'm going to have an assistant show you to your new quarters, Michael. Take it easy for the rest of this afternoon and this evening, and then I'd like for you to have breakfast with me in the morning. And relax, everything's going to work out just fine."

Michael just nodded and returned a rather weak smile. In the lobby everyone in the party split up. An assistant appeared, as promised, to guide Michael to his suite. Once in his new quarters, the young man realized just how exhausted he was, even though it was only about five in the afternoon. He thanked and dismissed the young staffer, and collapsed on his bed without even looking around. His thoughts again turned to Olivia for a few moments, and then quickly faded to a deep sleep.

Sometime later, he awoke with a start. As he lay in bed, the events of the day flooded back into his consciousness. Part of his mind wondered if some of his memories were imagined. He then noticed that the room was much darker; night must have fallen. He wondered what time it was. He started to ask his wrist Uplink for the time, and then remembered that his had been taken by Olivia the day before. (Or was it a hundred years ago?) So he just asked the room for the time, assuming a room monitor was online.

There was, and it responded in a smooth feminine voice, "The time is 11:37 PM, mountain standard."

He lay for a few minutes more then got up. Without asking the room lights to come on, he headed for the glimmer of light coming through the curtains. He asked the monitor to open them and it responded, flooding the room with a soft light from outside. As he approached the window, he was greeted by a stunning view of the Alexandria Library bathed in floodlights. His quarters were thirty floors up, so the view was panoramic.

Michael saw that he had a balcony, so he commanded the glass door to open. He walked outside and stood at the rail, breathing in the clean, crisp night air. Many buildings were already in place, along with streets and streetlights spreading out in all directions. Many more buildings and roads were still under construction, however, with floodlit cranes and construction equipment in view all around. He noticed that much of the equipment appeared to be in operation, even at this late hour. An entire city was being born, right before his eyes.

A short while later, Michael heard the door to his quarters slide open without the door chime having been sounded. A shiver went down his back as he wondered who could just walk into his room, and whether he might be once again in danger.

A silhouette stood at his doorway. "Hello Michael, it's just Mac."

"Come on in Mac, I'm out on the balcony," Michael responded.

Mac joined him outside. "Quite a view, huh. Sorry I didn't announce my presence before opening the door; I had a hunch you'd be awake but didn't want to disturb you if you were still asleep. And don't worry; only a few top security personnel have voiceprints that allow unrestricted access to all living quarters, and we don't abuse the privilege. After tonight, we would only enter your room without your permission in the event of a bona fide emergency. So how are you feeling?"

"Just fine Mac. If you can define confused, disoriented, disillusioned with myself, and banged up as fine, that is," the young man responded.

"Would you like to tell me what happened on the plane? I was rather preoccupied up front when you were knocked unconscious."

"Sure, Mac, what happened is that I panicked. When Olivia jumped the hijacker who was coming after you, her hands were still cuffed. So she tripped him and looped her arms around his neck from behind. He fell under her, face down. They landed in the aisle right in front of me. I knew that I should help, but I didn't know what to do. I froze. Then he twisted and slammed her against a seat. In an instant, he was on top and suddenly I saw a knife in his hand. I don't know where it came from. Finally, I moved; I tried to grab his hand with the knife, but he saw me and hit me between the eyes with his elbow, I think. I saw stars. I fell back into my seat. I was stunned but not unconscious. I watched him stab her and couldn't make myself move to help her. Then I saw you kick him just before I did pass out."

Both men were silent for a moment, and then Mac spoke, "Listen carefully to me, Michael. I've seen many men in combat for the first time, good men who have been well trained under the most realistic conditions possible. Some freeze. Many hesitate. Almost none behave like the veterans that most will eventually become. There simply is no substitute for training and experience."

Mac paused for effect, and then continued, "The important fact to consider is that you did initially act, and by doing so, you were willing to put your own life at risk. An unarmed man jumping someone with a knife approaches suicide, especially when he's untrained. You were lucky. One final, but all-important point is this: the moment's hesitation that you provided while Marcus was dealing with you just might have saved Olivia's life. One more stab wound might very well have been one too many."

Both men were silent again while Michael pondered that one.

Then Michael spoke up, "Thanks, Mac. I'm not sure if I believe everything you just told me, but it helps a bit. However, I do have one big favor to ask you."

"Name it," the older man responded.

"Train me. I want to know how to fight, to defend myself. I don't want to ever be in the position I was in on the plane again."

Mac shook his head, "Son, you'll be plenty busy with what Graham has planned for you, and that will be a lot more important than learning basic combat skills. Let me and my men take care of the fighting, if there is to be any. Michael, your destiny is to be a scholar, not a soldier."

"Mac, we may *all* have to be soldiers in the very near future…"

Mac knew the young man had a point. The future might just get pretty tough.

"Okay, then, train you we will," the old soldier finally responded and shook the younger man's hand.

10

Ghost Town

Before Valerian had departed on his great quest, he had been honored with a grand farewell festival held for him by the citizens of Aurora. In a series of feasts and receptions, which had lasted for three days, he had been invited into the homes of many of the Elympian capital's foremost citizens.

Finally, at sunset on the third day, the Council had formally presented Valerian with the last Cypher. To witness the ceremony, a large crowd had gathered around the raised platform in the center of the town square. Elympians had traveled from all of the other townships to participate. Many were from Antares, Valerian's hometown. His grandmother was seated on the platform with the other Elders. The young man also spotted his uncle standing unobtrusively at the back of the crowd.

The ceremony had begun with the ringing of the Town Bell...the very bell that he himself had rung not so very long ago.

Then Alera, the Council Tribune, addressed the large crowd, "Citizens of Elympias! I give you our new champion, Valerian, son of Josef and Rachel, both of whom died in the defense of their township and our People. Valerian, grandson of Elanor, one the most honored and respected of our Council Elders. Valerian, nephew of Sebastian, the legendary Captain of our Rangers, who turned back the Zealot invaders in the Northern Forest, thereby saving our lands and our People! Valerian, who, even as a young man, has passed the severest of challenges to prove his worthiness to accept this quest."

The crowd roared it approval.

"Valerian, first of all, our citizens have parting gifts that they hope will assist you on your long and dangerous journey. Delegates, please come forward."

With that, one by one, various representatives of the townships had approached Valerian with their gifts. The first was presented by a delegation of ladies from his home village. Although the hooded cloak seemed ordinary enough, the women proudly demonstrated its special qualities. Its mottled gray-green color was due to its treatment with dyes and resins that gave it the properties of both camouflage and water resistance; they would also serve to mask his scent from any wild beasts. The garment had also been fashioned in two layers so that the inner layer could be worn alone as a light summer cloak, or both layers could be worn together, to protect him from the harshest weather.

Next three Elders came forward from the western township of Capricorn to present Valerian with a knapsack. Its appearance was also deceptively commonplace. Made of deerskin, it was treated with the same mixture of dyes and resins as his cloak. They explained that it was packed with a variety of provisions, utensils, medicines and bandages.

However, what really made this knapsack special were its other contents. Packed away in the knapsack were small devices fabricated by the Ancients and collected by the citizens of the southern township of Cygnus. They included treasures such as: a roll of fishing line of great resilience, a magnifying glass for starting fires in daylight, an iron striker and pad that could readily do the same at night or during a cloudy day. Pockets sewn onto the front of the knapsack also held a priceless pair of small folding binoculars and a compass with a face that magically glowed in the dark. There was even a small folding leather pouch with pockets containing a comb, scissors, straight razor and toothbrush.

Then an old master blacksmith named Malcolm from the village of Orion came forward. He proudly presented Valerian with a fine lance made of polished oak and tipped with a razor sharp lance-head of steel. The wizened old man also gave him a long hunting knife and small hand axe that had been crafted with equal care.

At last, Valerian's uncle came forward to present his nephew with a new and beautifully crafted war bow. As the young man admired the weapon, Sebastian put a hand on his nephew's shoulder, "Lad, this weapon will help protect you and feed you. But, God willing, it's yo'r wits and the lessons I taught you in the forest that'll bring you home to us."

Valerian leaned forward and whispered, "Thank you, Uncle...still, I wish that you would join me..."

Sebastian didn't answer. He just hugged his nephew and said "Godspeed lad," before withdrawing back into the crowd.

Valerian's grandmother was the last to present the young man with a gift. It was a simple parchment and quill rolled up with a length of twine. "With this parchment, you can draw a simple map that will trace the path of your journey. On the back, you can keep a daily journal. A map drawn with care will help you find your way back to us."

The old woman had then held him close. Her voice was choked with emotion. "Your Mother and Father would be very proud of you this day, Valerian. Please return to us, Grandson, whether you reach Elympias or not." His grandmother wiped away the tears and seated herself.

Alera spoke once again, "Valerian of Elympias, today you have received gifts from your Clan that we all hope will help you to succeed in your quest. But never forget that the most important gift that you will take with you is the legacy of our ancestors. It is the gift of loyalty and self-discipline. It is the gift of citizenship and honesty, of charity and tolerance, of respect and curiosity. Most of all, Valerian of Elympias, the gift we bequeath you is the gift of...Honor and Courage!"

"Honor and Courage!"

As one, the crowd shouted the Elympian creed in response and cheered as Alera hung the precious Cypher around the young man's neck.

"Citizens of Elympias," Valerian had then addressed the enthusiastic crowd in a voice choked with emotion, "I hereby swear an oath to you...I will never waiver from this quest. I will persevere until I reach Elympias. I will unlock its secrets. Then I will restore to our people the secrets of our ancestors."

Valerian held the Cypher up for the entire crowd to see, for perhaps the very last time, and the crowd erupted in cheers once again...

* * *

Valerian had now been traveling for thirty-nine days. He knew it was precisely thirty-nine because of his grandmother's parchment, on which he had dutifully recorded the details of his journey each day. On the other side of the parchment, he had carefully drawn a map, recording distance and direction as accurately as he was able, along with details of each significant landmark.

So far, the young Elympian had run across several isolated settlements and two fairly large Zealot towns along the way. He had made a wide detour around the towns. He had also seen several Zealot scouting parties, but avoiding them was a relatively effortless task for the skilled young woodsman.

So far, his encounter with the wolf pack had been his closest call. Wolf packs remained a serious concern; he had seen their tracks more and more often. He had also heard them howling at night and had seen the remains of several of their kills. It seemed that they were much more plentiful and aggressive in the lands of the Zealots than in those of his own people.

However, a few days before, he had stumbled onto a grizzly mother and her cub, an equally dangerous situation. He had been lucky that time, as well. Lowering his lance, he had calmly backed away from the bear as she rose up with a roar. She had briefly charged at him, then stopped after several paces and returned to her cub, as the young man beat a hasty retreat.

Beyond his encounter with the wolf pack and the bear, the journey itself had been challenging enough. Indeed, the young man's endurance had been severely tested. He'd had to cross increasingly rugged foothills and one major mountain range.

Over the last several weeks, he had forded numerous rain-swollen streams and two rivers. Once, he had come across a river that had been too wide and deep to ford, so that he had followed it south until he had come across a small Zealot town. Late at night he had found a small rowboat tied to a dilapidated pier, slipped into it and quietly rowed across the river. He had left the boat on the far bank and gotten as much distance away from it as possible before dawn.

Overall, Valerian had walked countless miles, huddled shivering in countless storms, slogged through muddy bogs and scaled steep cliffs. The young traveler had largely run out of the provisions he had begun with; the salt, tea, corncakes, jerky and dried fruit were all long gone. Now he survived mostly on the fresh game that he had trapped or hunted, and whatever edible plants that he was able to gather along the way, (wild onions, dandelions, pine nuts...). He had found enough food to survive, but just enough, with little variety.

Occasionally he would brew a little tea from juniper twigs or pine needles, as his uncle had showed him. Or he might attempt a simple rabbit stew in his one small tin cook pot, flavoring the meat with wild onions and garlic. Still he missed more each day the hearty meals that his grandmother had treated him to over the years, the ham and eggs in the morning, the fresh bread, the stews, the roast duck.

Every week or so, he would stop and rest for a day or two, taking time to mend his torn garments, let his various blisters, cuts and scrapes heal a bit, snare a few rabbits or squirrels for fresh meat, gather some edible roots or plants. Nonetheless, he was footsore and weary, bored with the endless routine of walking, hiding and scrounging for the bare necessities for survival. But most of all, he was lonely. He hadn't talked to another soul in weeks. (Lately, he had noticed that he had even begun talking to himself.)

However, more than he would have ever imagined, the young traveler had been exposed during his journey to the abandoned and crumbling roads, towns and dwellings left by the Ancients. Within his own Clan's territories, most Ancient towns and buildings had long since been torn down or salvaged for anything of value, leaving little of interest. (The exceptions were a small Ancient city in the northern end of his valley, and a much larger city in the southern end, which were both strictly off limits to his people.)

In contrast, within the Zealot lands, most of the ruins of the Ancients had been left undisturbed. This was perhaps out of fear, Valerian had suspected, since the Zealots were supposed to be a highly superstitious folk. So far, young traveler had also given wide berth to these Ancient remains, as his uncle had counseled.

* * *

Now it was late afternoon and Valerian had decided to risk an early start, as he had seen no sign of Zealots in days. This day's march had led him across a heavily forested plateau. Coming over the crest of a ridge, he had stumbled onto the panoramic view of the ruins of a rather large Ancient town nestled below in a river valley. The young man was at first tempted to veer back into the depths of the forest. Instead, this time curiosity overruled his better judgment. He decided to cautiously explore the site.

Moving down into the valley, he had first passed miles of completely collapsed structures, all arranged in neat rows that he surmised had once been dwellings. Interspersed amongst the ruins were large oak trees and scattered shrubs. Running in front of these piles of wood and brick rubble were glimpses of smooth and even paved roads, largely covered now by runaway weeds and wild grasses.

Here and there, metal tubes, bent at wild angles, emerged from the roads; some had twisted shreds of green or red metal attached at their tops. Also scattered at intervals on the roads were rusted-out metal carriages, most with broken windows all around. A few, he noticed, still contained what appeared to be human skeletons.

Rats scuttled everywhere amongst the detritus and a multitude of feral cats stalked the rats. Here and there, packs of ragged and hungry wild dogs ran amongst the ruins. A few of the beasts approached him, but Valerian easily frightened them off with a shout and a wave of his lance.

After a time, the young traveler found what he assumed had once been the town square. At the center was a tight thicket of large trees and underbrush that almost completely obscured the remains of what might have once been a pavilion. Bordering this central area were the vestiges of a broad circular road. And arranged about the perimeter of this circle was a collection of larger buildings, most of which were constructed of brick or stone, metal and glass. Most seemed relatively intact.

Valerian had become even more cautious in this area, concerned that some of the buildings might still be inhabited. However, after scouting the area, he satisfied himself that there were no signs of current human habitation. As the sun hung low and red on the horizon, he carefully entered the largest building. It was an official looking structure made mostly of granite. Climbing a great flight of stone steps, he made his way between huge stone pillars up to the entrance. The entrance itself was wide open, as it had once been made of glass, which now littered the entryway in great piles. Carefully threading his way through the broken glass, he couldn't really look around until he was well inside the structure. What he saw took his breath away.

The inside of the building was huge, far larger than the interior of any structure he had ever seen before. Pigeons roosted high above and were startled into flight as he entered. The sounds of his steps echoed through the large, empty space.

He looked around with his jaw open. The floor was covered with large smooth stone tiles of green and black, the likes of which he had never seen before. Huge, faded murals and even larger cracked mirrors covered the walls. Hung from high above were many decorative objects made of hundreds of pieces of glass strung together. Scattered all about the floor were pieces of broken furniture made of heavy wood and metal. And amongst the pieces of furniture were the smashed remains of complex and intricate machines made of metal, glass and other strange materials that he could not identify. All was rather obscured by thick layers of dust and cobwebs. Four large staircases ran up to a second floor landing that extended all the way around.

Valerian pondered…truly, who had these people been that could fashion such wonders? Valerian turned up a large chair, dusted it off and sat down on it. He was amused to discover that it had rollers on the bottoms of its legs, allowing him to move around at will, even as he was seated. He opened the drawers of a desk and examined scraps of paper and pieces of books that disintegrated at his touch. He handled some of the strange devices, trying to fathom their function, without success. So fascinated was the young man by all of this that he did not immediately notice when the light began to fade. As the shadows stretched across the floor, he suddenly realized that he had stayed too long.

As the young man exited the building and began to descend the steps, he saw to his dismay that several packs of wild dogs had closed in on him, emboldened by the gathering gloom. Backing up, he looked for another exit. As he searched, he could hear some of the beasts coming up the steps. He hoped that the broken glass would slow them down, but he knew that he hadn't much time; if they rushed him in large enough numbers, he was done for.

Seeing one of the staircases in the dim light to his left, he decided to make his way to the second floor landing, which overlooked the main lobby. As he quickly made his way up the stairs, he could hear the first of the beasts entering the building behind him. At the top of the stairs was a large open area strewn with furniture and equipment. Along the back of the landing were several large oaken doors, which he surmised led to other rooms.

The first door had fallen off of its hinges. The next two would not open. However, the fourth door did creak open, revealing a large rectangular room. He quickly entered and closed the door behind him, just catching a glance of several dogs racing up after him. The door snapped shut, and a moment later, he could hear the animals padding about, growling, panting and clawing on the other side of the door.

He breathed a long sigh of relief and then looked around in the dim light. The room was spacious. It was perhaps twelve paces wide and almost as many deep. In its center was a large and heavy table that appeared to be made of stone. Situated around the table were several large leather and wooden chairs that were even more ornate than the ones he had seen below. On the wall to his left were bookshelves arranged around another door. The bookshelves were filled with the dusty remains of many books. Mounted on the wall to his right was a large flat device made of glass and metal.

The wall opposite was all glass, a window, he realized, that looked out over the town square. It appeared to Valerian to have been a meeting room. Overall, this meeting room appeared to have been undisturbed for many long years. Although there was a fine layer of dust on most surfaces, and a few cobwebs, the room appeared to be rather clean and orderly. Nothing had been broken or overturned.

The sun had now set and only a faint, dying light illuminated the room. He now took a moment to chide himself for stumbling into this predicament for no other reason than to satisfy his idle curiosity. He then determined to make the best of it. He decided to check the door by the bookshelves. It too creaked open, leading to an adjoining, smaller room. He peeked through and then immediately checked to see if its outer door was secured against the dogs outside; it was. In the gathering darkness, he saw, however, that this room's window had been smashed out, apparently by one of the chairs. He could also see that some time in the distant past, a small campfire made of books had been lit on the landing just outside the opening made by the broken window.

He decided that he would follow suit. Although he was not eager to light a fire in such an exposed spot, he was even less eager to spend the night in such a spooky, unfamiliar place in utter darkness. It was getting chilly too. Taking off his cloak, weapons and knapsack, he retrieved his flint and steel striker. With his hatchet, he then broke a small table up into kindling. The wood was fairly rotten but dry. Arranging the kindling with a few torn up books for tinder, he had started a small fire on the window ledge. He was pleased that a steady breeze seemed to be drafting most of the smoke out of the room.

As he busied himself with the fire, he could hear some of the wild dogs at the door. He wondered how many had remained. He realized that he would have to deal with them at dawn. It promised to be a long night.

Once he had a steady fire, the young man ate a few remaining scraps of food from his pack and quenched his thirst from his canteen. Restless and more than a bit nervous, he then decided to explore his surroundings. Breaking up a straight-backed chair, he fashioned a torch from one of its legs and some torn material from the chair's seat wrapped tightly around one end of the chair leg. He then used his makeshift torch to examine his surroundings.

The second, smaller room was about half the size of the meeting room. It contained a large desk and padded chair with wheels. Across the room was a large, decaying seat that could hold perhaps three persons side by side. There were also a few more chairs like the one he had broken up, as well as a few other small tables of different sizes. This room, unlike the first, had clearly been ransacked. Everything was overturned and scattered around, and all of the desk drawers had been pulled out. The weather had also taken its toll through the broken window. Dust, grime and cobwebs covered everything with a thick layer of filth. The wood of the furniture and bookshelves was all quite rotten. He began to sneeze from the dust.

Finally, leaving the door between the adjoining rooms open, so that some of the light from the fire would pass through, the young man retreated to the relatively cleaner meeting room. For additional light, he laid the torch on one end of the stone table with its burning end hanging over the tile floor. Still edgy, he wedged two of the still sturdy chairs against the outer door of each room to afford himself additional protection against... he wasn't sure just what.

Too restless to sleep, he then used the torch to examine the contents of the bookshelves. Some volumes were leather-bound; these bindings were still more or less intact. The pages, however, were very fragile, and crumbled at all but the most careful touch. Most contained nothing but the undecipherable script of the Ancients.

One set of books in a sealed glass case caught his attention, however. Theses books were also leather-bound, but they were in much better condition than those that lay unprotected on the bookshelves. He opened the case and selected a large, slim volume. It was a picture book.

The pictures themselves were a wonder. Many were so real that they looked more like windows to another world than images on a page. What they portrayed was even more incredible. One showed a street, much like the one below must have looked, with people attired in strange, complex clothing. Some walked; others seemed to be riding in carriages like the ruined ones he had seen. However, the carriages seemed to be moving along without any apparent means of locomotion, such as horses or oxen. Another picture showed a great machine in the clouds that looked rather like a metallic bird. An adjacent picture showed many people sitting in rows in what, he surmised, were the innards of the machine.

Page after page, wonder after wonder. Were these accurate portrayals of how the Ancients actually lived, Valerian wondered, or were some of them simply flights of fancy fabricated by the Ancient authors? (He decided that he was particularly skeptical of a flying machine that could carry dozens of people.)

Presently, the torch began to burn down, and he began to get drowsy. The beasts outside had grown quiet as well; he hoped that they had given up and left. Valerian put the picture book on the table and arranged two of the chairs so that they made a sort of cot. It wasn't precisely comfortable, but it would do well enough. Covering himself with his cloak, he drifted off to sleep. He dreamed…

It was perhaps the most vivid dream he had ever experienced. Suddenly he was walking down a street of the Ancients, except that everything was alive and new. As with some dreams, the perspective kept changing. One instant he was Valerian, a traveler from another time. The next, he was one of the Ancients himself, bemusedly watching the primitive visitor.

At first, the experience was exciting and exhilarating: watching the wondrous machines flashing by on the street and up in the sky, hearing a strange and complex, yet familiar, language actually being spoken, seeing the bright colors and textures of another world.

Then gradually he began to feel oppressed, all his senses overloaded. The sounds of machines were everywhere. Instead of the gentle sounds of birds singing or a breeze blowing through the trees, he heard the constant squeal of gears and wheels, the tinny sounds of machine music, the humming, clanking, and roaring of scores of devices all around.

The colors of the vehicles, of the buildings and the multitude of signs that covered them, even of the clothes that he and everyone else wore, were gaudy, garish…difficult to look at. Yet, when he looked up at the sky, he saw a dull gray-blue in place of the bright cobalt blue of his world. The few trees and shrubs were a dull and lifeless gray-green, as well. Even the air itself hung leaden and dirty. It was as if the Ancients had been compelled to manufacture bright colors to replace those that had been stripped away from nature itself.

Next came anxiety, as he noticed that everyone was in a rush, pushing past him without a greeting or even a nod. No one was smiling; everyone looked tense and distracted. He felt that he should be hurrying off to somewhere as well, but he didn't know where to go. He knew that he must be late for something, but for what he had no clue.

He felt the panic rise within himself. He wanted to escape this place, go back to his world, where life was infinitely simpler yet more profound. Then, suddenly, he was one of the Ancients again, chuckling at the simpleton dressed in a crude tunic and cloak, with what, a spear and a bow? Then everyone else on the street was looking at him, pointing, laughing at his expense...

He woke up with a start, almost falling out of his makeshift cot. His movements stirred complementary movements outside the door. His canine friends were still keeping him company. He rose and stretched. He was chilled and yet was clammy with sweat. The torch was out, and there were only a few dying embers remaining from the small campfire. However, both rooms were now illuminated by moonlight from the bright, nearly full moon that now hung high in the sky. He drank another sip from the canteen and walked over to the window.

The young man looked out over the ghostly ruins of the town square lit only by the silver light of the moon. He was reminded of nights like this as a small boy in his grandmother's cottage, looking out of the small window next to his bed. Late at night, sometimes he had awakened to see shadows moving in the moonlight under the swaying trees. Trying to go back to sleep, he had at times called out in fear to his grandmother. She would patiently come to his bed in her nightgown, comfort him, and assure him that what he saw was nothing more than the movements of the trees exaggerated by his overactive imagination.

At that moment Valerian felt intolerably alone. He missed the grandmother who had nurtured him for so many years with love and wisdom. He missed the strength and courage of his uncle. He missed the camaraderie of his friends in the village and the sacred bond of his entire Clan.

Valerian pondered his dream and thought that he had perhaps caught just a glimmer of what might have happened to the Ancients. Perhaps, he speculated, they had somehow simply forgotten who they were, as a people. Rather than relying on each other for support and protection, perhaps they had come to rely too much on the soulless wealth provided by their lifeless machines. First mastering nature, and then conquering it, it seemed that they had eventually despoiled it. Perhaps, as they had grown ever richer, they had also become ever more despondent. Perhaps, in the end, their lives had simply lost too much meaning for them to carry on...

How different it is with my people, my Clan, the young Elympian thought proudly. We stand together against all enemies, against all diversity. Every citizen is tested and every citizen knows his duty. Our people have little wealth, but what we have we share; not because we have to, but because we want to. Perhaps it is we who possess what the Ancients needed, rather than the other way around...perhaps that is the true secret of Elympias.

Well, Valerian supposed, *the final answers to these questions just might be waiting for me at the end of my quest.* But for now, he must simply wait for dawn...

* * *

The dawn that Valerian had feared turned out to be rather anticlimactic. At first light, gathering up his weapons and gear, Valerian had readied his lance and suddenly thrown the door open, ready for combat. Though most of the animals had already drifted silently away in the night, one of the remaining curs had leapt at him. The young man had simply poked it on its mangy side. It had yelped and run back down the stairs like it had been scalded. The young man had then suddenly charged the other beasts, and taking their cue from the first, they had all broken and run as well. Leaving the town had been quite uneventful after that...

11

Life in Olympus
May 7th, 2084

"Please wake up, Michael…It is now five-thirty AM Mountain Standard Time," the melodious female voice of his room monitor cooed.

Soothing music followed as the lights gradually came on. Nonetheless, Michael woke up in a grumpy mood, as he had practically every morning for the last six weeks. It just wasn't *normal* to wake up this early in the morning.

Chang didn't seem to share his Michael's master's grumpiness. The big Siamese just stretched and yawned at the foot of Michael's bed, then made a pass by Michael for a quick rub. Purring loudly, the cat jumped down and headed straight for his food bowl.

It really didn't help Michael's state of mind in the least that having to get up before dawn was his own fault. After all, he had asked Mac for military training and the veteran had graciously obliged. Less than a week after Michael had settled in at the Olympus facility, a sharp young Guardsman in the OSF (Olympus Security Force) had knocked on his door at six AM one morning and invited (ordered) him out for his first little bracing predawn three mile run. That first run had almost killed him;

since then it had become progressively less painful, but it was still a long way from resembling anything like pleasant.

As he stumbled into the sonic shower, he briefly reflected on how quickly he had settled into such a radically different lifestyle. Just a few months ago, he had been living the quiet, rather laid-back life of an associate professor of socio-history. Holding classes, grading essays, evenings with his friends and colleagues at the local cyber-pub, weekends hiking and biking in one or another of the city parks, had just about circumscribed his life. Writing and publishing his book had been the one exciting exception to his academic routine, but that excitement had passed quickly enough, as well.

Now, six days a week, his life consisted of a vigorous three hours of paramilitary training, followed by eight or more hours in the Think Tank, strategizing with some of the best analytical minds in the world on…how to save the world! Evenings were spent, as often as possible, with Olivia, helping her with her speech therapy exercises, having dinner with her at the medical center's café or just taking short walks with her around the hospital's grounds.

Olivia! There was no doubt that he was completely smitten with her. Her injuries, her vulnerability, had only served to make her seem more attractive to the young professor. How she felt about him, on the other hand, was far less clear. Certainly, she appreciated his kindness and attentiveness. She even seemed to genuinely enjoy his company. Beyond that, he could discern no deeper feelings from her. But first of all, he understood that she needed to focus her efforts on mending, both physically and emotionally, from her attack on the spaceplane. For the time being, he was more than content just to spend time with her.

Just thirty minutes after his wake up call, the young professor found himself in front of OSF's headquarters, in shorts and running shoes, lining up with the young men and women of the OSF Guard. The air was still chilled; daylight would not come until they had finished their run. Everyone was stretching and warming up.

Michael had been struck from the first at the contrast between these mostly young Guards, resolute, disciplined and clean cut, as compared to the rather disheveled and undisciplined intellectuals that he would be working with in a few hours. Both groups had been handpicked, but according to vastly different criteria. The Guards had been carefully recruited from the various Special Forces commands around the world. They had then been melded into an elite paramilitary unit. His fellow

'Think Tankers' had been some of the most brilliant individuals selected from universities, businesses and intelligence services from around the world. Much to his surprise, though, Michael had blended in about as well with the Guards as he had with the eggheads, for all the differences between the two groups.

At precisely 6:15 am, as always, McCafferty, the CO, showed up to lead the morning run. Everyone stood at attention. The Guards Sergeant-at-Arms reported all present and accounted for, and Mac briefly addressed the troops, giving them the news of the day. Asking for questions and receiving none, Mac had then taken off with over two hundred Guardsmen in his wake.

The run took less than thirty minutes and ended at OSF's canteen. Michael was pleased to realize that he was barely winded this morning, as he lined up for breakfast. Sitting down on a metal chair at a metal table with his metal breakfast tray, the young man was surprised to see McCafferty sitting down across from him. Both men had been quite busy over the last several weeks and had only seen each other occasionally, usually when visiting Olivia at the same time.

"Good morning Michael. How is the training agreeing with you? You're looking a bit more chipper than you did the first few weeks," the older man smiled. Michael hadn't known that Mac had noticed.

"Fine Mac. You're right; I was used to exercise before, but after work, never in the morning. Anyhow, I'm finally getting accustomed to it, more or less."

"What about the rest of your training?"

"My trainers are telling me that I'm a natural with small arms. That has come as a pretty big surprise to me; I've never held a gun, excuse me, weapon, before in my life. Hand-to-hand combat is another story; that's coming along very slowly," the gangly professor had to admit.

"Anyway, in another few weeks I should be ready for field exercises."

The Guard CO was aware of as much; Mac had followed the young academic's progress in the training reports. Considering that most of his other trainees came aboard already in possession of extensive military training, Michael really hadn't faired that badly as a complete novice.

"Glad to hear you're sticking with the program Michael, whether you ever need the training or not. Fitness and discipline will always stand you in good stead."

Michael agreed with the older man, but being able to handle himself effectively in a crisis still remained his primary objective.

"So Michael, today is the big day. Liv is being released this afternoon," Mac knew that Michael had been visiting the young woman at the Medical Center almost every day.

Mac thought that the two made an odd match, but in his experience unlikely matches sometimes made the most enduring ones. He had told the young woman as much not long ago. (Much to her chagrin!)

"Yep, I'm really happy for her; she's virtually back to 100%. Her internal injuries have healed completely, she has just a bit of numbness on her left side, but she's eliminated the slurring in her speech. She has put incredible effort into her therapy. The doctors and therapists are amazed at her progress."

What was left unsaid, however, was Michael's mixed emotions over her leaving the Medical Center. Of course, the young man wanted to see her healed, but he did have to admit to himself that he rather liked having a captive audience. Michael feared that once she was back at work, he would lose touch with her. Perhaps, he admitted to himself, she might even use her work to avoid him. Well, maybe he would find out where he stood tonight. He'd asked Olivia out to dinner this evening to celebrate her release, and she'd accepted…

The two men finished their breakfast and parted company. It was almost 0730, time for Michael to report to his small arms instructor and Mac to get back to conducting what had become nothing less than a covert war. By 0900 Michael had spent thirty minutes with a pulse rifle at the firing range and 45 minutes in the gym getting tossed around by a martial arts instructor. Thirty minutes more for a shave and a second shower, then Michael was on his way to the 'Tank'.

By 0930, Michael was at his desk. His cyber-station was situated in one of twenty "bullpens" that altogether made up the "Think Tank". Each bullpen contained six scholars or experts carefully selected for their complementary knowledge and ability. Michael's team consisted of a world famous economist, an obscure middle-aged professor of philosophy, an up-and-coming agronomist, and a former CIA analyst, (one position on his team remained to be filled).

"Anything new from Aristotle this morning?" (Aristotle was the name a few academics had pinned on ARIS, the Artificial Intelligence System, which managed all of the information, power and environmental systems at Olympus; the name had quickly become official).

His teammates caught him up on the news of the day, which, so far, was pretty routine. However, he found himself having a hard time focusing on their response; his mind was already drifting to speculation over just what fate might be revealed this night…

* * *

Mac was settling into his chair in his small office at the OSC Command Center at about the same time that Michael and his team were getting down to work. Like Michael, his first priority was a fresh cup of coffee. Unlike Michael, he wasn't simply looking for the latest news, however. He was just looking for something that would give him and his people an edge.

"Aristotle, please deliver my "Morning Intelligence Report," he spoke as he eased back in his swivel chair and took a sip.

"*Complying…Good morning, Mac. Your Morning Intelligence Report follows…*"

Mac sat back and listened for the next thirty minutes, interrupting occasionally to ask follow-up questions. Most information, as usual, was routine. As with each morning he listened primarily for two items: clues to the identity of their adversaries, and any intel on the latest activities of Marcus. As usual there were few clues as to whom it was that they were at war with. With all of the resources at Mac's and Aristotle's disposal, Mac was rather nonplussed that he had learned so little about their enemies over the last several weeks. Just the lack of good intelligence itself had to mean one important thing, however. They must be dealing with someone quite formidable.

As for Marcus, Mac had kept his word three weeks ago, releasing Marcus once the younger man had spilled his guts. Mac had learned that Marcus Sternhagen was actually Gregory Illych Constantine, a native of Cyprus. Marcus/Gregory had never served in the military. Rather, he was a seasoned veteran of the EuroMafia, the sophisticated and far-flung organized crime syndicate that had spread across Europe in the last quarter century.

Marcus/Constantine had been recruited by a shadowy affiliate of the Mafia and trained as an agent for over three years. Along with many other sophisticated espionage skills, he had learned to defeat the most sophisticated psychometric tests, producing the profile of an intelligent, honest and diligent individual…a far cry from his true persona. He was highly intelligent all right; that particular attribute couldn't be faked. But an accurate psychometric profile would have also revealed a completely amoral and self-centered individual motivated only by personal gain.

Mac had verified Marcus's story to the extent possible. He had then forced Marcus to explain in detail for the Olympus security experts his methods for faking the psychometric tests. (Based on this intelligence, the tests would be quickly altered, and all past tests would be carefully reviewed.)

Mac had then discussed the matter of granting Marcus/Gregory's freedom with Olivia. He had felt that for his own peace of mind, as someone who had suffered the most at the agent's hand, 'Liv deserved a vote in the matter. It turned out to be no problem; Olivia had readily concurred once she had heard Mac's plan for their "turncoat".

So Marcus had been given a false passport and ID, a ticket to Rio de Janeiro, and a small amount of money in an international cyber-account. He had then been released. (A virtually impossible to detect tracking device had also been surreptitiously installed under his skin, and one of Mac's best agents had been assigned full time to track him.) Perhaps, he would yet lead them to bigger "fish"…or perhaps not. In any case, Mac was certain, it would make for a rather interesting game of "cat and mouse"…

* * *

"Dr. Alvarez, it's an honor to meet you."

Graham ushered the professor into the ornate study of his penthouse suite at the top floor of the Alexandria Library.

"Dr. Vincent speaks most highly of you…as do some of my top researchers."

The two men settled into two high-backed leather chairs. Arrayed on two opposing walls were shelves that reached to the top of the twelve-foot ceiling, crammed with leather bound volumes of what the professor assumed were likely rare first editions. Tastefully arranged on the third wall were four paintings: a Degas, a Renoir, a Van Gogh and a Seurat; Dr. Alvarez suspected that these were originals, as well. The outer wall offered a panoramic view over top of the huge dome of the Library out to the center of the Olympus complex beyond.

"I hold Michael in equally high regard. And please, call me Louie, Mr. Graham," the small man replied.

Beyond Olympus

The professor was impressed but not awed by the surroundings. As the distinguished head of the Sociodynamics Department of a major university, Dr. Alvarez had seen his share of ornate drawing rooms; just as a former street urchin, Louie had seen more than his share of grimy flophouses and cantinas. That's why he liked being called Louie…to ensure that he never forget just from where he had come.

"Very well…Louie, and you can call me Jonathan. First of all, let me extend my sincere condolences over the recent death of your wife, Magdalena."

The professor involuntarily looked down at the mention of his wife's (soul mate's) name. They had been married for some thirty-five years and she had left him only some six months ago, taken by a rare form of cancer, one of the few varieties that still had no effective treatment. Since they had first married, her health had always been fragile, too fragile to bear children with him, now too fragile to grow old with him. But Maggie's gentle strength had been the foundation for all of his success, and now he felt like a sailing ship with its sails torn away, his life adrift…

"Louie…I have a very unique offer to make to you. Even though I am sure that Michael has maintained our security, I know that you and he have been in regular contact. I suspect that, by now, you must have deduced to some degree what our core purpose is here at Olympus."

The professor had indeed formulated something of a theory regarding the Olympus project, both from what could be inferred from his ongoing but rather guarded, conversations with Michael, (who had supposedly still been living in New York) as well as the independent research he had begun conducting on Graham Enterprises, once he had been informed by Michael that the younger man was suddenly leaving the university for a permanent position within Graham's organization. Very quickly, Louie's research had gravitated to the Olympus project itself and what its true purpose might be. However, just now he preferred to simply nod his head and let Graham continue. Graham took the hint.

"We here at Olympus believe that the fall of the modern technological civilization as we know it is imminent, is perhaps only a few decades away. I won't repeat what we believe are the underlying causes, since you know them as well as I do. The research that you assisted Michael with for his book drew the same conclusions that we came to, with a multimillion-dollar research project. What you couldn't have guessed, without access to our resources, was just how immediate the threat really was."

The diminutive academic leaned forward, "Yes, Mr. Graham... Jonathan, but what I still haven't been able to grasp is what you propose to do about it. Surely you don't plan on 'sweeping back the sea'? Even with your billions, your political power and your tens of thousands of employees, you don't really believe that you can actually change the course of history, do you?"

"Louie, not to boast, but it's *trillions* of dollars that I'm worth, and *hundreds of thousands* of employees that work for me, directly or indirectly; and amongst those are many thousands of the most brilliant, talented and capable individuals on the planet. Men with far less power have changed the course of history before."

Like Hitler and Napoleon, the professor thought to himself.

"Yes, but these men have changed history in the past through military conquest, for better or worse, or through profound technological breakthroughs. You are proposing nothing less than a fundamental transformation of the social and economic fabric that makes up our civilization. Can't be done."

"Perhaps, perhaps. But don't you think that it will be a worthy effort nonetheless? Olympus will be at the center of this effort. We will assemble the best minds and technology on the planet, right here. I am committing nothing less than everything that I have to this effort, all my fortune, all my power. What may we learn along the way, what else may we accomplish in the next fifteen or twenty years? Don't you think that something good must come of that?"

"So you are proposing to use all your resources to essentially undo your life's work, the creation of the largest financial empire the world has ever seen?"

"I understand your skepticism, I really do. Perhaps it would help to look at my motives in the light of some of history's other major philanthropists. Many rich and powerful men, having achieved the pinnacle of their success and perhaps having sacrificed virtually everything that they value along the way to achieve that success, have looked for a way later in life to find a justification for what they have accomplished. They have created foundations to underwrite worthy causes, or thrown themselves into charitable endeavors or backed idealistic political movements."

"I have three ex-wives, two ex-mistresses and six grown children; I'm hardly on speaking terms with any of them...in spite of the fact that I continue to support them all. I have no close personal friends or confidants, only colleagues, employees and competitors. Amassing any more wealth or power no longer bears any attraction for me whatsoever, particularly in light of what I believe is coming our way in the next few decades."

"Yet all my life I have been a driven man; that's far too engrained in my personality now to ever change. So to where can I redirect all my energy at this point? What's next for me? And what is my final legacy? Is it to be the man that contributed the most to the fall of modern civilization?"

"Every man needs a reason to live. I don't know where this project will lead, whether it will succeed or fail. But I am convinced that it is worthy effort and worthwhile way for me to spend my remaining years. I'll just put everything that I have into it, and let fate decide its eventual outcome."

"Now, what about you professor? You're roughly my age. You are now as alone as I am, I'm sorry to say. Would you like a new challenge, along with virtually unlimited resources to pursue your theories on social development? Or would you prefer to remain cloistered in your academic cocoon?"

The professor only paused to reflect a few moments. "Jonathan, I believe that I would like to accept your invitation."

The answer came out quickly, almost as surprise to the professor himself. Perhaps, he suddenly realized, he had already subconsciously made the decision before even entering the room with Graham; if an offer was made, he would take it. He knew in his heart that he desperately needed a clean break with his old life, every facet of which reminded him of his lost love…their home, their mutual friends, even the university that they had both taught at for so many years, now only served to haunt him with his loss.

Graham was somewhat taken aback by the professor's sudden acceptance as well. He had expected the typical give and take, the long philosophical discussions, the deliberation and uncertainty that he had become accustomed to with the other top candidates that he had personally recruited. Generally, it had taken days or weeks, occasionally months, to persuade the various Nobel Prize winners, renowned scientists and esteemed intellectuals to accept positions on his project. The ten minutes or so taken to recruit Dr. Alvarez would likely be a record that would remain unbroken.

Nonetheless, Graham was thrilled; he had a strange feeling about this small, modest man. He valued the opinion of his experts, but he valued his own intuition even more; indeed it had been one of the primary keys to his success over the years. And right now, even after this brief meeting with this man, his intuition was that this might be the most important addition yet to his team. It was nothing spoken, for they had spoken little. Perhaps it was the depth that Graham saw in the professor's eyes, the *gravitas* that the man projected…

"I'm pleased, Dr. Alvarez…Louie, that is. I know you won't regret your decision. Just out of curiosity, however, I wonder if I could ask you just one philosophical question, a ridiculous question, I fear; ridiculous, because there most likely is no simple answer. Nonetheless, I would like to ask this question, just to see how you would attempt answer it. The question is…*where did we go wrong? What is the fundamental flaw that has brought our civilization to the brink of disaster?*"

Once again, the professor did not hesitate with his response.

"Mr. Graham, I believe that there is indeed a simple answer. Any historian can tell you that that some combination of four basic factors is invariably the basis for the fall of any civilization: war, economic failure, the destruction of the environment and climate change. They are the true 'Four Horsemen' and we are seeing all four bearing down on us just now with a vengeance. However, it is the 'Fifth Horseman' that is the key."

"And would the 'Fifth Horseman' perhaps be a given society's ability, or rather, inability, to overcome those challenges?"

"Indeed, Jonathan. We have an almost mystical belief in the infallibility of democracy. However, we seem to have forgotten that the success of democracy is wholly dependent on the quality of the citizens that make up that democracy. Of course, modern society still harbors many citizens worthy of a strong democratic system. Unfortunately, we just no longer have enough of them, and more unfortunately still, they are not the ones we generally elect to lead us…"

I have a question for you too, Jonathan, the professor thought to himself. *But I'm going to wait for the right moment to ask it. The question is…just what is the real purpose behind Olympus?*

Graham nodded, "Professor, I believe that your answer will provide the basis for many fascinating discussions between the two of us in the upcoming months. But for now, let me have one of my assistants help you make whatever personal arrangements are necessary to have you relocated to Olympus."

Graham had learned long ago to cut a discussion short once he had gotten what he wanted; no point in giving them a chance to reconsider…

As his personal assistant escorted Dr. Alvarez out and the door closed behind them, Graham sat back in his expensive leather chair…in his ornate library surrounded by rare first editions and original masterpieces…at the top of his multi-billion dollar Library... overlooking his very own city under construction.

Graham had single-mindedly worshipped at the altar of money all his life, and the god of wealth had rewarded him beyond all comprehension. But now, late in life, he had become an apostate to that god. First he had begun to doubt this "deity" on a personal level; with the GRI report, he had eventually realized that it had, in fact, become the false god for virtually all of the rest of the civilized world, as well. And greed, materialism and ambition, all served as the false prophets for that god.

Could Graham actually change the course of history? Probably not; Louie was likely right about that. But he would, in whatever time he had remaining, certainly make whatever amends might still be possible....

* * *

That evening, Olivia waited at her new quarters to be picked up for dinner by Michael. Today had been a watershed for her. This afternoon, she had thanked her doctors, nurses and therapists, and checked out of the Medical Center. Then she had taken her luggage and valuables to the new quarters that Graham had arranged for her, in one of Olympus's twenty high-rise condos. Tomorrow, she would resume her old duties with Graham and Mac.

Now, tonight, she would try to let Michael down gently. Aside from the medical specialists working on her rehabilitation, at the Medical Center, her two links with the outside had been Mac and Michael. (Her parents had visited immediately after her injuries, but the young woman had been obliged to maintain security by presenting them with a cover story about a deranged lunatic on the flight. Olivia had been most uncomfortable with being less than honest with her mother and father, and her father had indeed seemed somewhat skeptical, although he had said nothing. Nonetheless, they had stayed long enough to be sure that she would fully recover, and then gone home.)

Olivia had looked forward to the visits from Mac, who had become something of a surrogate father for her, in her own father's absence. Mac and her father shared many qualities; both were intelligent, forceful ex-military individuals possessing a strong sense of duty.

She had looked forward to the visits from Michael as well, although with a great deal more ambivalence. If Mac was her surrogate father at

Olympus, she had come to look at Michael as the surrogate brother she had never had. The problem was that she knew that the young professor had much deeper feelings for her. So how was one to maintain a friendship with such a man without letting the relationship develop into something more? It was a puzzle that she felt ill equipped to solve. Over the years, she had had several serious romantic relationships. All of them had been intense; all had ended rather badly.

Olivia had long ago been forced to admit to herself that she seemed to have little skill at finding or creating the sort of enduring relationship that her parents had built. Perhaps, she was simply attracted to the wrong sort. Perhaps, the strong, independent men she was attracted to were eventually put off by her own strong-willed, independent nature. Perhaps in the end, it was her own subconscious desire for independence itself that impelled her to subvert each relationship when it had developed past a certain point.

In any case, even though Olivia was flattered by the effort that Michael had put into reinventing himself with his military training, to her he would always be the tall, rather awkward intellectual with the head of unruly hair; someone who could connect with her intellectually, rather than emotionally or physically.

So Olivia planned on a frank and honest, if somewhat difficult, conversation with Michael over dinner tonight. She thought too much of the young man to lead him on. They would be good friends, but only good friends. Olivia would pursue other relationships and she hoped that Michael would follow suite. Perhaps, there was still a "Mr. Right" out there, even for her.

The room monitor announced Michael's arrival. Olivia took a deep breath and opened the door...

12

The Caravan

Valerian had had been following a broad clear stream all night long. Dawn had broken just a short while before. Just when the young traveler had decided to begin looking for a new spot to camp, from around the next bend of the stream he heard a new, totally unexpected sound. At first, he wasn't sure if it was just his imagination, but he thought that he heard the laughter of children over the babbling of the water. Immediately, he took cover in some underbrush on the bank. Zealot children would mean Zealot parents!

Valerian dropped his cloak and all of his gear and crept cautiously forward. A short distance ahead he saw three young children playing in the water. Beyond, beneath a cluster of huge oak trees, he saw several large wagons circling an encampment. He could smell the smoke of cook fires. He could also smell bacon frying. Just the thought of bacon was enough to make him ravenous. Cautiously, he crept forward under the cover of the forest. Yes, just as he had hoped; it wasn't Zealots, but a Trademaster's Caravan.

Nonetheless, there remained the potential for danger; Zealot trading parties would be regularly visiting a Caravan…that was their purpose. And even though he had nothing to fear from the Tradesmen, he would expect any Zealot visitors to set upon an outsider without hesitation.

So the young man scouted the area carefully, not only watching the encampment, but all possible approaches to it. In a nearby meadow, he spied oxen and some horses grazing. He saw ten of the large Trademaster's wagons, perhaps twenty or so adults and a number of children. All of the adults wore the white tunics marked front and back with a red handprint, the garb reserved for those who had taken the Tradesman's Oath.

Most of the women were either preparing breakfast or organizing the camp. The men were mostly gathering firewood or setting out their merchandise for the day's trades. However, Valerian saw no sign of Zealots and he was encouraged by the fact that it was still early in the morning. Any Zealots in the area were probably having their own breakfasts and doing their own chores, right now. It was doubtful that any would appear before late morning. Finally, the young man went back to fetch his gear and then marched boldly into the Trademaster's camp.

Valerian raised his lance and shouted, "Greetings!"

Everyone in the camp, men, women and children turned his way in surprise. For an uncomfortable moment, they all just stood still and stared at him. Then, a big, barrel-chested man with a full black beard strode forward.

"Greetings traveler! Welcome to our humble Caravan! My name is Samuel. And what do you have to trade?" The big man's deep voice matched his frame. As he approached Valerian, his wide grin displayed a set of widely spaced teeth.

"My name is Valerian, and I have only my back and whatever wild game I can bring to you for trade," Valerian responded.

The young traveler knew that the Tradesmen were unfailingly honest and hospitable, but they never gave anything away. They and their families only had one means of survival, their trade goods. Those they could not afford to give away, so that charity was the one quality of character that Tradesmen chose not to exemplify.

"My wife, Greta, can work wonders with whatever game you can bring us. And if you can't bring in enough game, young man, I'm sure that we can work you hard enough to earn whatever it is that you need," Samuel responded, as he grabbed Valerian's shoulders with a pair of hands as big as hams.

"By your accent and clothing, I'll wager you're an Elympian, which means you're a dreadful long way from home. Where are you headed? And, speaking of heads, how have you managed to keep yours attached this deep into the Zealot lands?"

Greta strode up, a big woman with a huge bosom and wild head of auburn hair going gray. "I'm sure our young pilgrim will be happy to tell us his story once his belly's full...and perhaps once he's rested a bit...he looks about ready to keel over. Would you like some breakfast Valerian? You can pay with chores later."

Valerian simply nodded and responded," Thank you ma'am," as she led him to the cook fire.

"Sit down then, and Maya will fetch you a plate and a cup of tea," the big woman said and then went back to her chores.

A slender dark-haired girl of about sixteen or seventeen immediately busied herself with frying some eggs without so much as a look or a word to Valerian. The young man couldn't help but stare; he hadn't seen a girl in weeks. However, she shyly refused to return his stare and her full head of rather wild, wavy brown hair tended to obscure her face, so that he wasn't even sure what she looked like. (He suspected she was pretty.)

After a moment, Valerian dropped his lance, bow and quiver and took off his belt. He then removed his cloak, folded it on the ground and sat down on it cross-legged. He couldn't tell whether he was more tired, sleepy or hungry.

When the eggs were done, the girl added a few slices of leftover bacon and a couple of corncakes, then fetched him a tin cup of tea. Still without a word, she resumed her chores, leaving him to devour his meal alone. While he ate, Valerian noticed Samuel and two other men standing off to the side having an intense discussion. One of the men gestured toward Valerian. Samuel nodded and then came over just as the young man was finishing his last corn cake.

"My men are concerned about you, young pilgrim. If the Zealots show up with you here, they'll attack you for sure. We're not even sure what they might do to us."

"I thought that all of the Clans had to guarantee your safe passage through their lands...even the Zealots," Valerian responded as he stood up.

"Yes, but the Zealots are fanatics, therefore unpredictable, so we try not to provoke them," a tall thin man answered back, "and in any case, we certainly wouldn't be able to protect you," he added.

"I understand; I wouldn't want to endanger any of you. Would you mind if I just concealed myself in the forest nearby for a few days? I could hunt fresh game and trade you for hot meals and the provisions I need."

"First I have a few questions for you, Valerian. Are you indeed an Elympian and have you taken their Oath of Citizenship? If so, would you be willing to recite their 21 Laws for us?" Samuel asked.

Valerian nodded gravely, then without hesitation recited all of the 21 Laws of Elympias that guided his people.

"Fine indeed! In that case, Lemuel has a better idea." Samuel gestured to the tall man. "He suggests that you take the Tradesman's Oath. Any Elympian that follows the 21 Laws will have no trouble following the Tradesman's Code as well. You'd then be safe as one of us."

"That's a great honor and I appreciate your kindness, but I must be moving on in a few days."

"The Oath binds you for life to the Code of the Trade Guild, but you'll still be free to come and go as you please. And anywhere you meet a Caravan on your journey, you'll be taken in and given safe passage," Lemuel responded.

"In that case I'd be most honored," the young man answered.

"Well, fine then!" The big man slapped Valerian hard enough on the back to nearly knock him off of his feet.

"Zeke, fetch one of your spare tunics and the Sacraments and let's all gather around the fire here!" he shouted.

A big raw-boned teenager that Valerian suspected was Samuel's son headed for one of the wagons, while all of the adults dropped what they were doing and made a circle around Valerian and Samuel. Most of the children gathered behind the adults, as well. Presently Zeke returned with a plain white tunic folded over two other objects and joined the circle.

Samuel approached Valerian inside the circle. "Kneel right here," he commanded and the young man went to his knees.

"Valerian of Elympias, do you willingly now take the Oath of the Tradesman?"

"I do, "he responded.

"Do you swear for all your life to hold the welfare of your family first, the welfare of your brethren in the Trade Guild second and your own welfare third?"

"I swear," Valerian responded in the affirmative to this and the other eleven oaths that made up the Code of the Trade Guild.

They would indeed be easy to remember, he thought to himself, *since they are so similar the 21 Laws.*

With that, Zeke laid the white tunic in front of Valerian, who still knelt. The young man swayed a bit. He was beyond exhaustion and the whole ceremony had become a bit unreal for him.

Now Samuel turned away from Valerian and was handed two ceremonial objects. He turned back to Valerian with a shallow bronze bowl in one hand and a silver dagger in the other. He knelt in front of the young man, set down the bowl next to the clean tunic and asked the young man to hold out his right hand. Valerian noticed that the bowl contained a red liquid, but he was too tired to even hesitate; he just did as he was told. Samuel quickly cut Valerian's thumb and squeezed a single drop of blood into the bowl to mix with the red liquid that the bowl already held. Samuel then repeated the ritual with his own thumb and added another drop to the bowl.

"Now put your hand in the bowl and make your sign on the front of the tunic," the big man commanded as he moved the bowl aside. Valerian did so, dipping his hand in the red dye and then making his handprint on the center of the tunic. Samuel then had him repeat the process on the back of the tunic. He then picked up the tunic and stood up, bringing Valerian up with him; Greta handed him a wet rag to clean his hand.

Then, formally handing the tunic to the young man, Samuel said, "The handprints symbolize your blood connection to every one of your brethren in the Ancient Trade Guild. Tradesman Valerian of Elympias, Trademaster Samuel of Moab welcomes you to our Caravan!"

"Welcome to our Caravan!" everyone in the circle repeated together.

And with that, Samuel led Valerian around the circle to be introduced to each of his fellow members. He began with his own family. First came Greta, his wife, who gave him a big hug. Then they moved on to Zeke, Samuel's red-haired son, who enthusiastically shook his hand. Next he was formally introduced to the shy girl, Maya, Samuel's niece it turned out, who gently took his hand but still hardly looked up at him. *She is pretty after all*, he thought to himself. Then, one by one, he shook hands with all of the other members of his Caravan.

Finally, the ceremony was over. Valerian begged to be excused, explaining that he had been traveling all night. He then moved off a ways under a nearby oak, threw down his cloak and dropped his gear, changed into his new Tradesman's tunic, then promptly fell into a deep sleep…

* * *

"Wake up, Valerian," the voice came out of the darkness. "Aunt Greta says that if you sleep any longer, you'll miss out on whatever stew is left."

The voice was soft, feminine and melodic. The girl's hand gently prodded his shoulder as she spoke. Valerian, normally the lightest of sleepers, was completely sleep addled. For a few moments, he couldn't work out where he was, what was real and what had been a dream. Wolves, Tradesmen…a pretty girl hovering over him. Finally, he sat up and more or less focused his eyes.

Night had fallen completely; the only light came from a roaring bonfire in the center of the camp a ways off. How long had he slept? He could see people gathered around the fire; he heard someone telling a story, laughter, the chatter of children…fine sights and sounds to a lonely traveler.

"Thank you…Maya," he mumbled as he tried to rub the sleep away. Valerian could barely see the young girl in the dim glow of the firelight, but she looked lovely to him, nonetheless.

"Wait," he added as she rose and began to walk back to the fire. "Let me walk with you," he asked as he stood up to follow her.

She halted and waited without turning. He caught up with her and they walked together without another word. As they approached the bonfire, Samuel was in the midst of some tall tale. He held the others in rapt attention. But when he spied the young man, he interrupted his story to rise and shove a big mug into Valerian's hands.

"Drink up, young pilgrim!" Valerian took a sip; it was a strong, bitter ale.

Greta now stood up, filling a bowl from a large kettle hung over the fire, "Let's put some food in the boy before you fill his belly with drink, or he'll be back out again before we even get to hear his tale!"

Valerian sat down next to Samuel with his bowl of stew and his drink. (He was vaguely disappointed that Maya chose to sit on the other side of the fire next to her aunt.)

Valerian had eaten only had a few bites when Zeke spoke up, "Much as we love to hear your stories, Father, I'm sure that we'd all like to hear one that we hadn't already heard so many times before!"

Everyone laughed and the boy pointed at Valerian.

"Elympian, it's customary for a new member of the Caravan to tell his tale to his new mates. Would you do so now for us?"

Valerian looked at the expectant faces around the fire. He nodded his assent, took a swig of the ale for courage and began his tale. The young man had never been very outspoken or outgoing, even in his home village, where he had known almost everyone all his life. But there was a quality of warmth with this new adoptive family which gave him the confidence to speak up.

Valerian spoke quietly and steadily over the fire for a long time. He told them of the loss of his parents in the Zealot War as an infant. He told them of the loving grandmother that had raised him and the fearless uncle that had taught him the ways of the forest.

The young traveler described for his new family the three Trials of citizenship that all Elympians must pass to become full citizens…first, learning by heart as a boy the ten Elympian virtues…next, as a young man, actually demonstrating the ten virtues in a series of arduous tests…finally, learning and reciting the 21 Laws and taking the Oath of Citizenship, in order to become a full Elympian citizen.

Valerian told them the story of the twelve Cyphers and what they meant to the Elympian Clan. He recounted his proposal to the Council, the Challenge taken and passed. He even showed them the Cypher itself that hung around his neck. He recounted his journey thus far: the mountains and rivers crossed, his fight with the wolf pack, being trapped in the town of the Ancients. He concluded with his discovery of their Caravan.

The circle politely applauded as the young man finished his story. His stew had grown cold, but his cup of ale was empty. Samuel clapped him on his back.

"A fine tale, young traveler, and a fine adventure you've had so far."

"Let me see your bowl, so I can refill it with hot stew," Greta spoke up.

Zeke asked, "So when are you going to leave us to resume your quest? And would you like a companion on your journey?"

That drew a cuff from his mother. "The only quest you'll be going on is a quest to finish your chores in the morning!"

"I'm not sure; probably I'll need to move on in a few days", Valerian responded to Zeke's question.

The young man glanced at Maya, who had remained silent, but was now gazing steadily at him with her deep brown eyes. *Rather sad eyes*, he thought to himself. He returned her gaze for just a moment and for just a moment; everyone else disappeared.

"If you don't eat that stew it's going to get cold again!" Greta broke the silence. She wore a little smile and a knowing look. Valerian nodded and went to work on his supper.

Samuel refilled Valerian's cup then resumed his own story, "Where was I…"

The evening wore on. The fire crackled. Sparks lifted up into the black night and mixed with the sea of stars. More tales were told, mingled with friendly jibes and laughter. Valerian, not used to strong drink, was a bit groggy, but warm and relaxed. Crickets sang in the darkness.

Gradually, the group broke up. Maya and the other young folks cleaned up, washing the dishes and cookware in the nearby stream. Valerian offered to help, but was refused. Sentries were set to guard the camp and the livestock.

Samuel stayed with the young man, refilling both Valerian's cup and his own once more, as most of the other adults retreated to their wagons, turning in for the night. (Trademaster wagons were cleverly designed; shelves that held trade goods could be folded out so that there was room for a sleeping mat to be laid out on the floor for the adults. Children and the young slept underneath the wagon in bad weather or in the open in when the weather was fair.)

"So what do you think of our Maya?" Samuel asked, after everyone else had tuned in, just leaving the two of them in front of the dying fire.

Valerian was silent for few moments, and then finally answered, "She's pretty…and quiet…and nice. But she seems a bit sad."

"Yes lad. She's a good girl and she's right pretty as well. There are reasons for her sadness, but that story is not for me to tell. Perhaps she will tell you if you ask. She's taken with you, you know," the big man grinned at him.

Valerian blushed, hoping that Samuel couldn't see in the dim firelight.

"How would you know? She hasn't spoken three words to me since I've been here."

"Words aren't needed in these matters. Even a thickheaded youngster like yourself should have noticed how she's been looking at you, especially as you told your tale. Come to think of it, you had that same dreamy look whenever you looked at her, yourself!" he laughed.

"That was the ale! We don't drink much where I come from and our ale isn't nearly as strong!"

"Ah yes, the famed Elympian restraint…it's hard indeed to get an Elympian drunk, many times as I've tried, especially with that watered down stuff that they drink!"

"Our ale's as good as anyone's," he grew a bit defensive, "and self-discipline is one of the Ten Virtues."

"Elympian virtue…most admirable, but it can be a bit tiresome at times, as well. Nonetheless, our Caravan is headed west toward the Elympian lands, and we will be all too happy to leave our Zealot hosts in favor of our true Elympian friends."

Valerian stifled a yawn, he had slept all afternoon and half of the evening, but he had also eaten two large bowls of stew and drunk three mugs of ale. The fire was almost out now and most of the lamps in the wagons had been extinguished, as well. The only sounds left were the crickets and the occasional hoot of an owl in the distance. Nonetheless, although his family had turned in, Samuel showed no inclination to follow.

"What can you tell me of the Zealots, Samuel?" the young man asked after a time as he stirred the remaining embers in the fire. "We have been invaded by the Zealots, and we have fought and defeated them, but we know little about their ways. We know that they are fanatical warriors. We know that they all have long beards, wear white robes and are generally filthy and unkempt; other that that, it's just hearsay and rumors."

"As much as we have traveled through their lands, we know very little of their ways, Valerian. They aren't like the Elympians, or the Marmuns, the Northerners or any of the other Clans, for that matter. They will grudgingly trade with us because they really have no choice. But they won't break bread with us or trade stories with us over a bonfire, like the other Clans do. To them, we are heathens and therefore unclean; they fear being contaminated by our ways. They will only converse with us to conduct a trade or to try to convert us to their religion."

"We do know some things about them just by trading with them, however. They are filthy because they believe that cleanliness and grooming are signs of vanity, a mortal sin to them. The white robes and beards worn by the men signify they are 'Apostles', as opposed to young men in training, who wear the brown robes of 'Acolytes'. The women and children have no status whatever, and are rarely seen by outsiders."

"Their God, as far as I can tell, is an angry, vindictive, cruel God. And His followers do their absolute best to emulate Him. However, I must admit, the Zealots are scrupulously honest, they are hard working and they are disciplined. Their farms and villages are always neat and well-maintained," Samuel concluded, trying to depict them as evenhandedly as possible.

"You should see some close at hand tomorrow, Valerian. We heard from the last Zealot trading party that another is on its way. But I wouldn't speak to them, if I was you, as they might recognize your Elympian accent. No point in getting their suspicions up."

"And what have you learned in your travels of the fabled city of Elympias, Samuel? Do you have any idea where it is to be found?"

"Mostly just myths and rumors, like you. But here is what I have heard. About two weeks east of here lays the Great Mountain Range, which is also the eastern frontier of the Zealots. Crossing that range will be most difficult, even if the weather holds. On the other side, it is said that you will behold some of the most wondrous and beautiful lands ever seen by man. High waterfalls and crystal lakes, mountain meadows packed with moose, elk and deer, hot sulfurous springs that have healing properties, huge jets of water that spurt high in the sky. But you are also now in the Lawless Territories, where small bands of vicious bandits and raiders roam free, killing, raping, and stealing from anyone that they encounter, including each other."

"Once you have entered this land, you must turn south through the mountain passes for perhaps two weeks, perhaps four, looking for a place that was once known as the land of the twin lakes; the twin lakes are supposed to be near one of the largest mountains in all of those lands. On the shores of one of those lakes supposedly lies the city you seek."

"Have you been across those mountains, Samuel?"

"Never, although once every five years or so, a number of smaller Caravans will join up to form one great Caravan of perhaps a hundred wagons, with enough armed men to cross the Territories in relative safely, so that they can trade with the eastern Clans. These treks are very arduous and take many months to complete; however, the rewards can be great, as well," Samuel concluded with a yawn.

"And have you heard anything about the city itself"

"Most of the cities of the Ancients are truly horrible places. Our Caravan has skirted a few, but they are to be avoided at all costs. Their inhabitants are disease ridden scavengers who live in the filthy sewers and basements of what were once mighty buildings. However, the legends say that Elympias is completely uninhabited. Those few brave souls who claim to have seen it say that it is uninhabited because it is haunted. They say

Beyond Olympus

that at night strange lights play out across the city and eerie voices boom out in the darkness. They say that no one has ever dared spend the night there. But who knows, those are just the tales. I have never actually met anyone that had seen the city for himself."

Valerian stifled his own yawn. "One last question, if you please, Samuel, before we turn in. Have you ever heard of what happened to a force of Elympians under a man named Tobias? He tried to cross through the Zealot lands some twelve summers ago, in search of Elympias."

"As I said, the Zealots keep their tales to themselves, but I have heard stories from other Caravans, of an old battlefield at the base of the Great Mountains, where many Elympian artifacts have been found, lance heads, shields, armor and so forth. If you head due east, you may even come across it yourself."

With that, the two men bade each other good night. Samuel headed for his wagon and Valerian for his small campsite under the old oak tree. Under the tree, he saw that his cloak had been washed and neatly folded and his gear neatly arranged. Next to the cloak, a blanket and small pillow, a fresh bar of soap and a washcloth and towel had been neatly laid out for him. He took off his boots, spread out the blanket and pillow and lay down, wondering whether it was Maya or her aunt had been so thoughtful. Sleep came quickly, with dreams of a pretty brown-eyed girl.

* * *

He awoke at first dawn, but the camp was already a beehive of activity, with cook fires going and merchandise being laid out. He rose up and stretched, then headed down to the creek to wash up. Others were already there, doing the same. He looked for Maya, but assumed that she was already at work. He decided to find a bit of privacy downstream to take a proper bath. Perhaps the soap and washcloth had been as much a hint as a gift, he thought to himself.

Around the next bend of the stream was a sandy bank with no one else in sight, so he stripped off his tunic and undergarments. He shivered as he sat in the cold water and scrubbed himself down thoroughly. Drying himself and then brushing his teeth, he felt rejuvenated. He donned his new white tunic, gathered up his possessions and headed back along the stream to the camp.

Maya was at the stream near the camp, washing out some pots and utensils.

"Good morning...Maya. May I help?"

She continued scrubbing. "Woman's work...I'm sure that the men can find plenty of proper chores for you."

He knelt down next to her and picked up a dirty pot anyway.

"Where I come from, this is as proper a chore as any other for a man, especially since you fixed breakfast for me yesterday. And who knows, perhaps you might again this morning?"

With that, she turned to him with a little smile, *at last*! "That might be arranged. I haven't had breakfast yet either. I suppose I could throw in a few extra eggs for you whilst I'm frying mine..."

The two of them quickly finished washing and drying the pots and cook tools. They stood up together, and for a moment, they just looked at each other. The moment stretched and he was warmed by her gaze.

This morning, Maya's hair was pulled back in a ponytail, so that he could finally get a decent look at her. One errant strand of her long, wavy brown hair had fallen down from her smooth forehead and across one of her full cheeks. Valerian found himself gently brushing the hair back behind her ear. Yes, he realized, it was her eyes that made her special...big soulful brown eyes that seemed to hold warmth, strength and sadness in equal measure. He found himself lost in those eyes...When she spoke, it jolted him out of his reverie

"I'm very glad that it was our Caravan that you came across." Before he could think of how to respond, she turned and hurried back to the campsite with Valerian following.

After breakfast, a fair number of Zealot men and boys began arriving to trade. Just as Samuel had mentioned, there were no women or children to be seen. Nervous at the proximity of so many of his enemies, and bored with nothing to do, Valerian decided to hunt for fresh game. He determined that his new white tunic made him stand out too much for hunting, so he changed back into his old green tunic. Strapping his lance on his back, he strung his bow, and put on his quiver. He then crossed the stream and plunged into the forest.

Valerian was gone all day. He had to travel far from the sounds and smells of the camp before he began picking up on any promising signs of game. Finally, late in the afternoon, he encountered the fresh spoor of what he guessed was a very large stag. Finally, he caught sight of it in the distance. Circling around so that he was downwind, he patiently moved in, using the ample trees and underbrush to cover his approach. His patience was rewarded. Slowly rising up, he saw the big buck from its side, calmly grazing not twelve paces away. He aimed for its broad chest just behind its foreleg and hit clean. The big animal leaped straight up into the air and dropped like a stone.

By the time he made it back to the Caravan with the buck hung across his back, the sun was beginning to set. Valerian was tired, carrying the big deer for miles, but proud of himself. He knew that it would provide much fresh meat for his new family. Greta saw him first

"Look what the young pilgrim has brought in for us! Zeke, come over here and get to work! I want this fellow dressed out before dark. We were just about to start preparing dinner. I guess we'll have to delay it a bit. How about some fresh venison steaks, everyone?" the big women called out.

Samuel came over and clapped the youth on the shoulder. "This big fellow ought to settle your accounts right well for now, Valerian. But you have another small account that needs to be settled up pretty quick, as well."

Samuel pointed over to Maya, who was making herself busy shucking ears of corn.

"You didn't tell anyone where you'd gone. Maya didn't say anything, but when you were gone all day, she looked worried sick. We were all a little worried, truth to tell, thinking that maybe the Zealots had taken you, somehow."

As he walked over to the seated girl, the young man found himself completely befuddled. He had known this girl for just one day, had hardly talked to her at all, and she was angry at him for not letting her know what he was up to! *You'd have thought we were betrothed,* he thought to himself angrily. As he approached her, the corn shucking became a bit frantic. The young girl didn't look up.

"I'm sorry if I worried all of you," he said humbly. "I've been on my own for so long, it didn't occur to me to let any of you know what I'd be doing today." With that, he sat down in front of her stool.

She looked up at last, and the cool, bemused look she gave him, he knew well enough. It was the same look his grandmother had given him a thousand times, whenever he had done anything childish or foolhardy. He reached over to help her shuck the ears of corn.

"There you go, doin' women's work again. Pretty soon, the boys are going to start making fun of you."

"As soon as one of 'em brings in an eight point buck with a bow, he can make fun of me all he wants."

"All right then, but go wash up before you help. You smell like a deer."

Maya finally looked at him and smiled just a bit. Now she stopped with the corn so that Valerian could help. He hurried down to the stream, washed up and put his white tunic back on. Returning, he sat down in front of her again.

They all feasted that night on fresh venison steaks and roasted corn. After the dinner everyone cleaned up and collected around the nightly fire. But before Valerian could take his place at the fire, Maya asked him if he would like to take a walk. She took his hand as they moved into the darkness. They both had to endure friendly jibes from the youngsters and a warning from Greta not to stray to far.

The night was cool and clear as they walked down to the stream. Crickets and frogs sang a nighttime symphony. In the distance they could still see the dim light of the bonfire. It was a new moon, so the only other light came from the canopy of stars and the occasional flickering of fireflies.

I have been completely alone for weeks. Suddenly I find myself part of a Caravan, walking hand-in-hand in the darkness with a pretty girl. An awful lot can happen in a day, he thought to himself.

The young girl sat down on the bank of the stream, and Valerian sat down next to her. She was silent for a while, just looking into the darkness. Finally, without looking at him, she spoke.

"I'm an orphan like you are, Valerian, except that I was twelve when my family was taken from me, just five years ago. My father and my uncle Samuel were both Trademasters. They were partners in charge of a large Caravan of twenty wagons. We were on the eastern fringes of the lands belonging to the Zealots, near the Great Mountains. My father and Samuel decided to split the Caravan in two so that they could visit a pair of nearby Zealot towns at the same time."

"One day, after we had split from Samuel's party, we were encamped not far from the town that we had planned to trade with. Early that morning, I was out gathering firewood with a few other children when a raiding party attacked our camp. I fell to the ground and hid in some underbrush. The Raiders killed the men and children right away, raped and killed the women, took what they wanted and burned the wagons. I saw and heard everything."

Valerian was silent for a time. "I'm so sorry. I lost my parents, but I never really missed them in the way that you must miss yours, since I was an infant when it happened. Did the other children collecting firewood with you escape?"

"No, they cried out and the Raiders rode them down. One was only thirty paces from me when she fell."

"I didn't think that anyone ever dared raid in Zealot territories."

"Neither did we; that's why my father and Samuel felt safe splitting the Caravan. Nothing like this had happened for many years in Zealot lands."

"What did you do?"

"I knew where we were supposed to meet Samuel's group, so I just started walking. I was as afraid of being captured by the Zealots as by the Raiders. The Raiders would have raped and killed me; the Zealots would have enslaved me."

"Anyway, I walked for five days with no food and little water, until Samuel and a group of riders found me. They had become worried when my fathers group had not showed up at the rendezvous. Samuel had one of the riders take me back to their camp while the rest went on to bury my family and the others. Uncle Samuel still blames himself; it was his idea to split the Caravan."

"Do you?"

"No, I blame the Raiders. But they received their due in the end. Their mistake was burning our wagons. Much later, we learned that a large Zealot war band saw the smoke and investigated. They eventually caught up with the Raiders who were trying to escape back across the Great Mountains. The Zealots surrounded and killed most of them outright, then burned the few prisoners they took at the stake."

"I do miss my parents. I miss my father and mother and my little brother Jake. I miss my friends. And I will never be able to forget what I saw, what I heard."

They were both silent for a long while. Valerian wanted to say something, let her know how badly he felt about her loss. But he couldn't bring himself to say anything at all. So, finally he just put an arm around her shoulder and drew her in. She leaned against him and wept silently. After a time, she turned to face him and when they kissed, he could taste the tears...

13

The Farewell

Valerian had planned to stay with the Caravan for just a few days, but he had now been with them for twenty. His days with the Tradesmen had quickly settled into a sort of routine, hunting or trapping fresh game on one day, then helping with chores on the next, (helping to repair a wagon wheel, setting out merchandise, gathering firewood). Every other possible moment was spent with Maya, helping her with her own chores, walking through the forest with her, sometimes just sitting by the creek and talking. They talked for hours, about everything and nothing.

The young man was in a quandary. Valerian knew that sooner or later he must move on; the responsibility to his people was overwhelming. Yet, in spite of his best efforts, the bond with Maya had only grown stronger each day. So each day he had, in spite of himself, found some excuse to delay his departure.

Maya, for her part, desperately wanted to beg the young man to stay with her. She wanted to convince him that he could become a real Tradesman, marry her and eventually become the Trademaster of his own Caravan. But she resolutely stayed mute on the subject. She knew that Valerian would have to betray both himself and his people to give up his quest. As badly as she wanted him to stay, she couldn't bring herself to ask that of the young man, whom she now knew for certain that she loved. So with each passing day with him, she just hoped for one more…

Finally, the matter was settled for them both. Samuel announced early one evening that the area was traded out, and that the Caravan would be moving west in the morning. Maya just looked at her uncle for a moment, then turned and ran away, leaving Valerian standing forlornly in the center of the camp.

"Walk with me Valerian," the older man had placed his hand on Valerian's shoulder and pulled him along.

"It's time for you and our Caravan to go our separate ways. You have your duty to fulfill, and we have our families to provide for. Nevertheless, you have become a part of our family, and you will always remain so. Greta and I were much like you and Maya when we were young. The first moment we met, we knew that fate had ordained that we be together for life; everyone else around us knew it as well." The big man then pulled a small rolled up parchment from his tunic and handed it to Valerian.

"So, I have a going away gift for you, lad. This is a map that shows the journey that our Caravan has planned for the rest of this year. It shows the Zealot towns to the west that we plan to visit over the next few moons, then the Elympian towns we plan to visit thereafter. We should have reached Aurora in late summer, perhaps five moons from now."

Valerian unrolled the parchment. He noticed that Samuel had made the notes in Elympian rather than Samuel's own Trade-script.

"Now Valerian, take this map and find your young lady. Tell her that you must leave tonight. But, if you wish, you can give her your word that you will find her once you have completed your quest."

Valerian thanked the older man and turned to find Maya. He found her with Greta and Zeke at their wagon, packing in preparation for the morning's departure. He asked her to walk with him. As they walked into the darkness, he told her of Samuel's map.

"Maya, once I have found Elympias, I will return to find you, no matter what it takes, no matter how long it takes. I give you my word."

She turned to him in the darkness.

"I know you mean to come back to me, but who knows whether you will find Elympias or how long it may take? Who knows what will happen if and when you do? And…and who knows whether you will even survive your journey?"

"Who knows? No one knows. But Samuel told me tonight that he believes that it is our fate to be together. I believe that too. I'll make it back to you; I know it. Just promise me that you will wait for me."

"You know that I will. I don't understand these things very well, but I knew the first moment I saw you that you were the one. What I lost when my family was taken from me, I believe that you, and only you, can restore."

In silence, they held each other in the darkness for a long while. Finally, they returned to the camp, hand in hand. Greta and some of the other women had gathered Valerian's gear. They had packed his knapsack to overflowing with fresh provisions of every sort, dried meat, corn meal and corn cakes, dried fruit, salt, sugar, spices, and more. Earlier in the afternoon, they had also gathered up his cloak and tunic and washed them, as well; they had even cleaned and sharpened his weapons.

Everyone was packing now, breaking camp, and the mood was somber. Later, they shared a last, simple meal of dried meat, cheese and leftover bread. Samuel lifted his mug of ale for a farewell toast for Valerian and everyone around the fire followed suite. Valerian then made his way around the circle shaking hands with the men and boys, hugging the women and children. Tears were shed. It was time to leave. There was just one very painful farewell left to make. But as Valerian looked around the fire, Maya was nowhere to be seen. Rather, Greta approached the young man.

"Maya told me that you two had already said your farewells earlier this evening, and that she couldn't bear to do it again. She asked me to give this to you; it belonged to her father." Greta held out a ring to Valerian. It was a silver ring, intricately fashioned, with a tiny Tradesman's handprint carved on its surface. Valerian slipped on; it fit perfectly.

"Tell her that it will serve as a fine wedding ring when we are reunited."

The big women had tears in her eyes and gave him a final hug. Samuel followed suite. Changing from his Tradesman's tunic to his green woodsman's tunic, Valerian gathered up his gear. Giving everyone a final wave, the young man set out into the darkness without another word. He felt a strange mixture of relief and disappointment that Maya had not appeared to give him a final farewell. Soon he was alone…very alone.

Valerian headed east, following a game trail that ran along the stream. The wind kicked up and he could tell that the thunderheads that had hovered on the horizon all afternoon were beginning move in. He began seeing flashes of lightening and hearing the distant rumble of thunder.

Looks like it may be a cold, wet hike this night, he thought to himself. He set himself a brisk pace. He needed to be moving on.

As the hours passed, the gusting wind grew steadily stronger. He could smell rain now, but he was determined to keep moving. In spite of the weather, Valerian always stayed alert to his surroundings, as his uncle had taught him. That meant regularly looking and listening in all directions. With the wind in the trees, listening was difficult to impossible. Seeing anything in the darkness wasn't easy either, but he periodically scanned both sides of the trail and often turned to look behind, as well.

The lightening was growing closer and more frequent and rain began to sporadically fall. Valerian was beginning to consider stopping to fashion a shelter before the storm could hit him with its full force. Stopping for a moment, he looked around. Just as a flash of lightening lit up the sky in the distance, he thought that he caught a movement far behind on the trail. He stepped off of the trail and peered back into the darkness, but now saw nothing.

"*In the forest, to survive you must pay heed to every detail, every sign, every smell, every sound, and every movement…disregard nothing,*" his uncle had lectured him so many times in his youth.

So Valerian had hurried his pace across a clearing, and then stopped at a large oak tree whose limbs had reached over the trail. He then quickly dropped his gear and hid it in some underbrush. Next, he climbed the tree up to a spot where he had a good view back down the trail. He was now confident that he would be able to see who or whatever was coming up the trail after him without himself being seen.

What was it? A deer, perhaps a wolf, a Zealot scout…did the Zealots even have forest scouts? Or was it simply my imagination spurred by the wind and the lightning? Valerian wondered, as even the big oak swayed in the heavy winds.

Valerian wasn't very enthusiastic about being in a big tree in a thunderstorm. After a short time, he decided that perhaps his imagination had been playing tricks on him after all. But just as he was about to climb back down, he saw something approach through the branches. At first, it was too obscured by darkness and the tree's dense foliage to make out any detail. Then, as it moved closer into view between the branches, he saw that it was figure in a dark cloak, holding a lance or staff. The figure moved hesitantly, as if it was lost or confused.

In a few more moments, the figure passed almost directly under him. Valerian had almost decided that the safe strategy would be to just let

Beyond Olympus

the stranger pass, and then quietly resume his journey on another course, when a flash of lightning illuminated the figure from behind. A jolt of recognition hit him. He quickly jumped down from the tree and called out to the figure that had only moved ten or so paces down the trail.

"Maya!" The girl jumped, obviously startled, then turned, cried out and ran back into his arms. He returned her embrace, but then held her at arms length. He didn't know whether to laugh or cry.

"Are you completely mad?"

"Completely!" For her part, the young woman literally *was* laughing and crying, all at the same time.

"I thought that I was lost. I couldn't keep up with you and I knew that I could never find my way back. I didn't know what I would do. I had almost given up hope." With that she pulled herself to him and embraced him fiercely. The rain was beginning to come down steadily now. She shivered in his arms.

"I'm taking you back; there's no way that you can go with me. It will be far too difficult…and far too dangerous!"

"No Valerian, I've made up my mind and it won't be changed. If you try to take me back, I swear I'll fight you all the way! We'll never make it back before the Caravan leaves; they are going to break camp at first light."

"Not without you! Samuel and Greta would never leave you!"

"I left them a note telling them that I was going with you. I told them that they must leave without me. Now no more talk; get us out of the rain! I'm freezing!"

Indeed, it was pouring now and the winds were gusting fiercely. They both pulled their hoods over their heads and drew their cloaks about them. Valerian hesitated just a moment more, then after fetching his gear, he grabbed her wrist and began running. He had seen cliffs silhouetted against the night sky ahead and to his left. Reaching the foot of the cliff, he followed its base, hoping to find a cave or at least an outcropping that would provide some shelter. They were drenched now as they bent forward into the now violent storm.

Finally they found a recess in the cliff wall. It was only a few feet high, a few feet deep and several feet wide, but it sloped downhill so that it provided a decent, if minimal, shelter from the wind and rain. They dropped their gear at one end of the recess.

Valerian noted in the dim light that Maya had brought with her a rather large knapsack filled with provisions and a walking staff. She now wore what looked like a dark gray tunic with a rather serviceable looking hunting knife strapped on a wide leather belt. She also had on high leather boots much like his own, rather than the sandals that Tradesmen normally wore.

They both took their boots off and shook out the two cloaks. Valerian used his cloak, along with his lance and Maya's staff to fashion a crude lean-to that almost completely closed in their small shelter. Inside their little den, they rolled up together in Maya's cloak. They were both damp and cold at first, but as they snuggled closely together they were soon warmed. Entwined in their little cocoon with the storm raging around them was intoxicating for both of them.

So, huddled together, as the winds died and the rain continued to fall steadily, they talked long into the night. She told him how the idea of leaving with him had gradually germinated. But she knew that neither he nor Samuel and Greta would ever allow it. Finally, when Samuel had announced that they were breaking camp, she had decided on the spot what she would do.

First she had told Greta, that she was too upset to see anyone. She had then given her aunt her father's ring, asking her to give it to Valerian. Then, surreptitiously, while everyone else was eating, she had found a knapsack and quickly filled it with whatever provisions she could find close at hand. She gathered up from her own small trunk a few possessions, including a dark green tunic and cloak, as well as her old boots. She had pilfered the belt, staff and knife, and then left a note for Samuel and Greta in their wagon. In the note, she had told them of her plan and begged them forgiveness. She had told them that she loved them and hoped to see them again one day.

Slipping into the woods, the young girl had changed into the tunic and cloak and donned the belt and boots. Then she had waited in the darkness by the trail on which she had suspected that Valerian would depart. She had been correct, and she had carefully fallen in behind Valerian as he left the camp.

For a while, Maya had followed him without much trouble. But gradually, as the storm had kicked up, she had had trouble keeping him in sight. Eventually, she had lost him altogether and had become terrified, alone in the forest in the middle of a storm...

At last, towards dawn, the rain let up and the thunder and lightning moved off into the distance. Sounds of water dripping down the cliff and off of the trees mixed with the songs of the tree frogs. The couple lay together like spoons, with Valerian cradled against Maya's back. They both slept deeply…

* * *

Huddled in his own wet cloak under a nearby tree, the watcher in the forest finally slept, as well…

14

The Anniversary
March 26th, 2087

The evening promised to be a very special one for all of them. It had been Graham's idea. A month ago, it had occurred to him that the third anniversary of his party's arrival at Olympus was approaching. They hadn't celebrated the first or second anniversaries, since everyone had been so preoccupied with just getting the Olympus facility into full swing.

Now Graham had decided that it was finally time to celebrate their progress thus far. So, Graham had sent out engraved invitations to the fellow the passengers who had arrived with him on that fateful day. It was to be a formal affair in Graham's penthouse at the top of the Library.

Mac, Olivia and Michael arrived first that evening. Mac and Michael both looked handsome, though both seemed somewhat ill at ease in the tuxes that Graham had sent them. Olivia, however, looked absolutely resplendent in a full-length dark blue evening dress.

Dr. Raymond Fitzpatrick, Chief Medical Officer at Olympus arrived soon after; on his arm was Dr. Jacquelyn Ryder-Scott, Graham's CFO. Raymond and Jacquelyn made a very aristocratic couple in their formal attire; the tall, lean, gray-haired man in his tailored tux, and the trim, mature lady in her wine red evening gown and pearls. Equally impressive in their formal attire were Dr. Frederick Douglas Allen, who ran all of Olympus Operations, and Dr. John Tanaka, Chief Technical Officer.

Last to arrive were Dr. Luis Alvarez and Bill Atherton, the Olympus security chief, who had not been passengers on the plane, but two guests whom Graham nonetheless had felt were necessary to round out his party.

And now they all were seated around the large banquet table in Graham's private dining room. The view that night was spectacular. Construction of Olympus was now almost complete, and from the dining room, they could see most of the city lit up all around them. A full moon illuminating the night sky did its bit to add to the ambiance, as did the many candles in the ornate silver candelabras that were lit all around the dining room.

* * *

07:13 pm. The detail responsible for the security of Graham's dinner party consisted of three OSC guards: one lieutenant, one sergeant and one corporal. The three were located in the small, but very high tech Library Command Center in the basement of the huge building.

From the Command Center, they carefully monitored all of the approaches to Graham's quarters, and tracked the activity of all of Graham's support personnel in the area. (Although they were not allowed to monitor video or audio from within Graham's quarters, itself.)

The duty officer, one Lieutenant Susan Briggs, had been a member of the OSC in Olympus for just over a year. Susan, an ex-Marine, was a thirty year old, no-nonsense, rather boyish looking woman with short, blond hair and blue eyes. Seated at her command console, she suddenly bent over in pain. Sergeant Miller, seeing her distress, walked over to her.

"What's wrong Lieutenant? Do you need a medic?"

"Don't think so Miller. I think that it's just severe cramps…you know, *female stuff.* But please, take over the command console, and contact Greene; he's the backup duty officer. I think that I can manage until I'm relieved; I'll head to the clinic as soon as Greene gets here."

"OK, but you don't look so good."

The corporal was concerned. Nonetheless, he did as ordered; he had Aristotle contact Lieutenant Greene and ask him to report to the Command Center at once.

* * *

After everyone was seated, Graham made his entrance. He strode to the head of the table, as waiters arrived with bottles of champagne. Glasses were filled as Graham proposed a toast.

"To Olympus, the greatest city in the world, and to the Olympus Project, the greatest effort in the history of mankind!" Glasses were raised.

"I've invited all of you here tonight for several reasons, not the least of which is to simply take the opportunity to see all of you together socially, at long last. I also wanted an opportunity to personally thank all of you for your courage, hard work and sacrifice. You have all worked long hours. Many of you have sacrificed lucrative careers to be here. And regretfully, some of you have even been forced to endure physical danger."

"I also wished to give each of you an opportunity to share with us how well that you feel that you have adjusted to life here at Olympus, as well to give us your frank assessment of the progress of our project, so far. However, I'll only ask for those observations after enough alcohol has been consumed to ensure sufficient frankness, so drink up!"

Everyone chuckled.

"Lastly, I have an announcement to make, one that is meant for only those of you in this room. But first of all, let's savor the food, the drink and the camaraderie!"

* * *

07:22pm. Lieutenant Greene arrived at the Command Center looking a bit disheveled. He had been taken by surprise by Aristotle's alert, but had gotten there as quickly as possible, once Aristotle had apprised him that Briggs was in some sort of distress.

"Do you need help getting to the clinic, Briggs? Miller can help you while the corporal and I mind the store."

Gary L. Gibbs

"You know the rules, Lieutenant, minimum three in the Command Center, whenever Graham's quarters are occupied. Besides, I'm feeling a bit better now."

Green thought to himself that she still looked pretty bad, pale and in pain, but he grudgingly agreed. As she left the Command Center, Greene informed Aristotle at precisely 07:27 that he was officially taking over the watch. Routinely, Aristotle downloaded the information to 'Sherlock', one of its own subprograms, of the watch change along with the associated circumstances.

Sherlock, developed and named by Bill Atherton, the Olympus security chief, was a highly sophisticated security program intended to be Atherton's cybernetic alter ego. Bill had spent the last three years 'teaching' Sherlock the detective and deductive skills that he had accumulated over a long career in law enforcement…at least to the extent possible for a non-human AI.

* * *

It was a sparkling evening. They ate a meal fit for royalty, they drank the finest wines, and they socialized just as Graham had wished.

* * *

07:57pm. Sherlock suddenly came to life. It had been designed to look for suspicious patterns, and it had just detected one. An officer of the watch had suddenly gotten ill just as an event including most of the senior personnel at Olympus had begun. This in itself might be just a coincidence; but that officer had neither checked in at a clinic nor gone back to her quarters, and she had now had plenty of time to do either.

Sherlock tried to contact her on her Uplink, but was unable to hail her. It was possible that she was incapacitated or unconscious. At that point, the AI program alerted the Command Center. Greene considered contacting Mac or Atherton, but had been instructed to do so tonight only in the case of a serious emergency; he didn't think that this qualified. Neither did Sherlock, yet.

So Lieutenant Greene dispatched a roving security detail to retrace the woman's probable steps out from the Command Center, while Sherlock began to scan security cameras, as well as Lieutenant Brigg's voiceprint or implanted ID-chip access records to any of Olympus' facilities.

Simultaneously, Sherlock began a detailed analysis of the behavior of Lieutenant Briggs over the last thirty days, looking for any anomalous behavioral patterns. Even for an AI, this took time. Phone records were accessed and analyzed, not only for those of the Lieutenant, but of her friends, family, and acquaintances. Travel records and patterns of movements were scrutinized, as were finances. Searches were run on all media sources for any references to Susan Briggs or anyone associated to her.

* * *

When dessert was cleared away, some finished with coffee, others with a brandy. Finally, Graham excused the waiters and had the doors secured. It was time to talk.

"Now, I'd like to ask each of you to give me your thoughts. Within the bounds of privacy, I'd like for each of you to convey a bit to us where you are personally, before you move on to the bigger issues. Frederick, could we begin with you? How are you doing and how is your family?"

The big black man stood up and cleared his throat. He had a relaxed but forceful manner that commanded instant attention.

"Thank you, Jonathan. As some of you know, my wife Gloria has stayed back east to complete her research project at Columbia. However, last month she published her findings and is now anxious to move to Olympus as soon as possible. Our daughter, Alicia, already lives here at Olympus and works as a research assistant in the economics branch. All in all, we're doing fine, but it certainly will be nice when we're all reunited as a family once again."

"Now, on to the larger issues: Over the last three years, Olympus has blossomed into a vibrant city, with the construction of three fourths of the city completed, and two thirds of its planned twenty thousand residents in occupancy. The Alexandria Library, the stadium, the medical center, schools, research facilities, and living quarters are all now open and in full operation. So have many of its planned shops, restaurants and recreational facilities." He went on to describe the city's transportation, power, and food production facilities that were a model for the world.

"Wonderful, thank you Fred. Could we have your comments now Raymond," Graham continued.

And so it went around the table. Raymond offering up that he, a widower and Jacquelyn, a divorcee, had been seeing each other for some time…old news. Then he described the cutting edge technology deployed at the medical center.

Next Jacquelyn outlined the fantastic sums being expended to build Olympus, but assured everyone that the vast resources of Graham Enterprises could readily absorb the expenditures. John Tanaka updated everyone on the latest addition to his family…a third daughter, and then talked for a while about enhancements to Aristotle.

Mac came next, "On a personal level, there's not much to tell. You guys know me…no family, no hobbies, no outside interests. My life is my work."

"Wait a minute Mac," this from Olivia. "What about your lady friend? Whoa, are you blushing, Mac? Don't tell me our nail-biting, snake-eating chief of security is actually embarrassed?"

"Liv, keep it up and you're going to be pulling extra duty for a month!"

With that challenge, everyone around the table pounced on the poor man.

"Tell, us, who is it? Where did you meet her? How long ago?"

Graham came to his security chief's defense, holding his hands up, "Now everyone, we don't want to pry into anyone's private life. If Mac is uncomfortable discussing this, let's let him be."

Boos and cat calls from all around the table…

Mac relented, "All right, all right, I give up. Her name is Ellen Stockton; she's a high school history teacher…here at Olympus, of course. We met about six weeks ago, when she invited me to address one of her classes."

"What did you give your lecture on, Mac? Hand-to-hand combat?" Frederick chimed in now…they were all having a merry time at the big man's expense now.

"No, actually it was the Philippine insurrection. Ellen had somehow heard that I had participated in the peacekeeping effort with the U.N. forces years ago. Anyway, the lecture went over fairly well, and she invited me to have a cup of coffee after the class. It's progressed rather nicely from there, I must admit. She's a very fine lady."

"Now if we can move on to business," Mac cleared his throat, anxious to change the subject; he had never been comfortable with discussing his personal life.

"The good news is that, whoever our adversaries are, they seem to have abandoned violence, at least for the time being. Since the attempted hijacking three years ago, there have been no more overt attacks, kidnappings or sabotage. However, they are still opposing us now, just through more subtle means; the lawsuits, political resistance and bad publicity are unending. Just last week, a lawsuit was filed by the Environmental Justice Consortium to prevent the start up of our reactor. Several politicians and news outlets have already expressed support for the lawsuit. And we have traced funds transferred to the EJC as well as to some of those same politicians from a shadowy holding company overseas."

"Yes, but all they have accomplished so far is to slow us up a bit and cost us a great deal of otherwise unnecessary money to counter them," Graham pointed out.

Graham had been forced to counter-bribe any number of politicians, judges and news services to keep the project moving. But he was fine with that; he could play that game with the best of them.

"Correct, Jonathan. But the really bad news is that we still aren't certain who *they* are. We do have a good bit of circumstantial evidence that Gerhard Schmidt at Eurodynamics and Sergei Sergievich at TeleGrup are two of the ringleaders, but there is no solid proof, as yet. And we're concerned what their next move may be."

"We do have some intelligence regarding an enormous research project outside of St. Petersburg; we think that it may be some sort of response to the Olympus Project. However, so far, their intelligence has been virtually airtight, so even our best operatives have come up with few details."

"Thanks Mac. Olivia, I'm sure that we'd all like to hear your observations. And, I might add, you look simply stunning tonight."

As Olivia stood up, everyone around the table nodded and enthusiastically affirmed Graham's compliment.

"Thank you, Jonathan, thanks everyone, now it's my turn to blush. But first of all, let me just thank everyone that helped to save my life on plane on that terrible day. I especially owe my deepest appreciation for the courage of Mac and Michael, as well as the expertise of Dr.'s Fitzpatrick and Ryder-Scott. I also want to acknowledge the many medical specialists and therapists here at Olympus that assisted in my recovery. Finally, I'd like to thank Jonathan for the incredible support and generosity he has shown me over the years. There's never been a better boss!"

"Now, I have an announcement to make."

Olivia paused for dramatic effect, "Michael, I apologize for stealing your thunder, but I just can't wait any longer. Would you please stand by me?"

Michael rose as asked and Olivia took his hand. "Michael and I have decided that tonight would be the perfect occasion to announce our engagement!"

In the small banquet hall, there was applause and congratulations all around. Everyone rose to shake the young man's hand and hug the young woman...

It was Mac in the end that had finally brought them together. After Olivia had returned to work, she had quickly entered into a romantic relationship with an officer in the OSC. After that affair had self-destructed, she had moved on to an athletic director at the university; yet another OSC officer had soon followed. All three could have been from central casting; all were attractive, well built, confident male role models. In Mac's estimation, they had all also been, to varying degrees, egotistical, self-centered and shallow. Finding his own match in Ellen had given Mac the insight to give Olivia a bit of fatherly advice.

"Liv, if there's one thing that that I've finally learned after all these years, it's to stop trying to find a partner who measures up to some sort of ideal. Just find a relationship that seems to work...for whatever reason. Ellen and I have developed a great relationship, even though by any objective criteria we are a total mismatch. We have different interests, different personality traits, and different personal goals. We seem to only share one thing: we love spending time with each other."

Olivia had finally relented some six months ago. Out of the blue one day, she had called Michael and asked him out to dinner. Michael had long since more or less moved on; he had even chalked up a few failed relationships of his own. The called had utterly surprised him; nonetheless he had jumped without hesitation at Olivia's invitation.

After that first evening, their relationship had blossomed quickly and beyond all expectations. It was if all of Olivia's long repressed feelings for Michael had been suddenly released in a cascade of emotions. After that first day, the two had become virtually inseparable. Even the physical relationship had far exceeded any of her prior experiences, perhaps because of the emotional intensity that both now felt.

Michael, in turn, simply could not believe his good fortune. The young man had really known, deep down, that Olivia was the one for him from the first moment that they had met years ago in New York, in spite of the fact that he had feared all along that she would prove to be unattainable. He had never truly recovered when she had indeed rejected him, gently but unequivocally, almost three years ago. And now the reality of their relationship had exceeded even his own best expectations.

As for his part, Mac was feeling pretty smug about it all. Not only had he managed to find the first truly solid relationship in his own life, now the big tough guy had actually played Cupid, and got it right!

* * *

08:43pm. A warning alert tone sounded simultaneously in Mac and Bill's earpieces. It was Sherlock, informing them that it had autonomously instituted a stage three security alert in the vicinity of Graham's penthouse. It recommended immediate evacuation of all personnel from the area. Meanwhile, it informed them that a heavily armed fast response team had been dispatched to protect them, even though the exact nature of the threat was as yet unknown. ETA of the security detail was three minutes.

* * *

Mac and Bill quickly agreed not to wait for the security team. Both drew their personal weapons. Bill headed to the door, while Mac addressed the other guests.

"Everyone, no time to explain! Stand against that far wall, and then follow us immediately when we tell you. We're going down the express elevator. Let's move!"

Bill commanded the door to open as soon as he and Mac had gotten into in position with their weapons leveled. The door slid open, but no one was on the other side. They motioned the others to follow as soon as they had confirmed that no one was in the adjoining corridor.

Olivia, frustrated that she was unarmed in her evening dress, led the way. Quickly, they hustled everyone into the express elevator. As soon as it shut and the elevator began to descend, Bill instructed Sherlock to ensure that all of Graham's staff was immediately evacuated from the danger zone, as well. (The security program had already done so.) He next instructed Sherlock to redirect the security team to the fifth level basement "Crisis Center", where they were now headed.

Midway down to the basement, at precisely 08:50 pm, the elevator was rocked by an explosion from up above. The elevator lights flickered then went off and the elevator stopped. A moment later, the emergency lights came on, and soon after, the elevator continued its descent to the basement. Everyone was silent now.

* * *

Sherlock had located Lieutenant Susan Briggs, just seconds before it had sounded the alert. Initially, unable to locate her, it had performed a fast analysis of all access and entry records of any and everyone in Olympus. It was looking for any sort of anomaly or inconsistency, and it had found one after several minutes...

At 08:35, one Naomi Bennett, an Olympus maintenance technician (coincidentally, a thirty-two year old woman with short blond hair and blue eyes), had used her implanted ID-chip to board the nightly 08:45pm Olympus air-shuttle to Denver. The problem was that Naomi had also just used her ID-chip to access her quarters a few minutes ago, and had not left her quarters since.

Sherlock had immediately scanned the security cameras at the landing portal and had detected a person with Susan's facial patterns boarding the shuttle. It had immediately commanded the shuttle autopilot to lock its doors, shut its engines down and await further instructions. The AI program had then simultaneously alerted the Command Center, Mac and Bill.

* * *

The somewhat shaken guests from Graham's dinner party met the security team at the entrance of the Crisis Center in the Library's sub-basement. (The Crisis Center was an ultra secure complex of offices, meeting rooms and electronic command centers intended to be used in the event of any sort of natural or man-made disaster.)

On the way to the elevator, Bill and Mac had agreed that it was the perfect place for Graham's party to take refuge until the situation could be properly evaluated. The security team was deployed in the corridor outside the Crisis Center with instructions to let absolutely no one in.

At Mac's direction, the party assembled in one of the Crisis Center's larger conference rooms. It was about the same size as Graham's dining room and the table seated the same number as Graham's ornate oak banquet table, but that was where the similarities ended. This room was strictly utilitarian, holo-projections and maps on the walls rather than picture windows, simple swivel chairs rather than the high-backed expensive chairs upstairs.

After everyone was seated, Mac and Bill excused themselves; they had an emergency to manage. Before leaving the room they announced there had only been a few minor injuries upstairs. Everyone expressed relief.

As the two men left, Graham stood up, and with a grand gesture, held up a bottle of Dom Perignon that he had grabbed as they had fled the dining room.

"I didn't get where I am by losing my head in a crisis!"

Everyone applauded.

"Before we were so rudely interrupted, I was about to propose a toast to Olivia and Michael! Could someone find some glasses? I'm afraid that I didn't have time to salvage the crystal."

They were reduced to toasting the happy couple in plastic cups, but that didn't dampen the enthusiasm a bit. (Although Tanaka groused that drinking Dom out of a plastic cup must be some sort of a sacrilege.)

After a time, everyone settled down somewhat. The group was informed after a bit by Bill Atherton that they all might be asked to spend the next several hours in the Crisis Center. The security chief apologized, but asked Graham's party to be patient while they conducted a complete security assessment of the Library.

* * *

Shortly after the explosion, Sherlock had unearthed a rather minor story from a local Minneapolis news source. Three months ago, an individual identified as Terrence Briggs had been badly injured in a hit and run accident. Although he was expected to fully recover, he had received two broken legs, along with an assortment of other minor injuries. Upon further investigation, Sherlock determined that Terrence Briggs was the father of Lieutenant Briggs; he was, in fact, her only next of kin.

This led very quickly to another whole line of inquiry. Records of all calls made to or from Lieutenant Briggs's Uplink, over the last three weeks were carefully scrutinized. There had, of course been a flurry of calls just after the accident, to and from friends, relatives, etc. There were also Lieutenant Briggs' travel records indicating that she had visited her father for several days just after the accident.

Sherlock detected one anomaly, however. Just after the accident, and several times thereafter over the next few weeks, she had received calls from one Justin Ward. This in itself was not suspicious, as Justin Ward was listed as Terrence Briggs's next door neighbor. However, one of these calls had lasted twenty-two minutes, and during this particular call, Justin Ward had simultaneously originated another call across town.

It was a common intelligence practice to cover an agent's covert communications by disguising an Uplink call with a civilian's cloned Uplink ID. Without a doubt, Susan Briggs had been in contact with a covert agent just after her father's accident.

* * *

After the toast, Graham spoke again, "Well, it's not the surroundings but the company that makes for a fine dinner party, I always say. I would like to propose that we carry on from where we left off upstairs."

Everyone agreed.

"Louie, would you be so kind as to share some of your thoughts with us."

The small man stood up and spoke in his characteristically soft and accented, but rather hypnotic voice, "Thank you, Jonathan, I would be most pleased to do so. First of all, let me just say that, personally, this project has been nothing less than my salvation. I will never find a replacement for my beloved Maggie. But here, I have found renewed purpose to my life; here, I have finally learned how to move forward, once more."

"Now, onto the status of our research...together, we have learned much over the last two years. We now have a much deeper, clearer understanding of the root cause of society's self-destructive impetus. It is not economic in nature, neither is it political nor environmental. These factors are just the symptoms, rather than the cause of our plight."

"So what is that fundamental element that bears the seeds of our destruction? The one common attribute of all of history's great civilizations is that they have all produced citizens capable of overcoming any challenge. America was once such a society. In the last century, we won two world wars and perhaps an even more dangerous Cold War. We created unheard of prosperity for the vast majority of our population. We were responsible for most of the technological developments that are the foundation of our modern society."

"So, to look for the cause of our impending downfall, we must look inward, rather than outward. Of course, there are still many in our society who possess the intellectual and character traits that made our ancestors so capable...those in this room are proof of that. However, look at our nation's current leadership; look at our masses. Our leaders are obsessed with power and prosperity...their own, that is. The masses are equally obsessed with their own material well being...that is, those that haven't escaped to the alternate worlds of virtual reality or perhaps cults or fundamentalist beliefs. Who is left now to look after democracy, to protect the greater good?"

"So it is that we collectively continue to accept bad political, economic and environmental decisions because the only true core imperatives that are collectively instilled in all of us is self-aggrandizement and escapism," Frederick commented.

Now Michael stepped in; he had held himself in check up to now, not wanting to interrupt his mentor. "So, we are convinced that we understand the problem well enough. We even understand the necessary cure; we must simply change the core values that our children are taught. But then we're faced with the 'Gordian Knot', one that has stopped us all cold. How do you get a sophisticated society to completely break with the past in just twenty short years...before everything comes crashing down around our ears?"

"We have even begun experimental programs with our own children here in Olympus, and we are already beginning to see tangible results. However, gaining mass acceptance for such programs just seems out of the question."

Now Graham stood up. "Precisely, ladies and gentlemen. From the time of the original GRI report, we had suspected that there would be no way to reverse the course of history; the Olympus Project has thus far simply confirmed that fact. Consequently, I'm well aware that some of you have harbored doubts concerning the true purpose behind Olympus all along. You have asked yourselves, why the Herculean effort to save civilization, if it is essentially already beyond salvation? So now we come to the true and final purpose for tonight's dinner party..."

So Graham made his pronouncement, and the resulting discussion lasted far into the night. In fact, it was a bit of surprise to everyone when, with dawn fast approaching, Mac finally arrived to let everyone know that the area was secured and that they could at last be escorted back to their quarters. Graham shared his secret with Mac, as well, then bid farewell to his guests with a final warning that it was imperative that what they had heard that night must not be repeated…

*** * * ***

Bill Atherton and his erstwhile cybernetic partner, Sherlock, continued their investigation over the next few weeks. In truth, it had been pretty well wrapped up in a few days.

Susan had quickly confessed; enemy agents had intentionally hit her father. They had contacted Susan soon after; the choice that she had been given was stark. The 'accident' with her father had been staged to illustrate just how ruthless and powerful they were. If the OSC officer agreed to do their bidding without question, both she and her father would be given a new identity in another country, along with wealth beyond their imagination. Any other alternative would compel the agents to finish what they had started with her father, and then target her next. She was given convincing evidence that they could follow through with their threats, regardless of whatever protection was provided.

The explosives and remote actuator had been hidden in the four silver candelabras. Susan had arranged for their placement in Graham's dining room shortly after invitations had been sent out for his dinner party. This was easy enough for her to arrange, being in charge of one of Graham's security details. She hadn't been told what the candelabras contained, just that she must excuse herself and slip out of Olympus undetected on the 08:45 flight to Denver that night. She hadn't been told what would happen, but she had suspected…

In spite of her betrayal, Graham and Mac took a measure of pity on the young woman. They arranged for new identities for both Susan and her father, along with a couple of low-level jobs in one of Graham Enterprise's smaller subsidiaries. They wouldn't be rich, but they would be relatively safe and modestly comfortable.

15

Into the Mountains

The young couple had now reached the western foothills in sight of the Great Mountains. They had now been traveling for three weeks. Progress so far had been rather slow. This was partly because Maya was unused to walking such great distances, particularly at night. However, the real reason for their slow progress, Valerian had to admit to himself, was that traveling with this lovely young girl had become as much a romantic idyll as a single-minded quest to find Elympias.

Some days they would start their journey late in the evening, or stop well before dawn. Other days, finding a pretty spot in a meadow or by a waterfall, they would simply stop for an extra day or two to rest and enjoy each other's company. The journey could always wait one more day…

Today, they had encamped in a secluded spot on the bank of small lake filled with the cold, crystalline runoff from the nearby mountains. It was a lovely spot, made more so as the morning sun topped the mountain range. They had made better progress the night before; seeing the mountains silhouetted in the moonlit night sky over the trees had somehow prodded them onward through the darkness.

Now, seeing the huge snowcapped peaks nearby inspired equal measures of awe and dread in the young traveler. Could the two of them actually make it across? Scanning carefully from north to south, he could see no obvious passage. Well, that problem would have to be more carefully considered in a day or two, when they actually reached the mountains, he thought to himself.

When the sun had first come up, Valerian had noticed that the lake was teeming with fish. As Maya curled up in her cloak and quickly fell to sleep under a tree, Valerian had decided to spear a few trout and surprise the young girl with breakfast. She had only slept an hour or so when she awoke to the delicious smell of fresh fish frying on their small skillet.

Maya rose and stretched, catlike. Valerian glanced at the lovely young woman as he transferred the fish fillets over to a pair of tin plates. He was stuck, as always, by her grace and natural beauty. He was struck, as well, at her transformation from a shy, timid girl to a confident young woman in just the short time they had spent on their journey together. Could it be, he wondered, that it was simply his own perception of her that had changed?

"Sorry to wake you. Wash up in the lake, if you like, and let's have some breakfast. We can both sleep after."

As she yawned and went down to the water, Valerian added corn cakes from one of the packs to each plate and poured the tea he had brewed into their tin cups. The young girl sat down next to him, and they both ate quietly, but with gusto. Both plates were cleaned in moments.

"Heathens...stand up and turn around!"

In a flash, Valerian dropped his cup, grabbed his lance and whirled around to face four Zealots, who had somehow made a semicircle just four or five paces from him. He wondered miserably, how could they have they gotten so close without alerting him? His back was now to the lake and Maya had fallen behind him with her knife drawn.

The obvious leader in the center spoke again. He looked to be the eldest...and filthiest. His tangled beard reached to his stomach, and what teeth he had were rotten. The stench of his breath reached all the way over to Valerian as he spoke.

"Drop that lance and we'll dispatch you mercifully. Fight us and we'll burn you slow. The heathen bitch, we'll take for breeding stock."

"You'll have to kill me," Maya responded with quiet conviction as she brandished her hunting knife.

"Then it'll be a pleasure to burn you, as well," he growled

As they spoke, Valerian thought fast. Perhaps forgetting some of his uncle's lessons had gotten them into this predicament…using every one of the rest might still save them. As he pretended to hesitate he quickly took stock of his foes, as his uncle had taught him.

Looking from left to right, there was a tall, skinny dark-haired Zealot who looked like a real killer; he had a scar on his cheek and wore a vicious smile. Next to him stood a short, flabby man with a thin, scraggly beard. He looked nervous and uncertain, like he would rather be elsewhere. Then came the old man, who looked to be hard, confident and cruel. Finally, on Valerian's right was a youth in the brown robe of an Acolyte. He didn't appear to be either frightened or hateful, as the other men.

The three white robed Apostles were armed with the long curved knives, really short swords, which all Zealot warriors favored. The boy was unarmed.

"We are Tradesmen, separated from our Caravan; we have our white tunics."

Valerian knew that this wouldn't save them out here, but he wanted to stall for a moment before making his move. As he talked, he moved slightly forward and ever so subtly adopted a fighting stance.

"Tunics be damned boy! They could be stolen for all we know. Now drop that cursed weapon."

When you must defend yourself, always be the one to attack first, regardless of the odds. Do not hesitate, and provide no warning whatever. Once you attack, keep on attacking. Never let your foes recover. And before you attack, look into each man's eyes. Go after the leader first, the bravest next. The others may hesitate. Thrust! Parry! Slash!

How many times had he sparred with his uncle over the years? Eventually, he had become so adept with his lance that he could fight the older man to a draw nine times out of ten. Their matches became something to see, two lances flashing, stabbing and blocking so quickly that a spectator could have hardly made out what was happening…

Valerian, after another moment's hesitation, seemed to be laying his weapon down, when, in a flash, he leaped forward and drove its razor sharp point squarely into the center of the leader's chest. Before the old man had even fallen, the young warrior pulled the lance out, whirled and struck at the tall skinny one, who had only just begun to react.

But even before Valerian's lance had struck home, an arrow seemed to materialize in the Zealot's neck. A half heartbeat later, the fat one looked down at himself in horror to see an arrowhead protruding from the center of his chest. All three Zealots collapsed virtually at the same instant; none had made a sound.

Valerian, acting now on instinct and adrenaline dropped his lance, grabbed the youth and spun him violently facedown on the ground.

"Don't move if you want to live!" he shouted, as the boy cried out in terror.

"Valerian, stand aside and I'll take care of that one as well," his uncle had appeared from nowhere in the blink of an eye, knife in hand.

"No!"

Valerian had barely been able to croak the one word as he sat astride the boy. He raised his hand up to his uncle. His hand was shaking violently and his throat had now locked up completely. He flushed, embarrassed that his Uncle Sebastian should see him this way.

The big man pulled Valerian up by his arm. As he stood up, Maya dropped her knife and held her young man fiercely. The tough woodsman softened a bit.

"All right lad, we'll let the boy live if you wish, as long as he behaves. It's not a good idea by my reckoning; small serpents just grow into bigger ones one day, with that much more poison. But we'll find some way to release him when the time is right."

"Right now, we have much to do, and right fast. We need to find a crevice to throw these here carcasses into. We'll cover them with rocks, and then we'll cover all signs of the camp and the fight. Then we'll ride the horses as far up into the mountains as we can. It'll be right dangerous to travel by daylight, but we have to clear out before Zealot search parties begin looking for their mates."

Sebastian had pulled their young captive up as he spoke; he tied a leather thong about the youth's ankles with enough slack for him to walk but not run.

"Look here boy, if these are your family, I'll let you say some words over 'em after they're buried. But give me any problems and I'll be just as happy lettin' you join 'em!"

The youth, who had been mute up to now, finally spoke, "My name is Joshua of the Marmun Clan, and these creatures can burn in eternal hellfire, as far as I'm concerned!"

Joshua had then quickly told them that he had been taken as a young boy in a Zealot raid of his Marmun village. His parents and neighbors had been killed; a few other youngsters had been taken prisoners.

The young man, who appeared to be about fourteen summers in age, had pretended to convert, because death at the stake had been his only alternative. But he despised the Zealots and had secretly dreamed of escaping and finding his way home again one day. As proof of his story, he showed them the tattoo of a cross on the inside of his wrist, which was the sign of the Marmuns. It was partially obscured by scar tissue, where the Zealots had tried to burn it off, but it was still visible, nonetheless.

"Well that makes a difference. I'm still going to keep you hobbled for a bit, until I'm sure that I can trust you. But after a time, I reckon we'll let you loose."

"Thank you, sir. I promise I won't give you any trouble. In fact, I'll help you pitch this trash into a hole, if you'd like. I can also tell you that these Zealot scouts won't be missed 'til late evening, since that's how long they usually stay out. So search parties probably won't be sent out for them 'til the next morning."

"Fine then, Valerian, stay with your woman and settle down a bit whilst me and the boy here take care of these bodies."

The old warrior walked over to his nephew and clapped him on the shoulder. "Don't mind getting the shakes, lad; the first time for real combat does that to a man…happened to me too once upon a time. You did well in the fight, though I can't say much for your woodcraft gettin' caught flatfooted like that. But young love can make a man stupid; been there too, once upon a time…"

His uncle smiled a bit as he turned and grabbed the shoulders of one of the dead men as the boy grabbed his ankles. Carrying the first body, Sebastian and the boy soon found a rocky outcropping on the edge of the lake; it had a gap that was perhaps three feet wide and several feet deep. They dropped the body into the crevice and quickly added the other two. The big man then had the boy help him carry the trunk of a small fallen tree and drop it on top of the stacked corpses. They had then filled the gaps with large rocks, tree limbs and brush. Erasing their tracks, there was soon no trace left; even a skilled woodsman would have been hard pressed to find anything amiss.

Meanwhile, as the three bodies were disposed of by his uncle and the boy, Valerian and Maya had broken camp and thoroughly erased every trace of it, as well. Having traveled all night, all three, Valerian, Maya and even Sebastian were tired. However, the woodsman had no intention of letting anyone get any rest.

"Gather up your gear. The boy here will take us to their horses. Then we're going to head for the mountains. Now let's get moving!"

The boy led them through the forest to a small meadow where three horses and a mule were hobbled. The mounts were all fitted with bridles and crude saddles made of wood and cowhide. They were nothing like the well-crafted leather saddles that the Elympians favored, but they looked serviceable enough, Valerian decided. The animals were also outfitted with large rough saddle blankets, saddlebags and canteens. He and his uncle inspected the saddlebags and were pleased to find provisions, including sausages, hard bread and cheeses in each.

Valerian had a thousand questions for his uncle: When and why had his uncle changed his mind and decided to follow him all this way? How had the older man managed to track him so far, at night, through storms, across rivers? Why had he not just traveled along with Valerian rather than trail him? But he knew that now was not the time to ask these questions. Those would have to wait until their party was out of immediate danger.

Sebastian had them secure their knapsacks over the saddlebags. He made sure that all of their canteens were full. He showed Valerian how to tie their lances so that they could be readily retrieved while riding. Then he untied the youth's ankles, but tied one of his wrists to the pommel of the mule's saddle; he wasn't ready to completely trust the boy just yet. The big man mounted his horse, a big chestnut stallion, and grabbed the mule's reins. Valerian climbed up on his mount, a brown mare.

"Lass, do you know how to ride?"

"The name is Maya, Uncle, and I've ridden since I was a little girl," with that she swung lightly up on her mare, and expertly brought her around, "which way Uncle?"

Sebastian gave her a grin, then swung his own steed around, kicked him smartly, and took off up the trail at a gallop. The others followed; they were headed east toward the mountains. At first, the ride was exhilarating, swinging through forests and meadows, splashing through streams, galloping over hills.

But as the hours passed, their backsides and legs become more and more sore, and fatigue began to take its toll. Their mounts became lathered and winded as well, after a time. Yet Sebastian drove them on mercilessly, only stopping now and then for a few moments to let the animals drink in whatever streams or ponds they came across. For those few moments, he would let them dismount, stretch and drink from their canteens. Then, he would order them back up and off again.

Midday passed, and Valerian was sure that his uncle would stop and let them rest and eat, but the big man just kept pushing. The young man looked over at Joshua and back at Maya; both were just looking wearily ahead, trying to keep up. Neither was willing to complain, but both were clearly exhausted; so was Valerian after just a while longer.

Finally, at mid-afternoon, as they rode through a thick stand of cottonwoods and aspens, Valerian kicked his mount and caught up with the older man.

"Uncle, the animals are worn out, and so are we. We need to stop for a little while and rest up. Then we should be able to make it the rest of the way to the mountains without stopping again."

Reluctantly Sebastian reined in his mount; he didn't look the least bit tired. "I reckon you're right, lad. Looks like a stream up ahead with good cover. We'll water the horses, eat a bite or two and rest our backsides a bit."

The big man jumped down and cut Joshua loose. They all dismounted, led their mounts to the water and hobbled them. The animals drank eagerly and the three young people collapsed. Sebastian took a quick drink from a canteen, grabbed a sausage and his weapons and quickly disappeared into the forest.

"Where did he go?" Joshua asked as he wearily dragged himself up to get some food and water.

"He'll be scouting the area, like I should have done this morning," Valerian responded as the boy handed him a sausage and canteen.

Valerian passed the canteen to Maya, before taking any. The girl gulped down half the canteen, then collapsed onto her back; she waved the offered sausage away. The two youths ate, drank and then silently rested for a while.

Finally, sitting up, Joshua asked, "Where would you folks be headin', in the middle of Zealot lands?"

"We are on a journey that will take us over the mountains. More than that, I cannot say," Valerian responded.

"I understand. You don't know me yet; you've got no reason to trust me. Just the same, I hope that you'll take me with you, wherever you're going. I'll die before I go back to the Zealots, and I know I'd never make it back to the Marmun lands by myself."

"We'll see," was all Valerian would say.

They both lay quiet for a short while...

* * *

"Wake up, you three, time to get moving," Sebastian stood over them.

They had all fallen asleep, but not for long; Valerian noticed that the sun hadn't moved far in the sky. The young man rose first, nudging the boy with his toe and bending down to touch Maya's cheek. They all stretched then un-hobbled the animals. In moments, they were off again at a gallop behind Sebastian. This time he chose to let Joshua hold his own reins.

The mountains were now towering nearby. Finally they came to an open plain that led to the base of the nearest mountain. Riding behind his uncle, Valerian thought that he could make out the passage ahead that his Uncle was likely headed for. As they entered the plain, their pace quickened; the young man knew that his uncle wouldn't like being exposed as they were now and would want to get up into the mountains as quickly as possible.

Sure enough, halfway across the plain, his uncle wheeled his horse around and waived the others forward.

"Let 'em out!" he shouted, "Zealot party behind us! Move!"

Valerian glanced back, and there they were, just entering the plain, perhaps ten or fifteen of them. He kicked his mount to catch up with his uncle, who was now racing for the passage up the mountain. Maya stayed right up with him, side by side, determinedly looking forward. Joshua, however, gradually fell back on the slower mule.

Time slowed; it seemed that they would never make it to the trailhead at the mountain's base. Finally they did, although their mounts, which had been pushed all day, were winded and lathered again.

Joshua had finally caught up; his mule was slower, but had more stamina than the horses. However, the Zealots, on fresher mounts, had halved the distance to them. They were perhaps only three hundred paces behind. And now the trail up was steep and narrow and cluttered with large rocks. They would have to proceed slowly now, single file.

As they climbed, the Zealots closed the gap even more. Their pursuers were perhaps only two hundred paces behind when they made it to the trailhead below. For a time, the young riders just climbed onward, trying to keep up with the big man in front. They and their mounts were all completely exhausted once again.

Finally, they came around a bend in the trail to a fairly level, wider spot. Sebastian quickly dismounted and pulled off his pack and weapons.

"Keep them movin' upwards, lad. I'm going to hold these vermin here for awhile. Then I'll be along."

"We can't just leave you here Uncle!" Valerian cried out as he dismounted.

"Get back up there! It's those two you need to be worrying over, not me. Since when do you think a Ranger couldn't hold his own against a ragged bunch of flea-bitten Zealots?" the big man grinned and clapped his nephew on his shoulder.

"Now listen well, youngster. I may catch up or I may not. But just you remember everything I taught you and you'll all do all right. Take the animals as high as they can climb, then let 'em loose when they can't go any higher. Then you'll be back on foot. Keep the saddle blankets, though. It's gonna get cold up there. Now give me half of your arrows and…Godspeed young lad! I'm proud of you!"

Valerian threw his arms around the big man and hugged him with all his strength. It was like hugging the trunk of a tree. Then, without a word, he gave his uncle half of the twenty arrows in his quiver and jumped on Sebastian's stallion. He led the others off without looking back.

The big woodsman was now in his element. Alone, hidden, outnumbered, rather than fear or despair, he felt exhilaration. He might live or die this day, but for certain, these Zealots would come to believe that their God had deserted them by the morning…

These men were members of the same Clan that had taken the lives of his brother and sister-in-law, most of his friends and his beloved wife; the people that had invaded his lands without warning and with no reason or justification.

These Zealots were also the people that, years ago during the great Zealot War, had eventually come to believe that Sebastian and his Elympian Rangers were forest demons from Hell; demons that could appear from nowhere and kill them at will.

Staying out of sight, the Ranger could hear them stumbling up the trail on their horses. Although he was outnumbered by some twelve to one by his reckoning, he knew that he had his own advantages. First, he had the high ground, and they could only ride up single file. Secondly, he could climb and maneuver, (and even at his age, he could still climb like a mountain goat) while they would be loath to leave their mounts. Finally, he knew that Zealots, though vicious and relentless foes, were generally unskilled fighters. They were only armed with their crude curved knives and equally crude spears, and they barely knew how to use even those.

Sebastian waited around the bend until he reckoned from the sound that they were only about fifty paces away, and then boldly marched back down the trail. As the first rider came into view, without hesitation, the Ranger loosed an arrow from his powerful war bow that went clear through the chest of the lead rider.

As the Zealot fell back, instantly dead, the horse reared, and Sebastian put an arrow through the center of horse's chest as well. The beast reared again, whinnied and fell on its side across the trail. Its hooves kicked out wildly as it died. Sebastian felt no remorse for the man, but hated hurting a dumb animal. Nonetheless, it was necessary; this fight likely meant life or death for them all.

Chaos ensued behind the fallen horse and rider. Most of the men dismounted; some took cover, others moved forward to recover the body and push the horse's carcass off of the path. Standing calmly in the open some fifty paces up the trail, Sebastian pulled two more arrows from his quiver. He waited calmly.

After some time, with shouts and war cries, several of the bravest fighters broke cover and tried to rush him. The old warrior put an arrow through the belly of each of the two front men, almost simultaneously. As they dropped across the path, their falls broke the charge of the others. (Sebastian had coldly decided to wound rather than kill, since the wounded men would encumber even more of the fighters, as some would have to care for their wounded comrades.)

With another shout, brandishing their spears, more of the Zealots charged again, hoping to overwhelm whoever opposed them. Screaming and running now, they rounded the bend to the spot where the trail widened. There was no trace of anyone…

It took the Zealot party awhile to get reorganized. They had to push the dead horse off of the trail to get the others past. They also had to tend to the two wounded men, who were screaming in agony. Finally they were ready to move on; they left behind one uninjured fighter to take care of the two badly wounded men, along with their fallen comrade. They now had eight fighters left to move on, and those were furious for revenge. But already the sun was low on the horizon.

As the Zealots worked their way up the trail, they were now forced to move more slowly, constantly scanning above for the next ambush. They saw nothing for long while. The trail narrowed and steepened as the sun began to set. The going became both harder and slower, the drop-off below the trail was now sheer for several hundred feet. The horses became skittish as the shadows lengthened.

Suddenly, a rockslide broke loose above and just in front of the lead rider. His horse reared and stumbled. The beast twisted in terror, trying to avoid falling off of the cliff. It barely succeeded, but threw its rider in the process, falling on him. The man's right leg was crushed. As he screamed in agony, panic set in amongst the other riders, as they tried to rein in their mounts before they suffered the same fate. Finally, order was restored, as the men dismounted and some tended to the fallen rider.

Standing on a ledge far above far above, silently peering down at them was the lone warrior. With screams and shouts of anger, most of the Zealots gathered their weapons and began climbing towards him. The warrior didn't move or even look concerned.

The way up was arduous for the Zealots, especially with their ankle length robes. Still they fought their way up, scrambling and clawing up the steep slope, sliding back down, stumbling. Yet, every time they looked up, there the damnable heathen was just placidly looking down at them. They were delirious with fury now. Finally, they were just ten or so paces below him. Some drew their knives; others held their spears at the ready. His screams of agony would echo through the night!

Just moments before they reached him, his face disappeared over the top. They rushed forward, mounting the final rise, screaming and brandishing their weapons. He was gone. They fanned out, breathless, trying to find and close with him. He was nowhere to be found, and had left not a trace.

Darkness was now closing in; they were exhausted and beside themselves with rage. They began arguing with one another. Finally, one of the senior men commanded the others to settle down and climb back down the cliff. By the time they had made it back to the trail, darkness had settled in.

Now they found themselves on a narrow trail along a precipitous cliff with one badly injured man. They soon discovered that the lead horse had a broken foreleg as well. They unceremoniously cut its throat and pushed it off the cliff. The injured Zealot was tied across one of the other horses, howling in agony, to be led back down the trail.

Their party was now down to six, and at that point common sense should have dictated that they cut their losses and give up the chase. However, Zealots were known more for their fanaticism than for their common sense; they pushed onward. Above, in the moonlight, they continued to be scrutinized by a cool, implacable enemy. For them, the night's ordeal had only just begun…

* * *

The way up had been somewhat less eventful for Valerian's party; at least they had been unopposed. However, Valerian and Maya were beyond exhaustion, having traveled all through the night before. Their mounts were worn out, as well, and the young travelers finally decided to dismount and lead them, rather than take a chance that one of the tired animals might stumble on the narrow trail and take someone over the cliff.

Finally, late that night and perhaps two thirds of the way to the top of the pass, they reached a small plateau, covered by thick stand of spruce and fir. A small waterfall cascaded down into a pool of clear water. They led their animals to the pool and drank thirstily next to them.

"This place is perfect. Are we going to make camp here?" the young boy asked Valerian.

Maya was silent, but she looked at him expectantly, as well.

"I'm afraid not," the young man responded.

Valerian was trying think like his uncle now. *What would Sebastian do?*

"If the Zealots get past Uncle, we'd be completely exposed here. You two rest; I'm going to scout ahead to find the best way up."

Maya rose wearily. Valerian expected her to beg him to stay there, rest and make camp. Instead, she held him and comforted him, "I know that you're worried about your uncle; I know that you want to go back to help him. But he was right, we need you more."

He held her tightly for a moment without speaking, and then mounted the stallion. "Maya, you and the boy need to rest and eat something while you have the chance. I'll be back soon," he said, as he set off into the moonlight to scout ahead.

The young man started off by going back to the top of the trail they had just climbed. He scanned below for a while, looking for any sign of either his uncle or their pursuers. He saw nothing. *Well, at least Uncle must have delayed them,* he thought to himself.

Then he led his mount around the perimeter of their plateau. What he found was troubling. On one side was the sheer drop back down the cliff.

The rest of the perimeter was bounded by roughly semicircular rock wall all around. At first, he thought that they had truly ridden into a trap.

However, as he rode back slowly along the rock face, peering into the dim moonlight, he thought that he made out a break several paces away. Dismounting, he led his mount to the spot. Tethering the horse to a convenient branch, he explored further. He found a narrow steep path that started out almost straight up for several feet, and then seemed to level off. He scrambled up the nearly vertical path. Then, once over the top, he jogged ahead quickly for a hundred paces. Yes! Even in the moonlight, he could see a wide, gradually inclined trail that seemed to extend far into the distance between the two peaks on either side.

The problem was…how would they get the animals up that first steep incline? He decided to try with the stallion, the biggest and strongest of the three horses; the beast would have no part of it. Valerian wedged himself above and pulled and tugged on the reins, then he got behind and tried to whip the beast on the rump to drive him up. He pleaded, shouted, cajoled, all to no avail. The animal responded by rearing and bucking; once or twice the beast almost got away from him altogether.

Totally exhausted now, the young man gave it up. Wearily, he calmed the horse, mounted up and rode back to his compatriots. He found them both laid out, exhausted. However, both rose as he approached.

"I found a way up, but we're going to have to leave the animals."

"Not Sam; she can go anywhere we can," Joshua asserted, "besides, I'm not leaving her."

"Who's Sam?" Maya asked wearily.

"Sam…Samantha, my mule; I raised her. She ain't much to look at, but she'll do anything I ask."

"Well, she better be part mountain goat," Valerian responded, "let's mount up."

They rode the short distance to the narrow opening. Valerian had them take the saddlebags and gear off of the horses, but leave them saddled. He then directed Joshua to pull everything off of Samantha but her bridle. He showed the boy the way up.

"Still think she can make it?"

"Won't be easy, but I think so. Just give us some room and let me talk to her."

The boy led his mule to the path; it was almost vertical. He spoke to her softly and calmly, stroking her nose. She nuzzled him in return. He began to climb up backwards, facing her. He led her up, but didn't pull on the reins. He just let her follow him, offering her encouragement with each step. The mule calmly searched in the darkness for one foothold, then another. Several times she slipped or stumbled, each time the boy released the reins so that she could recover, then gently led her back up.

Valerian and Maya watched in wonder, as the boy and the mule seemed to climb straight up. Then suddenly, both scrambled, and they were over the top. Maya clapped her hands in delight as, up above, Joshua patted Sam's rump and praised her.

"Good work, Joshua! Tether her up there and come back down. I want to load all of the saddlebags and knapsacks on Samantha. Then we're going to lead the horses off, cut 'em loose and cover our tracks."

So they hauled the saddlebags, knapsacks and weapons up to the top. Then while Joshua stowed their provisions on his mule, Valerian and Maya led the horses away. Near the cliff, they unsaddled the mounts and took off their bridles. They released the horses and threw the gear over the cliff, only keeping the saddle blankets.

On the way back to the trailhead, Valerian tried to cover their tracks as thoroughly as possible in the darkness. He paid particular attention to the trailhead, using a rotten log and some brush to disguise their exit path. With a little luck, any Zealots following wouldn't be able to find the way up at all; and even if they did, Valerian was confident that none of their mounts could manage to go where Samantha had.

Dawn's first light was just beginning to show over the mountains. As Valerian and Maya climbed to the top of the trailhead, they both petted Sam and spoke to her. He noted that the boy had done a good job of packing the gear on her; they carefully strapped the three saddle blankets on top of the other provisions. The young man realized that the mule had suddenly become their companion, rather than just a beast of burden.

Looking back from where they had come, in the emerging light they had a panoramic view all the way back down to the plains below. Still there was no sign of his uncle or their pursuers. Valerian pulled the small pair of folding binoculars from his pack and searched down the side of the mountain again. Nothing.

Maya read his mind, "He'll be all right, Valerian. He'll catch up in his own time. But it's time to go now."

Indeed it was. He turned and headed up the trail, with Maya at his side and Joshua behind, leading his mule. They stumbled wearily along the trail until midmorning. After a time, Maya had begun leaning on Valerian. Once he looked down at her and she seemed to be asleep as she walked.

Finally, she just stopped, "Valerian, I'm sorry, but I can go no farther."

"All right, Maya, I'm worn out too. Joshua, stay here with her. I'm going to scout ahead a bit and find a place to camp."

To his right, he had noticed a line of small hills, covered with brush. He scrambled up a likely one nearby and found what he was looking for right away. It was a gully, sheltered on all sides by hills, saplings and underbrush. By the time he made it back, Maya was curled up by the side of the path, sound asleep but shivering. Joshua was lying on his back next to his mule, which was calmly grazing.

Although he was wiped out, the young man picked the sleeping girl up and slowly led the boy and his mule over the hill to the gully. Once at the bottom, he made one more trip back over the hill. Cutting off some brush, he swept their tracks to the gully clear.

By the time Valerian made it back, both Maya and Joshua were fast asleep, and Samantha was standing still, placidly chewing. He bent down to Maya, who was still shivering in her sleep. At this altitude, it was chilly, even at midmorning. He took off his gear, belt and boots, put his cloak over hers, and then curled up underneath them with her. That was the last thing he remembered until almost dusk.

16

The Cottage

Whatever hardships Valerian had endured in his journey prior to the mountains, it had been a leisurely stroll compared to his little party's arduous trek across the Great Mountains. Most days were comfortable enough, at least when the weather was dry. But every night at this altitude was bitterly cold, and when it rained, the nights were almost unendurable. And it rained often; thunderstorms would regularly roll in late in the afternoon and buffet them as they sought whatever meager shelter that they could in the bare mountain passes. Game was scarce, as well, just an occasional rabbit or bird to augment their diminishing rations. Even fires were hard to start in the thin air, and firewood was often scarce, in any case.

As the days, then weeks, passed in the mountains, their frustration grew in equal measure with their fatigue, as they crested each ridge only to see yet another line of mountains in the distance. Adding to their frustration, on several occasions the mountain passes that they followed turned out to be dead ends, and they were forced to backtrack for miles.

Nonetheless, Valerian was proud of his little party. He, Maya and Joshua had steadily hardened in the mountains. His companions rarely complained, silently marching behind him up and down steep mountain trails for hours each day. And it was by day that they marched now; they had decided that the danger of running into a scouting party in the daylight was much less than the risk of negotiating the treacherous mountain passes in the darkness. In this regard, they had been fortunate; so far, they had encountered no one else, and precious few signs of anyone else's passing, in these mountains.

Now, it was late in the afternoon, and they were approaching the crest of yet another ridge. Joshua was in front, leading Samantha. (Every day Valerian blessed the fact that they had been able to bring the mule; he could hardly imagine how they could have made it this far without her.) Maya followed Joshua and his mule by several paces, and Valerian brought up the rear, as usual. He liked to have a clear view behind them, in equal measures hoping that he might catch sight of his uncle and fearing that he might still see signs of their pursuers. Joshua stopped at the top of the crest above.

"Back up a bit Joshua, you'll be silhouetted against the sky up there!" Valerian was still trying to teach the youth good woodcraft, (Valerian himself had paid much better attention to his uncle's lessons after the encounter with the Zealots.) Valerian and Maya hurried to catch up with the young man. Was this it, the far side of the mountain range? Were they finally over?

...It wasn't, but it was the next best thing: a deep and narrow mountain valley. Far below they saw a thick forest of perhaps a few hundred acres, apparently bounded by high peaks on all sides. Through the center of the valley, between the trees, they could just make out a large stream or river that seemed to open up to a small lake. Best of all, they could see no signs of habitation. It looked like the perfect place to rest up and prepare themselves for what would, hopefully, be the final push to the other side of the mountain range.

"If we hurry, we should just about be able to make it to that lake before darkness falls," Valerian pointed out.

"Then let's get moving. Perhaps you can catch us some fish for breakfast in the morning, Valerian...and maybe we can all bathe and wash our clothes tomorrow morning, as well. I can barely stand to smell myself, much less you two," Maya responded.

With that, they all began to pick their way down the trail. They made good time going down into the valley, for the trail was fairly wide and smooth. They reached the shore of the small lake well before dusk. All three of the weary travelers and their mule bent down to drink of its cold, crystalline waters.

"Maya and Joshua, please unload Samantha and make camp. I want to scout the area before we light a fire."

"Be careful, Valerian," Maya responded as she and the boy set to work.

Valerian left at a trot; he was tired, but he wanted to cover as much area as possible before darkness fell. Although the young man had seen nothing to be concerned with while approaching the valley from the trail above, he wanted to take no chances. He began by following the lakeshore southward. For a long while, he detected nothing of concern. Then, suddenly, he caught a faint whiff of smoke in the late afternoon breeze. He slowed and began moving cautiously toward the smell. He moved silently now, taking maximum advantage of the terrain for concealment.

Gradually the odor of wood smoke became stronger, and as it did, Valerian became more wary. Finally, through the trees, he caught sight of a small cove off of the main body of the lake. Just on the other side of the cove, he spotted a small log cabin. Dusk was beginning to settle over the valley as, with great stealth, he made his way around the cove toward the small cottage.

As he approached, Valerian was just able to make out, against the gathering darkness, the flickering light of a fireplace through the cabin's one small window. A new smell now reached his nostrils blended with that of the fire: meat cooking. *A roast, or maybe a stew*, the hungry young man thought to himself, as his mouth began to water. He decided to risk a look through the window. He approached silently as a ghost.

At first, he couldn't make out much, as the window glass was cloudy, and the firelight was dim. But after a few moments, he was just able to make out the backside of what looked to be a very old woman stirring a kettle hung over the fireplace fire.

Without warning, the face of a great beast appeared on the other side of the window, growling and barking, with fangs bared and ears pulled back. Valerian stumbled back in surprise and unconsciously held his lance forward in defense. Through the window, he saw an old black woman come forward and pull the dog down. She cupped her eyes, trying to see out of the window, but, peering into the darkness outside, she didn't seem to be able to make anything out. Valerian considered just melting away into the forest, but decided to stay put.

"Hello in there; my name is Valerian! I am a traveler from far away and I mean you no harm."

After a moment, the door opened, with the old woman silhouetted against the doorway. She was holding back the huge animal, (who looked to be more wolf than dog), by his collar.

"Aye, young traveler, and I doubt that Clancy here would let you give us much trouble even if you wanted to. He's a bit long in the tooth now, his eyes and nose ain't what they used to be, but he ain't too old to take down a bear, iffin he wants to..."

Looking at the great beast, Valerian believed her. Clancy made the wolves that had attacked him look like mere pups.

"Yes ma'am, I'm sure that's true. My party is camped on the other side of the lake. We plan on staying just a few days to rest up before we push on. Is there anyone else in the valley that we have to worry about?"

"Clancy, be still!" the old woman commanded. "Sit down in your corner!"

The animal grudgingly obeyed and curled up in his corner near the fire.

"It's getting chilly out here, young man, come on in, and we'll talk over by the fire."

Valerian came in, dropping his cloak and weapons just inside the door. (Though he decided to keep the big knife on his belt at the ready; the old lady seemed harmless enough, but he still wasn't too sure about the wolf dog.) The cottage was small. Nonetheless, it was clean and neat...Valerian also found it cozy and welcoming.

The old woman dragged over a straight-backed wooden chair next to the old rocking chair that already sat in front of the fireplace. She sat on the rocker and beckoned to the chair. He settled down next to her. The fire warmed him and, as he relaxed, his hunger stirred again.

"How about a bowl of stew, young man? You look like you could just about eat Clancy over there." The big animal raised his massive head a bit when he heard his name, and then lowered it back down on his outstretched paws.

"Thank you, but no ma'am. I need to get back to my two friends before they get worried about me." It was hard to decline the offer; the food smelled delicious.

"Is there anything that we have to worry about in this valley?"

"Not that I know of, sonny; I pretty much have this little valley to myself, now that my husband's passed on and our two sons have flown the coop. I reckon this little valley's too small and isolated for anyone else to try to settle. And it's truly cut off all through the winter, when the passes are snowed over. Only time I git any company is once in a blue moon, when a wayfarer or two, like yourself, drops in."

"By the way, my name is Isabel, but you can call me Izzy."

"Pleased to meet you, Izzy. Like I said, my name is Valerian."

"I reckon by your name and accent, that you must be Elympian. Am I right?"

Valerian was a bit surprised that she knew anything of the Elympians.

"Yes ma'am. What do you know of the Elympian clan?"

"Young feller, you make it to my age and you get to know a little bit about just about everything."

She did indeed look as old as the hills. Her back was stooped and her gray hair was pulled back in a bun. Her ebony face and hands were seamed by countless wrinkles. Yet her cheeks were full, her smile was wide and her dark brown eyes twinkled with good humor. Valerian decided on the spot that he liked her.

"Well, Izzy, I really must get back to my friends now. Might we pay you a visit in the morning? There are just three of us, a girl my age and a young boy..."

"Better yet, why don't you go back and fetch your friends right now? I'll chop up some more carrots and taters and put 'em in the stew. When your bellies are full, you all can sleep right here. It'll be a mite crowded, but two of you can bed down in the loft, where my boys used to sleep, and the other can curl up on the floor in front of the fireplace."

"Thank you ma'am, but..."

"But nothing, young man. Grant an old woman a favor; it's been a long time since I've had any company."

Valerian gave in rather easily; he could hardly wait to bring his friends back to share a good hot meal, as well as to give them a warm place to sleep. He thanked Izzy again and made his leave. As the young man picked up his gear and opened the door, Clancy jumped up and bounded over to him; the young man stiffened a bit, in spite of himself. But the great beast just muzzled his hand, as if to say farewell. Apparently, Valerian had found himself two new friends.

Darkness had fallen completely by the time that Valerian had made it back to the camp. He hailed his comrades as he approached, so that they wouldn't be frightened. He could see in the faint moonlight that the camp was well set up and organized. Samantha had been unpacked, the saddle blankets and gear had been laid out, and a campfire had been built, (though not lit). Maya ran up and gave him a hug.

"Did you see anything? Can we build a fire now? It's getting chilly and we're hungry."

"Sorry, Maya, but we've got to break camp; let's get Samantha packed back up."

"What? We just finished setting the camp up," Joshua responded.

"Don't worry Joshua; it'll be worth it, I promise. I have someone that I want the both of you to meet."

Valerian refused to elaborate; he just began breaking down the new camp. After a moment's hesitation, Maya and Joshua pitched in. The march back to the cottage was slower. They followed the lakeshore, but, in the darkness, they had to move slowly and carefully. Maya was persistent, asking Valerian regularly where they were headed; he was equally stubborn, not wanting to spoil the surprise.

Finally, late in the evening, they reached the cove. The firelight from the one window stood out like a beacon in the darkness; its glow was reflected across the still water. Seeing their destination, unconsciously, their pace quickened. This time, Clancy heard their approach, and his deep-pitched barking shattered the peaceful night. Samantha almost bolted, but Joshua managed to quiet her. From inside the cottage, they could hear an old woman scolding the beast and he soon quieted.

After a moment, the door opened, and light flooded the grassy area in front of the cottage. The old woman beckoned them in.

"Welcome travelers, come on in and help yourselves to some of Miss Izzy's delicious rabbit stew."

Valerian introduced Maya and Joshua to Miss Izzy. Joshua stayed back to unpack Samantha. He then tethered her to a hitching rail on the side of the cabin. The mule was still a bit nervous in such proximity to the dog inside, so the young man spent a few more moments comforting her.

After he had settled his mule down a bit, Joshua followed his friends inside. The youth was greeted by warmth and the homey smell of a freshly cooked dinner. Valerian and Maya were already seated at a tiny table in one corner of the cabin, devouring stew from wooden bowls. The old woman sat him down, introduced herself, and handed him a bowl, as well.

"Whew. It's nice to have company, but we're going to have to get you three washed up tomorrow. No offense, but y'all smell a bit gamey."

Maya laughed, almost choking on a mouthful of stew. "Miss Izzy, none taken. I can hardly wait to get cleaned up. I plan on jumping into that lake with some soap, first thing in the morning. I'll make sure the boys do the same right after."

"Better yet, young lady, there's an old tub in back that I made my husband lug over the mountains some forty odd years ago. We'll boil some water over on that there woodstove and you can have a hot bath."

Maya practically shivered in anticipation. "Ma'am, you have no idea what that would mean to me…"

"Yes I do, little missy. That's why I wouldn't agree to come to this valley in the first place, less'n my husband agreed to bring me a bathtub."

While they finished their meal, Miss Izzy heated some water in an old teapot on her little woodstove. Meanwhile, Clancy sat down on his haunches next to Joshua's leg, wagged his tail and softly whined. The young boy rewarded him with a chunk of rabbit from the stew.

After they had eaten and cleaned up, the three pulled their chairs near the fireplace and made a little semi-circle next to Miss Izzy's rocker. The old lady then served each hot tea in battered old tin cups. She then settled down in her rocker with an old chipped cup that might once have been fine china. Clancy rested his massive head on her lap; she stroked him with one hand while she sipped from her teacup with the other.

"It's been a long spell since I've had any company up here. Trappers come up every so often, and I'll trade provisions, flour, tea, salt and the like, for room and board. Raiders from the territories come through every now and again, too, and I'll give 'em a hot meal or two for trade goods."

Maya shuddered at the mention of Raiders. "Aren't you afraid of them, Miss Izzy, that they'll just take what you have?"

"Take what? Don't have much, and I always tell 'em that they're welcome to whatever they need or want. Even to the Raiders, it always made more sense to leave us be, as a way-station for 'em up here in the mountains; my husband and me figured that out long ago. It's all in God's hands, anyhow."

"I guess it don't hurt much having Clancy around to remind folks to behave, either," Joshua pointed out.

The old woman cackled, "Guess it don't, at that."

Clancy turned to the boy and let out a little "woof" at the sound of his name. Soon enough, they had all finished their tea. Miss Izzy rose.

"You young 'uns will have to excuse me now. An old lady like yours truly needs her rest. I'll pull out some blankets and pillers, and you all can bed down when you're ready. We can all talk some more in the mornin'."

"I'm ready to turn in right now too, Miss Izzy" Maya responded, "I'm exhausted, and I can't wait to sleep in a real bed. How about you, Valerian?"

"Me too; let's all turn in. It's been a long day."

Joshua just yawned and stretched; Clancy responded with a yawn of his own. They all chuckled at that. The old woman fetched their bedding: old, moth-eaten blankets and ancient feather pillows. Soon, Miss Izzy had retired to the little bedroom in the back of the cabin.

Joshua made a pad in front of the fireplace and curled up next to Clancy. Maya and Valerian climbed the little homemade ladder up to the tiny loft just above Miss Izzy's bedroom. It was just large enough to accommodate the straw mattress on its floor. They made up their little bed, stripped down to their undergarments, and curled up together under the old blanket. The straw mattress was thin and hard, the blanket smelled moldy and the pillows were lumpy. Yet a palace could hardly have seemed any more luxurious. In a moment they were both sound asleep...

*** * * ***

The smells woke them early the next morning: eggs frying, biscuits baking... and was that the smell of fried chicken? Maya and Valerian threw on their tunics and climbed down the stairs. Miss Izzy had a small feast laid out for them. She and her little wood stove had been busy this morning. Joshua was already at the table, having a cup of tea.

"I thought that you two were going to sleep all morning," he said, "I was afraid that we were going to have to start without you."

"Miss Izzy, you must have gotten up long before dawn to have this all ready. Thank you so much!" Maya had spoken before Valerian.

"It's a curse of the old that we have to go to sleep early in the evening and wake up even earlier in the morn. Anyhow, the boy helped; I had him fetch some eggs from the coop out back. Then I had him wring the necks of a couple of chickens and pluck 'em whilst I made the biscuits."

"Well then, thank you too, Joshua," Maya added. "How can I help Miss Izzy?"

"You and Valerian wash up out back, and then you can come in and set the table."

The meal was the best that Maya and Valerian had had since they had left the Caravan. (Living as a slave of the Zealots, it was the best that Joshua had had in years.) After they had stuffed themselves and cleaned up, Miss Izzy had them move the chairs and her rocker out to the front porch, which extended the entire length of the cabin. The morning sun still hung low over the lake.

The old woman fetched them all a fresh cup of tea. Valerian and Maya sat down with Miss Izzy, while Joshua tended to his mule. Clancy bounded out the front door, relieved himself on one corner of the cabin, and then headed to the old wooden bowl that held scraps from their breakfast.

"Miss Izzy, how long have you lived here, all by yourself?" Maya asked.

"Well, I'm not really alone, iffin you count Clancy. My husband, Lucius was his name, passed on some six seasons back. The boys have been gone over thirty."

"Where did your sons go?" Valerian asked.

"They were a fine pair of lads, Will and Aaron, named after Lucius's father and mine. I had 'em two years apart. When they had pretty well grow'd up, they wanted to leave and see the world, like most young men do, I reckon. We couldn't see how we could stop 'em, so we tried to teach 'em all we could about how to make their way in the Territories. Then we gave 'em all the supplies we could spare, along with our last two mules, and sent 'em on their way. It was the last we ever saw of 'em. "

"Could you teach us too, Miss Izzy? I mean, teach us how to make our way in the Territories," Maya asked.

"I suppose I could learn you a few things. I grew up in the Territories. Had a homestead there with Lucius for nine years, but it's been more than forty since we left. A lot can change in that much time. What I can't understand is: why in the world would you young folks want to go there? From what we've always heard, the Elympian lands are a heck of a lot better place to live than the Territories."

"Why did you folks leave to come up here and live all alone?" Valerian asked.

Joshua had returned. He had staked his mule out in a meadow by the lake to graze. The boy grabbed a stick from a stack of firewood and tossed it for Clancy. The old dog chased it down and brought it back with the enthusiasm of a pup.

Valerian had already decided that he could trust the old woman with their secret. "We're on a quest to find the homeland of my ancestors and uncover its secrets."

Miss Izzy looked at him for a long moment. "Then you're on a fool's errand, young man. Elympias is a cursed place in a cursed land."

"What do you know of it, Miss Izzy? Have you seen it?" Maya asked.

"Yes, I've seen it." Her face took on a faraway look; she didn't answer the question directly...

"When my husband was young, he was a big, powerful black man, a trapper right up in these here mountains. And I was a young girl living in one of the townships, when he swept me off my feet. I was a pretty little thing back in those days too, although you wouldn't know it now. We moved into a little abandoned farmstead just outside of my town, and built ourselves a nice little home. Had our two boys."

"We were raided from time to time, like everyone else, but that was to be expected. Usually, the Raiders don't hurt no one; they just take what they want and move on. They have a saying: 'Butcher the sheep, and you can't sheer 'em next season.'"

"Don't you have any protection in the townships?" Valerian asked.

"We had a Magistrate and militia like most townships, but they were more interested in raiding other towns than protecting ours."

"Anyhow, one spring we were raided, when the boys were still young. One of the varmints insulted me, and Lucius lost his temper and hit him. Next thing I knew, Lucius had been beat to within an inch of his life, and I had been raped by their leader."

"I could have lived with it; iffin you're a young woman in the Territories, you can pretty well expect it to happen sooner or later," the old woman looked hard at Maya, "but Lucius couldn't; he blamed hissself."

"He told me about this fine little valley that he had found when he was trappin'. We could raise up our family far away from the Lawless Lands, keep what we raised, without havin' to worry about being beaten, robbed or raped."

"I was young and dumb, back then...and in love. I was pretty much ready to do whatever Lucius thought best. So, we sold everything we had left. Bought two good wagons and some mules to pull 'em. A milk cow, too. Filled the wagons with tools, seed grain, cages with chickens and rabbits, just the essentials...cept'n my bathtub," she smiled at the memory, "then we carved a home out of the wilderness, just us four. And a fine home it was, too."

"I'm sure it was, Miss Izzy. But what can you tell us of Elympias?" Maya asked again.

"I'll get to that, in due time. But this is more talkin' than I've done in years. Let me rest my tongue for a spell and let's give you that bath, right now. The boys can bathe after they finish their chores."

"Chores?" Joshua asked.

Maya was eager to hear of Elympias, but even more so to take that bath...

* * *

The sun now hung low on the western horizon. The three young people were all tired, but pleasantly so, after a hard days work. Miss Izzy had welcomed them with generosity, but had expected them to work for their keep. She had reminded them that she was an old woman and had had no one to help her with her farmstead in a very long time.

So Valerian had chopped wood until his hands had blistered, repaired the chicken coops and rabbit cages and patched the cabin's old wood shingle roof. Maya had helped Miss Izzy clean out the cabin from top to bottom, and then had fed the chickens and rabbits. Joshua had weeded the vegetable garden, cut the high grass all around the cabin with a sickle and fetched water from the lake for supper and their baths.

Finally, late in the afternoon, the old woman had let the young men stop and take turns bathing. While each bathed, she had Maya wash all of their clothes in the lake. While the clothes dried, Miss Izzy provided all three with some ragged but clean old clothes that had once belonged to her husband and sons.

Dinner that night was simple fare, corncakes and a vegetable soup with a little leftover chicken thrown in; it was still delicious. After the dinner table was cleared, they made a circle around the fireplace with their cups of tea, just as they had the night before. Clancy curled up next to Joshua's chair.

Valerian asked the old woman as she settled into her rocker, "Miss Izzy, now can you tell us of Elympias?"

The old woman chuckled, and then her face once again took on that faraway look. "Reckon so, but I don't think you all will be happy with what you hear...Lucius had warned me that, on our journey into the mountains, we would have to pass near the 'haunted city', as he called it. He told me that he hoped we could pass by it during the daylight and camp as far away from it as possible. Lucius was a fearless man; it surprised me to hear him talking that way. Anyhow, I had always been a lot more curious than I was superstitious. His warning had just made me that much more determined to get a good look at the place."

"Anyhow, many days into our journey, Lucius stopped his wagon and walked back to the rig I was driving with the boys. It was late in the afternoon. He pointed to some foothills and told me that the 'haunted city' was just on the other side. Told me that we needed to push on and get as much distance between us and that place as we could before sunset. I told him I wanted to see it first. He said no, but I was stubborn back then, and could always get what I wanted from him, iffin I wanted it bad enough."

"We made a right turn and went up into the foothills. When we finally came over the last rise and saw the city, it was near sunset. The sight took my breath away. Great buildings, dozens of 'em, maybe hundreds, all shapes and sizes, towered up into the sky. Great, broad roads ran between the buildings in perfect straight lines, with trees planted in neat rows along most of them. A great white wall went around the whole city, which lay between two crystal blue lakes. Right in the middle of the city stood a grand dome of a building, the biggest, most beautiful thing made by man you ever saw. There was just one thing missing."

"People?" Maya asked.

"That's right, little lady. People. The city didn't look like the abandoned towns of the Ancients, all falling apart and filthy, with scavengers lurking about. There was no sign at all that anyone still lived there. No sounds, no movement. It was like everyone had just up and left the day before."

"So what was so scary about that?" Joshua asked.

"I'm gettin' to that young fella," the old woman continued, "talked Lucius into making camp right there on that hill. He didn't want to, but I told him we were all tired. Taunted him too; asked him, how come a big such a big, strong man was such a 'fraidy-cat' when his dainty little woman wasn't afraid at all."

"Everythin' seemed just fine for a while. We unhitched the mules and made camp. Fixed supper over a campfire; laid out our bedding. It was a full moon, I remember, so's we could still see the city in the moonlight, which made it seem even more beautiful, almost like in a dream. But, soon enough, the dream turned into a nightmare..."

"How so?" Maya asked.

"We had just bedded down for the night. The sounds came first; faint sounds coming up into the hills. At first, I thought it was our imagination. Voices, music, crying, shouts. Then lights dancing over the hills. White at first, then colors. Soon enough, we got up and looked toward the city. It was lit up all over. Now and again, beams of light shot up into the night sky. Then we began to see ghostly images in the city and nearby, phantoms moving around, appearing and disappearing."

"I can tell you, we spent the night huddled together, me huddled against Lucius and the boys curled up close to me. None of us slept a wink. At first light, we hitched up the mules and got ourselves out of there, pronto," she chuckled, "It was one of the few times I ever had to apologize to my husband."

Valerian was undaunted, although he could see some fear and uncertainty in both Maya and Joshua's eyes.

"Can you help us find our way there?" he asked.

The old woman cackled, "Well, I tried my darnedest to scare you off. It's been many a long year, but yes, I reckon I can still remember the way well enough to help you…"

* * *

As with Valerian's time with the Caravan, the days had soon stretched into weeks. Very quickly, the little cabin and the little old lady had come to mean "home" to the three weary travelers. They were all now well rested; their blisters, bruises and scrapes had healed, their bellies were full, and their travel clothes were cleaned and mended. In return, it had been many years since Miss Izzy's little homestead had looked so well tended, her larder so well stocked with smoked venison from the forest and fish from the lake.

Valerian had known for days now that it was time to push on, but each day they had procrastinated. Finally, one afternoon, Valerian announced that they would leave in the morning. He was met with silent acquiescence from Maya and Joshua, good-natured acceptance from Miss Izzy.

"I knew this time was a'comin' directly. I'll miss you three; so will Clancy. Just make sure that you stop and see us on the way back. And keep an eye out for my boys. I expect that they'd be a couple of big handsome black men by now."

"That's a promise, Miss Izzy," Valerian responded.

That evening, after dinner, they prepared for the morning's departure. They packed fresh provisions and stowed their gear, cleaned and sharpened their weapons. Finally, their preparations complete, they gathered for one last time around the fireplace for their nightly cup of tea. They were all silent for a while.

Even Clancy, sensing that something was up, seemed pensive and restless. Suddenly, the beast's ears perked up. A moment later he was on his feet jumping up to the window, barking madly. Valerian, fearing an incursion by a bear or wolves, quickly strapped on his belt, with its ax and knife, threw his quiver and bow to Maya, and grabbed his lance.

"Joshua!" he commanded, "Hold Clancy back until we see what's out there. Then let him loose if I tell you!"

The boy grabbed the huge beast's collar with both hands and hung on for dear life. Holding his lance at the ready, Valerian threw the door open, ready for combat. Looking out, he saw...nothing. He carefully moved out to the porch and peered into the darkness, listening for any movement. He heard nothing...

"Hush Clancy up so's I can hear!" Valerian whispered.

In response, Miss Izzy commanded the big animal to be silent. His barking stopped, though his growling continued. Now Valerian moved off the porch onto the yard, watching and listening.

"Valerian, be careful," Maya called out urgently, holding the bow with an arrow nocked at the ready. Maya moved out to the porch with Joshua and Clancy just behind her. Suddenly, Valerian threw his lance down and ran into the darkness.

"Valerian!" Maya called out in exasperation as he disappeared into the darkness.

For a few minutes, only silence, then suddenly, Valerian's laughter blended with that of another, far deeper voice. Clancy began barking again as Valerian re-entered the light of the front door helping the big man, who was limping badly. It was Sebastian, Valerian's uncle, looking much the worse for wear, but at least he was alive! Maya dropped the bow, ran up and threw her arms around the big man...

17

Cat and Mouse
August 16th, 2087

The attractive young woman passed her hand through the passport scanner at the Zurich Transnational Airport. The scanner read the Identichip implanted in the tip of her right index finger, identifying her as one Genevieve Carpentier, a staff journalist with the international cyber-press organization, ACI, (a Graham Enterprise subsidiary). As a further precaution taken with all passengers on international flights, Ms. Carpentier's DNA was simultaneously analyzed by the same scanner to further verify her identity.

The scanner compared the young lady's DNA with her personal data stored in the International Archives; it confirmed a positive match. If her retinal patterns, fingerprints, or basic facial patterns had been checked, they too would have matched those on record for Ms. Carpentier...in spite of the fact that the lady in question was indeed not Ms. Carpentier, at all. The scans were positive because this young lady's personal data had been surreptitiously substituted for Ms. Carpentier's in the primary databank of the Archives...a supposedly impossible feat.

With the scanner's permission, the glass doors ahead of her automatically opened, allowing her access to the main terminal of the airport. She crossed the terminal, and then caught a drop tube to the air-shuttle departure area. She found a small commuter air-shuttle with the distinctive logo of the Regency Suisse Hotel. Boarding the small craft, she pressed her index to the touchpad at the doorway. The shuttle's auto-attendant welcomed Ms. Carpentier in her native language, (French) and verified that her bags had already been transferred aboard. Settling into the soft leather seat and allowing the seat restraint to adjust itself around her, she relaxed just a bit. So far, so good...

As the young women waited for lift-off, she reflected on the circumstances that had brought her to this place. Her target, under constant surveillance for over three years in Rio, had suddenly disappeared without a trace, along with the experienced agent assigned to track him. Over those three years, Gregory Constantine had tended bar part time, hung out on the beach, picked up the odd hooker or occasional lady tourist, and apparently done little else of note.

Olympus Security had considered dropping surveillance on him altogether, when suddenly...he was gone. Backup teams had been sent to Brazil to try to determine what had become of Constantine and their agent, but had so far come up empty-handed.

Their one ace-in-the-hole was the tracking device. It had been surreptitiously implanted in Constantine's arm along with the routine inoculation required for his passport to Brazil. The device was a tiny technological wonder. At random intervals once a day, it transmitted a three-microsecond signal that would be picked up by the nearest cyber-network receiver. Any monitoring equipment would only detect a spike of noise. However, the GRI worldwide decryption network could detect the signal and record the cell site from which it had originated. (The tiny device would even automatically shut down whenever it detected the presence of a scan.)

For a number of days, no signal had been detected. Then suddenly, a signal was received from a cell site near the Zurich Airport; the next day, another fix near the Regency Suisse. After that, over the last three weeks, the signal had been detected at various points around Zurich, but most often at the Regency and downtown at the headquarters of the Eurobanque International, a subsidiary of Eurodynamics. An operation by Olympus Security had been mounted.

Mac had summoned Olivia to his office. "Liv, I'm sure that you've seen the report on Constantine. How would you like to help us 'reacquire' him?"

Olivia had instantly agreed. The young woman had long since been returned to full duty under Graham, but the routine that she had settled into over the last few years had become increasingly frustrating to her. Although, her relationship with Michael had only grown stronger, she found little satisfaction in her work. She was essentially a woman that craved action, with perhaps just a bit of danger thrown in. And except for the bombing incident, there had been precious little excitement at Olympus. These days, she was functioning as little more than an overqualified executive assistant for Graham.

Mac had dismissed Olivia that afternoon, but set up another appointment for the next day. "We'll brief you on the plan at that time," he had told her with a grin that got her curiosity up. "You can't tell Michael about this, Liv, but you can let him know that you may be traveling in a few weeks and may be gone for some time."

That night, she and Michael had their first major argument. (After announcing their engagement, they had soon moved in together.) She had followed Mac's orders, but Michael had instantly read in her eyes that something serious was up. He had pressed her for details and had gotten nothing out of her. The rest of the evening had consisted of icy silence.

The next day, again in Mac's office, Olivia had been introduced to an attractive young woman. Both Mac and the woman had smiled at each other at the introduction, as if they were sharing a private joke. Olivia didn't get it. Then Mac had simply walked up between the two women and turned them toward the window. She still didn't get it at first. Then she saw her faint reflection next to the other young lady. Same height and similar builds, although the other women had perhaps a slightly fuller figure. The other women's hair was fair and cut short, while Olivia's was dark brown and pulled back. However, their features were very similar. They certainly wouldn't be mistaken for twins, but they could easily pass as sisters.

"As you're well aware, Liv, Graham Enterprises employs hundreds of thousands of men and women worldwide. We simply ran your profile against all other women employees and reviewed the closest matches. There were actually several better matches, as far as appearance goes. However, Ms. Carpentier has some additional assets that may prove to be very valuable. She is a journalist, which is a perfect cover for you. She is a French national and you happen to be quite fluent in French. Last, and certainly not least, she is unattached and quite willing to help us with this operation. Genevieve has agreed to stay here with us in Olympus, incommunicado, while you gallivant around Europe in her place."

"Great Mac, but what about biological scans?"

Mac had then explained how their profiles would be swapped in the International Archives. Olivia was utterly shocked that this was possible; the data in the Archives was universally considered sacrosanct.

"We will need to alter your appearance a bit, however. Rather that swapping your facial scan data, we have decided to alter your appearance to more closely match that of Genevieve. As a result, we are hoping that you will be able to recognize Constantine much more readily than he might recognize you. We have experts that will help you with hair and makeup to minimize differences in your appearance. Other specialists can inject small amounts of biogel, which is virtually undetectable, to subtly alter the shape of your cheeks and jaw line to more closely resemble Genevieve's. Are you still game?"

"I'm in," she nodded confidently.

"Then have a nice romantic dinner with Michael tonight, and bid farewell to him in the morning. Tell him that I will act as a conduit for messages between you two whenever possible, and extend to him my apologies. Then for the next two weeks, I want you and Genevieve to be joined at the hip. I want you to learn her accent and speech patterns, her mannerisms, and as much of her history as possible. We will have intelligence specialists who will coach you."

And so it had transpired; the next few weeks had been quite intensive. Voice coaches had sharpened Olivia's dialect to more nearly match her French counterpart's. Plastic surgeons had made a series of subtle alterations to Olivia's features. Hair and makeup experts had showed her how to further enhance her similarities and minimize her differences with her "sister". Meanwhile, Olivia and Genevieve had spent virtually every waking moment together; the two women had soon become quite good friends.

At the end of the two weeks, the pair met with Mac, who had not seen them since their initial meeting. He had been impressed, indeed, rather confused. The two women had lowered the lights a bit in the meeting room and partially closed the blinds. They had stood with their backs at the window, facing the door through which Mac had entered.

Genevieve had spoken first in her soft Parisian accent, presenting her new 'doppelganger' with a flourish. *"Monsieur McCafferty, are you not impressed with Olivia's transformation?"*

Mac had peered at Olivia...she looked more like Genevieve than Genevieve! No wait...she really was Genevieve, wasn't she? Yes, now he got it. The two women looked at each other and chuckled at Mac's expense. The young lady who had spoken had actually been Olivia...and he had almost been fooled, in spite of the fact that he had worked with Olivia on a daily basis for years!

Although a family member or close friend would doubtless be able to distinguish the two, a casual acquaintance likely wouldn't. The individual changes to Olivia were subtle, but the overall effect was striking. Olivia's hair was now light brown and short. Her lips were a bit fuller and her cheeks somewhat higher. Her jaw line was softer. She had even added a few pounds to her lithe figure to more closely resemble that of Genevieve's.

* * *

Now, in Zurich, as the shuttle lifted off bound for her hotel, Olivia/Genevieve began to prepare herself mentally for her mission. Although she had been an agent for years now, her specialties had been surveillance and counter-intelligence. She had never actually operated as an undercover agent before. She would have to stay sharp. The people she would be up against had repeatedly proven to be absolutely ruthless.

Checking into the hotel had been uneventful. Once in her room, she had immediately run scans with her specially modified, hand-held Uplink to identify any surveillance equipment in the room; it detected none. Then she had the GRI network check for any traces on Genevieve's Uplink; again, none were detected. She then sent a short coded message back to Olympus security to confirm that all had gone as planned, so far. Finally relaxing a bit, the young woman unpacked, then showered and carefully reapplied the makeup that enhanced her disguise. She then changed into a cocktail dress and checked her handbag.

The handbag had been issued to her shortly before her departure from Olympus. When introduced to it by a security department briefer, she had been rather amused. It was like something from a cheap spy thriller. Nonetheless, she was glad to have it, since carrying a firearm in Switzerland was not an option. The small, innocent looking bag contained a hairbrush whose handle cleverly concealed a stiletto. It held a small can of hairspray, which actually dispensed a gas under high pressure that could instantly incapacitate any attacker. With a special twist, a small penlight could emit a pulse of high intensity light that could blind an opponent. Finally, a small compact doubled as a stun grenade.

However, her greatest protection could be summoned by uttering just three magic words: *Don't touch me!* Those three words would activate all three of her Uplinks: her pocket, wrist and ear units. A panic signal would be instantly transmitted to a fast response team that shadowed her constantly. It had been guaranteed that they could be at her side in no more than three minutes, day or night.

Olivia headed downstairs to the hotel bar. Although Constantine was not registered in this hotel, or any other hotel in Zurich, for that matter, they had picked up the tracking device's signal near the Regency on three more occasions in the last two weeks. So, he was either using a room in the hotel registered to someone else, or perhaps he had simply been frequenting the hotel or its bar for some reason. (Olympus Security could only speculate how Constantine had entered the country without registering anywhere or without even possessing a valid passport. Perhaps, they had speculated, he had been smuggled onboard a private aircraft.)

*In any case, now the hunt begins...*Olivia/Genevieve thought to herself as she settled onto a barstool in the classy mahogany paneled bar and subtly scanned the surroundings as she ordered her first cocktail...

* * *

Across town a few days later, Constantine could be found taking dinner with his handler, a man he knew only as Wolfgang. He was fairly certain that Wolfgang wasn't the man's true name, but what did that matter? The important thing was that, after three long years, the Organization had finally located him in Rio, and rather than liquidating him as he had feared, had taken him back into the fold. (They had, however, disposed of agent that had been shadowing him, before spiriting Constantine aboard a private hyper-jet bound for Paris.)

When the two big men had shown up at the door to Constantine's shabby third floor apartment in downtown Rio, he had almost bolted. "Wait, wait," the bigger of the two had said. "If we had wanted you dead, you'd be dead already. The Organization just wants to debrief you, and then reinstate you as an agent. However," they had shown him their weapons under their coats, "if you prefer, we can simply terminate your employment right now."

He wasn't a fool; he went along. However, he had still been extremely wary when he had first met with Wolfgang in a nondescript office in Paris. "Welcome back to our little 'family', Gregory," the swarthy, heavyset man had said after he had introduced himself.

"Sit down, sit down. Would you like something to drink? You have nothing to fear from us, you know. You see, we understand why you gave up everything you knew to Graham's security people. It was the only logical choice, was it not? After all, you are just a mercenary...as are we all. Either a small stipend and an anonymous life or perhaps a rather difficult and painful death...what's to choose?"

Constantine had said nothing in response, maintaining his best poker face. He knew that it was still possible that the rough, crafty looking agent sitting across from him might just be drawing him out, learning what he could before torturing him to extract the rest.

"I see that you still aren't completely convinced. Understandable. But, you see, we are prepared to make you a much better offer than you received from Graham's organization. Just tell us every detail of what transpired with the hijacking. Then tell us everything that you know about Graham's security organization and everything that you told them about ours. In return you will be fully reinstated."

"You see, Gregory, you are very valuable to us. We spent years and a small fortune to train you. And you, in turn, have become a truly gifted professional. After all, you penetrated Graham's security apparatus at the highest level, and came within a whisker of hijacking Graham himself along with his whole executive team. How many men on this planet could have even attempted such a thing?"

In the end, Constantine had told his new handler everything. He'd really had no choice, had he? And somewhat to his surprise, Wolfgang had been as good as his word. After a thorough debriefing that had taken over a week, he had been accompanied by Wolfgang on another private jet to Zurich. Wolfgang had reserved a two bedroom suite at the posh Regency Suisse, taking one bedroom for himself and giving the other to Constantine. (He was being treated well enough, he observed, but he was nonetheless being kept on a short leash.)

* * *

Now dining in a dimly lit booth in a quiet French restaurant, Wolfgang briefed him on his first mission.

"Consider this a remedial assignment, Gregory, a relatively simple task to get you back into the game", the big man attacked his roast duck before continuing, "we want you to simply act as bait for a while."

Constantine simply nodded. "Go on."

Wolfgang washed a mouthful of the duck down with a big swig of white wine.

"It seems we had a stroke of luck when we brought you here. These days, the Organization carefully watches the comings and goings of each and every individual to and from Olympus, as you might imagine. Five days after we spirited you out of Brazil, a journalist in a Graham wire service based in Paris was suddenly summoned to Olympus."

"So?"

"So nothing...at first. However, 'coincidentally', that same journalist arrived a few days ago in Zurich...and can you believe this? She's staying at our hotel!"

Constantine's interest was up now. He, for one, didn't believe in coincidences. However, he had a concern. "But how could Graham's people possibly have located me? You smuggled me into the country, and we have carefully avoided all identity scans ever since. I'm not registered at the hotel. I've had absolutely no outside communications. The Organization has provided me with a false Identichip, though I haven't even been required to use it yet. And your security people have checked me from head to foot for tracking devices and found nothing."

"Yes indeed. Of course, one working hypothesis might be that you have been turned and have somehow contacted them." Wolfgang was pleased to see the color drain from Constantine's face. "Then again, perhaps it is just a simple coincidence after all. In any case, once you help us capture her, we intend to ask her, in the most forceful manner."

"Wolfgang, I can assure you..."

"Yes, yes. Assurances aren't necessary, my friend. The mystery will be solved once we have the young lady in hand."

Looking at his rack of lamb, Constantine suddenly realized that he had lost his appetite. *If they captured this bitch and she falsely implicated him out of spite...*

"Do you have a Holo of the woman?"

"Of course." The handler pulled his pocket Uplink and called up the journalist's picture. He held it low so that only Constantine could see.

"Her name is Genevieve Carpentier. Rather attractive, is she not? A sadist might actually enjoy interrogating her. But, of course, we are not sadists, are we?"

Constantine studied the Holo. Although he was certain that he had never met her, she seemed disturbingly familiar to him, somehow. He just couldn't put his finger on precisely how.

"The interesting thing about Mademoiselle Carpentier is that we can find no evidence whatever that she has ever been an agent. These last few days, we have done a most thorough investigation of her background, and by all accounts, she is nothing more than a conventional journalist. Either Graham's organization has recruited a legitimate journalist to do a little bit of overt investigation for them, or she is in very deep cover indeed."

"So what do you propose?"

"We assume that she is looking for you. So, I suggest that we let her find you. Who knows, perhaps you can amuse yourself with her a bit before you lure her off quietly to a secure facility where she can be interrogated."

"And how will I let her find me?"

"We could simply trace her Uplink and put you in her path. However, we are concerned that a trace might alert her somehow. We are still wondering how our agents were detected when they were trailing that young professor in New York three years ago. (Constantine had wondered about that as well. When he had casually asked McCafferty, he had been rebuffed on the basis of 'need to know'.) Doubtless, if you spend some time in the hotel lobby, the hotel bar and its restaurants, you will stumble into her. All that will be required is a bit of patience. We have no reason to hurry."

"Very well, then, let the hunt begin."

The two men clinked their wine glasses and finished their dinner...

* * *

It was ironic; two experienced agents looking for each other in a narrowly defined area, and still it took five days for them to stumble into one another. For her part, Olivia had hung around the hotel and its facilities a great deal, frequented some of the nearby bars and cafes and had even taken the time to maintain her cover by playing the part of a journalist. Genevieve, her alter ego, had set her up with a few appointments with banking executives concerning an international merger that they were each involved in. Both men had seemed happy enough to be interviewed by the attractive young "journalist". One of them, an overweight, balding old goat, had even had the temerity to proposition her...

Constantine had spent his time in much the same way. Eventually, it was Olivia that had spotted Constantine first. It was after ten pm. She had been sitting in the lobby for hours, pretending to work on her pocket Uplink, looking the part of a young businesswoman working late with a glass of wine.

Olivia had seen him crossing the lobby toward the bar. Seeing him somewhat from behind, she hadn't been entirely certain that it was actually Constantine, but she decided that it was definitely worth investigating. She waited for a bit so that it wouldn't appear that she had followed him. Then she casually got up and sauntered towards the bar. As she approached its entrance, she had to suppress the unexpected surge of adrenaline. After all, this might be the man who had stabbed and almost killed her three years ago. *Calm down, Olivia,* she thought to herself, *if we stay cool, perhaps we could administer a bit of payback...*

She could see him seated at the bar, but in the dim lighting she still couldn't be completely certain that it was Constantine. Careful not to give the man more than a passing glance, she sat down on a stool two seats away from her intended quarry. The bar was fairly quiet, as it was a workday evening; there were perhaps just three or four other patrons scattered about. Pretending to ignore him, she ordered a cocktail. She could see out of the corner of her eye that he was already nursing a beer.

When he spoke, there was no doubt that it was Constantine. "Pretty quiet tonight, isn't it? Do you perhaps speak English?" The man spoke to her with a mid-western American accent, as if he were a typical up and coming young American businessman.

She pretended disinterest as she fought to stay outwardly calm. She took a drink, paused for a moment as if she were trying to decide whether to respond to an obvious pick-up attempt, and then answered nonchalantly, "*Oui monsieur,* it is my second language, but I am comfortable enough with it."

Olivia worked at adopting the softer tenor of Genevieve's voice, afraid that Constantine might recognize Olivia's own voice, even through the accent. She also avoided direct eye contact with the man, suddenly certain that he would see right through her disguise.

But he seemed totally without suspicion, giving her a big innocent grin. "Great, because I don't speak much French. Do you mind?" He gestured to the seat next to her. Again she hesitated a moment, adopting an air of Gallic indifference.

"I suppose not *monsieur*, although I must tell you that I had planned just this one drink before turning in for the night...I am very tired."

"That's OK; it's been a long day for me too. What are you doing here in Zurich, if I might ask?"

"*Certainement,* I am a journalist on, I fear, a very boring assignment... to report on the progress of business merger between a large French agribusiness and a Swiss investment house. *Et vous?*"

"Eh? Oh, me? I'm here on business too; I'm a sales executive for an AI development firm in Indianapolis. My boss and I are meeting with a prospective European distributor. Are you staying here at the hotel?"

"Perhaps. But forgive me, *monsieur*; a single woman must be very careful when talking to strangers, especially in an unfamiliar city, *n'est pas?*"

"Sure, I understand, so let's just take care of that. My name is Todd Allen...and your name is?" He held out his hand to her, flashing another boyish grin.

She took his hand and responded, "Genevieve...Genevieve Carpentier. *Enchanté, Monsieur* Allen." She returned his smile, though, once again, she was careful not to make direct eye contact.

"Pleased to meet you Ms. Carpentier," "Todd" responded.

"Have you had time to see the sights in Zurich, yet?"

"I'm afraid not, *Monsieur* Allen, I have only had time for work so far, although I have had dinner with a few of the persons that I have interviewed for my story. *Et vous?*

"Please call me Todd. My boss and I have had a little free time. We've explored Old Town down by the river. It's a quaint part of the city, with narrow cobbled streets and lots of great little shops and cafes..."

The innocuous small talk continued for awhile. Genevieve/Olivia maintained her reserved but cautiously friendly persona, while Todd/Gregory continued to play the part of the young mid-westerner-in-the-big city. Eventually, the young woman finished her martini.

"Would you let me buy you another drink?"

"*Merci, mais non;* I am very tired and I have an early conference call in the morning with my home office. I fear that I must excuse myself, *monsieur,*" she held out her hand to him, "I have enjoyed our little conversation...Todd. I hope that you enjoy the rest of your stay here in Zurich."

As the young woman rose to leave, Todd held her hand for just an extra moment. "Would you consider having dinner with me tomorrow evening? There's a fine little restaurant in Old Town with a beautiful view of the river. You wouldn't want to leave Zurich before you've at least seen just a bit of the city, would you?"

She hesitated for a long moment as he held her hand, as if trying to decide. *Perfect, all I have to do is to gently set the hook,* she thought to herself.

"Well...I am only going to be here a few more days. Perhaps... *oui* ...I would like that very much. *Merci.*"

"Great! It's settled then."

"Todd" stood up, still holding her hand, perhaps squeezing it just a bit harder...and standing a bit nearer.

"It's called *The Mondgaststätte.* How about eight o'clock tomorrow evening?"

"That sounds fine, Todd. I have an interview late tomorrow afternoon. So, if you don't mind, I'll just meet you at the restaurant bar at eight. And now if you will excuse me...*bonsoir, monsieur.*"

"*Bonsoir*, Genevieve. It's been a pleasure; I look forward to tomorrow evening. Could we exchange access codes just in case there is a change in plans?"

The young woman simply nodded and held out her wrist unit. Touching his wrist unit to hers, the access codes for each Uplink was automatically transferred to the other's unit. With that, she made her leave. The young man stayed behind, ordering himself another beer.

*　　　＊　＊　＊*

Well, that was easy enough, Gregory thought to himself as he nursed his beer. *Wasn't that much more difficult than picking up one of those rich tourist babes down in Rio.* The only thing that bothered him was that he just couldn't shake the feeling that he had seen her somewhere before. Maybe he had caught her image in a Cybercast ...he wondered if she had also spent time as a broadcast reporter; she certainly had the looks to be one.

Maybe he could ask her over dinner. *Anyhow, so far so good*, he thought to himself...

* * *

Olivia finally allowed herself to breathe a sigh of relief as soon as the door to her hotel room closed behind her. She had never fully appreciated just how stressful the life of a covert agent could be. Successfully maintaining a phony identity in itself was arduous enough, even before considering the fact that failure could result in one's torture or death.

And pleasantly shaking hands with the man who had shoved a knife into her body! The thought of it still sent shivers down her spine. It was a small miracle that she had managed to maintain her composure when they had first actually touched.

Well, one more evening and perhaps this will all be over, she thought to herself as she keyed the encrypted message into her pocket Uplink:

> *"Contact made with target. Have the surveillance teams into position by 19:30 local time tomorrow at The Mondgaststätte restaurant on the River Limmat in Old Town."*

So far, so good, she thought to herself as she stepped into a very hot shower...

* * *

The next day was a long one for Olivia. She had stayed in her room most of the morning. Getting restless, around noon she had decided to head down to Old Town for lunch. *Mac says that it's always vital to know the lay of the land before a battle...I guess that his advice would apply even to a battle of wits*, she had thought to herself as she headed for the drop tube to the lobby. The afternoon had been pleasant enough, the late summer day cool and crisp, marred only by the absence of Michael and the anticipation of dinner with a mortal enemy. She had walked along the river, had lunch in a small café, and browsed in some of the quaint little shops in Old Town. She had walked past *The Mondgaststätt*, paying attention to the entrances and exits, as well as the surrounding streets and alleys.

* * *

Now it was eight-fifteen, as Olivia/Genevieve entered the restaurant wearing a casual but classy dark green evening dress. (She had purposefully arrived late to limit the pre-dinner small talk, as well as to put the man a bit on the defensive.)

Heading toward the restaurant's bar, she saw Constantine seated on a stool at its near end. (She was pleased to observe that both the bar and the restaurant were dimly lit.) Todd/Gregory jumped up to meet her.

"I was getting a bit worried that you might stand me up!" he said as he took her hand and led her to the bar.

"*Je suis desole*...I am so sorry. The interview lasted longer than anticipated. And I still had to return to the hotel to change."

"That's okay, you're here now; that's the important thing. Would you like a drink? Or if you prefer, a table is waiting for us."

"I could, how you say...eat a cow? Let us take our table, *si vous plait*. I am famished."

He laughed his boyish laugh. "I think that the phrase is 'eat a horse', but I get the point. Let me get someone to seat us."

They were seated by a window upstairs overlooking the river. It was lovely, looking at the lights of the traffic moving up and down the river, with a full moon's light reflected on the dark water. *I'd like to bring Michael here someday*, she thought to herself absently, as they were seated.

They had a fine continental meal and shared some excellent chardonnay. They talked and laughed, each lying about their backgrounds, their jobs, their family and how they had spent the day. Into their second bottle, as she had talked to him, she had casually put her hand on his leg in a gesture of intimacy, attaching a micro-transmitter to his trousers. Another time, she had leaned in close to tell him a racy joke, putting a hand on his shoulder, (and another bug on his coat).

They had finished with coffee and a shared dessert. The meal had been leisurely; two hours had been consumed, as well as over two bottles of wine. Olivia/Genevieve didn't have to feign being tired or sleepy. The food, alcohol and hidden stress had exhausted her. But her mission was almost done now. Constantine would be followed back to his room by the surveillance team, where, before the micro-bugs planted on him had self-destructed overnight, much more sophisticated surveillance methods would have been deployed against him. Meanwhile, Olivia's own backup team would follow her back to her hotel room. Then home in the morning... and Michael. It was almost over.

"How about a nightcap back at the hotel?"

"I would love to, but I am very tired and I have yet another interview early in the morning," before he could protest, she continued, "however, I truly had a lovely time this evening. Would you like to share dinner again tomorrow evening, *avec moi*?"

He seemed very pleased with that. "Now that's an offer that I could hardly refuse. That would be just great! Could you at least take an auto-cab back to the hotel with me?" he raised a hand, "I know, I know, you haven't even told me what hotel you're staying in, but I suspect that it's somewhere near the Regency, am I right?"

She really didn't want to ride anywhere with him, but she could think of no graceful way to decline the offer. After all, she had just invited him to dinner, hadn't she? Why would she refuse to ride in a cab with him?

"*Mais oui*, I would be my pleasure."

She just hoped that he didn't plan on making any moves on her in the privacy of the cab. It gave her the shivers thinking of this man groping her. So Todd/Gregory had settled the bill and escorted her out of the restaurant to the cabstand. (These new European auto-cabs were fully automated, unlike American cabs, which still carried a human driver as a backup.) Closing the hatch of the cab, he settled in next to Olivia/Genevieve, giving its autopilot the Regency as their destination.

"Todd" turned towards her and smiled warmly as the cab smoothly left the curb. She returned his smile in the dim light of the cab's cabin. She felt a stinging sensation in her leg.

Olivia was able to utter just one word, "Don't..." before darkness enveloped her.

* * *

Consciousness returned in stages. At first disjointed images: lights above, like an operating room, the feel of hard cold steel below her, voices around her that she couldn't quite make out. She couldn't move at first, because of the drugs, she supposed. Later, she became aware of leather restraints on her wrists and ankles. Eventually some clarity returned, but she continued to feign unconsciousness, hoping that someone would say something that would give her a clue about what was happening to her.

"Don't bother; we know that you're awake, Olivia. We have you on a neuro-scanner. Welcome back." It was Constantine. The young man seemed to be in a jaunty mood.

"Well, what do you think of our latest designer drug? It induces practically instant catatonia. You sit there with your eyes open, totally unaware, yet you can be stood up and led around like the proverbial zombie. Unfortunately, its effects also suppress all other cognitive functions, so we had to neutralize it before we could interrogate you."

"Now, I must admit, you really had me going there. Obviously, you knew who I was all along, but I had no clue just who you really were until we got you here. Even then, it took us a while to correctly ID you. All of your biological markers matched those of Ms. Carpentier, so how could it not be her? In the end, it was good old human intuition that saved the day. I just knew that I'd seen you somewhere before. Seeing you strapped down on this table, it finally hit me. I'd seen you before just like that, looking down on you in the plane, with my knife between your ribs."

She spat in his face...he'd gotten just a little too close to her. A flash of anger crossed his face, but then he smiled as he wiped off the spittle with a handkerchief.

"*Touché*, my dear. I suppose you deserve that, considering what you have already endured, not to mention what horrors you must still face."

The adrenaline had finally cleared her mind. "You bastard. We turn you over to our side and then you just flip back to theirs the first chance you get."

Constantine slapped her. Nonetheless, she had scored the first point...

18

The Mission

The small corporate hyperjet began to make its descent from the suborbital trajectory that had taken it across the Atlantic Ocean. Taking off from Kennedy International, the flight had lasted just a little over an hour and a half. As the craft approached the coast of France, it slowed to subsonic speed. In just another hour, it would begin its final approach toward the international airport at Bern, Switzerland.

The plane had been chartered just twelve hours ago by a venerable Swiss investment-banking firm. If anyone had checked its flight manifest, they would have discovered that it carried six executives of the Swiss firm, four of whom were Swiss citizens and two of whom were American.

However, there was actually just one executive onboard, and he worked for Graham Enterprises, rather than some Swiss banking firm. And the five men that accompanied him were not fellow executives. Rather, they were highly skilled ex-commandos recruited by Graham Enterprises over the last three years from some of most elite Special Forces commands from around the world.

The executive was Daniel Patrick McCafferty, the head of Graham Security, and just now, he was a man possessed. He had taken Graham's own hyperjet from Olympus to New York, accompanied by just one operative, a big retired SAS regimental sergeant major named Will Stirling. Rendezvousing with the other four agents at Kennedy, they had covertly boarded the plane bound for Europe. On each leg of his journey, the intelligence chief had spent every possible minute gathering intelligence and drawing up plans for a rescue mission.

Mac had been in the Olympus Command Center just eighteen hours ago, around 3 pm MST the day before, when Olivia had disappeared. She had vanished along with Constantine, although they had been closely shadowed by no less than four of Graham Security's best agents.

But then, less than an hour later, they had had their one stroke of good luck. Although all of the external tracking devices on both Olivia and Constantine had clearly been discarded or disabled, at around 4 pm that same afternoon, the micro-device that had been injected into Constantine's arm three years earlier had transmitted its little three microsecond signal. The signal was detected from two Uplink cell sites in a warehouse district in the outskirts of Zurich. Even as Mac had assembled a strike team, intelligence specialists had pinpointed a particular closed warehouse, owned by Eurodynamics, as the likely source of the signal.

Graham himself had tried to talk Mac out of personally heading the mission; Mac would hear none of it. "Boss, I got her into this, and I'm getting her out of it."

"Mac, you know as well as I do that there are two excellent reasons for someone else rather than you leading the team. First of all, let's face it; you just aren't getting any younger. I know you're still a pretty tough customer; you proved that well enough on the hyperjet three years ago. Nonetheless, you just aren't trained up at the level your best men are any more. Secondly, you are just too emotionally involved."

Mac had raised his hand in protest, but Graham had persisted. "Don't deny it, Mac; Olivia is the proverbial daughter you never had."

In the end, Graham had relented. Despite his concerns, he knew that Mac would have resigned his position and led his own private mission, rather than stand down. So the wealthy man had simply offered Mac his blessing, along with any resource that Graham Enterprises could provide in order to help him accomplish his mission.

As soon as the hyperjet crossed the border into Switzerland, claiming a minor mechanical problem, its pilot requested permission from Swiss air traffic control to divert from its original flight plan. With ATC approval, the craft turned to begin its final approach to a small UN/NATO military facility some 80 kilometers southwest of Bern, just north of Lake Geneva. Staging from the secure NATO facility would allow Mac and his team to effectively circumvent Swiss Customs and Security. (The Supreme Commander of NATO, it turned out, was an old friend of McCafferty, and owed Mac a favor or two.)

The craft was directed by the base tower to land by a small, unused maintenance hanger on the isolated northern perimeter of the base. The base commander had been ordered to allow these civilians free access to and use of this part of his facility, with no questions asked. (He had been given to assume that they were part of some classified NATO operation.)

No sooner than his plane had touched down next to the hanger, Mac and his team hustled down the ramp and into the hanger. Inside the hanger, an advance team based in Europe had already set up an impressive array of communications and surveillance equipment, as well as a stockpile of weapons and assault gear.

As Mac's strike team headed over to begin sorting out and inspecting their equipment, Mac approached the advance team's leader, a Frenchman named Jean Paul Cheval. Years ago, Jean Paul had been Mac's S2 (intelligence officer) in one of his last U.N. command postings. He looked much the same as Mac had remembered him from ten years back: tall and lean, with a long and pronounced Gallic nose. The gray that now had begun to show at the retired U.N. officer's temples only served to enhance his aristocratic profile. The two men trusted each other completely.

"Jean Paul, it's good to see you after all these years, in spite of the circumstances. Can you give me the most current sitrep?"

"*Bon jour, Colonel.*" Cheval almost saluted his old superior out of habit.

"It is très *bien* to see you as well. As you can see, we have most of the command and control gear set up. The two surveillance teams already deployed in Zurich, as you know, have already set up secure positions to observe the warehouse at close range. They are quite motivated, since they are very embarrassed by what has transpired; all four agents desire to make amends."

"A supply air-shuttle from Geneva is enroute to Zurich and should arrive with a half dozen microdrones within the hour. (Microdrones were battery-powered hovercraft the approximate size of sparrows, equipped with tiny optical and infrared sensors. Virtually undetectable, they could remain on station for hours, providing close-in intelligence.)"

"The surveillance teams have already set up electronic sensors near the building to pick up audio or electronic communications, but so far, they have picked up absolutely nothing. This, of course, only reinforces the suspicion that we have targeted the correct building, since it must be thoroughly shielded for security purposes, unusual for an ordinary warehouse."

"Right, Jean Paul, I presume that you have already studied the blueprints of the building, as I was able to do on the flight over. What do you say that you, I and Will go over to that office over there, get each of ourselves a strong cup of coffee, and make a plan?"

"*Certainement.*"

Mac gestured at Stirling, who already had his men getting organized with brisk efficiency. Two were ex-Delta, one was ex-SAS and one was an ex-SEAL; all had been detached to the U.N Special Forces Command and had served in that unit under Colonel McCafferty at one time or another. Stirling gave a few more terse orders to the men, then joined Mac and Jean Paul in a maintenance office looking out over the hanger. Will and Jean Paul shook hands; they too had served together in years past. They joined Mac at the auto-coffee maker.

"Right, then; gentlemen, I don't need to tell you that we are in a race against time. I want to rescue Olivia before she is permanently injured, either physically or psychologically. Our one advantage in that regard is that they probably don't believe that they need to hurry the interrogation, since they are probably certain that we have no idea where she is currently being held captive. Standard procedure would be to begin with drugs, fear and sleep deprivation for a few days to soften her up, before moving on to harsher methods; I propose that we extract her before they have a chance to move on to those methods."

"So we are going to be thorough in our planning, but we are also going to move fast. I want an assault on the warehouse to begin no later than 0400 local time, day after tomorrow. Secondary to the rescue, our goals will be to gather what intelligence we can, as well as to strike back forcefully. Graham personnel and facilities have been attacked repeatedly over the last four or five years...it's time that we provide a deterrent to further attacks."

The two other men looked at each other. It was now almost 1800 local time. That would give them the rest of the evening and the next day to plan and execute a highly dangerous, complex mission. Well, they had better get cracking; tonight promised to be a very long night indeed!

* * *

Olivia had not been allowed to sleep, eat or drink since her capture eighteen hours ago. Strapped to a metal gurney, her whole body cried out, her arms and legs had long ago grown numb from lack of circulation; the back of her head and her hips ached terribly. Dressed in only a hospital gown, she was cold. She was also parched. Once she had cried out in the empty cell that she needed to urinate. After a time, a male guard had come in to let her use a bedpan; the only consideration that she had been given, so far.

After the slap from Constantine, he had ordered her moved to a small holding cell. Presumably, he had gone to get a good night's sleep, while she was softened up. The naked light bulb in the ceiling shinning right in her eyes conspired with the cold in the room to keep her sleepless through the endless night.

At the military academy, years ago, Olivia had taken a course in meditation. It was a "gimme" class in her sophomore year, intended to give her a bit of a break between serious classes such as physics and advanced calculus. She had, rather to her own surprise, gotten hooked, practicing meditation techniques off and on over the years to handle stress. That knowledge now proved to be vital to her survival. She cleared her mind, slowed her breathing, and just put the pain and fear aside. She would endure.

Finally, after an eternity, two guards wheeled the young woman into what seemed to be an interrogation room. Waiting in the room were Constantine and two other men, strangers, one a stocky, dark complexioned man dressed in an ill-fitting suit, and the other a pinched-faced, evil looking old man wearing a doctor's white smock.

Constantine looked rested and seemed to still be in good spirits. However, Olivia thought that she also detected just a hint of fear, uncertainty perhaps, in his eyes as well. Maybe he was still under suspicion here; she would try to exploit that.

"Well, you seem to have had a rather rough night, my dear," Constantine feigned compassion, "let us help you. Here, we are going to put e-cuffs on your hands, then let you sit in a nice comfortable chair while we have a little chat. Don't try to do anything stupid; the punishment would be beyond your worst nightmares."

The two guards un-strapped her wrists, then sat her up. They cuffed her, then un-strapped her ankles and helped her stand. All five men grinned and leered as her gown rode up, exposing her as she was pulled off of the gurney. In spite of herself, she felt raw anger course through her. The wild, fierce glare that she fixed on Constantine actually forced him to look away for just a moment.

The guards had to hold her up by her elbows, since her legs were completely numb. They walked her to a metal chair and sat her down, strapping her ankles to the chair legs. They were taking no chances. Constantine handed her a cup of water and a straw.

"I imagine that your mouth must be very dry; you'll need this before you can do much more than croak."

She took the water and drained the cup, throwing it on the floor. Constantine smiled.

"Ah, a feeble act of defiance, littering our humble facility. But enough of such nonsense; let's get right down to business shall we? To my left is a man that you can call Wolfgang, one of my superiors in our organization. Behind me is a man that we will only refer to as 'the Doctor'. 'The Doctor' is renowned in the intelligence community for his ability to extract information from even the most unwilling of subjects."

"We know that you have been well trained in counter-interrogation techniques, so I won't play games with you. I will tell you exactly what to expect. We will ask you questions, and you will lie to us, at first. We will drug you and make you ever more uncomfortable with cold, thirst, hunger and lack of sleep. We will ask you the questions again and again, and you will still attempt to lie to us, but you will begin to have difficulty remembering your lies."

"Then the torture and humiliation will begin. Pain will be administered beyond any human being's ability to endure. You will be raped repeatedly and then mutilated. Eventually, you will beg us to let you tell us everything you know. In the end you will plead with us to end your life. And when we believe that we have every single scrape of information that you possess, we will give you what you want...oblivion"

"The sad irony of all this is that we would be forced to go through this entire process, even if you were determined to tell us everything you know right now. For in that event, how could we be certain that you had told us absolutely everything?"

And with that, 'the Doctor' moved in to inject a psychoactive drug into her exposed thigh. Then the questions began...and the lies...

* * *

"Saddle up!" Will shouted to his men.

It was two am, two hours before the assault was to begin, and time to board the combat cruiser, which had been painted and rigged to look more or less like one of Zurich's tactical police skycraft. The flight would take less than an hour.

As the day before had drawn to a close, they had been forced to conclude, after a day and night of planning, that their assault plan, sketchy as it was, was about as good as it would ever get. This was due to the unfortunate fact that they had so little intelligence about the warehouse itself, or what they would find inside. They knew the original layout of the facility, but they didn't know how it might have been modified or hardened.

They had closely tracked the movements of the two security guards that were stationed outside behind a chain link fence that surrounded the warehouse. However, no one else had been observed entering or leaving the facility in the last two days, so they had no idea how many adversaries they would confront once inside. Then too, the warehouse's shielding continued to stymie their attempts to gather any electronic intelligence.

Another issue had arisen during the day's planning. Will had addressed it straightforwardly, as was his natural inclination. "Colonel McCafferty, you're my boss and the best C.O. I ever had from the old days; you know that I...that all of the team will follow your orders without question. However, the team has trained together for hundreds of hours in both 'sim' and 'real world' environments with the prototype weapons that Graham Research has provided for us. You've had just a little 'sim' time for familiarization's sake. You're more apt to get in the way than contribute to our effectiveness. Would you consider staying here at the C&C to coordinate the assault with Jean Paul?"

Mac had responded immediately, "Will, I respect your concerns. However, we don't even know how many bad guys we're going to find inside. Five men may not be enough to cover all of the bases. Don't worry, though, you are the team leader; I'll just be one of your grunts on this mission. I'm not sure how much help that I will be with all of this new gear, but I guarantee that I won't get in the way."

Mac hadn't kidded himself; he knew that Will was probably right. Nonetheless, in his younger days, Mac had been very good at this sort of thing. He was confident that his experience would carry him through tonight. It would have to...

In the end, because of their lack of intel, they had decided that total surprise, teamwork and the ability to adapt quickly to whatever situation they were confronted with would have to do. So as the departure time had approached, the men had all attempted to take a quick catnap before dust-off. And now they were on their way...

* * *

A bodyguard of lies, Olivia thought absently to herself, *who had said that? Was it Roosevelt or Churchill? Churchill, I think... yes, it was Winston Churchill, for certain.* Between the endless interrogation sessions, she still tried to meditate, to find some relief, but it was difficult, with the drugs serving to keep her constantly disoriented. However, ironically, Constantine had inadvertently given her additional motivation to hold out at all costs. He had assured her that she would be tortured and killed, regardless of whether she cooperated or not. In consequence, all she left to cling to was her determination deny them the one thing that they wanted...the truth.

So her lies became subtler, more believable, as she pretended to be even more strung out and exhausted than she actually was. The three men took turns interrogating her, and she had seen that each had his own individual style. Constantine exhibited an oily sort of cruelty, arrogant and smug. 'The Doctor' was cold and clinical, treating her like a specimen in a jar.

Just now it was Wolfgang's turn. He was clearly the sadist, although so far his cruelties were small; he pinched her, slapped her, and poked her at every opportunity. She knew that he would be the worst, once the interrogation reached its next level. How long before that happened, she had no idea, because she had lost all track of time; she didn't know whether she had been under interrogation for hours or days.

* * *

As the craft sped through the night sky, the men suited up and checked out their gear. Each man wore cutting edge body armor made of lightweight composite material that was virtually indestructible against conventional weapons. The suits and gear were also coated with a light sensing "chameleon" coating that adapted to the brightness and hues of its surroundings. The men then donned helmets that enabled them to continuously communicate with their C&C as well as each other. Lowering their visors, they checked out their infrared and lowlight displays, as well as targeting data for their primary weapons. These were prototype EM rifles that used high-energy electromagnetic pulses to fire tiny explosive-tipped projectiles with incredible velocity and accuracy. These weapons generated absolutely no sound or flash, yet were devastatingly effective.

As the assault team approached Zurich, each man strapped on and checked out his descent harness. The descent harness looked like a pair of stubby wings that jutted about a foot out from each man's shoulders. Mounted on the end of each wing was a small pod, a micro-turbine. Their descent harnesses could lower them to a gentle and accurate landing from an altitude of several thousand feet. Both the descent turbines and the EM rifles were powered by a high capacity fuel cell worn on each man's back.

Mac knew, though, that with all of the high tech gear, the success or failure of this rescue mission would ultimately rest with the skill and courage of the team itself. And regarding this, he could hardly have had more confidence, for he had carefully handpicked each of these men himself, and they were the best of the best. Will Stirling, the team leader, had served for 20 years in the SAS, still one of the most elite fighting forces in the world. Retired while still in his early forties, Will, a quiet, intelligent and resourceful leader, had jumped at the chance to work with his old C.O. again.

The two Delta operators were both highly skilled at infiltration and hostage rescue. One, Jimmy Park, was a Korean-American who also served as the team's electronics and communications specialist. The other, Mike Willis, was a rugged blond Mid-Westerner who was also served as the team's demolitions expert. The ex-SEAL, Harris Young, was a tall and lean black New Yorker who had been a star college athlete. He now also served as the team's paramedic. Finally, there was Brian Herlihy, a tough little Irishman from Dublin who had been a staff sergeant in the SAS and was the team's most skillful sniper. Though these men could hardly have been more different in temperament or background, they had been melding into a tight, efficient assault team by Stirling over the last three years. The men looked ready to Mac.

* * *

Now it was "the Doctor's" turn, apparently. Wolfgang had left some time ago. Olivia had been left strapped to a straight-backed metal chair bolted to the concrete floor for hours now. She was handcuffed and her lower back screamed at her.

"I need to pee."

"Then pee," the old man replied absently, as he studied the pharmacological supplies in the medicine cabinet across the room.

Finding what he was looking for, he prepared an old style hypodermic, with a very large needle. He crossed over to her, showed her the needle and then inserted it in her neck in slow motion. She refused to flinch, meeting him eye to eye. She controlled her breathing, keeping her muscles relaxed.

"I have concluded from the neuro-scanner readouts that you must be familiar with advanced meditation techniques. That is good; I like the challenge."

The drug, whatever it was, began to kick in. At first, she felt warmth spreading out from the site of the injection, followed closely by euphoria. Then heat, agonizing heat, she was burning up all over, from the inside out.

In the midst of excruciating agony, seemingly out of nowhere, an inner peace began to take hold of her, based on a deep conviction. *Mac...no way he would leave me like this...no way...he would move heaven and earth to find me...and when he does...oh how these bastards will pay!*

Convulsing, she looked through a red haze at her tormenter and met his cold gaze. Her eyes narrowed and she actually smiled at him. "The Doctor" was rather perplexed, in spite of himself...

* * *

The big warehouse had a large open area with a roof perhaps three stories high. Pallets of heavy equipment were scattered about on its concrete floor. On one side of the warehouse was a row of old offices that had been converted into living quarters for the guards, along with a holding cell and the "interrogation room" that had been set up for their newly arrived prisoner. On the opposite end of the warehouse, a large office had been converted into a security and communications control center, staffed by two armed surveillance specialists.

From the control center, the surveillance specialists continuously monitored an extensive array of internal and external sensors that presumably ensured an airtight operation. In addition to the two control center guards, two external guards and two roving internal guards patrolled the facility continually. Two more guards were stationed in close proximity to their new "guest". Eight men, in all, but these men were no ordinary rent-a-cops. Rather, they were all highly trained ex-special forces personnel, mostly from Eastern block nations. Now employed by "the Organization", they were all heavily armed and well paid to ensure that this particular secure facility stay that way.

The entire security team had been placed on high alert with the arrival of their sole prisoner. Nonetheless, the men in the control room were bored and sleepy. It was almost 4 am, and they had picked up absolutely nothing on their sensors since midnight. Suddenly, at the extreme range of their sensors, one of their Holo displays showed a slowly approaching skycraft. One of the guards queried its transponder, and received the encoded ID of a police patrol vehicle. They had surreptitious access to the Zurich PD databank, so, as a routine precaution they verified its ID. It checked out; no worries.

* * *

The four Graham agents had deployed five of the six micro-drones the day before from two nearby rooftops. Since then, the five tiny surveillance probes had provided the C&C back at the NATO facility with a continuous stream of close-in intelligence all around the warehouse.

Now, fifteen minutes before H hour, one of the two agent teams released the sixth drone from the same rooftop. This drone was a much larger machine than the other five; it was closer to the size of a large vulture than that of a sparrow. Though relatively stealthy, it was not completely invisible to sensors as the smaller probes had been. It also had a very special purpose. As it approached the warehouse, the other probes retreated to a safe distance.

* * *

"Hey, is that another bogie? Is that a bird or something?"

In the warehouse control center, their sensors now picked up a trace image approaching at very slow speed. After several minutes, it was almost directly overhead. Then, suddenly it disappeared...along with everything else. After a moment of confusion, the men suddenly realized that they had lost all visibility outside of the facility, although all the internal sensors seemed to be working just fine. According to procedure, they instantly sounded the alarm, alerting both their fellow guards and their Command Center in Warsaw. The guards inside the facility instantly grabbed their weapons, donned their body armor and deployed to their prearranged combat stations.

Meanwhile, outside the facility, the two guards looked around in confusion; they had lost all contact with the men inside and with each other. The floodlights around the warehouse had gone out, along with all of their personal communications and surveillance equipment. They were, literally, left in the dark.

* * *

"EMP drone successfully activated. All external lights and sensors appear to be neutralized. Warehouse shielding has likely protected internal systems, as expected," Jean Paul back at C&C calmly reported to the assault team.

A powerful electromagnetic pulse from the drone had fried every microcircuit within a 150-meter radius of the warehouse. The combat vehicle now sped up, though not enough to attract the attention of metropolitan traffic control or the real police. The men readied themselves on the final approach. Visors were lowered and lit up, weapons and assault packs were strapped securely, and hand-controls for the descent harnesses were gripped tightly. The craft descended from five to two thousand feet, and dropped its rear ramp as it slowed to a near hover directly over the warehouse.

"Go! Go! Go!" Jean Paul called out over the encrypted headsets as soon as the vehicle reached the right altitude and position.

Will tapped each man on the shoulder as his turn came, keeping him at precise intervals. He tapped Mac last and then leapt into the darkness himself exactly three seconds later. As soon as Will cleared the ramp, the craft smoothly pulled away, landing on a secure rooftop a kilometer away, to await the extraction phase. The entire combat drop had taken less than a minute.

The drop was giddy for Mac. As a trooper, he had made many combat drops using high-aspect collapsible parasails. In the last few years, he had also made a few "sim" drops with the new descent harnesses. However, a real combat drop at night with one of these "Buck Rogers" rigs was really something else. Mac's harness allowed him to freefall for a seemingly endless five seconds, and then automatically stabilized him and began to slow his descent.

Spotting the string of nearly invisible troopers descending below with the lowlight/IR display on his visor, the old veteran oriented himself and then activated the hand-controls for his descent harness. Shaky with the unfamiliar controls, he overcorrected to the left and right, drifting high then low. He fell far behind. To his left, he saw Will shoot by to fall quickly into line with the tight formation that was now approaching the large roof of the warehouse below.

The rest of the team landed noiselessly and within a few seconds of one another. Mac was hardly aware of this as he concentrated on just making it to the rooftop in one piece. He made it clumsily, but at least managed to stay on his feet...if just barely.

The team was already at work. Herlihy, the designated sniper, was already at the rooftop's edge lining up on one of the guards loitering outside. Willis, the demo man, had dropped his large chest pack and was firing up a plasma torch, while Will marked a rough white circle, two meters in diameter, at a precise, predetermined spot on the roof. As Mac gathered his wits, he noted with satisfaction how swiftly and efficiently the team operated. There was no wasted effort, no lost time.

Mac heard a small muffled explosion down below, and saw Herlihy quickly change position. A moment later, he heard another; both outside guards had been taken out, without a doubt. Simultaneously, Willis ran the torch around the white circle, cutting through the steel roof like a hot knife through butter. He skipped a few spots, to keep the section intact until the team was ready. He then attached a small shaped charge to the center of the cut section.

Everyone got into position just outside the circle, facing away from it. Willis activated the charge, and with a bang, the circle of steel was blown downward. It hit the warehouse floor below with a loud crash an instant later. Only Willis moved; he wasn't finished just yet. He quickly activated a device about the size of a football and tossed it through the hole in the roof. Halfway to the floor, it went off, blowing bomblets in all directions. A split second later, the bomblets exploded all over the interior of the warehouse, filling it instantly with a dense riot gas.

Time to jump again! Park went first, then Willis, Herlihy, Young and Mac in quick succession, with Will going last again. As they dropped, the men intentionally scattered, landing all around the large warehouse floor. On the way down, Herlihy actually managed to take out one of the guards caught in the open by the sudden attack. Mac came down more smoothly this time, but landed hard enough so that he had to go down on a knee. He quickly recovered, however, and hit the quick release on the descent harness, dropping it on the floor, as the other men had already done.

In three pre-arranged pairs, the six men split up. Park and Willis headed to the source of signal traffic that indicated a command center. Mac and Herlihy raced to the opposite side of the warehouse towards what appeared to be the entrance to a complex of offices; Will and Young sprinted to another to a different entrance on the same side of the building. Though the gas was still dense, the assault team was largely unaffected, with their helmet filtration systems and visor displays.

As Mac neared the entrance, with Herlihy just ahead, he could already hear the staccato explosions of the EM projectiles interspersed with the chatter of pulse rifles on the other side of the warehouse. A firefight was already in progress.

Suddenly, the door they had almost reached whipped open. As Herlihy swung his weapon up, Mac shoved him out of the way and grabbed the barrel of a pulse rifle just as the guard pulled the trigger. The burst passed just over Mac's shoulder. There wasn't a second burst, because Mac's boot had almost simultaneously slammed into the guard's solar plexus. Jerking the rifle out of his hand, Mac slammed his opponent's helmeted head against the doorjamb and threw him to the floor. Meanwhile, Herlihy quickly recovered and dove through the door, looking for any other bad guys...none were in sight.

"You better speak English, or you're a dead man!" Mac had straddled the guard and had his combat knife at the terrified man's throat. "The only way that you live, is if she lives."

Mac didn't intend to waste words; there wasn't time. "Show us where she is."

The guard nodded emphatically, "Da, da; I show you. Do not kill!"

* * *

It wasn't the klaxon that caught the poor creature's attention, at first. Just now, she wasn't really functioning on the level of a sentient being; in the midst of the endless, excruciating pain, she had been effectively reduced to the level of a dumb beast. She was dimly aware of her surroundings, but incapable of coherent thought. Rather, what grabbed her attention was the sudden, wholly unexpected look of pure terror that had appeared on the face of her tormentor.

Then, suddenly, the door to the interrogation room was thrown open and three men rushed into the room, slamming and securing the door behind them. Two were vaguely familiar, her other two tormentors. The third was a big, heavily armed man. All seemed breathless and confused... so was she. They were shouting at each other. She tried to understand what was happening, with little success. And what were those angry, constant sounds?

"I say finish her off now, while we still have the chance!"

"Constantine, you fool, she is our only bargaining chip! Do you want to die for sure?" the big heavyset man responded.

"The Doctor" just shrank back into a corner and stayed silent. The guard faced the door, holding his weapon ready, uncertain of what to do next. Suddenly, a muffled explosion, and the big metal door was blown inward, right into the face of the guard. The guard was slammed to the floor, partially covered by the heavy door.

Without thinking, Mac plunged through the door ahead of Herlihy, but stopped short. There was Olivia, strapped to a chair two meters dead ahead. Two men stood a meter or so behind her. One was a terrified old man cowering in one corner; the other was a big heavyset man standing calmly with his hands behind his neck. However, a third was crouching behind Olivia with a knife at her throat. He recognized the face, even though it was largely covered by Olivia's head.

Constantine spoke first, "Drop that fucking weapon and back off, or so help me I'll finish her off!"

Mac lowered his weapon, but didn't drop it. Slowly raising his free hand, he popped his visor up. The riot gas that had made its way down the corridor instantly stung his eyes.

Mac spoke calmly, "My men are all over, Constantine. The only, and I mean only, way you make it out of here is to let her go and give yourself up."

"Well, well, Mac!" Constantine had just recognized his old nemesis as Mac's visor had come up.

"Aren't you getting a bit long in the tooth to be playing at these commando games? But I guess this one's a bit personal for you, huh? You always did have a bit of a thing for this little lady, didn't you? Well, I guess that just gives me that much of a better bargaining position."

Olivia looked up into Mac's eyes, uncomprehending. She looked very bad to Mac. Her sweat-soaked hair was plastered to her scalp and face. Her skin was deathly white with very dark circles under her eyes. And her eyes…she had the "thousand yard stare" that he had seen over the years on troopers who had been completely overcome by combat fatigue. He managed to contain his fury, but just barely.

"Well, are you going to be reasonable?" Constantine growled.

Before he could respond, Mac, still looking at Olivia, saw a hint of awareness appear in her eyes. She recognized him! Suddenly her head jerked down and to the side, completely exposing Constantine behind her. Mac hesitated for a heartbeat, as did Constantine. Herlihy, standing just behind Mac and to his left, didn't. Cat quick, the Irishman aimed and fired a single shot.

The projectile hit precisely between Constantine's eyes, exploding with a sharp, muffled bang. His shattered head was slammed back as if it had been hit with a well-aimed sledgehammer. The knife at Olivia's throat was thrown out and away from her neck, as the lifeless body fell back almost to the feet of the horrified old man.

"The Doctor", in turn, panicked and bolted for the back door to the interrogation room. A second well-aimed projectile from Herlihy's weapon had much the same effect on the old man; his lifeless body slammed against the unopened door. The big man at the back of the room never budged. It was all over in a few seconds.

"Beggin' your pardon, Colonel. We're trained to take our shot when we get th' chance…" Herlihy, a man of few words, nonetheless felt the need to explain himself.

"Right, Sergeant; good work. Now you!" Mac pointed at their lone conscious prisoner, the big man standing at the back of the room, "Where is the controller for her e-cuffs?"

He still did not move, but responded calmly, "In that cabinet drawer over there, I think," he pointed with his head, keeping his fingers locked behind his neck. "Let me just say that you will have my complete cooperation, I will gladly give up everything I know, as long as I am not harmed."

Mac ignored the man as he holstered his weapon and retrieved the controller. Freeing Olivia from the chair, he gently lifted and held her. She returned his embrace, but weakly; he could tell that she could barely stand. He supported her.

Mac tried to keep his voice from choking, as he gave terse commands over his helmet mike, "Hostage safely recovered. Harris, to my position for medical response. Will, are we ready to begin the extraction phase?"

"Very nearly, sir. Jimmy is just finishing up and all guards are accounted for…either dead or in custody. Your extraction vehicle is enroute. We will cordon your area while Harris stabilizes our girl, then we'll exit through the north loading dock, as planned."

"Very well. Good work Will."

"Sir, begging your pardon, I'd really prefer we'd not congratulate ourselves until we're safely away…" Will was superstitious about such things; he'd seen too many missions go awry at the last minute.

"Roger that, Will. So then, let's be away with alacrity…"

"Affirmative, sir."

Mac helped Olivia to the room's gurney, as Herlihy rounded up their three prisoners: the big man at the back of the room, the injured guard who had been knocked down at the door and the other guard that they had e-cuffed facedown in the corridor before blowing the door.

However, before Mac could put the girl up on the gurney, she suddenly tore herself free and staggered to the man she knew as Wolfgang. Wolfgang, his hands now e-cuffed, gave her an expression of sincere regret and shrugged his shoulders.

"I would like to express my most humble…"

Olivia slapped him…hard. Not a ladylike slap on the cheek, but a slap that snapped the big man's head back and almost took him to his knees. A slap that broke his nose and caused it to gush a small torrent of blood. The effort almost took her to her knees as well. Mac pulled her back and laid her down on the gurney; she didn't resist this time.

As Mac covered her with a blanket, he found himself grinning. As he looked at Herlihy leading the shaken prisoner away, he noted that the small, tough Irishman was grinning, as well…

19

Aftermath

Standing on the balcony at dawn, the young woman looked out over Lake Geneva. The view was spectacular. The sky was lit up in a beautiful blend of reds and oranges as the sun just topped the snowcapped peaks across the lake. The lake itself was like a vast mirror, as hardly a ripple showed in the still and cool morning air. The only sounds to be heard were the occasional cries of birds that echoed across the water.

From a distance, the young woman herself would have seemed a vision of serenity and beauty to match her surroundings, standing peacefully at the railing of her balcony, her soft brown hair and white silk dressing gown lit by the morning sun. However, up close, one's impression might have changed. The young woman's attractive face was marred by eyes reddened and rimmed by dark circles from lack of sleep. Her cheeks were sunken from stress and a lack of appetite. Up close, the picture of the young woman would have, perhaps, been more nearly one of sadness, anger and regret.

After Olivia's rescue, the original plan had been to immediately return her to Olympus. However, Graham had had a small inspiration. One of Graham Enterprises' vast array of holdings was a luxury spa on the edge of

Lake Geneva. The facility itself resembled a fairytale palace; only the most elite could afford its luxurious services. For Olivia's rest and recuperation, Graham had reserved an entire wing, staffed with the appropriate medical and security personnel.

A few days later, Michael, after being briefed, had been flown over to join his fiancée. Dr. Alvarez accompanied him, for moral support. All of this was handled surreptitiously; the cover story was that a celebrity and her retinue had been checked in anonymously for rehab.

Backing away from the railing, Olivia opened the French doors to her suite and parted the sheer curtains to look in at Michael. He was still soundly asleep in the big, four-poster bed. She had initially been thrilled to see him when he had first arrived. They had embraced each other fiercely and the tears had flowed. Little by little, she had told him her story as the days had passed.

However, their relationship had soon grown strained. She had snapped at him over the most minor provocations. Rather that responding with patience, as he knew he should, Michael had often snapped back. He had had his own suppressed anger to deal with. Olivia had left him to go on a very dangerous mission without his knowledge or permission. They were supposed to be partners; didn't she understand that she had jeopardized his future as well as her own?

Olivia quietly changed from her gown to a jumpsuit, careful not to wake Michael. Perhaps a solitary walk along the lakeshore would do her a bit of good, she thought to herself. The truth was that she just wanted to be left alone. She was already dreading her first daily therapy session in a few hours. Carefully closing the door behind her, she headed for the stairs to the courtyard. There she planned to fetch herself a mug of coffee from the little café and then head down to the lake for a long, quiet walk.

As she entered the courtyard, she almost ran into Dr. Alvarez, who was just sitting down at one of the patio tables with a decanter of tea. *Blast*, she thought to herself as she greeted the small man, *there goes my quiet morning*.

"*Buenos días, señorita!* How pleased I am to see you this lovely morning! Would you like a cup of very fine Earl Grey?"

The professor rose and took her hand with both of his. When she hesitated, he looked into her eyes. His gaze was warm and sympathetic.

"Please, please, would you give just a few moments to a lonely old man? I haven't had a chance to speak to you alone since I arrived with Michael almost a week ago."

She relented, silently giving up her plans for the morning. Somehow she knew that she would be giving him more than just a few moments. She sat down at his table as he fetched a cup and saucer for her and poured some tea. She added some lemon and sugar; it was indeed very good, she admitted to herself. She smiled at the professor and said so.

For a time, nothing else was said by either; they both just shared the tranquil morning as they sipped their tea. Gradually, she relaxed, almost in spite of herself. The crisp morning air, the spectacular view and most of all, the aura of serenity that seemed to emanate from the small man seated across from her, conspired to drive away her angst, at least temporarily.

After a very long time, the professor spoke, "So, Olivia, what do you think of your therapists here? Or, more succinctly, how do you *feel* about your therapists? Are they helping you?"

Absently, she thought to herself how pleasant his soft spoken Latin accent was to her ears this morning; *almost hypnotic*, she thought, *Perhaps it's simply the contrast with the clinical techno-jargon I keep getting from my therapists.*

"Fine, Dr. Alvarez…well, not really. They are all well meaning enough; I know that they are just trying to help me. But I am really bored with having to hear about post-traumatic stress, repressed hostility, serotonin imbalances and so forth. I just feel like I need some quiet time alone to lick my wounds. And they keep trying to drug me. I had my fill of that during the interrogation sessions. If a glass of red wine won't do the trick, I'm not interested."

"I quite agree, Olivia," (that surprised her a bit).

"Forgive me, but may I ask you a very personal question?"

"No, please forgive me professor, I know that you just want to help, too, but I would prefer to just sit here and enjoy the moment. Over the last several days, I've had just about all of the advice and counseling that I can stand."

"Ah, but that is precisely the point, don't you see?"

"What's the point, Professor?"

"That you should just be enjoying the moment, every moment…"

"And?"

"Are the horrible experiences that you suffered through still vividly real to you?"

"What would you think professor? They're real enough to keep me up every night… real enough to dominate every waking minute of every day.

Dr. Alvarez, they hurt me, they violated me, they stripped away every shred of dignity that I possess!"

Damn! Against her will, the hot tears began to course down her cheeks, yet again. The anger began to rise up in her; this time directed against the little man placidly gazing at her with compassion. Why couldn't he have just let her enjoy a quiet moment with her cup of tea? He handed her a handkerchief.

"But you see, those experiences aren't real at all, strictly speaking. They are, in fact, a mental and emotional construct…a figment of your imagination, if you will."

She really wasn't in the mood for this. She stood up. "Professor, please excuse me, but I think that I'm ready to take my walk now."

The little man rose and took her hand again. "*Por favor, señorita*! Indulge me for just a few moments more."

Olivia hesitated for a moment, and then relented, sitting back down. She decided that she would politely endure the lecture and then just as politely take her leave.

"I have an advanced degree in philosophy, but it was an old priest that taught me a very profound secret, when I was still a very young man. *He taught me that the past has no meaning but that which we give it.* I was an angry and bitter youth, abandoned by my parents, beaten and abused by the prostitutes that, more or less, raised me, as well as the corrupt officers that took payoffs from them. When I was old enough, I joined a gang, at first for protection, later to provide me with whatever I wanted, through criminal acts. I robbed people; I sold drugs; I did whatever they told me to, without hesitation or regret."

"One day, I was wounded while narrowly escaping the police. I hid in a small chapel. An old priest found me. Rather than turn me over to the authorities, he tended to me. First he tended to my wounds, and later to my spirit. He made me understand one simple fact; that my fate was truly in my own hands. The past need have no bearing in what my future would be, unless I let it be so. He told me what a wise old philosopher once said: 'Letting your past guide your actions was like steering a boat by looking back at its wake.'"

"The choice itself is simple enough; it *is understanding that one really has a choice* that is so difficult. I was a stubborn youth; it took the old padre a long time to make me see the truth. But then, in the end, he was even more stubborn than I was."

"Eventually, the priest asked me the one great question: What sort of future did I really want? He told me to completely disregard whatever I thought might be possible, to just answer the question honestly."

"I half jokingly told him that I wanted to be a professor at a great university, married to a wonderful, brilliant woman. He looked at me for a long time; his eyes seemed to look into my soul. Finally, he swore to me that, together, we would make it so. And in time, with much effort, he and I did make it so. His name was Father Alvarez."

"Alvarez...was he related to you?"

"I had no last name; on the street they just called me Luis or Louie. To go back to school I needed a last name, so he gave me his as my own."

"A wonderful story professor, but..."

"But what, *señorita*? Less than a year ago, I lost the love of my life. Should I be bitter that she is gone, or rejoice in the years that we had together? It's a simple choice is it not? And the choice is mine alone to make."

"So you are saying that it is my choice to simply disregard what has happened to me?"

"*Sí*, but first you must come to understand that the choice is truly yours to make; that is the difficult part. And you don't need specialists or drugs to help you come to that understanding."

They were both silent for a long while. He poured them both a little more tea. The sun had come up now and shone brightly across the lake. It was going to be a beautiful day.

Finally, the littlie man asked her one more question, "And just what future do you desire, *señorita*?"

The young woman immediately thought of Michael. "If you would excuse me now professor, I think that I'll just go back up to my room. Michael may not be up just yet."

The old man had a twinkle in his eye. "*Excelente*, a much better way to spend the morning than a solitary walk along the lake, I should think. Would you like me to cancel your appointment for this morning?"

"Yes, I think that would be a good idea. *Gracias*, Professor Alvarez." This time the young woman stood and took his hand in both of hers.

"*De nada...vía con dios, señorita.*"

Olivia left and the little professor sat back down. He knew that the young woman had only made a small first step in her recovery, but it was a very important step, nonetheless. Oh, how he missed Maggie at times such as this!

* * *

That very morning, some eight hundred kilometers away, another individual sat viewing the sunrise from his own balcony, overlooking the spectacular, cultivated gardens of his palatial estate just outside of Vienna. The aristocratic gentleman sipped at his coffee as he waited for his breakfast to be fetched by one of his servants. To bide the time, he scanned the news on his tabletop Holo. The man was Gerhardt Schmidt, owner of Eurodynamics, and therefore one of the richest and most powerful men in the world.

Schmidt was in his fifties, a tall man with thick hair that had gone completely gray. He was handsome in a vaguely cruel way, with blue-gray eyes that seemed to look right through a person. He inspired awe and respect in virtually everyone he met, along with some degree of fear in most. On the other hand, his looks, (along with his wealth and power) had proved irresistible to many women over the years, and he had taken full advantage of this fact. He had had a few wives, (primarily to provide him with heirs), along with several mistresses and countless casual lovers.

Just now, the cruelty showed a bit more than usual, for he was in a foul mood. The news was reporting once again on the explosion and fire at the Eurodynamics warehouse in Zurich, followed closely by the cyber-attack on his corporate network. The destruction of the warehouse had been a minor affair, a few million Euros and a few low level employees cremated. However, the sophisticated cyber-attack had disrupted Eurodynamics' financial and operations systems across Europe for days, costing his corporation billions. ACT, the Alliance of Cybernetic Terrorists, had claimed responsibility for both attacks, but, of course, he damn well knew better...it was Graham.

Just then, his servant arrived with his breakfast. As the servant arranged Schmidt's table, he noticed that the man also held a VR visor and gloves.

"What are those for, Stefan?"

"Sir, Mr. Graham and his chief of security have requested a VR conference with you at your earliest convenience. I brought these just in case you might want to meet with him after breakfast."

"Take those back and tell Mr. Graham that he can go through channels to set up an appointment some time next week." Schmidt let his irritation show. (He noticed with satisfaction that, in response, Stefan's hands were shaking just a bit.) *That bastard Graham wants to gloat; well, he'll just have to do it on my terms,* he thought to himself.

"Yes sir, but Mr. Graham said that it was a matter of utmost urgency. He said that he had information regarding your personal security and that he was concerned for your safety."

I'll bet, he thought to himself. Nonetheless, he decided to play out this little game. "Very well, then. Leave the visor and gloves and inform Mr. Graham that I will meet with him after breakfast, at, say, 9:15."

"Very well, sir."

With that, Stefan left the wealthy man to his solitary breakfast. After Schmidt had finished a leisurely morning meal and the table was cleared, he dismissed his servant. Moving inside to his office, he sat down at his desk and grudgingly donned the visor and gloves; he hated the things, in spite of the fact that they were necessary for a proper conference in virtual reality. Switching on the visor, he was instantly transported to a conference room in VR. Graham and a man that he surmised was Graham's security chief were seated across a conference table.

Graham spoke first, "Ah, Gerhard, you have arrived! Thank you for joining us with so little notice."

"Yes, yes, Jonathan; I'm afraid that I have a very busy schedule this morning, so I can only spare a little time."

Jonathan's VR avatar smiled warmly. "Of course, we will try to take as little of your time as possible."

Graham motioned to the other man. "Permit me to introduce Daniel Patrick McCafferty, my head of security."

McCafferty's avatar merely nodded, as did Schmidt's in return.

"At my direction, Mr. McCafferty and a small team of his intelligence experts have investigated the acts of terrorism committed against your corporation last week. As you can imagine, we are quite concerned that Graham Enterprises might be the next target of the terrorists. Although we have had little success, so far, in identifying the culprits, we do believe that we have stumbled across a plot to attack you personally."

Was this bastard threatening him? Schmidt wondered. "Jonathon, I appreciate your concern, but I can assure you that my own organization provides absolutely airtight security for myself and those near to me. I can further assure you that when we identify the culprits, *whoever they are*, we will respond most forcefully. If you have any hard intelligence, of course, you can have Mr. McCafferty pass it along to my organization through appropriate channels. Now then, if that is all, I must regretfully excuse myself."

Jonathan's image projected a look of sincere disappointment. "My friend, I was hoping that this crisis could open a new chapter in our relationship. Even though our companies compete with one another most aggressively in the fields of commerce and politics, I believe that we should nonetheless strive to ensure the heath and safety of those in each other's organizations. After all, we are all civilized, do you not agree?"

"Yes, yes. Nonetheless, I am quite satisfied with the status quo. You look after your people, Jonathan, and I will look after mine. Now, if you will forgive me, Jonathan...Mr. McCafferty, I must take my leave."

Jonathan and Mac barely had time to respond before Schmidt's avatar vanished as he switched off. Schmidt angrily stripped the visor and gloves off and threw them on his desk, then contacted Stefan on his wrist Uplink.

"Ready my sky cruiser, Stefan; I will be leaving for my corporate office within the hour." *Incredible! I have just been physically threatened! If Graham thinks he can intimidate me, he has miscalculated on a grand scale. Today, the gloves really come off!* Schmidt thought to himself as he hurriedly dressed. He planned to call an all-hands staff meeting of his department heads as soon as he arrived at headquarters. This very morning, an all-out war on Graham Enterprises would be declared.

* * *

"Well, Schmidt responded to our overture just about as you predicted, Jonathan. Arrogant bastard, isn't he?" Mac said as they each removed their VR visors.

"Mac, you only know the half of it..."

"So, I presume that we are authorized to activate project M.A.D.?"

"Immediately."

Mac quickly made a call, and headed down to the Command Center to set the plan in motion.

* * *

A few minutes after ten am, local time, Schmidt took the drop tube up to his private rooftop landing pad. The great man was meticulously dressed and groomed, as usual. He wore an elegant Italian suit tailored perfectly to his tall and well-proportioned frame. His gray hair, cut rather long, was nonetheless combed and trimmed perfectly. Schmidt was a man of meticulous detail and the attention he paid to his appearance was no exception.

The tycoon's sleek blue and white corporate sky cruiser waited with its engines idling. The Eurodynamics logo shone on each of the craft's twin vertical tails. A liveried flight attendant waited for him at the ramp. Boarding the craft, Gerhardt took his seat and allowed the restraints to conform to his body. To anyone else, the pure white leather interior with gold and mahogany trim would have seemed incredibly luxurious; the wealthy man took it all for granted. As he settled in, the attendant immediately served him a cup of the finest Guatemalan coffee in a cup and saucer of the best china. He gave a nod to the attendant, who ordered the cruiser's autopilot to depart its landing pad.

The craft's cockpit held a very experienced pilot and copilot, though their role was merely to act as a backup to the craft's cyber-systems. The flight from Schmidt's estate three hundred kilometers outside of Vienna to the roof of the Eurodynamics building in the center of the city would be controlled from takeoff to landing by the cruiser's cybernetic AI flight control system. The craft's AI, in turn, operated in concert with the regional air traffic system, which was itself totally automated.

The craft quickly and smoothly ascended to a cruising altitude of five thousand feet. The flight would take only a half hour. That would give Schmidt just enough time to finish his second cup of coffee of the morning...

* * *

During the assault on the warehouse one week prior, Jimmy Park had been assigned a task secondary to the actual rescue. The plan was for him to quickly make his way to the warehouse's presumed command center and try to find an open, unsecured channel into their adversaries' corporate network. Although standard security protocol would be for the security personnel to lock down any such channels, it was hoped that the speed and surprise of the assault might prevent such steps from being taken.

As Park and his partner, Willis, had assaulted the command center, they had quickly killed one guard and captured the other. However, all security channels had already been locked down. Nonetheless, it had only taken Willis a few intense moments with the surviving guard to convince him to log back on to the network; that was the good thing about mercenaries, their sense of loyalty was generally limited to their own personal well being.

Park had worked quickly; before the network security systems could respond, he had downloaded an intrusion program prepared by Graham's best cybernetic specialists. The program was designed to wreak havoc with all of the host's systems. Complete recovery, it was estimated, would take eight to ten days.

However, the damage was not an end in itself; rather, it was a cover. While the network security systems tried to deal with the initial damage, another, much more elusive program had insinuated itself into the enemy network. This program would surreptitiously intercept classified data, copy it and divert it to GRI's network. It was hoped that it might take days or weeks for Eurodynamics to identify and eliminate this program. In the meantime, it was hoped that GRI would reap a goldmine of intelligence.

* * *

As the craft glided through the morning sky, Schmidt sipped his coffee and mentally rehearsed what he would say to his senior staff. He would make it very clear to one and all that their future in his organization would be tied very directly to the single-minded ruthlessness that each individual demonstrated in this struggle with their declared enemy.

Suddenly, his reverie was interrupted as the craft was buffeted violently. The cup and saucer flew out of his hand and hot coffee was sprayed all over the seats as well as his suit. The attendant, who was just walking down the aisle to freshen his boss's coffee, was thrown to his knees. He had dropped the decanter of coffee. He looked at Schmidt, terrified.

After a few seconds, the craft seemed to go completely out of control. Schmidt tried to raise the autopilot or the flight crew, without any response. The cruiser began to plummet. Crazily, Schmidt thought of an amusement park ride that his wealthy parents had taken him on when he had been a small child. The ride had immediately dropped several hundred feet, making him sick and afraid. This was the same; only this time the fall seemed endless. The attendant was holding on to the bottoms of one of the seats, staring at Schmidt, his face ghostly white. The man's eyes were held almost comically wide in terror. Schmidt looked back at the man, thinking, *I'm going to die, staring at this fool.*

Then, just as suddenly, the craft stabilized. Schmidt looked out his window. The cruiser was skimming along just above the treetops. It had been that close.

Schmidt raised the pilot, letting his fury disguise his terror, "What the hell happened?"

"Sir, we have no idea at this time," the pilot's voice almost cracked in fear, as well, "All systems went down without warning a few moments ago, then restored themselves just in time."

Suddenly, one word came into Schmidt's mind...*Graham*...

* * *

"Mission accomplished," Mac, in the Command Center, relayed the information to Graham in his study.

"All appears to have gone exactly as planned."

Graham had dubbed the project M.A.D., after the old Cold War acronym: *m*utually *a*ssured *d*estruction. They had just demonstrated that force would henceforth be met with force, violence with violence, all the way to the top, if necessary.

"Good work, Mac; tell everyone how much I appreciate their efforts, and tell that young man Hammond to expect a bonus."

"With pleasure, sir."

Hammond was a junior cyber-analyst, one of many that had been assigned to the vast project of evaluating the massive amounts of supposedly secure data that GRI had begun surreptitiously snagging over the last several days from the Eurodynamics network.

While most of the senior analysts focused on the treasure trove of executive data streaming out of the corporate headquarters, young Hammond had spotted seemingly unimportant files containing the cyber-codes for the entire Eurodynamics corporate fleet. These were the Uplink codes that interfaced all of Eurodynamics craft with the international air traffic network.

Even Hammond's superiors hadn't recognized the import of these codes, at first. Hammond had; he had pointed out that with these codes, Graham Security could patch into the air traffic network and, literally, take remote control of any Eurodynamics' skycraft, including Schmidt's own personal cruiser. The information had quickly made its way to Mac and then Graham.

"Jonathan, we can take Schmidt himself out." Mac, after seeing what had been done to Olivia, had been in no mood for restraint.

"No Mac, we may all have to be soldiers in this conflict, but we really don't want to become assassins, do we? Besides, kill someone like Schmidt and, likely as not, someone will replace him that's even worse. I have a better idea."

Graham had then gone on to describe his plan to his security chief. First they would offer Schmidt an olive branch, which would, in actuality, be a thinly disguised ultimatum. Schmidt would doubtless refuse their offer and they would quickly respond with a demonstration that would prove that they could readily make good on their threat. Schmidt was no fool; when he realized that they could actually get to him at will, he would back off. He would doubtless continue to impede their project by every *peaceful* means at his disposal, but he would now be forced to accept the fact that he could employ violent methods only at his own peril. Mac had liked the plan.

* * *

They all sat down to a private candlelit dinner at the spa. The intimate dining room looked out over the dark expanse of Lake Geneva. The view was lovely; a crescent moon and a sea of stars were reflected on the black waters of the lake. Olivia and Michael were there, looking very much in love. Dr. Alvarez sat next across from the young couple, looking very pleased with himself.

Mac and his fiancée, Ellen, were also there. They had arrived the day before; after the excitement and success of the last few weeks, Graham had insisted that Mac and Ellen take a much-deserved vacation there, as well. The last dinner guest was the great man himself; Graham had just flown in that afternoon.

"Here's to Olivia, to her courage, to her resilience, and most of all, to her future happiness with Michael!" Graham raised his glass and they all responded with enthusiasm.

"Olivia, let me also say how much Jonathan and I regret the situation that we put you in, and how much you have suffered as a result." Mac's voice trembled a bit with emotion as he spoke.

Olivia responded by standing up; Michael thought that she looked both lovely and regal in the soft candlelight. (So did everyone else.) She stood silent for a moment, gathering her thoughts.

"Professor Alvarez, bless his heart, helped me put all of this in the proper perspective. Mac, without your courage, my life would have ended days ago. Thank you for my life. Jonathan, you have given me the chance to participate in what may be one of the most important efforts in history. Thank you for that opportunity. Finally, Michael you have given me something that I never really expected to experience in my life, unconditional love. Thank you for your love."

Olivia began to sit down, and then hesitated. "I hate to steal Michael's thunder yet again, but I have an announcement to make." She looked down at her fiancée, who was smiling at her and nodding.

"Michael, please stand by me." The young professor rose and put an arm around her.

"Michael and I have decided that this would be the perfect spot to be married, so we would like to invite all of you to our wedding this Saturday."

They all stood and raised their glasses once more to Olivia and Michael. As they congratulated the young couple, Olivia noticed Mac whispering something rather urgently in Ellen's ear. Ellen looked at Mac, nodded and then threw her arms around his neck, embracing him tightly. Mac raised his hands for silence.

"Ellen I and I would like to ask the two of you if you would mind very much if we made this a double wedding."

They all cheered at that...

* * *

The next morning was gray and overcast. Graham had invited just Olivia and Michael to a quiet continental breakfast on the patio overlooking the lake. After the three had been served and Graham had dismissed the waiter, he spoke to the young couple.

"I just wanted the both of you to understand clearly what your sacrifices have accomplished. First of all, we have already received quiet assurances from Gerhardt Schmidt that that any further physical attacks against us will cease, henceforth. He has even given us assurances that his partner organizations, such as TeleGrup, will cease any such hostile activity. That he is able to give such assurances on their behalf is telling in itself."

"We have also now confirmed, beyond any doubt, that Schmidt at Eurodynamics and Sergei Sergievich, the head of TeleGrup, are the ringleaders in the conspiracy against us. The heads of East Asia and Aramcorp appeared to be participants, as well, but seem to have a much more passive role."

"However, perhaps most important is what we have learned through the intercepts of Schmidt's own executive communications. We now understand the true motive behind the attacks. We had been led believe that the other "Great Powers" had been convinced that the GRI Report predicting a worldwide collapse was actually a ploy by Graham Enterprises to achieve worldwide economic domination. We now have evidence that, to the contrary, experts within both Eurodynamics and Telegrup have independently verified the conclusions drawn by the GRI Report."

Michael frowned in consternation. "Then, why in the world are they fighting us, rather than helping us?"

"They just don't want us to interfere with their plans. They are convinced that the worldwide collapse is inevitable, just as we are. Consequently, rather than engaging in what they believe is a futile effort to forestall the inevitable, they intend to try to shape the disaster in order to achieve their own ends. We now believe that they may actually try to hasten the collapse on their own terms, so that it is their organization that achieves domination over what is left of civilization...in another words, to create a new world order."

"Even if it's dominion over a new Dark Age?" Michael asked.

Olivia suddenly spoke up, "How does the old quote go? 'Tis better to reign in Hell than serve in Heaven...'"

Both men nodded gravely. All three were then silent for a while, looking out over the somber, fog-shrouded waters...

20

The Territories

As their party crested the eastern ridge of Miss Izzy's little valley, they each took one last look back. The old lady's little cabin was now well out of sight, but they could still see the lake that it lay next to, as well as the forest meadow that they knew it was nestled in.

Almost another month had passed since Valerian, Maya and Joshua had first prepared to leave; it had taken that long for Sebastian to recover fully from his wounds. When they had first brought the injured man into Miss Izzy's cabin, his broken leg had only partially mended, although he had managed to set it himself and had fashioned a splint out of small saplings. The big man was still feverish from his various wounds, the worst of which had become infected. Valerian had never seen his uncle look so pale or gaunt.

The two women had immediately set to work nursing Sebastian back to health, though the big woodsman had protested. They had cleaned him up and fed him just broth that first evening. Then, the next day, Miss Izzy had made poultices for his wounds and treated his fever with tea laced with herbs gathered from the forest. He had soon begun to regain his strength.

Several days later, as they had all sipped tea on the porch at sunset, Valerian had asked his uncle what had happened after they had left him behind on the mountainside.

"I harried the Zealot's all that afternoon, and all through the night. Killed some, and wounded most of the others. They were pretty stubborn; it was near dawn before them what was left had finally had enough. They just packed their mounts with their dead and wounded, and headed back down the trail. I was watching from an outcropping up above."

"It was still fairly dark and the Zealots were out of sight before I turned to follow you three. Then I got careless. The outcropping I was perched on gave way and I fell all the way down the cliff to the trail. If the Zealots had heard, I'da been done for."

"Anyway, I was hurt pretty bad, but by just mid mornin' I had managed to drag myself to the little plateau where it appeared you three had stopped to rest the night before. Camped by the little pool with the waterfall and patched myself up as best I could. Waited for a few days 'til I had got a bit of my strength back, then set out to follow you, using my war bow as a crutch."

"I'm surprised you were able to track us Uncle; I tried to cover our tracks pretty well, in case it was the Zealots who were still following us."

"You did right well in that regard, Valerian. Part of why it took me so long to catch up with you was that I had so much trouble picking up and following your trail. Don't think the Zealots would have ever managed it."

That note of approval, coming from his uncle, had given the young man a sense of quiet satisfaction.

"So, uncle, you never told me why you finally decided to follow me from home, or why you didn't just travel with me, instead of tracking me at a distance."

The older man didn't answer for a time. Finally, he spoke, "Didn't really decide until a few days after you left, lad. Tried to just go about my business, but discovered that I just couldn't get my mind off wonderin' where you where, what you were doin'."

"Or whether I was going to get myself into some sort of trouble that I couldn't get out of?"

"That too," the tough old Ranger admitted.

"Anyhow, I went to visit your Grandma to talk it over."

"And what did she say?"

"What do you reckon, lad? When I told her I was fretting over you, she ordered me in no uncertain terms to do somethin' about it. Told me to get my big old rear end movin' and follow you. You know, I've always pretty much gone my own way, cept'n when my Marian or your Grandma had made up their mind about somethin'."

Valerian hoped that his uncle couldn't see him grinning in the gathering darkness, at the thought of his strong-willed, little old grandma ordering his hard-headed, independent uncle about.

"Anyhow, I didn't catch up with you until the Caravan...almost lost your trail a few times too."

"Why didn't you just join me then, Uncle?"

"Figured I could cover your backside a bit better iffin I just trailed you."

"Looks like you were right about that, Uncle," the younger man admitted.

"Anyway, I sure am glad you're with us now."

* * *

And now they were on their way again. Valerian, like his two young companions, regretted leaving the little valley. However, with Sebastian by his side, Valerian's confidence in their ability to reach their destination had soared; the young man simply believed that his uncle was virtually invincible.

They soon settled back into a routine, except that now Sebastian typically ranged far ahead, marking a trail for them during the day, then joined them at dusk each day to make camp. Miss Izzy had told them that they would reach the eastern foothills in a fortnight; in fact they made it in a little over a week.

At long last, they reached the top of the last high ridge and were suddenly presented with a magnificent panorama of foothills and plains, covered with dense forests interspersed with rolling grasslands. In the distance they could make out two wide rivers and several lakes and smaller bodies of water. It seemed that flocks of wild birds covered the skies, and they could just make out a herd of elk and another of buffalo on the distant plains below. On the horizon, far to the east, were snowcapped peaks that seemed to dwarf even the mountain range they had just crossed.

It was late afternoon when they finally reached the bottom of the mountain trail. Sebastian was waiting for them there. He had ranged far ahead into the foothills, then had doubled back to lead them to a good, secluded spot that he had found for a campsite.

"We'll have to be right careful from here on in," the Ranger cautioned.

"I saw lots of man-signs hereabouts, horse tracks and such. We had better start traveling at night again. We'll turn south from here tomorrow, and if Miss Izzy was right, with any luck, we should find Elympias in a month or two."

They made camp late in that afternoon in a perfect little spot that Sebastian had discovered. It was a tiny meadow surrounded by steep hills that were covered by a dense thicket of brush and saplings. A small mountain stream traversed the meadow. At one end of the meadow, the stream opened into clear, rock-lined pond. Any intruder would have to either crash through the underbrush or splash up the creek to approach them; either way, they would have ample warning.

Maya started a small campfire as Joshua unpacked Samantha and set her out to graze. Sebastian and Valerian cut a few young saplings down and rigged them with lines and hooks from their packs. Then, as the sun began to set, they moved off to a likely spot to try to catch their dinner. They sat down by the pond, tossed their lines into the water and spoke in low tones so as not to scare the fish.

"I want you three to wait here until tomorrow night. Rest up and get some food in you. I'll scout ahead and see what I see. Then I'll be back for you tomorrow evening. Then we'll all head out together."

* * *

Their journey south was uneventful for the next several days. The going was slow, since Sebastian was determined to steer them through the densest forests that he could find, traveling only at night to lessen the possibility of their being discovered. Finally, they came to a wide river that crossed their path. They camped on a secluded bank while Sebastian ranged upriver looking for a spot shallow enough for them to ford.

The Ranger finally returned just before dawn, two days later. Maya and Valerian had already lit a small campfire and were heating a small pot of water for tea. Maya fetched Sebastian a hot cup of tea as he dropped his gear and sat down.

"Thank you lass, I haven't had anything but water, jerky and corncakes, since I left."

"Any luck, Uncle?" Valerian asked, as Maya also handed the young man a cup of tea and sat down next to him with her own cup.

Joshua, who had just awakened, was tending to his mule.

"Not what we hoped for lad. This river seems to stay wide and deep for many miles. However, I did find two farmsteads along the river with a few small boats, and a town with a ferry barge."

"Are either of the boats large enough to carry a mule," Joshua asked, as he came over and sat down with the others.

"Nope. In fact, either of them would be hard pressed to carry more than two of us with our gear."

"Then, how about the ferry?" Maya asked.

"Well, we could try, but it's likely to be right dangerous. We could just walk up to the ferryman and ask if we could pay to cross. The problem is, we have no idea how the townspeople around here treat strangers. For that matter, we don't even know how we would pay."

"Miss Izzy gave me some coins that she said would be good in most of the townships. She also said that most townspeople usually mind their own business around strangers," Maya responded.

"Is there any other way, Uncle?" Valerian didn't like the idea of just walking into a town filled with potentially hostile strangers.

"Well, we could try our luck downriver. But the river just seems to get even wider in that direction."

"So, what do you think we should do?" Valerian asked.

"Let me go into town, alone. See how I'm treated. Talk to the ferryman. If all looks well, I'll come back and fetch all of you. If I don't return, you three can go downriver and find another way."

"And just leave you, again?" Valerian asked.

"Lad, just what will it take to convince you that I can take care of myself?" the big man smiled.

In the end, they all agreed to the plan, (Valerian grudgingly). They then waited for nightfall and headed upriver. On his first reconnaissance, Sebastian had found another good, secluded campsite by the river just a half-day's march from the town. Valerian and his party would wait there for his uncle's return. Arriving at their new campsite before dawn, they unpacked, started a fire and made tea. Sebastian drank his tea with a corn cake, and then shouldered his pack and weapons.

"Wait two days for me lad, no more, no less. Iffin I don't show up by nightfall on the second day, head downriver. And good luck to you."

"Come back to us, Uncle." Valerian hugged the big man, as did Maya. The Ranger then headed out without further ado.

The two days passed, slowly but uneventfully. Nightfall arrived on the second day, and there was no sign of his uncle. Valerian paced back and forth in front of the campfire, as Maya roasted a rabbit that Valerian had snared earlier in the day.

"Sit down, Valerian. The rabbit is almost ready. And worrying won't help. Eat now and you can go into town after midnight to try to find your uncle..." Maya said.

"What?"

"You know that is what you want to do. You'll never forgive yourself if you leave him again," Maya responded.

"And what happens to you two if something happens to me, as well?"

"Well, just don't let anything happen to you. But if it does, Joshua and I will just have to manage."

For the rest of the evening, the young man was torn. In equal measure, he wanted to find his uncle and stay to protect Maya and Joshua. Though Maya served him some of the rabbit, he had lost his appetite.

In the end, it was Maya who was resolute. Late that night, after Joshua had fallen asleep, she kissed her young man, held him, and then handed him his cloak and weapons.

"Go my beloved, fetch your uncle, and then come back to me."

Valerian held her tightly. "I'll be back soon; that's a promise."

Without another word, he set off into the darkness. It was still well before dawn when he arrived at the outskirts of the town. All was quiet. Here and there, oil lamps were set at the corners of streets. Most had burned out, but a few still sent out a flickering light onto the dirt streets. A dog barked far in the distance, but Valerian reckoned that the far off noise posed little threat.

In the darkness of a back alley, the young man hid his pack and weapons, except for the knife and hand ax on his belt. Pulling the hood of his cloak over his head, he then boldly strode out onto one of the side streets. He headed toward the center of town, not sure what he was looking for. Soon, he reached the town square. There were more lamps here, most of which were still lit. So far, he had seen no one.

Looking about the square, he saw numerous wooden buildings that looked to be shops or residences. However, at the far side of the square, he saw one two-story building that appeared to be much larger than the others. It had two flags mounted on either side of the entrance. Then he noticed two uniformed guards standing at the entrance. He casually changed direction and headed back into the darkness.

Although it was only an educated guess, he suspected that if his uncle had been captured in the town, he very well might be a prisoner in that particular building. He decided to scout it out and see if there might be a window or back entrance that he could use to gain entry. Using utmost caution, in the shadows, he patiently worked his way to the back of the building. There was a back door, but when he tried it, he discovered without surprise that it was latched from within. There were side windows, but they too were latched, and he was sure that there was no way that he could force them without alerting the guards at the front entrance. Looking up from the back alley, he saw two open windows, but they were well out of reach from below.

However, he remembered that he had seen a drainpipe on one side of the building. Looking again, he saw that he could scale it to the roof. From the roof, he just might be able to make it to one of the open windows. Without hesitation, he quietly made his way to the drainpipe and began climbing. In just moments he was up and over the edge of the roof...so far, so good.

But as the young man looked out over the town from his perch, he noticed the first gray light of dawn had appeared on the horizon. He would have to hurry. Moving to the edge of the roof, he peered over the edge. Directly below was the sill of one of the open windows...far below. The distance between the edge of the roof and the window sill appeared much greater that it had from the ground. He thought that he just might be able to swing down, drop and grab the window ledge, but the resulting racket would surely alert the guards, or whoever might be sleeping inside. He wished he had a rope.

However, he was steadying himself at the edge of the roof by holding onto small a chimney pipe. Perhaps he could tie his cloak to the pipe and lower himself to the sill, he thought. He tried it, and in just a short time he had clambered through the window. Although he had made a bit of a racket, he didn't think that it was enough to have alerted the guards out front.

The room he had entered was dark and unoccupied. It appeared to be some sort of office. Carefully, he made his way to the door and cracked it open. There were a few lamps in the hallway. Across the hallway were two doors with iron bars...cells! He crossed his fingers. Looking both ways down the hall, he quietly opened the door and entered the hallway.

"Uncle!" he whispered into each cell.

"Valerian, you young fool; you should be miles away from here by now!" his uncle replied from the second cell.

The young man ignored the admonishment. "I'm going to get you out of here, Uncle. I'll try to find the keys downstairs."

"There are guards downstairs, lad," his uncle hissed, "get out now whilst you still can!"

Even as his uncle whispered his warning, Valerian moved to the stairs. Dawn was coming; he needed to move fast. Looking down the stairs, he saw...two guards coming up the stairs with swords drawn! Spinning quickly, he made for the window in the back room, with the guards running up the stairs close behind. Looking out the window, he looked down only two see two more guards below waiting for him.

Out of options, the young man turned. In an instant, one guard held a very wicked looking sword at his chest. Meanwhile, the other disarmed him, held his wrists from behind and pushed him roughly into the other cell. As they locked him up, Valerian asked the guards what they were going to do with him and his uncle.

"Our Town Magistrate will see the both of you the morning," the guard responded, "and the Commander of the Territorial Militia is supposed to arrive today, to boot. Between the two of 'em, I reckon they'll decide what to do with you."

Valerian lay down on his cot. After the guards had returned to their posts, the young man spoke up. "Sorry Uncle, I should have heeded your advice."

"That's all right Valerian. All may not be lost. These folks seem right civilized, almost like Elympians. Notice how the guards have proper uniforms. They just locked me up me because they think I'm a Raider. Seems I wouldn't tell a couple of inquisitive militiamen that crossed paths with me who I was or what I was up to. Still, they didn't treat me badly... they've even fed me good meals. We still may be able to straighten this all out."

Sure enough, in a while, their captors brought them a hearty breakfast. Shortly after, the guards bound the two prisoners' hands in front of them, and led them downstairs to the Magistrate's office. The Magistrate was elderly, tall and rather rotund, with gray hair and a large gray beard. He projected an air of authority, yet seemed friendly enough. He motioned to two chairs across from his large oaken desk.

"Gentlemen, please be seated. I apologize that we must keep you bound for the time being. However, we must be cautious until we understand a bit more about where you are from and what your intentions are."

"I can tell you that we are Elympians from across the mountains, but in return I will tell you no more until I understand your own intentions," Sebastian countered.

The Magistrate smiled. "Elympians, indeed. I would find that hard to believe, except possibly for the strangeness of your speech and dress. No one has ever seen an Elympian that I know of. In any case, let me begin with introductions. My name is Jebedia Smythe, Magistrate of the township of Marlt'n. And how should I address you two?"

"I am called Sebastian, and this be my nephew, Valerian."

"Pleased to meet you both. Now, since the two of you are supposedly strangers from far away, let me tell you just a bit about the situation that we are faced with hereabouts. As you perhaps know, the Territories have also been known as the Lawless Lands for as far back as anyone can remember…and with good reason. For countless years, Raiders crisscrossed the Territories robbing, raping and sometimes killing at will."

"All of that began to change some ten years ago. The Magistrates of three townships north of here met and drew up a treaty of mutual protection. They combined their small militias into one larger territorial militia, and then set about driving the Raiders out of their lands. A young militia officer named Rawlins was named Commander of the combined Territorial Militia. He turned out to be a brilliant military leader; and had soon succeeded in achieving an unheard of peace and stability for their combined territories. As the years have passed, many other townships have joined the alliance, including our own."

"The townships are still independent, but the Northern Territories now have a representative assembly that meets twice a year, courts and a large Territorial Militia, which remains under the command of Rawlins."

"However, restoring peace and the rule of law hasn't been easy. The Raiders have organized as well, and a guerilla war has developed with the Southern Territories under their control. Because our townships are open, the Raiders have found it easy to gather intelligence; hence, our suspicion of strangers."

"I see; so you thought we were spies."

"Suspected as much, yes. As luck would have it, the Commander Rawlins is encamped with a detachment nearby. Word was sent to him of your capture and word has already come back that he would like to interrogate you himself. We expect his arrival sometime this afternoon. If you are who you say you are, then you should have nothing to worry about."

With that, Sebastian and his nephew were led back to their cells. Valerian had already begun to worry about Maya and Joshua. "I shouldn't have left them alone, Uncle."

"Don't worry too much, just yet, Valerian. The lass a good head on her shoulders. She'll lie low and wait for us for a good long while. Hopefully, we'll get this sorted out today and we'll be let loose to fetch her directly..."

Nonetheless, the hours dragged by slowly, interrupted only when their guards brought them a simple midday meal of cheese and bread. Finally, in late afternoon, the guards once again tied their hands and led them back to the Magistrate's office.

The Magistrate was seated at his desk, as before, but next to the desk stood a uniformed black man cut from an altogether cloth. To Valerian, he looked something like a younger, leaner version of his own uncle. This man was tall, with ebony skin that covered a rugged, muscular frame. He had a broad, easy smile, which in no way diminished the authority that he projected. His clean but well-worn uniform consisted of a dark blue tunic and trousers, with high black riding boots and a broad black belt. The uniform bore no insignia or medals, though a short saber hung at his side.

As the Magistrate had before, this new man beckoned them to their seats.

"Gentlemen, my name is Commander Rawlins. The Magistrate has told me your story. If you are who you say you are, then you have nothing to fear from us. However, if you are Raider spies, you would do well to admit so now. At this point, you might still find some leniency. However, keeping to a false story will lead you very quickly to a hangman's rope."

"We be of the Elympian Clan, Commander, and we would have nothing to do with any Raiders," Sebastian responded.

"Then what would your business be?" the Commander asked.

"That I cannot say," the Ranger answered.

"If you cannot say, how would you expect us to believe you?"

"As the Magistrate said, just witness our foreign clothes and speech."

"That might make a good disguise for Raider agents, don't you think?" the Commander countered.

"We could recite the 21 Laws of Elympias..." Valerian spoke up.

"Never heard of 'em; wouldn't mean a thing to me."

They seemed to be at an impasse. Neither Sebastian nor Valerian could think of a way to convince the Commander that they were who they said they were. Valerian was considering just telling the two men of his quest when the Commander spoke again.

"I have been fighting the Raiders and the chaos they bring for some thirty years now. In that time, I have seen every form of deceit and skullduggery you two can imagine. Still, I want to keep an open mind; I can remember how my brother and I had to fight for trust and acceptance when we first came down from the mountains so many years ago."

Valerian and his uncle just looked at each other. They both smiled. Could it be? The Commander frowned.

"Did I say something humorous, gentlemen?"

Valerian answered, "No sir, begging your pardon. May I ask your first name, sir?"

Now it was the Commander and the Magistrate that looked at each other, "I don't see why not. It's Aaron."

Now the two Elympians laughed. Valerian responded, "And your brother's name is Will, I expect. Commander Rawlins, Aaron, your mother, Miss Izzy, says hello."

* * *

Valerian and his uncle mounted up now; guards had fetched their weapons and gear, (someone had even recovered Valerian's cloak from the roof). A dozen of the Commander's elite personal cavalry escorted them. The sun was low on the horizon, but they hoped that if they rode fast enough, they could reach Maya and Joshua before darkness had fallen. They set out at a gallop.

The hard-bitten Commander had looked near tears when Valerian had told him of his mother. Years before, a pair of trappers had told Rawlins that they had had found the bodies of his mother and father in his parent's cabin. He had believed the story back then and now could only wonder why the trappers had lied to him. Meanwhile, over the years, he had been consumed with the conflict that had eventually taken his brother's life.

Valerian's heart pounded as they neared the campsite. The sun was now setting. Once their party was reunited and they had all returned to the town, Valerian planned to tell the Commander of his quest. With luck, the young man hoped that they might have an armed escort all the way to Elympias. His goal now looked nearer and more attainable than ever.

His uncle first spotted the site in the gathering darkness. Valerian kicked his mount and took the lead. As he neared the site, he shouted Maya's name. He heard nothing in return. The young man quickly dismounted and ran through the thicket that had hidden the campsite, even as his uncle shouted for him to wait. Ignoring the older man he broke through the brush to see...nothing.

The site was abandoned. The campfire still smoldered. Had they left for some reason, or had something worse happened? Valerian looked for clues, but could make nothing out in the darkness. His uncle arrived in a moment.

"Valerian, rushing ahead like that was foolhardy; there could have been an ambush set."

"Can you tell what happened, uncle?"

"Too dark, we need to make torches."

Sebastian waved the cavalrymen back so that they wouldn't disturb any signs, and directed them to make torches. After this was done, the old woodsman returned to the site with his nephew on his heels. He studied every square foot of the camp and the surrounding area. The news wasn't good.

"I make the tracks of eight or ten men. They surrounded the campsite, and then moved in. Someone, probably Maya, almost escaped, but they brought her down by the river bank. There was a struggle. Then they brought their mounts from the woods over there, and headed west at a trot."

"How long ago, uncle?"

"I'd say this happened around about mid-day."

"So they have about six hours on us. Let's go!"

"Wait," interrupted the captain of the cavalry, a tall, taciturn man named Hawkins, "following them in the darkness would be suicide. Eight or ten men would make a small Raider scouting party. They would probably have joined up with a much larger group hidden deep in the forest. If we blundered into them in the darkness we'd be cut to pieces,"

"The captain's right, Valerian. We'll leave at first light. Meanwhile, perhaps the captain can send word back to town to ask his commander to send a larger detachment to follow us."

The captain nodded. "With pleasure, sir. We'd love to track down these vermin."

Valerian wouldn't be deterred. "That's fine, then. I'll leave now and mark a trail. The rest of you can follow in the morning."

His uncle shook his head in exasperation. "No lad, you're a good tracker and fair woodsman, but not that good. There is only a quarter moon and the stars to light the way; following their trail would tax even my skills, much less yours. Besides, even if you did manage to track them down, likely as not you'd just get yourself killed."

"Nonetheless..."

The old warrior sighed, "Nonetheless, I'll try to track them tonight, lad, and mark a trail. You follow with these men at first light, but not before."

Valerian finally relented. He knew that if Maya and Joshua could be rescued, their best hope lay with his uncle's extraordinary abilities. Sebastian soon left on foot at a trot, the only way he could track in the darkness. The old woodsman could keep a steady pace throughout the night, covering many miles.

The young man and the cavalry detachment made camp. The men lit a small campfire for tea and ate cold rations. Valerian had no appetite. Posting sentries, most of the men soon turned in. Wrapped in his cloak, Valerian lay wide-awake. He looked up at the brilliant canopy of stars and listened to the murmuring of the river nearby. Nothing mattered to him now, but the safe return of the girl he loved, not his quest, not even his own life. He would still be wide-awake at the sun's first light...

21

The Encampment

The old woodsman was definitely feeling his age this night; his recently mended leg especially pained him. However, he ignored his aches and pains and kept up a relentless dogtrot through the night, hour after hour. Periodically, he would make an "X" on a tree trunk, the pre-arranged sign for those who would follow. Occasionally, he would also pause and kneel for just a moment, making sure that he still had the trail. In this regard, he was lucky; even though there was little light, the ground was soft and the tracks of the mounted party were fresh and clear.

Around midnight, the trail entered a more densely forested area. The thick foliage cut the moonlight even further; nonetheless, the trail remained blessedly easy to follow. He came to a stream. He could tell that the raiding party had stopped there to water their horses and rest. It was obvious to him that they had dismounted for some time. A few Raiders had backtracked a ways on foot, presumably to see if they were being followed.

Sebastian himself stopped for just a moment to drink from the stream and splash some water on his face. He took the time to gather his thoughts, as well. The Raiders had begun with a five or six hour lead. The signs indicated that they had stopped here for perhaps an hour or so. In this forest, they would probably have wanted to reach their base camp by nightfall, (riding through here in the darkness would be a good way to get your neck broken!) Therefore, doing the math, he estimated that if he pushed on, he should be catching up with them in an hour or two, at most.

Sebastian crossed the stream, but could not readily find the tracks on the other side. He splashed downstream a ways, but found nothing. He now became concerned that he would again fall behind if it took too long to pick up their trail again. He turned and headed upstream now. After a time, in the dim light, he spotted some underbrush slightly disturbed on the other side of the stream. It was their trail, and he had only lost perhaps a half hour! (That they had taken such an effort to cover their tracks was another sign that their camp must be near.)

So, he pushed on, but he gradually began to trade speed for stealth; the last thing he wanted was to blunder into the Raider's camp and alert them. In any case, the best time to scout the camp would be in the early morning hours.

A few hours later, now moving at just a brisk walk, he caught the first faint signs of an encampment: the smells of campfires, followed closely by the boisterous sounds of drunken men and women. Pickets would most likely be set along any likely points of access to the encampment, so the old Ranger quickly moved off of the trail, and instantly became little more than a wraith in the forest.

Sure enough, after a short while, he observed two sentries "hidden" near the trail, on the side of a hill. He glided past them effortlessly in the darkness. At the crest of the hill, concealed in a thicket, he came upon the encampment.

The Raider camp was much larger than he had expected. There were dozens of campfires lit in the small valley below, surrounded by hundreds of makeshift tents. So, now Sebastian's concern was to try pinpoint in this large camp precisely where Maya and Joshua were being held prisoner before the rescue party arrived.

* * *

Nearing dawn, the young girl had gradually come to realize that she had become no more than the grand prize in a game of chance. She was gagged and her hands were bound to a small sapling behind her back. She sat perhaps ten paces from one of the many campfires, next to which squatted a half dozen drunken men playing some unfamiliar game of chance with dice and cards. Perhaps another dozen spectators surrounded the gamblers. All were foul smelling, filthy brutes, men and women alike, swilling ale from large mugs, laughing and punching one another as each hand was played. As one or another player seemed to get the upper hand, he would look to her with hungry eyes; some would make obscene gestures in her direction, as well.

Maya could just make out Joshua's bound and inert form on the other side of the campfire. The youth had fought courageously when they had first been ambushed at their own camp. He had almost created enough of a distraction for her to escape; she had broken for the river, but had been tackled by one of the Raiders just before she was able to dive in.

For his efforts, Joshua had been badly beaten. He might have been killed if the leader of the Raiders hadn't intervened.

"Enough...th' stripling has sand, he'll make a good Raider, onc't he's broke in," he had said with the Raider's barely intelligible dialect.

They had thrown the youth's unconscious body across Samantha. Then they had gagged and blindfolded Maya and tied her hands around one of the mounted riders, a massive man who smelled like he had probably never once in his life been washed. The ride had been an endless nightmare.

At the camp, a few old hags had removed her blindfold and gag, and then retied her hands in front of her. They had allowed her to relieve herself behind some bushes and then had given her some water, which she had gulped down. Bound to the sapling as darkness fell, one of the toothless old women had tried to feed her some broth. The stuff was disgusting and the girl had spit it out. The old women had looked at her blankly for a moment, and then slapped her hard with the back of her hand. The girl had tasted the blood of her split lip as the hag replaced the gag and stalked away without a word.

The feasting, drinking and gambling had commenced as darkness fell. As Maya looked around, she had noticed that other women and youths were tied to nearby trees and posts, doubtless captured by other raiding parties.

Maya dreaded what she knew must come soon. She had already seen it happen at two other nearby campfires. A player would win a final hand, to the raucous cheers and jeers from players and spectators alike. The winner would then rise in triumph, strut over to a prisoner, cut her loose and then drag her wailing into a tent.

One drunken Raider, a big bearded man, staggered out of the darkness towards Maya. She stiffened, not knowing what to expect, but he just gave her a passing glance and stumbled on, upending a huge mug of ale as he passed back into the darkness.

A short while later, a huge cheer from the gamblers as one stood up, raising his arms in victory. He threw his cards down and turned towards Maya with a big smile, rubbing his hands together. He staggered over to her, pulling a knife as he approached. As he bent down and cut her loose from the sapling, his face came near hers. He was a young man, tall and thin, but his breath reeked of ale and bad food and his eyes were glazed by drunkenness.

His speech was so slurred, that, together with his accent, she could barely understand him. "C'mon li'l one...b'have y'self and I'll take go' care of ye."

The drunken Raider dragged her up and shoved her roughly towards a nearby tent. Her hands were still tied behind her. She stumbled ahead, praying that in his drunken stupor, he might prove careless. She decided to feign submission and wait for her chance. If she could just get to his knife...

It was complete darkness inside the tent. The man shoved her down and fell down on top of her. He groped her and tried to undress her. She kept her legs locked together, desperately trying to resist without angering him. The struggle in the darkness seemed to last forever. Then suddenly, blessedly, it was over. He relaxed and then began breathing regularly. Soon he was snoring loudly. In spite of herself, she whimpered and then began to quietly weep.

He was lying across her so that she could barely move. She finally gained control of herself. She tried to gradually work her way out from under him, but it was no good. Every time she pushed too hard, he shifted, threatening to wake up. She waited in misery for the dawn...

* * *

It was Maya, without a doubt. He had passed to within a few paces of her and even she had not recognized him. He had spotted the boy a short distance away, as well. He had watched in the darkness as the girl had been led into the tent. It had pained him, but he knew he must be patient. There were just too many people still awake all around. Even with his skills, attempting to get her out of that tent right now would doubtless mean death for them both.

Sebastian meandered toward the outer edge of the encampment, continuing to feign drunkenness. He needed to move quickly now; dawn's first light was no more than a few hours away. In a dense thicket, he recovered his tunic and gear. The body of a big Raider was concealed just a few paces away. The man had provided the old Ranger with the typical floppy hat, trousers and jacket of a Raider.

It had been easy enough; Sebastian had just waited for one of the drunks, (a big one about his size) to head into the darkness to relieve himself. Several moments later, Sebastian had emerged looking, for all of the world like a Raider; his victim had even provided him with a half-filled mug of ale, (nasty stuff, but it had at least quenched his thirst...and provided him with a prop.)

Quickly, now, he melted back into the forest, slipping effortlessly past the sleepy pickets. Soon he had found the trail back. Now, though tired, he let out the stops, setting himself a killing pace. He wanted to meet the rescue party as far away from the enemy encampment as possible. He just hoped that the cavalry was indeed on their way...

* * *

It was just an hour or so after dawn, and Valerian now rode at the head of a column of a hundred and twenty cavalrymen. They seemed to be a tough, disciplined lot, dressed in the dark blue trousers, tunics and the bronze and leather helmets of the Territorial Militia. All were armed with lances, war bows and sabers.

Just ahead of Valerian rode Hawkins and Commander Rawlins; the young man had been shocked when Rawlins himself had arrived with his men at dawn.

"Sorry that it took this long to get here, lad. By the time the messenger arrived in town and we had sent for a couple of cavalry companies, it was already quite late in the evening. We had to push on through the night to get here by dawn," Rawlins had explained.

Valerian had thanked the Commander, and explained that his uncle had ranged ahead during the night in pursuit of the Raiders. Rawlins had immediately sent several scouts at a fast gallop to follow. The scouts would try to follow Sebastian's trail, watching out for signs of either Sebastian or an ambush.

After perhaps three hours, Valerian and Rawlins spotted two riders returning at a gallop. As they neared, Valerian realized that one of the riders was his uncle. He kicked his mount to meet them, as did the Commander and Hawkins. The three intercepted Sebastian and the scout perhaps a hundred paces ahead of the column.

"Uncle! What news have you?" Valerian almost shouted as he and his uncle embraced while still on horseback.

The older man looked tired but determined. He dismounted, as did the other men. Hawkins handed Sebastian a canteen and some jerky from his saddlebag. The big man gulped some water and splashed more on his face before he spoke.

"The girl and boy are still safe for now, lad, although I think that the boy is hurt. I've seen 'em both close up inside the camp. But Commander, it's a mighty big encampment, I'm not sure iffin you have enough men to take 'em on. I estimate that they have better'n three times as many fighting men as you do."

"Hmm...must be a major base for the Raiders. We could deal them a serious blow in this region if we destroy the camp. Still, though my men are good, three to one would be pushing it," Rawlins replied, "unless, that is, if we took 'em completely by surprise..."

Sebastian looked up and gave the man a big grin. "Well, Commander, that just happens to be my speciality!"

With that, before mounting back up, the two men worked out a hasty plan. Soon, Sebastian was headed back once again toward the Raider encampment, with Valerian and six more scouts close on his heals. Riding hard, Valerian was still amazed by his uncle's stamina. The older man had run through the night for hours, infiltrated an enemy encampment and then run and rode back for hours more.

After a time, they caught up with the four forward scouts, who had waited for them. Together, they moved ahead, until Sebastian had estimated that they were within a half-mile of the encampment. The Ranger then ordered most of the scouts to conceal themselves well away from the trail. By now it was mid-morning and he was afraid that the Raiders might soon be sending out their own scouting or raiding parties.

Sebastian had told the leader of the scouts, "Iffin you spot a raiding party headed out from the camp and think you can take 'em, do it. Just don't let any survivors loose to come back and warn the rest."

Then Sebastian, Valerian and two of the scouts headed toward the encampment on foot. Soon, the four were within a hundred paces of where the Ranger knew they would find the first pickets. Now they must wait; the old warrior knew that timing was crucial. If they took out the sentries too soon, the odds would be too great that they would be missed. He had paid careful attention to the distance traveled, so he had a pretty good idea how long it would take for Rawlins and his men to catch up.

When it was time, the Ranger had the two scouts conceal themselves nearby, (he wasn't sure enough of their woodsman's skills to use them just yet). Then he took his nephew forward until they saw the first sentry.

"Can you do it, lad? It must be done silently and without hesitation," the older man whispered.

"They have Maya in there, Uncle. I'll do whatever it takes," the younger man whispered back.

The look in Valerian's eyes told the Ranger all he needed to know.

"Then wait for the hoot of an owl and make yo'r move."

In an instant his uncle had disappeared.

*** * * ***

Maya woke up just after the sun had risen. Somehow, exhaustion had overcome fear and, sometime before dawn, she had fallen asleep. The Raider was still asleep and snoring loudly. He had rolled off of her in the night, but lay right across the entrance to the tent.

She sat up awkwardly, with her hands still bound behind her. Her hands and arms screamed at her. She looked about for the knife, but saw nothing. She assumed the man had concealed it somewhere in his clothes. She looked about inside the tent for anything else she could use to cut herself free. There wasn't much: a few old saddle blankets, a candle in an old brass holder, some coins in one corner along with some playing cards, an almost empty liquor bottle. Nothing useful.

The young girl shifted so that she could just see outside the tent. People were moving about sluggishly, starting cook fires, and drinking tea for their hangovers. She could hear a mule braying in the distance and wondered whether it was Samantha. She looked where Joshua had lain the night before, but couldn't see any sign of him. She lay back and curled up in misery.

She wondered what had become of Valerian and his uncle. She prayed that they were safe. She despaired that Valerian would ever know what had happened to her. What a fine time they had had together! Even if the worst happened, it was worth it...how she loved him! Even now, thinking of him brought a faint smile to her pretty face. A single tear rolled down her cheek.

Out of nowhere a vision came to her...a big man staggering towards her in the darkness, his face covered by a big floppy hat. An instant's hesitation, then moving on. Something familiar...about his walk, maybe. Could it have been? No, it must be just wishful thinking...

* * *

The owl hooted. It sounded exactly like an owl too, Valerian noted to himself as he moved in. Although he could have readily struck the sentry with an arrow, he couldn't take the chance that his victim might cry out. So he would use the knife. Leaving his other weapons behind, the young woodsman crept through the underbrush, slowly, carefully. He took his time, making no sound, angling out of the sentry's line of sight, using every ounce of cover to hide his approach. He became a ghost in the forest...just as his uncle had taught him.

He stood up right behind the sentry; the man held a lance in one hand and looked to be chewing on a turkey leg with the other. He had no inkling that it would be his last meal. Valerian rose up, and without hesitation drove the knife into the man's lower back, as he simultaneously covered his victim's mouth with his other hand. The big man grunted softly then collapsed. Valerian caught him and lowered him gently, so that not even the noise of his fall disturbed the silence of the forest. He dragged the body into a nearby thicket and quickly concealed all traces of the struggle. He then slipped back to where he had left his weapons. He was surprised at how calm he had remained.

The owl hooted softly again. Valerian moved toward the sound, silently and almost invisibly. His uncle appeared out of nowhere, tapping him on the shoulder, startling him. Without doubt the other sentry was dead.

The Ranger motioned to his nephew to follow; they slipped back to where they had left the scouts. The two scouts were also surprised when the two woodsmen seemed to materialize out of nowhere. Sebastian put a hand on one man's shoulder.

"Get on back to yo'r Commander and tell him that the way's open. Move fast. Me and the lad are going to scout about and take care of anyone else who might sound the alarm. Just tell Rawlins to hit 'em hard and fast."

"I won't need to tell him that, sir," the young man replied, "that's they only way he knows how to do it." With that he and his partner moved out, at a run.

"Let's go lad..."

* * *

One of the camp hags (as Maya had come to think of them) opened the flap of the tent and kicked the young Raider in the head.

"Wake up, Crowe, iffin y'want vittles fer you and your li'l plaything." The old woman leered at Maya as she kicked him again.

"As fer you, y'er highness, soon's ya eat some slops, it's to work." The flap dropped back down as the young man stirred, cursed and sat up.

"Damn m' head hurts...gotta piss." He finally seemed to remember Maya, looked over at her and gave her a cruel smile.

"Oh yea, m' prize...not sure, but I don't think we got our bidness done last night...s'okay, we'll take care of it soon's we eat." With that, the young Raider reached over and grabbed her thigh. She yelped, in spite of herself, and recoiled in horror. He laughed and went to the side of the tent to relieve himself. The young woman resolved to either kill him or herself at the first opportunity.

After he had eaten, Crowe returned with a bowl of porridge and a cup of tea. Before he cut her hands free, he tied her ankles with a leather strap; he was taking no chances. She stretched and tried to get the circulation back into her arms and hands. Grudgingly she took the tin cup of tea; she couldn't resist. As she drank the hot liquid, she actually began to feel a little human again, but she refused the porridge.

"Eat...y'er goin' t need y'er stren'th directly." He leered at her again.

Maya threw the bowl down as angry tears rolled down her cheeks. In response, surprisingly, he softened. "Never could deal w' a woman bawl'n. Tell'ya what, jus' eat and I'll give ya' a day or two to get used to th' ide' that y'er m'woman."

She didn't speak, but she nodded and picked up the bowl. There was no spoon, so she had to pick at it with her fingers. She even forced a little pained smile for him. Really looking at the young man for the first time, she even managed to feel a bit sorry for him. He might have even been good looking except for his bad teeth, his wild hair and beard and his filthy clothes. Still, she shivered at the thought of his touch. He sat across from her, just looking at her eat, as he finished his own cup of tea. He realized, in his own coarse way, that he was smitten with her.

* * *

The two men were well concealed in a thicket at the top of the hill. The older man had pointed out to the younger the tent where he hoped that Maya was still held captive. Once the battle started they would make their way directly to the tent as quickly as possible.

Sebastian was fretting just now. He and Valerian had had successfully intercepted two more sentries coming over the hill, presumably to relieve the two they had already eliminated. Sooner or later, the first two would be expected back at the camp. The Ranger just hoped that the Militia would arrive first.

A short while later, (though it seemed an eternity), Sebastian heard the faint sounds of mounted riders. The old warrior noted with satisfaction the discipline of the cavalrymen; there was no talking, no rattling of weapons or equipment, just the muffled sound of horses' hooves on the soft ground.

He sent Valerian down to meet the riders, as he continued to watch the camp. So far, the camp remained quiet. Sebastian surmised that the Raiders and their followers were still trying to shake off their collective hangover. Directly, Rawlins, Hawkins and his nephew joined the Ranger at the crest of the hill. The Commander took out some Ancient field glasses and quickly assessed the layout of the encampment.

"Do you know where your friends are?" he whispered.

Sebastian pointed out the tent that he suspected held the girl. He had no idea where the boy was now held. "Commander, tell your men to take care; there are many women and children held captive down there."

"We always do. Raider camps generally hold many prisoners. We only kill those who fight us. Hawkins, we'll perform an envelopment. You lead one company to the right; I'll lead the other to the left. We'll circle around.

Then, on my signal, we'll attack to the center. It'll look like we're comin' at 'em from all directions."

Hawkins smiled, saluted and immediately headed downhill to prepare the men.

"Ranger, I'm assigning all ten scouts to you; they're some of my best men. I'm putting two other men on foot so you can have their horses. Godspeed!"

"And to you, Commander." Sebastian shook his hand before they all headed downhill. In a few minutes, they had all mounted up and headed back up the hill in two columns. Sebastian thought to himself, as he rode up, that these men looked like they could even give an Elympian cavalry unit a hard time.

At the crest of the hill, the Commander and Hawkins split and spurred their mounts forward at a gallop, with their men close behind. As planned, one column swung to the left, the other to the right, beginning the encirclement of the camp. Still, none of the cavalrymen made a sound... no war cries, no shouts.

Meanwhile, Sebastian and Valerian, with their scouts following closely, broke straight into the center of the encampment at a dead run. They were dimly aware of Raiders scattered about them, first being taken completely by surprise, hesitating in confusion, then shouting out alarms and running for their weapons.

Valerian took the lead, racing for the one he loved. Raiders began to come at him from both sides with hastily recovered swords or lances, but he rode past before they could reach him. Sebastian, just behind his nephew, ran interference as best he could, riding down some of the attacking Raiders and using his lance on others. The scouts, who had formed a ragged wedge behind the two leaders, followed suit.

Even as he fought, the Ranger, no stranger to the battlefield, kept a part of his attention on how the battle around him was developing. The Raiders, at first running and attempting to fight in all directions, were gradually being organized into a perimeter by their leaders, who recognized that the primary threat was from the main body of cavalry that was quickly encircling their camp. This helped their progress, as Raiders, who had been attacking in their direction were ordered to form a line.

Nonetheless, Sebastian and the scouts had their hands full with the remaining attackers, falling behind Valerian as he flew ahead.

"Valerian! Stay back with us or you'll be cut off!" the big man bellowed, but his voiced was instantly drowned out by the rising sounds of battle.

Just as Sebastian shouted, a Raider on foot rushed forward, driving a lance into the chest of the Ranger's mount. As the big man fell, the scout behind him instantly skewered the Raider himself. The horse collapsed forward and the old warrior was just barely able to roll off without being caught underneath.

Suddenly, all was chaos, as other Raiders, seeing one of the enemy go down, rushed forward to press the attack. In a split second, the scouts were surrounded and fighting for their lives. Sebastian quickly leapt to his feet. He had lost his lance in the fall, the bow on back was useless in close-in fighting, but the old warrior was equally deadly with the long knife and hatchet at his belt.

In a flash, the big man had pulled both weapons and charged at the first Raider that had come his way. The man was tall and thin and carried a short sword. The Ranger parried a swing of the sword with his hatchet and drove his knife into the man's side. A hatchet blow to the head finished him. Then old warrior turned to attack the next adversary. They were now surrounded by a mob of Raiders.

As the Ranger fought on foot, the scouts' leader shouted, "Dismount! Sabers!" The men leapt down, driving their mounts into their opponents, while pulling their sabers. Together with Sebastian, they quickly formed a rough circle of flashing steel, facing outward. Just then, a bugle sounded in the distance, followed by the shout of a hundred men in unison. Many in the mob turned to face outward, as the cavalry, which had completed its encirclement, charged towards the center.

Meanwhile, Valerian, with all of his attention focused on finding the tent where Maya was held captive, had only come to realize that he was alone as he dismounted by the tent. However, his luck had held for the moment; in the confusion, no one seemed to notice the lone rider. Leaping off his horse, the young man dove into the tent. It was empty. *Perhaps it's the wrong tent*, he thought desperately.

"Maya, Maya!" he shouted at the top of his lungs, as he remounted.

Just then the bugle sounded...

* * *

In the tent, just moments earlier, they had both heard the commotion: the shouts, the screams, people running about. When Crowe ducked out of the tent, Maya had instantly thrown her bowl of porridge down and tried desperately to untie the thong securing her ankles. In the confusion, she hoped that she might be able to escape. Just as she seemed to make progress with her restraints, Crowe rushed back in.

"We be'n raided!" he fairly shouted, "Gimme y'er han's!"

Maya pulled back, but Crowe roughly grabbed her wrists. She struggled to get free. He slapped her hard, stunning her. Desperate now, he tied her wrists with a long leather thong and cut the one around her ankles. He led her out of the tent, pulling her by the thong around her wrists. He ran and she was forced to stumble behind. The young man didn't want to lose his new prize. They had almost made it to the perimeter of the camp, when a big bearded man grabbed Crowe.

"Where ya' goin', boy? Drop that bitch down an' fall inta line!"

Crowe tried to force his way past, but the Raider leader grabbed his shirt, pulled a big knife and put its point under the younger man's chin. "Do watta say, or I'll finish ya' here!"

The young Raider relented. Unexpectedly, he turned and hit Maya hard in the solar plexus, knocking to her knees. As Crowe ran to fall into the line of Raiders that was forming nearby, he shouted back to her, "Try ta run off an' I'll kill ya'!"

Someone shoved a lance into his hands.

Maya, desperate to escape, tried to get up, but the wind had been knocked out of her; she was still stunned from the first blow as well. Everything swirled around her in total confusion. She fell to the ground on her face. She sensed, dimly, people running to and fro past her, some leaping right over her.

Gasping, she finally took a few deep breaths and then raised her head up. She looked about; Crowe was nowhere to be seen. She raised herself to her knees and then stood up. Her legs were still wobbly and she could barely breathe. Her ears were ringing. Chaos reigned all about her. She turned in a circle, looking for the most promising direction to escape. Toward the nearest edge of the encampment, through dust and smoke, she finally made out the men in uniform with lances raised. She had no idea who they were. Then a bugle sounded and, as one, the soldiers lowered their lances with a shout. She ran...

*** * * ***

The battle unfolded in two concentric circles. A small, highly disciplined inner circle of Territorial scouts fought roughly in the center of the camp within a much larger, incompletely formed circle of Raiders. Both circles faced outward toward the outermost ring of cavalrymen. On the second bugle call, the militiamen charged as one, driving right through the ragged ranks of the Raiders. Many of the cavalrymen lost or broke their lances in the bodies of their victims. They wheeled their horses, drew their sabers and charged the line from the other side.

Their perimeter broken, many Raiders fled in all directions. Others, however, reformed into smaller units and fought on tenaciously. Most of these men were the veteran Raiders, tough, experienced fighters who had fought in countless battles.

The pressure on Sebastian and his scouts lessened as the cavalrymen approached. Many of the Raiders that had surrounded them had begun to flee. A pile of bodies was strewn around them, the largest concentration in the vicinity of the old Ranger. He was covered in blood, but most of it was not his own. Though wounded in several places, all of his wounds were minor. Some of the scouts were wounded, as well, a few badly. Two appeared slain.

As they drove off the last of their attackers, Sebastian looked toward where his Valerian had ridden. He could see nothing.

"I'm goin' to find my nephew," the Ranger shouted to his men, and then took off at a run. Most of the scouts still able quickly followed him.

On the other side of the camp, Valerian had run his horse in circles throughout the beginning stages of the battle, shouting for Maya. Along the way, he had wounded one Raider and killed another with his lance, losing the weapon in the second man's chest. Moments later, he had then almost been skewered himself by a cavalryman, who had only recognized him at the last instant. Shouting Maya's name again and again, his calls had finally been answered, but by a boy.

"Valerian, over here!" Joshua shouted. The youth, hands and feet bound, was tied to a post driven into the ground. He had been badly beaten; his face and body was a patchwork of cuts and bruises. Valerian leapt off of his horse to free the youth, his anger swelling. How could they do this to a child?

Just then, a Raider charged the young Elympian with a cutlass. Valerian ducked a vicious slash from the weapon, his own knife already drawn. The wild swing had unbalanced the Raider, and Valerian had sprung on him before he could recover. The younger, smaller man drove his knife into

Beyond Olympus

his opponent's chest and threw him to the ground, quickly finishing him with a slash to the throat. He rose in fury and triumph, taking the man's cutlass and cutting Joshua free with it.

"Have you seen Maya?" he shouted over the din of battle, as he hugged the youth.

"Not since last night Valerian. A man dragged her into that tent over yonder." Joshua pointed to the tent that Valerian had already searched. "But I haven't seen her since!"

"Help me find her!"

"I will, sir, but let me fetch Samantha first. I heard her braying just over there." The youth pointed towards the edge of the camp. "Me and Samantha will help you find her!"

Valerian nodded. "All right, but hurry! And watch yourself!"

The youth limped off and Valerian chased down his horse and remounted, still gripping the captured cutlass. The battle raged all around him. Some men shouted war cries, as others screamed in agony. Many others, women and inexperienced Raiders, fled in all directions, trying to take refuge in the surrounding forest. Where was Maya?

* * *

Maya, her hands still bound, ran toward the forest, right toward the charging cavalrymen. She prayed that they would concentrate on the Raiders and ride past her...they did. Two riders passed right by on either side of her, and either could have easily run her down or taken her with a lance.

The young girl soon stumbled into a thicket and ran on, brush and limbs slapping her, cutting at her legs, her arms, her face. She disregarded all of it as she ran on. Soon she tripped into a small gully, falling on her face. She rolled over, out of breath, covered with dirt and leaves. She pushed herself into some underbrush. Every now and then, someone would thrash by, but no one was interested in her; all were intent on fleeing deep into the forest.

Suddenly, Maya realized that the sounds of the battle had faded. Her heart still racing, she tried to relax a bit and gather her wits. She slowed her breathing. She tried to better conceal herself. Then she began to chew at the thongs at her wrists...

* * *

The battle reached a crescendo of intensity, and then ended rather abruptly. As the militiamen loosed scores of well-aimed arrows into the small knots of Raiders still fighting, the survivors soon dropped their weapons in surrender. Most hung their heads in despair, for they knew that a hangman's noose would likely be their eventual fate.

Relative quiet descended over the encampment, punctuated only by the occasional moan of a wounded man, or the wail of a Raider's woman who had lost her mate. The Cavalrymen now began to round up their captives.

One other sound that could now be heard all over the camp was the shouts of Valerian and Joshua calling out Maya's name. The shouts had alerted the young man's uncle, who had finally caught up with his mounted nephew.

"Thank goodness yo'r in one piece, lad. The gods sure do look after the foolhardy at times, I reckon."

Valerian had jumped off his horse and embraced the older man. "Are you all right Uncle? You look pretty used up."

"I look a far sight better'n them who bled all over me, I reckon. I do confess I'm pretty well worn out, though."

"I can't find her, Uncle; I've looked everywhere!" Valerian's voice caught in his throat.

"Hold yourself together, lad. We'll find her sure enough, in due time," the older man told his anguished nephew. (What he thought, but didn't say, was that he wasn't certain whether she would be alive or dead when they did find her.)

Valerian simply mounted back up and rode around the perimeter of the camp once more, shouting Maya's name. Joshua followed suite, riding Samantha in the opposite direction, calling out her name, as well. Even the grizzled old Ranger was touched by the forlorn spectacle of the two young riders circling the camp, calling out for the missing girl.

"Scout, could you and yo'r men help me search every square foot of this camp? We'd be lookin' for a sweet-faced, dark haired girl of about sixteen summers."

"Yessir, right away, sir," the scout saluted. The tough young soldier had been as impressed as hell by the big stranger who had fought like a mountain lion at his side. He got moving.

* * *

She had lain hidden for a while now, as the sounds of the battle had faded. Curled up in a thicket, she was loath to move just yet, for fear of attracting attention. In any case, she was simply too exhausted and terrified to move. She had slept or eaten little for the last few days and she hurt all over. At least she had finally worked her way out of the leather straps that had bound her wrists.

Every now and again, through the trees she heard someone shout one word, though it was too faint to make out. It sounded like a young man's voice, but the sound was so distant that she couldn't be certain of that, either. She began to fade, exhaustion finally taking her to the edge of sleep.

It might have been a trick of the wind. Or maybe the young man had shouted at just the right spot so that his voice had found its way unimpeded through the dense foliage. Then again, perhaps it was simply fate. In any case, just as her head relaxed onto a pillow of dry leaves, her own name carried through to her ears, clear and unmistakable...

"Maya!"

Instantly she arose, wide-awake. Without thinking, she shouted back in joy, at the top of her lungs, "Valerian!"

She began to run back toward the encampment, shouting his name over and over. She never saw the man chasing her down from behind. He tackled her, spun her to her back and pinned her down with his legs, cupping a hand over her mouth.

""M' li'l prize!" Crowe's breath stank of liquor and fear. His cheek was bleeding and his forearm was cut badly.

He whispered urgently, "Saw'd you run oft inta the woods over yar. Thought I'da lost ya. Thanks fer callin' out, but make another sound, an' I'll hafta hurt ya agin."

She struggled desperately, but couldn't budge. Tears rolled down her cheeks in desperation. Her young man was so close! Finally, she relaxed in defeat. He rolled her over, shoving her face into the forest floor. He pulled her hands behind her back, producing yet another damnable leather thong. He quickly tied her hands once again.

The young Raider was in the process of cutting a piece of cloth from her tunic for a gag, when he looked up to see a horse charging at him through the trees. The rider reigned in almost on top of them, and leapt down with a drawn sword. But just as the young man dismounted, the Raider suddenly leapt up at him, taking him off balance.

Valerian fell, with Crowe on top. The young Elympian tried to bring the sword into play, but the Raider caught his wrist with one hand, as he produced a knife from his belt with the other. Now Valerian grabbed Crowe's own wrist with his free hand.

Locked in silent and furious combat, the two young men rolled and twisted on the ground. Then, suddenly, Crowe kneed the young Elympian in the groin and Valerian's hand slipped off of the Raider's wrist. In an instant, Crowe plunged the knife deep into Valerian's side. The pain seared through the young man, but as his opponent raised the knife for a killing blow, Valerian grabbed his opponent's wrist again with his last reserves of strength. They struggled furiously for another few moments, as Valerian's strength slowly but inexorably faded. Maya, who had rolled over, called out in anguish.

Suddenly, another rider appeared, this time on a mule. Joshua jumped off directly on the Raider's back, pulling him off of Valerian. The man spun in fury and rolled on top of the youth. This was no contest; the lad was half the Raider's size. Crowe plunged the knife into Joshua's chest; the boy howled in agony...

The Raider looked up just in time to see one of Samantha's back hooves smash him between the eyes. The blow propelled him a full five paces away from the youth's body. The enraged mule, braying madly, leapt over her master, and went at the body of the unconscious Raider as if it were a serpent. By the time she was done, the body was barely recognizable as a human corpse.

Her hands still tied behind her back, Maya stumbled and collapsed next to Valerian, resting her head on his chest. She sobbed uncontrollably. Valerian, fading into shock, held her weakly and comforted her as best he could. He caressed her cheek. The young man was strangely at peace. As the darkness enveloped him, it occurred to him that, if he had to die, that this would be as good a way as any.

Likewise, Samantha approached her young master and nuzzled him. Joshua weakly caressed the beast's muzzle and whispered, "That's a good ol' girl, Sam." The lad's hand dropped as he too lost consciousness. The mule continued to gently nudge her master's body with her muzzle as if to wake him back up.

Maya heard the riders approach. She stood up clumsily and cried out as she saw Sebastian in the lead. Seeing his nephew down, the big man spurred his mount forward and leapt from the saddle on the run. Kneeling down by the young man, he was all business. He tore Valerian's tunic open and looked carefully at the wound. The blood was bright red, rather than dark, to his relief. He quickly cut a large piece of cloth from his nephew's tunic and pressed it against the wound.

"Scout, does the company have a surgeon?"

"No sir, but we have a medic who's plenty good with battle wounds."

"Fetch him, and be fast about it, if you please!"

"Yessir!"

The scout saluted and spun his mount, taking it through the trees at a wildly reckless pace. One of the other scouts had cut Maya loose, while two others tended to Joshua. Still weeping, the girl embraced Sebastian. She then dropped to hold Valerian's head in her lap.

"Will he live Uncle?" she asked in anguish.

"Don't rightly know lass," the big man replied gently, as he inspected the wound again, "he's bleedin' pretty bad, but I don't reckon any organs were cut. There's hope, but I reckon it's in God's hands now..."

22

The Birthday
September 14th, 2095

They had all ridden up into the mountains to celebrate Daniel's seventh birthday. It was the youngster's idea; the aspens had just changed, and he had wanted to admire their beauty up close. As usual, Michael thought to himself in wonder, it was an idea both unique and creative for such a young boy. So he and Olivia had ridden up with their son. Mac and Ellen, both avid riders, had joined them, along with Professor Alvarez. The old professor, now into his early seventies, had gamely done his best to keep up, though he had clearly looked quite awkward on the back of a horse.

As they reached a small clearing on the mountainside, Daniel deftly dismounted. "This is it," the youth exclaimed, "We can have our picnic right here!"

Michael was still amazed by his and Olivia's young son, Daniel Luis Vincent. He was one of the first "Pathfinder" children, raised carefully from birth according to the social principles that Michael, Professor Alvarez and the rest of the Olympian researchers had carefully developed.

In the beginning, the Pathfinder program had not been without controversy; even some of the citizens of Olympus had challenged it as a potential form of brainwashing. Some had even compared it with the Hitler Youth! However, Dr. Alvarez and his followers had convincingly argued that it was no such sinister thing. He had argued that their approach was nothing more than a synthesis of the wisdom accumulated by all of the great societies on how best to raise children to be strong individuals and worthy citizens. The Olympian youth program's only distinction was that it was perhaps more methodical in its approach than any of its predecessors.

They all dismounted; Professor Alvarez rubbed his backside in relief. Everyone looked around, admiring their surroundings. They were on a small plateau, high up on the side of a mountain. The aspens formed a semi-circle of bright yellows and greens, punctuated by their straight white trunks. On one side, however, they were rewarded with a panoramic view of Olympus nestled below in its little valley, between its two blue lakes. Everyone approved; Daniel had indeed picked the perfect spot for a picnic.

"Let's unpack the horses and have our lunch. I don't know about the rest of you, but after that ride, I'm famished!" Olivia said as soon as her feet hit the ground.

They had all agreed and tethered the horses on one side of the small meadow, then laid out the blankets a short distance away. The women took charge of the food, unpacking the sandwiches, fruit and drinks. Olivia carefully set down the basket of birthday cupcakes that she had personally baked from scratch and decorated by hand. She was ridiculously proud of those cupcakes. Domesticity had never come easily to her, but she had made a gallant effort for benefit of the young son who, along with Michael, had become the center of her universe.

With the retirement of Bill Atherton three years earlier, Mac had promoted Olivia to head of security for all of Olympus. She had plunged into the new position with enthusiasm. However, she had done her best to balance the demands of that role with those of a wife and mother. This was not only tolerated, but expected of all Pathfinder parents, who were considered an integral part of the program.

Mac, out of habit, had pulled a pulse rifle from its saddle scabbard, and proceeded to scout the surrounding woods. Michael, unarmed, had followed him.

"Looking for terrorists Mac?" he asked with a grin.

"You never know, Michael. Though actually, I had something more like bears in mind, or maybe wolves. Both have been sighted up here on occasion, in case you hadn't heard..."

"Can I come too, uncle? " Daniel had asked, running to catch up.

"Certainly lad; after all, you're likely a better woodsman than your dad," now Mac grinned back at Michael.

Daniel smiled too, in spite of himself. *More likely true than not,* Michael thought to himself wryly. A key element of the Pathfinder program was to teach the children self-sufficiency. Even at his tender age, Daniel had already spent many days in the forests surrounding Olympus, learning survival skills from Olympus's experts.

The three proceeded to scout the woods, a pleasant enough little hike as it turned out. Michael noticed that Mac let the boy take the lead. Daniel did so with confidence, walking silently and staying alert to his surroundings. He seemed to have no apparent doubt as to what direction to lead them. The only beasts that they encountered were a few squirrels and a chattering blue jay. After a time, they circled back and re-entered their little meadow.

"It's about time that you three frontiersmen returned. We were about to begin lunch without you!" Ellen called out.

"Wouldn't have done to start without the birthday boy," Mac responded as he walked up, setting his rifle down carefully and giving his wife a big hug.

Louie had already opened a good bottle of Pinot for the adults...Daniel would have to settle for apple juice. They all ate a hearty lunch. Even ordinary sandwiches seemed special up here in the mountains, Michael thought.

After finishing lunch and clearing the remains, Olivia brought out her precious cupcakes, handing the first to her son, then one to each of the others. She then put a candle in Daniel's cupcake, lit it, and forced the boy to endure a clumsy rendition of "Happy Birthday!"

The boy made his wish and blew out the candle. They all ate Olivia's cupcakes with gusto. Luckily, there were extras; everyone except Dr. Alvarez asked for seconds. (He was, with little success, trying to keep his expanding waistline in check.)

Now, seemingly out of nowhere, small gifts appeared for the young boy. Not the elaborate electronic gadgets or outlandish clothes that well-off children out in the world would typically expect. Pathfinder children had been taught to have little regard for such personal possessions.

Rather, from Professor Alvarez, there was a vintage leather-bound volume of Robinson Crusoe. Mac presented the boy with a small survival knife that held a compass, matches, and fishing line stored in its hollow handle. The knife was sheathed in a beautiful leather scabbard hand-crafted by Ellen.

"Be careful with this, young man," Mac cautioned, "the gift of a knife is supposed to be bad luck, but just such a gift saved my life, once upon a time."

"It saved your Mom and Dad's life, as well," Olivia added as she handed her son a small package, "now open mine."

It was a complete set of artist's pencils and a small drawing pad. Daniel was delighted; he had shown a facility for sketching at an early age and his Mother wanted to encourage his interest in art.

Finally, Michael handed his son a small card; Daniel opened it eagerly. It held three plane tickets…to anywhere. "Son, in all your seven years, the farthest that you've been away from Olympus is up in these mountains. Your mother and I would like to show you a bit of the world; you pick the spot: Disneyland, Greece, a Caribbean Island, Hawaii. You name it. Just choose wisely, for it may be a very long time before we get to do this again."

Or maybe never…

He and Olivia had discussed this gift at length. They would have preferred to take Daniel out to see a bit of the world when he was a little older, perhaps twelve, or ten, at least. However, world events were unfolding quickly now. Daniel's parents were afraid that there wasn't that much time left.

The president of the United States had just resigned…the third to do so in the last six years. The federal government was now officially bankrupt; only a financial bailout by Graham Enterprises and the other Great Powers allowed it to continue to function as a viable institution. The EU was on the verge of breaking up, and terrorism was rampant across the continent. A variety of brushfire wars in the Middle East had finally grown into a general conflagration. Starvation in Africa, South America and much of Asia had reached apocalyptic proportions. And on and on…

Nonetheless, the young couple had agreed that they wanted their young son to see something of the old world while it still existed, and while it was still relatively safe to travel. If nothing else, they hoped that it would help him to better understand what had been lost, when the end finally came. No one at Olympus now had any illusions that they could stop, or even delay the inevitable.

The youth thanked everyone for the gifts. He seemed delighted with all of them, but particularly the last. Daniel assured his mother and father that he would carefully consider the destination for their first real family vacation.

"Anybody up for a game of catch?" Mac asked. "I brought a ball and gloves."

"Me!" Daniel responded.

"Me too!" Olivia chimed in.

Professor Alvarez preferred to sit on one of the blankets with a book and a good glass of wine. Michael offered to help Ellen finish cleaning up the remains of their little picnic. After they finished cleaning up, they followed suit with the professor, fetching their own books and glasses of wine. Sitting on a blanket, Michael watched Mac, his son and his wife play catch. The sky was crystal blue...life was good.

"I'd call this a perfect day," he said to no one in particular.

"Yes, Michael, don't you just wish it just go on forever?" Ellen responded, sitting down on her own blanket.

"Treasure these days. We will need to hold onto memories such as these when the dark days come," Professor Alvarez observed lightly.

Ellen and Michael both nodded in agreement. Michael sipped his wine, but left his book unread on the blanket. *How far we've come*, he thought to himself. *Amazing. We've been here almost ten years now. We've become a family, not just Olivia, Daniel and me, but all of us, everyone at Olympus...a real extended family. And just look at Daniel. On the surface he looks like an ordinary boy. Yet in some subtle but powerful way, he is very different from my generation...stronger, more introspective, more confident...*

* * *

Gerhard Schmidt switched off his VR visor and gloves and settled back into the big leather chair in his study. (For sound reasons, he now preferred to conduct most business from his estate, traveling by air only when absolutely necessary.) He smiled to himself; the conference with his development team outside of St. Petersburg had gone exceedingly well. The project was proceeding right on schedule, although its costs were growing exponentially. However, Schmidt was unconcerned with the cost;

Eurodynamics had the resources to fund a project such as this, expensive as it was, several times over

The tycoon had to laugh at himself at how much time and effort that he had wasted trying to thwart Graham's own project...Olympus. He had assumed that his adversary was intending to make his own power play at the appropriate time. However, he was now convinced that the whole Olympus Project was merely a fuzzy-headed attempt to create some sort of Utopian community in the mountains. He was happy enough to let Graham build whatever he desired, as long as Graham did not attempt to interfere with Schmidt's own rather more ambitious plans.

For Schmidt considered his own plan rather more pragmatic than Graham's. His scheme, once put into motion, would actually trigger the apocalypse, but on Schmidt's own timetable and terms. It would allow him and his partners to seize power in their respective regions, just as the rival centers of power, such as Graham Enterprises, the EU and the U.S. government, all collapsed.

Schmidt had absolutely no qualms over his own agenda. Compared with the absolute chaos that would reign after the collapse occurred elsewhere around the world, he was certain that the masses under his control would eventually welcome his authoritarian rule with open arms.

However, it was the timing that was now crucial. If the end was allowed to occur of its own accord, only universal chaos would ensue, to no one's benefit. Schmidt's project *must* be completed and put into effect, first. And it would be a close thing. Most of his experts reckoned the collapse would occur in three to five years; his project would be completed in no less than three.

Schmidt had mandated that the project should remain unnamed for security purposes. However, much to his chagrin, a nickname for the project had begun to widely circulate within the development team. He had been tempted to mandate that the use of name be strictly forbidden. However, the name had even grown on Schmidt, and before long he too was using it, in spite of himself. After all, it did seem particularly apropos... Project Lucifer...

* * *

Olivia took a break, letting Mac and her boy continue to play catch. She trotted over to Michael and flopped on his lap, almost spilling his wine.

"Watch it!" he chuckled as he held the glass out.

"Gimmee that," she responded, snatching the glass and finishing it off in one gulp.

"Very rude, young lady. Now you'll have to refill it."

"Yessir, your highness." Before she could rise, Michael pulled her down for a long kiss.

"All right, you two...there are children present...one, at least," Ellen adopted her most authoritarian schoolmarm's voice.

"Sorry, ma'am, we forgot ourselves in the heat of the moment," Olivia answered when she finally came up for air. She rose at last to fetch Michael his wine. As she poured them both a glass, she thought to herself, *how could it possibly have taken me so long to see that this was the perfect man for me?*

These days were bittersweet for Olivia. Her job as chief of Olympus Security was challenging, and her marriage and family life was nothing less than idyllic. But always, over all their heads loomed the dark clouds of the cataclysm that everyone at Olympus now accepted as inevitable. She knew that it could be upon them in as soon as three or four years, or, with some luck, as far away as ten, (though few had any hope that it would be that far distant).

Olivia had tried to convince her parents to move to Olympus; the Olympus Council that now governed their community had in recent years granted a number of waivers to accept next of kin. However, the now elderly couple had stubbornly refused. They had already moved into a secluded home in the rolling hills of Maryland's countryside. Though they had remained skeptical of their daughter's dire warnings of the terrible times to come, they had at least taken some rudimentary steps towards making their home relatively self-sufficient...just in case. Michael had had no better luck with his mother.

*　*　*

The sun now hung low on the horizon; time to mount up and head for home. Olivia smiled as she watched her son and his father settle into their saddles simultaneously. Her love for Michael had developed slowly, almost against her will, at least at first. But perhaps it was all the deeper now because of that, she thought to herself.

Young Daniel led the way, confidently guiding his mount down the trail. Still pregnant with Daniel, Olivia had been amongst the skeptics when Professor Alvarez and Michael had proposed the Pathfinder program almost eight years ago to the newly formed Olympus Council…

"It is our fate to weather the coming storm," Professor Alvarez had told the Council, "but it is our children who will truly inherit the new, darker world that will soon reveal itself. Therefore, we must bequeath to them far more than this facility and the knowledge that it contains. We must give the next generation here at Olympus the strength, the wisdom and the courage to face mankind's greatest challenge."

"So Michael and I now propose the Pathfinder program. It will be voluntary, but will be open to all youth here at Olympus. Systematically, Pathfinder children will be taught from birth through young adulthood the social and survival skills necessary to overcome any of the future challenges they may meet. The program will be a joint effort of parents, educators, religious leaders and various experts in many fields…"

The professor had proceeded to outline the program, which, after some debate, had been approved by the Council. Soon, the Pathfinder program had become the new cornerstone of the Olympus Project…

* * *

From his office atop of the Alexandria Library, Jonathan Graham looked out over the nearby mountains. He assumed that his "family" was riding back down those mountains by now. Jonathan had been invited to accompany them, but had graciously deferred. Instead, the great man had countered with an invitation for all of them to attend a quiet dinner party that evening to celebrate young Master Daniel's birthday.

One more irony to add to a life filled with ironies, he thought to himself, *is that, for all my wealth, all my power, the great satisfaction in my twilight years is a "family" that bears no blood relation to me whatsoever. Louie, Mac and Ellen, Michael and Olivia, and most of all, my godson, young Daniel, have added a dimension to my life that I would have never thought possible.*

Graham had not even relocated to Olympus before he had been forced to concede that saving civilization was simply not a realistic possibility, even with all of the resources at his disposal. As a more realistic alternative, he had, along with his inner circle, secretly devised an alternative plan. Project Olympus had morphed into the creation of a vast repository for all of civilization's knowledge to be safeguarded, for centuries if necessary, to aid in the rebirth of some future civilization. The citizens of Olympus would become the caretakers of this repository and little more.

Then Professor Alvarez and Michael had made their proposal for the Pathfinder program. Graham had been as skeptical as the Council when the program had been proposed; only his great respect for the two professors had mitigated that skepticism. However, his doubts had gradually faded as the oldest children had begun to mature. (Some had been as old as five when they had been enrolled in the program; they were twelve now.)

These youths all still possessed the varied traits one would expect to observe in ordinary children. Some were creative; others were practical. Some were quiet; others were boisterous. In fact, a casual observer might have initially noticed little difference between a group of Pathfinder children and any other group of contemporary children. However, a more cautious observer, (like Graham, for instance) would soon have discerned subtle but nonetheless powerful differences...these youths were, as a whole, more earnest, more self-possessed, more *capable* than any group of contemporary youths.

As for Graham himself, he had gradually become, at least seemingly, little more than a bystander since the Olympus Council had been elected, (although he still managed to pull quite a few strings at Olympus behind the scenes) He was now a very vigorous and healthy seventy-two, (with the help of secret gene therapy treatments administered some ten years ago, which had largely arrested the ageing process).

Nonetheless, Graham now had to largely content himself, much like a proud parent beholding his new grown child, with hoping that his finest creation, Olympus, would somehow fulfill its destiny in ways even he might not yet foresee...

* * *

William Robertson Powell, the sixty-second President of the United States. He had to admit to himself that he liked the sound of it. Truth be told, he was still rather astounded at the sound of it...even though his old friends back in Boise still called him Billy Bob. He really didn't care what they called him; the fact was that he was now the most powerful man in the most powerful nation in the world.

It could be nothing less than God's own will, he thought to himself as he sat alone behind his desk in the oval office. Only eight years ago he had been a divorced and bankrupted insurance salesman in Boise. Exasperated with Powell's chronic alcohol and drug abuse, his wife had taken their two children back to her parents' home in California. She had vowed to never return. His life in tatters, in desperation, Billy Bob had been "born again".

Though a late-blooming convert, Powell had quickly become a vocal and radical fundamentalist. Soon he had found his true calling. He became a full time activist for the National Alliance of Fundamentalists, whose stated purpose was nothing less than the building of an overt Christian theocracy in America. Powell had risen rapidly in the organization's hierarchy, becoming its National Communications Coordinator in just two years. Soon after, he was surreptitiously indoctrinated into NAF's ultra-secret cabal, the "Brethren".

Powell soon discovered with his newfound passion, undiscovered abilities within himself that had heretofore lain dormant. He became a compelling speaker, projecting a charismatic personality that quickly made him a national (though highly controversial) figure. Soon, he officially parted ways with NAF, and joined one of the national political parties.

The subsequent political ride was giddying. After one term as a Congressman and a half a term as a U.S. Senator, Powell was selected as the running mate to a presidential candidate with a somewhat checkered past. It was hoped that Powell's persona as a born-again Christian would help to balance the presidential candidate's rather questionable personal history.

The ploy had worked; the mismatched pair was elected in a landslide. At least it worked for almost two years, until Marine Two, the president's air-shuttle, was brought down by a ground-to-air missile. ACT, the cyber-terrorist organization, had claimed responsibility. Now, shockingly and unexpectedly, Powell was the new president. God's will.

Powell had quickly appointed a highly respected veteran senator as VP, much to everyone's relief. He would soon do likewise with the major Cabinet positions, to convince one and all that, even with his administration, politics would largely be "business as usual". However, his key advisors would be largely made up of unknown cronies from home. Nothing unusual about that, other than the fact that every one of these men was secretly a member of the "Brethren".

God's will be done...

23

Marlt'n

The ride in the wagon seemed interminable to the wounded young man. Every bump in the narrow forest trail was agony to Valerian, who periodically passed into and out of consciousness all afternoon. Next to him sat Maya, who cared for him as best she could, giving him water or wiping his face with a wet rag. Crowded into the wagon were a few other wounded cavalrymen, who were also tended to by the young girl. Towards the front of the wagon slept Sebastian, snoring loudly. With only minor wounds, the old Ranger had resisted being loaded into the wagon with the other injured men, but the Commander, taking one look at the exhausted man, had insisted.

    They rode in one of several captured Raider wagons that the Militia had loaded up with wounded men, militiamen and Raiders alike, along with freed Raider captives and captured supplies. Behind the wagons walked a long column of prisoners, men and women, whose hands were bound. The prisoners were tied to one another at their necks, front to back. All around rode cavalrymen, guiding the long caravan back to Marlt'n.

    The attack on the Raider encampment had been a major victory for the Militia. Only a few of the cavalrymen had been killed or wounded, while they, in turn, had slain or captured better than half of the Raiders. They had also rescued some two dozen women and children captives, taken in earlier raids on the townships and outlying homesteads.

The Raiders who had escaped were scattered in flight throughout the forest. Commander Rawlins had left behind most of his scouts and half of his men to hunt down as many of the fugitive Raiders as possible. He would send more men back later to this area to make sure that these Raiders would never have the chance to regroup. Meanwhile, the Militia had burned everything in the camp that they had not taken with them.

The young Elympian was weak from loss of blood, although the Militia's medic had likely saved his life with prompt first aid. Young Joshua had not been so fortunate; his life had drained away even before the medic had arrived. Maya had cried for the young boy, even as she held her own critically wounded young man. As the company medic tended to Valerian, Sebastian had buried the boy on a small hill under a big oak tree.

Samantha was now tethered to the back of their wagon, following placidly behind. For a while, only Maya had been able to approach the beast, once her master's body had been carried away.

As they finally exited the forest, Commander Rawlins noted that the sun was hanging low on the horizon. Finding a meadow with a wide stream coursing through it, he ordered the column to halt. They would camp there tonight and return to Marlt'n the next day. The wagons were formed into a circle, with the prisoners gathered into a tight knot in the center. A number of militiamen formed a wide perimeter of sentries; others were dispatched to scout the surrounding area for hostiles. The remaining soldiers ate and rested, tending to the captives and injured. They would look after the Raider prisoners last.

Sebastian had finally woken when the wagons had stopped. With the help of Maya and a few of the soldiers he had gently lifted Valerian and the other wounded men on blankets set out on the ground. Valerian now slept peacefully, not even waking when he was moved. The Ranger checked on the young man's wound. At least the bleeding seemed to have stopped, although he was worried about internal bleeding. *Well, there's nothing to be done about that,* he thought to himself.

Stretching, he left to fetch food and drink for Maya, who stayed by her young man's side. Seeing the Commander, Sebastian walked over to him. Just then, he was directing Hawkins and a few other senior men in the disposition of the encampment.

"Well, Ranger, you look a far sight better than you did when we set out this afternoon!" Rawlings observed as he handed the big man his own canteen.

Sebastian took a long swallow before he answered, "Thank you kindly, Commander. And, if you please, give my regards to yo'r men, especially the scouts. Ceptin' our own Elympian cavalry and Rangers, these are the best fightin' men I've ever seen...and I've seen my share."

"I appreciate the observation, Ranger; I'll pass it along to the men. It'll carry some weight, too, judging by the stories about you that I've already heard amongst the men. Seems you made quite an impression on my scouts during the battle, yourself."

The two men shook hands and Sebastian set out to fetch food and drink. By the time he had returned, the sun was setting and Maya slept soundly, curled up at Valerians side. The big man did not disturb her. He just put a blanket over them both and took care of the other wounded men.

* * *

Toward dawn, Valerian woke both Maya and his uncle, thrashing about and mumbling deliriously. Maya put a hand lightly on his forehead and was distressed at the heat. He was burning up!

"Is there anything we can do, Uncle?"

The big man, who had gently felt around his nephew's wound, replied, "I was afraid of this, little one. The wound was deep and made with a dirty weapon. Even though that young medic did a fair job of cleaning it out, it's infected. I'll go fetch him and see iffin he can do anything. Meanwhile, you bath him with some cool water from that stream over yonder."

In the half-light just before dawn, the medic had checked the feverish young man's wound, cleaning and redressing it as best he could. He had then forced a little herb tea down his throat.

"This will help a little with the pain and fever," the medic had told the big Ranger and the young girl, "but the infection looks serious. We'll have the town surgeon, who's a real doctor, look at him as soon as we get into town. But I suspect that there won't be much else that he can do either. We'll just have to let the infection run its course. In four or five days, either he'll begin to recover...or he won't."

"Meanwhile, just keep doing what you've been doing. Keep him cool and keep him as comfortable as you can," the medic rose up to check on some of the other wounded men.

Maya had turned away, but not before the tough old man had seen the tears coursing down her cheeks. He moved to put an arm around her shoulders, but before he could, she had already laid down next to her young man again. So instead, he moved off to check on Samantha, who was hobbled in the meadow nearby. Later he would fetch some tea and breakfast for himself and the young girl. If he had to, he would *make* her eat, whether she wanted to or not...

✳ ✳ ✳

The young man awoke in the middle of the night. Moonlight streamed through an open window accompanied by a cool, pleasant breeze. Curtains, which framed the large window at the foot of the bed, fluttered softly. As he lay in the soft bed, gradually he became aware of his surroundings. Although he was otherwise cool and comfortable, he noticed that the sheet that he lay upon, as well as the one that covered him, were both soaking wet. Instinctively, he moved to the edge of the bed, where the sheets were still dry. Realizing that the soft pillow that his head rested upon was also damp, he flipped it over. That's when he became aware of the sharp pain at his side.

He put a hand to his ribs and felt the bandages wrapped tightly around his midsection, also damp. One spot was very tender indeed. Lying there quietly, his senses came somewhat back into focus. He became aware of the faint sound of regular breathing from the other side of the bed. He raised himself up on an elbow, (there was that sharp pain again!). And there lay Maya; the moonlight illuminating her face. She looked like an angel, sleeping peacefully.

He moved to her side and snuggled next to her, gently putting an arm around her waist, in spite of the pain it caused. She stirred but did not awaken. At that moment, he had no idea where he was or how he had gotten here. Just now, however, he really didn't care. He soon fell back into a deep, tranquil sleep.

✳ ✳ ✳

Beyond Olympus

The next time he awoke, sunlight was streaming through the window and a hand was gently stroking his cheek. For a long moment, he kept his eyes closed feigning sleep, so that he could luxuriate in the soft loving touch, in the warmth of the sunlight, in just being alive.

He finally opened his eyes, and the first image that that greeted him was that of her warm brown eyes gazing back at him. Her hand stayed at his cheek.

"Welcome back, Valerian. Your fever must have broken in the night, thanks be to God," she bent down to kiss him softly and he kissed her back.

"I'm starving! I love you!" he blurted out when their lips parted.

She laughed and her eyes sparkled. "Just like a man; food first, then romance."

He started to reply, but she put a finger to his lips. "Just rest my love. You are still very weak. You haven't eaten in six days."

"Six days! I've been out six days?" As if to prove her point, he sat up and almost fainted. He quickly lowered his head back onto the pillow.

"Yes, and by the fourth, we thought that we were surely going to lose you. But I talked to you. I begged you to stay with me. They said you couldn't hear me, but I think that some part of you did, for you wouldn't let go. You fought..." Her eyes glistened with tears.

"Where are we?" he quickly asked to change the subject.

"We've returned to Marlt'n with the Militia. You're in a guestroom in Doc Meriwether's home. He's been taking care of you."

"Is Sebastian all right? How about Joshua? What happened to the man who stabbed me?"

"Your Uncle is fine. The man who hurt you is dead..."

"And Joshua?"

She didn't speak, but looked away; it was answer enough. They were both silent for a while.

"He was a fine lad."

"He was indeed; he saved both our lives. Now enough talk, let me get you some broth and some tea," she turned to leave.

"Broth! How about eggs...with ham?"

She laughed and turned again as she reached the door to the bedroom.

"Soon enough, you can have whatever your heart desires. But for now, broth will have to do."

* * *

Days passed. Soon, he sat up in bed. Not much later, he took a few halting steps around it. Maya nursed him, shaved him, even bathed him...an embarrassing if not altogether unpleasant experience for the young man.

Visitors came. Doc Meriwether checked in on him regularly. Sebastian hung around to harass him into getting up and around. Various townspeople dropped in to satisfy their curiosity; all were friendly enough. Most of the women visitors brought home-cooked food. Maya eyed a few of the younger, unattached women suspiciously.

Magistrate Smythe paid a visit, as did Commander Rawlins, eager to glean all that he could from the young man about his mother, Miss Izzy. Soon after, Rawlins left town with a few fresh companies of militiamen to track down as many of the fugitive Raiders as possible. Sebastian, chaffing at being stuck in town with nothing to do, accompanied the troops as a scout.

Finally, one evening, Valerian had regained enough strength to take his first walk through town, with Maya to steady him. She had obtained clean new clothes for her young man, having discarded his bloody and ragged tunic. The clothes consisted of black trousers that fell over his boots, a simple white cotton shirt and a black woolen jacket. Compared to his tunic, the clothes felt bulky and awkward. They were itchy too. Nonetheless, Maya thought that her young man looked handsome in his new outfit, though he drew the line at the floppy hat that most townspeople wore.

Maya had also adopted the dress of the townspeople. She now wore a low cut velvet dress with a long loose skirt, a gift from the Magistrate's wife. It had belonged to her daughter and fit Maya perfectly. The young girl's long brown hair was tied back with a matching ribbon, in the fashion of many of the town's younger women. A shawl fell across her smooth shoulders. She looked more beautiful than ever to Valerian. As he walked arm and arm down the street with her, he was in equal parts proud and jealous to notice that virtually every young man turned to watch the lovely young woman as she passed them by...

* * *

Beyond Olympus

"Long day, Commander." Sebastian sat on the ground next to Rawlins, in front of the campfire. He poured himself a cup of hot tea from the kettle.

"Yes indeed, Ranger, but a productive one," Rawlins responded as he glanced over at the dozen or so prisoners huddled nearby that they had bagged just that afternoon. "You are quite a tracker, Sebastian. Are you sure you won't take my offer as chief of scouts?" (It was the third time that the Commander had made the offer in the last five days.)

"Like I said, Commander, that's a mighty interesting offer. I haven't enjoyed myself this much in years. Problem is, I've still got unfinished business elsewhere..."

"And when do you think that you'll be able to trust me enough to let me know just what that business might be?" Commander Rawlins gave the old Ranger a steady look in the dim firelight. Sebastian could barely make out the other man's features, with his black skin blending into the darkness.

Nonetheless, the Ranger returned the Commander's stare for a long moment before answering. "Well sir, I suppose that would be right now. The truth is that I'm takin' the boy to Elympias, or, to be honest, he's takin' me," the Ranger finally replied

The Commander absorbed his answer for a moment, then leaned his head back and laughed loud and long enough so that the militiamen all about stopped and stared. "No wonder you didn't want to tell me what you were up to, Sebastian. I don't expect that it's easy for a man like you to admit you're on a fool's errand."

The big man found himself growing a bit defensive, in spite of himself. "I admit that it may sound a bit mad, but Elympias is the homeland of our ancestors. And my nephew has sworn an oath to return to it for the sake of his people."

"Yes, and you may meet some of your ancestors in person if you do make it there... which you likely won't. Did my mother tell you that we saw the place?"

"Yes she did; said the place terrified all of you, even your pa."

"It did indeed. I was a small boy and I had nightmares about the place for years after. Elympias is truly haunted."

"But there is a more immediate reason that your journey is hopeless," the Commander continued, "Across the Green River, to the east and south of here, is a no man's land ruled, more or less, by the Raider clans. It's lucky enough for you that you didn't find your way across the river, for they ruthlessly hunt down and kill everyone that crosses from this side. Remember, we have been at war with them for years now. Someday, I'm going to cross that river with an army large enough to crush them all. However, that may be many years from now, I fear."

"How many days march from the river do you think Elympias lies, Commander?"

"I'd say another forty or fifty days at least, and did I mention that your little trek would be over some of the most inhospitable, mountainous terrain you can imagine?"

"Well Commander, that's the best news you've given me. The rougher the country, the better the chance we have to stay hid in it. And I might remind you that we made it clean across the Zealot lands, as well as the Great Mountains, in one piece."

"Well, you do have a point or two there, Ranger. But I reckon the last leg of your journey may be the toughest of all. Since this war began, the Raiders have created a real hell on Earth in the Southern Territories. They have a warlord, name of Deacon, who has consolidated power over most of the Raider bands. In the process, he's created a serious guerilla army to challenge us. He and his army have turned the farmers and townspeople in the south into little more than slaves. The Raiders over there can do as they please, taking whatever they want...food, money, women. We have a constant stream of refugees from the south risking life and limb to make it to this side of the river. Trouble is that there are always Raiders infiltrating in amongst them."

"Believe me, Sebastian, if they capture you like we did, they'll torture you for information and then kill you, right off," the Commander hesitated for a moment, lost in thought, "Tell you what, Ranger; how about we make a deal?"

"What sort of deal, Commander?"

"Call me Aaron, Sebastian. I have agents of my own on the other side, people that I trust. I will get one or more of them to help you. I will also have a map made that will mark out the safest route to Elympias."

"In return for what, Aaron?"

"In return, you will simply gather intelligence on the Southern Territories for me, going out and, God willing, coming back. Keep a particular eye out for any large Raider parties getting' ready to cross to this side. Oh yes, and I'll also ask you to reconsider my offer to take that position with the scouts, someday."

"It's a deal, Aaron, but I can't guarantee I can take that position. I'll still have to get the lad and his young lady back to our homeland."

"I understand; just think it over."

The two tough men agreed and shook hands.

"I have just one more question Sebastian. Just what in the world do you and the lad expect to find in Elympias, anyway."

"Well, Commander, if I had the faintest idea, I'd be happy to let you know…"

* * *

It was late evening and the young couple could be seen strolling down the main street, back to Doc Meriwether's home. They had just finished a long and more or less pleasant dinner with one of the town Eldermen, a rather corpulent shopkeeper named Josiah Gault, his wife and two teenaged sons. The Gaults were both talkative, good-natured folk who loved to share the town gossip with the young couple. The two sons were quiet and respectful, (except for the fact that they couldn't keep their eyes off Maya the entire evening).

Valerian and Maya had become much sought after dinner guests in Marlt'n, treated with a mixture of curiosity and respect. Everyone wanted to know about the Elympian Clan as well as life amongst the Tradesmen. Valerian and Maya were happy to tell tales of their respective peoples and past. Everyone was also curious about why they had come to their town and where they were going. About these things, the young couple stayed mum; this only added to the curiosity that surrounded them.

With all this attention, Maya had blossomed even further as a young lady. The shy reclusive girl that Valerian had first met now seemed a distant memory. She clearly welcomed being the center of attention, chatting with the ladies and receiving the silent but open admiration of the young men. The townspeople's esteem for her had increased even further as she had repaid the old doctor's kindness by serving as a very capable nurse.

On the other hand, Valerian was becoming increasingly uncomfortable with their stay in town. Each day he became more eager to push on to their ultimate destination. The young man had to admit to himself that there was another reason behind his impatience to leave. It was in no small part the result of his growing awareness of the contrast between his own people with those that he now lived amongst.

These folk, though for the most part kind and good-natured, were clearly just this side of civilized. Unheard of in his homeland, these people smoked the leaves of some dried plant in long-stemmed things they called "pipes". They practiced this disgusting habit even in their homes, leaving a noxious stench all around.

They drank ale, much like the Elympians, as well as a strong clear liquor made from corn that was unknown to him. Unlike Elympians, however, they often drank to excess. Drunks, both men and women, could be seen practically any time of the day or night walking up and down the streets.

Taverns were commonplace in Marlt'n, as were brothels. Of course, there were a fair number of taverns in Valerian's homeland, as well. There they served as quiet meeting places for friends to socialize a bit over a mug of ale. Here they were smoky, raucous places where drunkenness, gambling and prostitution were the normal pursuits. Gambling and prostitution were unheard of in Valerian's homeland.

Even the town itself seemed somehow foreign to him. Each Elympian township had wide, tree lined avenues that radiated out from a large town square. Large public buildings of brick or stone anchored most corners, with neat whitewashed wooden homes, shops or taverns in between. In contrast, Marlt'n was a hodgepodge of new wooden buildings built amongst ramshackle Ancient structures of brick or steel in various states of disrepair. Streets and narrow back alleys were laid out in no discernable order.

Tolerance and respect were two of the virtues that had been deeply ingrained in Valerian's nature. In any case, he actually enjoyed the townspeople's company for the most part. The young traveler found most of them to be warm and generous, not to mention boisterous and fun loving. Nonetheless, the very fact that these folk seemed to possess no set of fundamental virtues to guide them, tended to make him feel out of place. Basically, he missed his home; he was eager to move on.

Maya, though just as aware of the townspeople's shortcomings, seemed more comfortable with just accepting them as they were. However, she understood the discomfort her young man felt, as well as his desire to resume their journey. She too would be ready, whenever he was, to continue his quest...now their quest.

* * *

"Wake up, lad."

Dawn was still an hour or so away and Valerian had been sound asleep. He was in his soft bed, between clean sheets, curled up with a beautiful girl. But just now a huge silhouette loomed over the young man, shaking his shoulder.

"Uncle? What is it?" Valerian croaked. The young man rubbed his eyes and tried to focus.

"What it is, nephew, is time for you to get back into fighting trim…that is if you still intend to reach Elympias. I reckon you still do, don't you?"

"Yessir, I do."

"Well then, hop out of this here soft bed. I had the local tailor make you proper tunic, since I don't suppose you want to be traipsin' through the woods in them city clothes. Had yo'r gear cleaned, yo'r weapons sharpened and fresh provisions packed into yo'r knapsack, too. So let's get you outfitted and let's be off. Tell yo'r little lady friend that we'll be back when we git back."

"Yessir." The youth knew well better than to question his uncle. He quickly got up and got dressed, washed his face and rinsed his mouth in the wash basin. He tied his hair back, then bent down to Maya and kissed her.

"I'm going out with uncle for a while, Maya. Don't worry; I'll be back in a few days."

"More likely a few weeks, lass. Me and the lad are going to get yo'r man back into shape. Judging by how thick his waist is and how thin his arms and legs are, that may be a while."

"Come back soon Valerian. Be careful…I love you," the girl responded, still half asleep. She put an arm around his neck and kissed him back.

They left town at a trot with Sebastian in the lead. The first rays of sunlight were just breaking over the eastern horizon. Valerian was exhilarated to be back in his element. That lasted just about until they had reached the outskirts of town. Then his legs started burning and he began gasping for air. He was shocked at his lack of stamina. He had to slow to a walk.

His uncle didn't stop or look back. He just kept a steady pace straight ahead, pulling gradually away. As soon as the young man had caught his breath, he broke back into a trot. Soon, he had to slow again. He had a hitch in his side. After a while, his uncle had left the road and had cut over to a small trail that led into the forest. Valerian knew better than to call out for Sebastian to slow down or wait for him. Eventually, he lost sight of the older man altogether. He then had to track his uncle...no small chore.

By midday, the young man was thoroughly exhausted. He was hungry and thirsty; his legs ached and his feet were sore. Then, around a bend in the trail, he caught sight of his uncle. The Ranger was seated on a log, brewing tea over a small fire. He didn't even look up. Valerian dropped his knapsack and weapons. He took off his cloak, laid it on the ground and collapsed on it. His uncle handed him a cup of tea.

"Lad, I'm only going this easy on you 'cause it's yo'r first day out. Don't expect it to be this easy tomorrow."

Valerian just gave his uncle a pained smile. He was far too tired to reply. The big man handed him a corn cake and a bit of jerky. Soon enough, they would be off again.

* * *

They had been out for weeks now. Valerian had lost count of just how many. He missed Maya, but their little expedition had begun to yield its intended results. He was deeply tanned once again. The many miles they had traveled at a run had hardened his legs and restored his stamina. Hours of sparring with his uncle and practicing with his powerful war bow had tightened his arms and chest.

During one of their hand-to-hand sparring sessions, Valerian's uncle had struck him hard enough in the chest to really anger him. Without thinking, the younger man had struck back with all his strength. With Valerian unbalanced for an instant, the old Ranger had smoothly moved in, tripped him and pinned him firmly to the ground.

Holding him face down, the old warrior had asked his nephew, "And what did we just learn yet again, lad?"

"To keep a cool head, Uncle..."he had responded in frustration, "uh, can you let me up now?"

"Not just yet. I'd like the lesson to soak in a might better, first. Valerian, I know how you feel about the lass. Can't say I blame you. But more than once, you've lost yo'r head when you thought she was in danger. As a result, you came within a cat's whisker of getting' yo'rself dead...her too. Before I let you up, I'd like your oath that you'll keep a cool head from here on in, no matter what. It just might save yo'r life the next time. Just might save her life too."

The young man hesitated for a moment. An Elympian giving his or her oath for any reason was a most serious matter. "You have my word of honor Uncle," he answered.

With that, the big man pulled his nephew to his feet and slapped him on his back. "Then let's make camp and have our supper."

The campfire that evening warmed them. A half moon and stars shined down on the two men through the trees in the clearing. They roasted a rabbit that Valerian had brought down that afternoon with a well-aimed arrow.

"I reckon yo'r almost ready lad. That's the thing about you confounded youngsters; you can bounce back pretty fast when you put yo'r minds to it."

Valerian took the Ranger's comments as high praise.

"So, does that mean we can go back to fetch Maya now, Uncle, and resume our journey?"

The big man chuckled, "Miss her a bit, do you?"

"Yessir, I do."

"Well, I've been meanin' to talk to you about that, lad. I think that you might want to consider leavin' her in Marlt'n whilst we push on for Elympias."

The young man was taken by surprise. Leaving her behind had simply never occurred to him. He started to reply, but the older man stopped him.

"Hear me out, lad. The Commander tells me that the last part of our trip through the Lawless Lands will be by far the most dangerous. He thinks it'll be even tougher than what we've already been through. Now, Maya is fine young lass and a first class travel companion. She has more courage, spunk and resourcefulness than most men that I've fought with. But do you really want to put her at such risk, again?" Sebastian asked.

Valerian was silent for a while. He thought back to how he had so nearly lost her to the Raiders. Could he risk her to a fate such as that, yet again? Would he ever forgive himself if anything did happen to her?

* * *

It was near sunset one day when the two woodsmen finally strode back into town. They had been gone for well over a month. Townspeople, recognizing the two Elympians, tipped their hats or waved in greeting.

Then, there she was, running down the street toward them. Valerian dropped his gear in the street just before Maya leapt into his arms, her legs wrapping around his waist. Overcome with emotion, neither spoke. They kissed and she finally climbed down. The young woman stood back a pace to admire her young man, now tanned and lean.

"Now that's the Valerian I fell in love with," she observed with approval.

Meanwhile, the young man's eyes feasted on the lovely young woman. Her wavy brown hair was pulled back in a ponytail. She once again wore a tunic, rather than a dress. But it was new, forest green with tan stitching and a new wide leather belt. She saw that he noticed.

"I had it made for when we resume our journey. I was hoping you'd be back soon. Do you like it?" She gave him a coy little turn. He said nothing of the journey.

"You look even more beautiful that when I left, and I didn't think that possible."

That night, the three had dinner with Doc Meriwether, served by the Doc's old housekeeper, Else. After dinner, they all took tea on the doctor's front porch. Finally, after darkness had fallen, Valerian asked Maya to walk with him. The young couple strolled arm-in-arm down the street in silence for a while.

Finally, Valerian spoke, "Maya, I have to ask something of you that will be very difficult for the both of us."

She stopped and looked up at him. "What would that be, love?"

The words would hardly come out. "Sebastian and I believe that it would be best if you stayed here in Marlt'n, while he and I continue the journey to Elympias," he finally blurted out.

Fearing her response, he stumbled on, "We have heard that the danger across the river would be even greater than any we have yet seen. I couldn't bear to have anything happen to you. I would never forgive myself if something happened to you. Please consider doing this for both our sakes."

The young man had in no way anticipated the response she gave him. Rather than delivering the outburst he had braced himself for, she just looked at him coolly in the dim light of the streetlamps for a long while. Then she smiled at him warmly and kissed him lightly.

"No Valerian," she answered calmly, "here is what's going to happen. You are going to marry me. Right here in this town. Then we are going to leave for Elympias. Together...husband and wife...and you will never speak of leaving me behind...ever again. If something terrible happens to me, it will be at your side...right where I want to be. If I die, it will be by your side...right where I belong. Is there anything else that you'd like to discuss with me this fair night, my love?"

Suddenly, he felt like a little boy again, being sternly talked to by his grandmother. He just couldn't come up with anything sensible to say. Looking into her eyes, he knew that there was simply nothing he could do. If he left her, she would follow...alone, if need be. And looking at the quiet determination in those eyes, he knew that she would never be persuaded to stay behind, ever. In any case, the honest truth was that he didn't really want to leave her behind, anyway.

"Yes ma'am; no ma'am. I mean...will you marry me?" he stammered.

She laughed, threw her arms around him and kissed him...hard, this time.

* * *

The wedding ceremony was held in the Marlt'n town square. Though it was a simple ceremony, most of the town turned out. The Magistrate conducted the ceremony. The young couple was flanked by Sebastian on one side and Commander Rawlins on the other. Rawlins had brought along a company of cavalry, decked out in freshly cleaned and pressed blue uniforms, to act as an honor guard.

Valerian squirmed in a nice black suit that had been loaned to him. Maya was radiant in a rose-colored velvet gown that had been presented to her by the ladies of the town. Her hair had been tied back with ribbons of silk. In Elympias, weddings were conducted by Spiritual Elders; here, weddings were civil affairs. Nonetheless, the Magistrate did a fine job; all the women cried, including Maya.

That evening, the town let out all the stops, hosting the biggest wedding feast in anyone's memory. As the revelry continued late into the night, Rawlins asked Sebastian to take a walk with him. Once they were alone, he stopped and looked at the Ranger.

"So do you three still plan to leave in the morning?"

"Yes we do, Aaron. I reckon everyone will sleep a little later in the mornin' after this bash. So we'll just fade away into the forest without any fuss. Then, when the time is right, we'll find a way to slip across the river."

"Well then, come with me to the good doctor's house. I have something to show you"

Once in Doc Meriwether's house, Rawlins carried a lamp to the dinner table. Out of his tunic, he took out a small rolled up map. "So you boys couldn't talk the little lady into staying behind?" Rawlins smiled at the Ranger and Sebastian responded with a rueful smile of his own.

"Kinda reminds me of my woman that way. Once she set her mind about somethin'..."the big man just shook his head, "anyway, she's a resourceful young lass; I reckon she can carry her own weight. The rest is in the hands of the Maker."

The Commander shook his head, as well. Then he turned back to the map and pointed to a spot on it.

"Here is Marlt'n. Head down the main road south along the river. Right on the river, five or six days march south of here is a small fishing village with a garrison of my troops; village name of Jamest'n. A fisherman, name of Marley, has a little cabin just outside of town. Everyone in the village knows him. He also has a pretty good little fishing boat. He'll be expecting you. So is the garrison's captain, a man named Valdez. They'll get you across the river, but you'll have to wait for a moonless night. On the other side, a guide name of Santiago will take you up into the mountains. All the territories to the south and east of the Green River are the Lawless Lands. You're on your own from there on."

The Commander pointed to another spot on the map. "Right here, just to the south of those mountains, is where Elympias lies. You might make it there in a month, maybe two, depending on what gets in your way."

The big Ranger rolled the map back up and shook Rawlins's hand. "I don't know how to thank you, Aaron."

"You can thank me by not gettin' yourselves killed," the big black man answered with a smile.

"Aaron, I have to ask; what is it that's driven you to fight for so long and so hard against the Raiders?"

The Commander looked at his friend for a long moment before answering. "You know what happened to my Ma, don't you?"

"Yes, I'm afraid I do," Sebastian replied.

"I was just a small lad when that happened. My brother and I had to watch it happen, too."

"Well, when me and Will came down out of the mountains, we both worked in a small town north of here. After a time, we'd earned enough money to rent a small farmstead. Then I met a girl in town, name of

Maudie...sweet girl, pretty too. Married her and she moved in with me and Will on the farmstead. Then, not long after, the Raiders came. Burned out our place and took Maudie while my brother and I were out in the fields."

"Pa had taught us to be pretty fair trackers. Will and I joined up with a militia outfit and we tracked 'em down. To frighten us off their trail, the Raiders killed some of their captives and left them so's we'd find them and get discouraged. Maudie was one of them."

"It was a bad idea on their part. We tracked them for weeks after that. I would have tracked 'em to the ends of the earth. When we caught up with 'em, we took 'em by complete surprise. We killed some of 'em outright but captured most, including some of their women. I was hell bent on executin' all of them on the spot, men and women alike. Most of the militia agreed with me."

"But my brother, Will, wouldn't let us. Said if we did that, we'd be no better than them. Stood his ground. In the end, it was the rest of us that backed down. We brought 'em all back into town. Tried the men and hung most of 'em, except some of the younger ones. Them and the Raider women were sentenced to indentured servitude as punishment."

"We Elympians have a saying: *'Justice is the true foe of evil; revenge is nothing more than its accomplice.'* It was a hard lesson for me to swallow, after I lost most of my friends and family to the Zealots. Aaron, I've had my own losses. Someday I'll tell you of mine. And someday, God willing, I'll repay your kindness as well."

The Commander nodded gravely and concluded, "After what we'd been through, Will and I were done with farmin'. We stayed with the militia, determined to drive the Raiders out of our lands for good. Just five years ago, my brother, Will, was killed in a Raider ambush. But I'm not stoppin' 'til the Raider's day is done, once and for all...both here and across the river."

The Commander rose, straightened his tunic, and took the Ranger's hand. "Godspeed Sebastian. I hope you and the youngsters find what you're looking for."

With that, the soldier turned and left out the front door into the darkness...

* * *

They were all set. All three were dressed in tunics and wide belts. All three wore gray-green hooded woodsman cloaks, and all three wore high boots of deerskin. The two men each had a hatchet hung on one side of their belts and a large hunting knife in a scabbard on the other. The girl carried only a hunting knife. The men each had large war bows and quivers hung across their backs. The girl now also wore a lighter bow given to her by Sebastian, paid for with the wages he had earned as a scout. All three also carried knapsacks carefully packed with fresh provisions. The girl's knapsack was only a bit lighter. All three carried lances now, as well. Again, the girl's lance was only a tad smaller.

In the weeks leading up to the wedding, Valerian had taken Maya on vigorous hikes in the nearby forest almost every day. Both knew that life in the town had softened her as well. Often the two would camp out under the stars. Often he would have her practice for hours with her new bow. To his surprise, he had discovered that she was something of a prodigy with the weapon; soon her skills as an archer rivaled his own.

Sebastian checked the straps for Samantha's packs one last time. Even the mule seemed eager to be off. Maya scratched her behind her ears and spoke to her softly. The beast nuzzled the young woman in return. They had debated whether to bring Samantha. The mule would allow them to bring more provisions. Yet this benefit was offset by the fact that a pack mule would make it much more difficult for them to travel without being discovered. In the end, it was their heart rather than their heads that prevailed. She had become a part of their little party and they just couldn't bear to leave her behind.

Dawn would soon be breaking. Maya turned and hugged her young man. "Well, husband, what are we waiting for? I'm anxious to enjoy my honeymoon in Elympias, so let's be off!"

Both men smiled and nodded. And with that, the three set out to complete their journey, God willing, to Elympias at long last...

24

Snow Falls on Olympus
January 31st, 2098

Michael sat alone at his desk in the "Think Tank". It was early evening and tonight he was the last to leave the bullpen. The role of his research group had changed dramatically since the early days. Back then, there had still been a sliver of hope that they could somehow delay or at least mitigate Armageddon. Now, all their hopes had turned inward. They now aspired to create in Olympus a small, but durable, lifeboat for civilization. After all of the death and destruction had run its course, they hoped that their city would rise up out of the ashes, as a shining beacon to lead the world to a new Renaissance.

Soon, Michael would leave to join Olivia and his son Daniel for dinner. This evening, they would be celebrating their son's successfully graduation from the novice "Sparrow" into the intermediate "Falcon" level of the Pathfinder program. To do so, their son had been required to pass a series of rigorous mental and physical challenges. The challenges had been designed to test his character as much as his ability. The ten year old had passed all of the tests with flying colors.

Before leaving, the professor took one last depressing look at the daily cyber-news reports. They showed a world quickly descending into chaos. Last August, a mega-hurricane had laid waste to practically the entire Florida peninsula. Ever since, chaos had ruled throughout the region. President Powell, using the emergency as justification, had declared martial law and had suspended habeas corpus. To announce these Draconian steps, he had made a bizarre speech before Congress, almost seeming to welcome Armageddon as part of God's plan to restore His will on earth.

The news from around the world was no better. Nuclear weapons had finally, perhaps inevitably, been unleashed in the Middle East. Hundreds of thousands had died. Another exchange might take millions. Meanwhile the Eurowar had, thankfully, stayed conventional, at least so far. But who knew for how long, with the Eastern Alliance gradually pushing NATO forces back all along the Eastern front. Without American aide, (which Powell had announced would not be forthcoming), there seemed to be little hope that the western powers could hold out for long. How long before NATO, in desperation, resorted to tactical nukes, as well?

Michael was glad that he and Olivia had taken their son on their grand vacation while they had still had the chance. Three years ago, the world had still held itself together, if even then, by only a thread. They had toured the ruins of Greece and Rome...the Parthenon, Delphi, the Coliseum, Pompeii.

Viewing the fallen remains of once mighty civilizations, young Daniel had asked, "Will this be all that is left of our cities someday, Father?"

Michael had exchanged a look with Olivia and answered truthfully, "Perhaps, son, but no one can truly know what the future holds." Michael was glad that they had concluded their trip by savoring the eternal beauty of the south of France.

Michael slipped on his hooded jacket. It would be very cold outside tonight. He could have made it to the restaurant by walking through a series of tunnels and walkways that connected the various buildings. However, it had been snowing all afternoon and he still took an almost boyish delight in walking in the snow. With its broad tree-lined avenues and majestic buildings, Olympus was a magical place on any evening. Covered in snow, the city became positively ethereal.

* * *

That evening, Graham looked out from high up in his study. He watched the snow fall over his city...he still thought of it as "his" city. But it really wasn't anymore, was it? No, now it truly belonged to the people that worked and lived there. Savoring a snifter of good brandy by the window, the great man was in a contemplative mood this evening.

Just then Aristotle announced that his guest had arrived, *"Mr. Graham, would you like for me to permit Dr. Alvarez entrance to your study?"*

"Aristotle, thank you, but I would prefer to greet Professor Alvarez at the door myself," Graham responded as he rose and walked up to the big double doors, (the new explosion-proof doors that had replaced the originals, which had been blown off their hinges in the explosion some ten years ago.

Graham commanded the doors to open. "Louie, so good of you to see me tonight!" He greeted the small man with a warm two-handed handshake. "Please come into the study and relax by the fireplace. Here, give me your coat."

"*Gracias*, Jonathan. I thoroughly enjoyed the walk to the Library in the snow. The city is *muy bonito* tonight with its *manta* of white. But my aged bones do not like the cold so much, I think." The old professor settled into the big overstuffed leather chair.

"Would you like a glass of brandy to warm up those old bones a bit, professor?"

"If you please, Jonathan, a hot cup of Earl Grey would be much more to my liking."

"Done... Aristotle, would you please serve up a cup of Earl Grey for the professor?"

"*Complying, Mr. Graham. It will be delivered momentarily,*" the AI program responded.

After Graham had retrieved the cup of tea from the study's dumbwaiter and handed it to his friend, he settled into the leather chair across from the professor. Graham took another sip of his brandy as Professor Alvarez followed suit with his tea. Both men stared silently into the fire for a while, each lost in his thoughts.

After a time, Graham spoke, "Louie, I can't tell you how much I've come to look forward to these visits. Your life's history, your philosophy, your perspective on life have enriched and broadened my own thoughts and perceptions more than I can say."

"*Gracias*, Jonathan. These visits have been most rewarding for me, as well. I suppose it is not so unusual for a pair of lonely old goats like us to enjoy each other's company in their waning years. At another time and place I could imagine the two of us spending quiet afternoons playing chess in a park somewhere, is it not so?"

"Quite, Louie. Tonight, however, I have something both personal and confidential to share with you...and an offer to make."

"Louie, let us for a moment consider the concept of immortality. How many people have dreamed of it over the ages? Many have tried to achieve a sort of immortality through great works. I must admit, I myself have done so. Others have yearned for it in a more literal sense. It's a very seductive concept is it not?"

"*Sí*, Jonathan, very seductive indeed. But you see, I already believe that immortality is quite attainable...in a spiritual sense."

"Yes, I understand Louie, although I must admit that I have always been perplexed that a man of science can also have the capacity to believe with such assurance in the existence of a God and a hereafter."

"*Mi compadre*, it is far easier than you might imagine. Science and faith are but different facets of the one and only truth. I have never seen the contradiction...I leave that to the fundamentalists and radicals...of both science and religion."

"Yes, but how would you feel about the possibility of *physical* immortality?"

"For myself, I would not be interested. For others, if such a thing was possible, I would leave it to their conscience."

"Of course, Louie. As you are aware, some of the world's foremost genetic biologists have been working on such a possibility for generations. From time to time, breakthroughs are announced but, in the end, the results have invariably been disappointing. Nonetheless, slow and steady progress has been made in retarding the aging process. That's partly why the median age, for at least the upper classes, now hovers around ninety."

"So now, Jonathan, you wish to tell me that immortality has truly become a possibility?"

"Yes indeed Louie, and I may be the first person to have achieved it, literally. The geneticists have confirmed that my body's aging process has been totally arrested. It's taken years of research and treatments, and billions of dollars, but my biological clock appears to have been stopped cold at about sixty-five...to bad it couldn't have been thirty-five!"

"Nonetheless, the experts say that, theoretically, I could live for thousands of years. That's if my mind holds out. No one knows what the psychological effects of immortality might be."

"Jonathan, are you suggesting that you could share this breakthrough with the rest of the citizens of Olympus?"

"I'm afraid not, Louie. The process remains very complex, expensive and time-consuming. Doing it on a large scale would be very impractical. However, we could replicate it with a select few others, such as you and Mac, for instance. Let's be frank, my friend. You are seventy-seven years old, and your health could be better. Without taking steps, you may not be with us much longer. May I ask why you would not be interested?"

"*Compadre*, I know that my time on this earth is near an end, but I do not despair. Rather, I look forward to the transition. For I believe, fervently, that I will be reunited on that blessed day with that which is most precious to me...my beloved Magdalena."

Graham responded, "Believing as you do, I suppose that I can understand your answer...even though, believing as I do, your answer is a little hard to accept."

"But Jonathan, may I turn the question about, and ask specifically what it is about immortality that appeals to you so much?"

"I presume that you are asking...Why would anyone want to live to endure the bleak future we all now anticipate? But, you see, that's precisely why I do want to live on. I contributed more than perhaps any other individual to coming catastrophe. Now I've done what I could to make amends."

"Professor, I am, quite simply, obsessed with the desire to know how this story will play out. How far will civilization fall? Will it come back some day? If so, in how may years? Will Olympus survive? I want to know these things more than anything that I have ever wanted in my life. I'm even willing to risk insanity to see what the future holds."

"Beyond all that, I have a responsibility to protect this city. President Powell is a lunatic; that much is clear. I will tell you that I know to a far greater extent than anyone else just how great a madman our new president truly is. And no one else knows to what degree it is my money that is keeping him at bay. Without huge infusions of cash from Graham Enterprises, the U.S. would certainly be bankrupt by now. But without this leverage, Powell would likely become a very dangerous enemy to Olympus."

"Then you have Schmidt and Sergievich. I know that they are somehow behind the European war. They are using it to deplete the rival political and military centers of power in their region, so that they can more readily consolidate their own control and influence. They will soon make their move. I just wish I could find out where and how..."

"Jonathan, I must admit that I too am determined to remain with our friends until I have made whatever contribution that I can to ensure their survival. Therefore, I will accept your offer in a very limited way. I do not wish for immortality, but I would like to ensure my health until we have seen our way through the coming crisis. Is such a thing possible?"

"Yes, my friend, I believe that it is. My understanding is that the aging process can be reversed to some degree and then temporarily arrested."

"Then, *gracias*, such an offer I will accept. And, of course, your own secret will be safe with me."

"Wonderful Louie! Of course, I knew I could trust you to keep my confidence. Now then, if you would also be so kind, would you also accept my invitation to dinner?"

"There is no need to carefully examine that particular offer, *mi amigo. Tengo muy hambre!*"

"Very well then, my friend; let us adjourn to the dining room..."

✱ ✱ ✱

Olivia and Michael had dinner that evening with their son at "The Canteen". The café was a quaint little retro place decorated to look like an early 21st century eatery. They ordered up hamburgers, fries and shakes that at least looked like the real thing.

"Tell us about the Pathfinder Challenges, Daniel. We've hardly seen you since they began five days ago," Olivia asked as she took a hesitant slurp of the milkshake. (She was more of a yogurt and salad person.)

"It was mostly fun, Mom, but some of it was pretty tough and scary, too. The first day was all oral exams in VR. Teaching avatars would pose ethical issues, and we would try to address them off the top of our heads."

"Issues like what, Daniel? Give us an example," Michael asked, (even though he had helped to design most of the tests).

"You know Dad," the boy paused to take a hearty bite out of his burger, "like, if you had the chance to steal money from a criminal that you could give to the needy, would you...should you?"

"And how did you answer?" Olivia asked.

"Aw Mom, you know our answers are supposed to be confidential."

"Sorry, Daniel...then what?"

"On the second and third days were the individual challenges. Those were the most fun for me. We had to pass tests in martial arts, long distance running, woodcraft, mountain climbing and so forth. Each of us had to demonstrate personal courage, endurance and self-discipline."

"Then, on the fourth and fifth days, we had the teamwork and leadership challenges. Each of us was assigned to a team of six classmates. I was on the Alpha team. Each team was given a series of exercises in the classroom and in the field. Each member was required to demonstrate his or her ability to help the team pass each challenge. If the team failed any of them, all of its members failed."

"Your Mother and I are very proud that you did so well Daniel."

"Thanks Dad. Can you pass the catsup?"

* * *

"Well, let's hear it."

Schmidt had already seen the reports, but he wanted to hear it straight from the development team. Consequently, he had scheduled a 7AM VR conference.

"I very much regret to inform you that we have indeed encountered a significant setback, Herr Schmidt," the Project Leader, Dr. Koderesku replied. Even the project leader's avatar seemed to be trembling.

"The entity itself, we believe, is virtually irresistible. That is precisely the problem. Once it is unleashed, we have not determined a way to reliably control or restrain it."

Schmidt's avatar slammed its fist on the VR conference table. "I'm not interested in hearing about your problems, doctor. I was led to believe that this project was nearing completion. Just tell me how much longer it will take to get your problems solved."

Dr. Koderesku hesitated for a long moment before answering, "Two years, Herr Schmidt, perhaps three..." The project leader went on to describe how Lucifer was the most complex, ambitious project undertaken in modern times. It would take a truly monumental effort to bring it to completion.

Schmidt's avatar could mimic facial expressions, but it was not designed to register changes in facial color. His real face turned beet red, while his digital simulation merely glared at the good doctor's avatar. "And just what makes you think that this project will even be relevant in two or three years, doctor?"

The project leader did not know how to reply...

> * * *

President Powell had just concluded a very raucous late night cabinet meeting. The Attorney General had threatened to resign. The Secretary of Homeland Defense had hinted that he just might do the same. Very well, then. If they did resign, so be it. If they didn't, he might just ask for their resignations anyway. He had Brethren waiting in the wings ready to replace them.

Powell had been the very picture of moderation after he had succeeded his fallen predecessor. Even his harshest critics had been forced to admit that the new president had done an excellent job in restoring stability in the wake of two presidential resignations and an assassination in just a few short years. He gone on to run a masterful campaign in '96 and had won the election rather handily. His radical past had largely been forgotten. But now, the facade was beginning to wear thin.

Congressional impeachment hearings were gearing up over his declaration of martial law. Let them. He had bought enough of the congressmen on the Judiciary committee with Graham's money to ensure that they would never approve the articles of impeachment. Then there was the Supreme Court review of his suspension of habeas corpus. But guess what? He had half the judges in his back pocket too.

Powell was at peace with himself. While most presidents had suffered under the weight of the office, Powell had welcomed its tribulations. He understood that the worse things got, the greater was the opportunity for transformation.

The president had seen the classified intelligence reports; Apocalypse was drawing near and he must be ready. His government would act as the right hand of the Lord; when the time was right, it would protect the righteous and destroy the corrupt. And when the Antichrist appeared, Powell would be ready with twenty thousand nuclear weapons to smite him down.

However, more changes were necessary before he would hold the requisite power to do God's bidding, unfettered. Martial law was a good first step, but it was only a temporary measure. Somehow it needed to be codified into permanent law. How could that be accomplished? He already had the press and the other branches of government up in arms.

Powell's cyber-polls were below twenty percent and his term was up in two years. Re-election seemed out of the question. It would take a miracle for him to consolidate his power beyond the present Constitutional or electoral constraints. A miracle...perhaps in the guise of a national disaster?

* * *

After dinner, the three walked home in the snow. Michael and Olivia walked arm-in-arm under the streetlights. Daniel ran ahead, enjoying the crunch of his boots in the snow. It was late and very cold, so they had the broad avenue largely to themselves.

The couple stopped and kissed...only to be interrupted by a well-aimed snowball tossed by their son. His parents instantly broke apart and retaliated. Finally, after a time, covered in snow and laughing so hard he could barely speak, the young boy surrendered. "I give, I give!"

"And let that be a lesson to you, young man! Never, ever challenge your elders!" Olivia shouted, breathless from laughter as well.

Michael looked at his wife's profile in the dim glow of the streetlight. Her cheeks were flushed and the end of her nose was red. The steam of her breath glowed in the lamplight against the darkness. He had never seen anything so beautiful.

"I love you," he whispered.

Olivia stopped laughing and turned to gaze up at him. Her eyed were wide. She smiled and embraced him...only to be hit by another snowball!

"Gotcha!" the boy laughed as he ran ahead to get out of range...

* * *

Mac threw another log on the fire and settled down next to Ellen. Other than the fireplace in Jonathan's study, they had probably the only real fireplace in Olympus. Plenty of other condos and restaurants had fireplaces, but the rest were all virtual. Mac had had to get a special construction permit to install this one. *But it was worth the trouble*, he thought to himself as he put an arm around his wife, who snuggled up against him in response.

Dinner had been excellent, hand prepared by Ellen, who remained blessedly old-school about such things. Now they each savored a cup of rich coffee...their evening routine.

"So how was your first Olympian Council meeting, husband? I would never have imagined that you would turn into a bureaucrat in your old age."

"Nor I, wife. It was pretty boring I must admit, not really my cup of tea...discussing fines for littering, reviewing food production statistics, looking at updates on construction projects... those sorts of things. I still can't figure out why I ran for the position in the first place."

"You ran because everyone you knew insisted that you run. Remember? We all told you that you were the best man for the job. You are, you know, whether you want to hear it or not."

"Maybe...we'll see. In any case, I found one element of the meeting quite interesting, fascinating even."

"What was that, dear?"

"The Pathfinder Council meets in parallel with our own. They meet in the same hall, just on the other side. Their Council of seven is made up of twelve to fifteen year old youths elected by their peers, much like ours."

"Yes, I'm familiar with all that."

"The Pathfinder Council meets while we do, and then presents a report to the senior Council before we adjourn."

"Yes, go on."

"Well, Ellen, the report just doesn't seem like something a bunch of kids would produce. It's a serious report, which includes careful analysis leading to thoughtful and creative suggestions. Matter of fact, I'd have to say that, in may ways, the Pathfinder Council seems to be rather more relevant and more creative than our own is..."

"That is interesting, but for me perhaps, not really all that surprising. Remember, I've been working with these kids for years." Ellen, as a teacher, had spent more time than most with many of the Pathfinder children. As such, she had become well aware of their potential.

"How about another log on the fire, dear? With the snow, this cold really seems to go right down to your bones..."

"Only if you'll fetch me a couple of those cookies you baked this afternoon, to go with my coffee."

"Deal."

25

Across the River

It took five days, traveling south along the river through the densest part of the forest, to reach the little fishing village of Jamest'n. Although, according to Rawlins, it would have been safe enough to travel right down the road that led to the town, Sebastian preferred to take a less exposed route. He worried that spies might spot them and alert Raiders across the river. He hoped that they could slip into the village and then across the river as quietly as possible.

The three made camp just outside of town in a secluded little spot along the river. After a late dinner of freshly caught trout and corncakes, Sebastian fetched his gear. "Like we discussed, lad, stay here and lie low. I'll find the garrison, and Captain Valdez will lead me to the fisherman's cottage. Once everything's arranged, I'll come fetch you two."

Maya gave the big man a hug. "Be careful Uncle. I don't want to have to send Valerian out to rescue you again. We all know how well that turned out last time."

Sebastian laughed, "Little lady, iffin I need rescuin', just send Samantha next time. I reckon I'd trust that jackass more to get the job done than this here wet-behind-the-ears nephew of mine." Samantha pricked up her ears and snorted when she heard her name, then returned to grazing.

Valerian shot back, "Maybe if I get the chance to rescue you a few more times, Uncle, I'll get better at it."

"Let's just see if we can skirt the need for anybody to have to rescue anybody for a spell. I'll be off now; take care, youngsters."

With that, the Ranger disappeared into the night. The young couple sat back down by the fire, which had almost died down to embers. With darkness, a breeze had kicked up and the air had chilled significantly. When he noticed that Maya was shivering, Valerian threw a few small pieces of firewood on the fire and got it going again. When she continued to shake, he fetched her cloak and put it over her shoulders. She looked up at him with her big brown eyes.

"Husband, it would probably work a lot better if you were in here with me..."

The young man quickly settled in next to her as she opened her cloak and pulled him in.

* * *

It was near midnight by the time the Ranger had located the garrison just outside of town. Moving like an apparition, he had scouted the entire area until he was satisfied that everything was as it should be. The garrison was complex of several buildings and a corral surrounded by a high wooden palisade that was perhaps a hundred or so paces on each side. He could see what was inside because the large front gate was thrown wide open and the grounds inside were well lit with hanging lanterns. However, he could also see that if the gates were barred shut, the garrison would make a stout fortress. He guessed that the complex would be large enough to hold sixty or so men and their mounts.

The Ranger saw two sentries posted at the entrance, with two or three more manning each wall. Additionally, he had spotted at least three pairs of mounted sentries patrolling the general area. Once again, these men seemed to demonstrate admirable military discipline and vigilance.

When he thought the time was right, Sebastian simply appeared out of the darkness right in front of the sentries at the main gate. He raised his hands in greeting, but was immediately challenged, nonetheless.

"My name be Sebastian. If you please, fetch y'or captain, who would be expectin' me."

"Yessir, Capt'n told us to be on the lookout for a big stranger. Didn't give us y'er name, but I reckon ye'd be a big enough specimen to be him, all right. Just leave y'er gear with Private Kearns here and I'll escort you to Capt'n Valdez's quarters. My name be Corporal Benteen."

The big Ranger rather grudgingly dropped his weapons, cloak and gear behind the gate and followed the corporal across the compound. They headed towards a long low building that appeared to be the barracks. On one end was a door that Sebastian presumed was the captain's quarters. He could see the dim glow of a lamplight through the adjacent window. The corporal knocked at the door.

"Beggin' y'er pardon, Capt'n. You have a visitor out here, name of Sebastian."

The door opened and a short, lean, dark-skinned man peered into the dim light of the compound. He stuck his hand out in greeting and Sebastian took it. As with most of Commander Rawlins's troopers, this man looked both tough and disciplined. His leathery face was deeply lined from the sun. His close-cropped hair was jet black with just a bit of gray at the temples. He wore trooper's pants and boots, and a simple white shirt that hung out at the waist.

"So you're the fellow. Come in, come in; have a seat. Thank you corporal; that'll be all."

The corporal saluted and spun on his heels to return to his post. Sebastian sat down on a straight-backed wooden chair in front of the captain's small wooden desk. He glanced at the surroundings. The quarters were spare but neat, with a simple bed on one side of the room and the desk on the other. There was a piece of paper on the desk with fresh scribblings. It looked like the captain had been writing a report or perhaps a letter when he had been interrupted.

Captain Valdez opened a desk drawer and pulled out a bottle and two small glasses. "Would you care to have a drink? I reckon you must have worked up a thirst traipsin' through the forest out there."

"Thank you, captain; don't mind if I do."

Sebastian took the glass of clear liquid. When Valdez swallowed his drink in one smooth gulp, the Ranger followed suite. The fiery liquid almost caused the big man to choke. It was all he could do to keep himself from spraying it out on the officer's desk.

"Care for another?"

Sebastian just shook his head and waved it off. He was afraid to talk just yet. Valdez just laughed good-naturedly.

"The dispatch from the Commander said you were a Ranger from across the mountains. Looks like they don't have good corn-licker where you come from."

Finally Sebastian sputtered, "Right you are Captain, we have good ale, and wine on occasion, but we don't have anything that matches the hammer blow of that there fire water."

"Well, let's get right down to business, Ranger. I received a dispatch a few days ago from one of the Commander's personal scouts. It included orders from the Commander to make arrangements with a fisherman name of Marley to get you and your party safely across the river into the Lawless Lands."

"That's right Captain."

"I presume that the Commander made sure you know just how dangerous it is over there, didn't he?"

"I'm afraid that he did indeed, sir."

"Then I'm sure that you have good reason for going, and the Commander's got good reason for helpin' you. That'll be good enough for me. May I ask about where your party is camped? And how many are in your party"

"We're camped about two hour's march northwest of here. And there are two others beside myself."

"Then it'd be about an hour or so on horseback," he muttered to himself. "So here's what we're goin' to do. I'm going to have Corporal Benteen relieved at his post and saddle up two of our mounts. Benteen's one of my best men…he also knows how to keep his mouth shut if I order him to."

"You lead him back to your campsite. Then you all can double up on the two mounts and the corporal will take you to Marley's place on the river. If we get you going now, you should make it there before dawn."

"Sounds good, captain. I'm much obliged."

The officer stood up and smiled.

"Don't thank me, Ranger; I'm just following orders. But one more thing…When you get one look at Marley, you'll probably want to be right leery of the man. He's a rough old bird. Used to be a Raider hisself, once upon a time. But some Raiders from another band took his woman many years ago, and the man does hold a grudge. What I'm saying is that you can trust him with your life, if you make it no secret that the Raiders are your sworn enemy."

"Thanks for the advice, Captain. I'll put it to good use, I assure you. And thanks ag'in for your hospitality, but I'd best be on my way."

The two men shook hands and parted ways.

* * *

When Sebastian and Corporal Benteen arrived at the campsite, the Ranger was pleased to see that his nephew and Maya were nowhere to be seen.

"You youngsters can come out; it's just your uncle and a new friend!"

"We're right behind you, Uncle."

Valerian appeared out of the darkness, with his bow at the ready. Maya appeared just behind and to the side of her mate, with an arrow nocked on her bowstring, as well. The two men dismounted. In the dim moonlight, Sebastian introduced the corporal to Valerian and Maya. With a smile, the older man noticed that the young corporal was staring slack-jawed at the lovely young woman. *Not surprising,* he thought to himself, *in the moonlight, she looks like a warrior goddess, with her long, sleep-tousled hair, her bow and her short tunic. Young feller probably never saw such a vision in his life; probably never will again, for that matter.*

"Pleased t' meet ya ma'am," the young soldier stammered. He took the hand Maya had offered, then shook Valerian's hand as well, without really taking his eyes off of the girl.

"Well, enough for pleasantries. Let's get the camp broke down and get packed up. The corporal here is going to take us to Marley's place. If we move smartly, we'll get there before dawn."

Directly, Samantha had been packed and all traces of the campsite had been erased. Sebastian and Benteen mounted up. Much to the corporal's disappointment, Valerian hopped up behind him as Maya swung up behind Sebastian. They headed out without any further ado...

* * *

The sky to the east had just begun to lighten as they topped a small ridge and came into the sight of a run-down cabin on the river. As they approached the cabin, a ramshackle pier came into view just behind, with a small fishing boat moored up to it. A thin column of smoke rose from the pipe that served as a chimney for the cabin.

"Marley, it's Corporal Benteen! You got some visitors. Come on out and say hello…" the corporal shouted as they dismounted.

No response was forthcoming, so the corporal banged on the flimsy door.

"Marley! Are you in there?"

Still no answer. The soldier shook the door, trying to open it. However, it was securely latched from the inside. Then, suddenly, as he rattled the door, it swung inward. A face appeared from the darkness, more of an apparition, actually. It was a man, but just barely so. The old man had an eye patch over his left eye and about a week's stubble on his chin. Wild, thinning hair framed his almost bald head. His clothes were filthy and wrinkled, and his breath reeked of liquor.

The old rogue emerged from the doorway onto the rotting planks of his porch. To round out the image, he was stoop-shouldered, as well. "Wake me b'fore dawn, do ye? How's a hard workin' man supposed ta git his rest?"

Sebastian stepped forward and held out his hand. "I be Sebastian and this be my companions. I reckon you've been told to expect us."

Marley grinned and shook Sebastian's big, powerful hand with a bony, gnarled paw. He turned and leered at Maya with his one eye, ignoring Valerian altogether. "Rawlin's rider din't tell me ye'd have a pretty young lass w' ye. What be y'er name, little lady?"

Marley grinned at the young girl, showing a mouth with few teeth. Valerian stepped protectively between her and the old man. "My name is Valerian. Pleased to meet you."

Marley absently shook the young man's hand. The corporal mounted back up and took the reigns of his other horse. "The capt'n ordered me to deliver you folks and git back to the stockade straightaway, so's I best be off. It was a pleasure to meet you folks. Godspeed. Pleasure ma'am." The soldier saluted the young girl and gave her one last smile. He then turned and rode off over the hill.

"Would you folks like ta come in? I fear it's a bit cramped inside."

Sebastian had looked inside through the door. The cabin looked a pigpen and smelled even worse. "That's right hospitable of you Marley, but I'd just as soon let you have your privacy. If you don't mind, I think that we'll just make camp in that stand of trees by the river over yonder.

Directly, we'll have some tea brewed and some breakfast cooked. We'll fetch you to join us when it's ready, iffin you like."

"Well that's right kindly of you, sir. I'd be most obliged. But let me fetch a few smoked salmon that I reckon will be to y'er likin', along with a few eggs from the coop out back. Then we kin all have us a right proper breakfast. Meanwhile, I'll just clean up a bit and have my morning snort."

They had quickly set up camp in a secluded spot amongst the trees. Soon, they had unpacked Samantha and set her out to graze. They started a campfire and Maya made breakfast. Just as she had finished, Marley appeared through the trees. "Smells right good."

Sebastian stepped forward and handed the old man a tin plate and fork when he noticed the girl unconsciously slinking back. "Join us by the fire Marley, the morning still carries a bit of chill with it. Care for a cup of tea?"

"I prefer somethin' a bit stronger t' git my blood goin' in th' morn." The old man raised a clay jug that he'd carried with him.

"But I'll be pleased t' warm m'self by y'er fire. Care for a snort y'self Ranger? How about ye, lad? Missy, I know ye'd like it if ye'd jus' try it..." Marley leered at the young girl again. Sebastian and Valerian politely declined. Maya just shook her head and sat as far away from the filthy old man as she could. The men sat down around the fire, as well.

All were silent for a bit as they ate breakfast. Marley had discarded the fork and ate the salmon and fried eggs with his fingers. He ate with gusto, slurping, belching and licking his fingers. Maya could barely hide her disgust.

Setting his plate down, the old pirate licked his fingers one last time, wiped his hands on his filthy trousers and took a swig from the jug to wash down the last of his breakfast. "Ah, missy, that was a fine breakfast! Iffin ye' ever git tired of wanderin' about wi' these gents, ye'd be welcome to stay and rest up w' old Marley fer a spell. Ye' never did tell me y'er name, little missy. I reckon ye' must be a touch shy 'round strangers, ain't ye?"

"My name is Maya."

"Well that's a right pretty name fer a right pretty lass." Grinning, he stared at her with his one eye until she turned away. He just chuckled.

"So Marley," Sebastian broke in, "I hear tell you aren't too fond of the Raiders."

"No indeed. Used t' be a Raider m'self, as you prob'ly know. But I grew tired of ramblin' and raid'n' whilst I was still in m' prime. Fancied a whore from a town near here. Built a cabin and talked her inta movin' in w' me. Bought a fishin' boat with m' ill-gotten gains. Fished a little bit with it too…but mostly made m' livin' smugglin' for the Raiders. Smugglin' trade goods to the other side and smugglin' some of them Raiders back across to this side."

"Had a son. You'll meet him directly; he still runs the boat with me. Lives downriver w' his own woman. Well, when the boy was only half grow'd, we brought some Raiders across one night. I could tell their leader took a fancy to my woman right off. Offered to buy her onc't we made it to shore. Should'a took the money. When I refused, he just took her with him anyway. I couldn't do anythin' about it; there was six of 'em. What really stuck in my craw was that she went with 'em of her own accord; seemed like she fancied him too. They just left me an' th' boy standin' there on th' river bank with our boat."

"Well, I had m' revenge. Found out from another smuggler when they were plannin' on goin' back across th' river, and turned 'em in to the Militia. Most were killed or captured in an ambush. Never did find out what happened t' m' woman, though."

"Anyway, the Militia paid me a handsome reward. Offered to pay me even more if I'd let 'em know whenever I could find out Raiders was comin' across. They even gave me license to keep on smugglin'. That's still how we make a livin' these days, me and th' boy: smugglin' fer th' Raiders 'n spyin' for the Commander."

"So, Ranger, I hear tell ye helped the Commander hunt down a passel of Raiders ye'self."

"That we did, Marley. Raiders took our Maya. Me and the lad fetched her back and made some Raiders suffer fer it right well in the bargain. The lad was almost killed in the process; had a knife stuck between his ribs."

Marley seemed to look at Valerian with a bit of newfound respect. "Well then, I'm y'er man. But I reckon y'er goin' to have ta lie low for a week or so, 'til we git a new moon."

"Can you navigate the river even without moonlight?" Valerian asked.

"Sonny, I could run that river w' a patch over m' one good eye."

* * *

A week at Marley's cabin had passed quickly and uneventfully. Now, just past midnight on the first moonless night, they found themselves gliding silently through the darkness on Marley's "fishing boat". Marley's son, a big, blonde, rugged fellow, stood lookout at the bow. While Marley worked the tiller, his son used a long pole to probe ahead for obstructions. Marley stationed Sebastian and his nephew as lookouts on either side of the bow as well. They needed no sails; they just let the current take them downstream at a leisurely pace.

"Better to move slow through the darkness anyhow, 'case we hit a log or some other flotsam," Marley had pointed out.

Sebastian had been rather surprised when he had first gotten a close look at the boat. Though, from a distance, it looked as ramshackle as Marley's cabin, (or Marley himself, for that matter) upon closer inspection, the Ranger had noted that the boat appeared to be quite well maintained. No rotted timbers were apparent, the sail was well-mended, and the boat itself seemed quite watertight, overall.

"Ol' 'Bonnie Doone' don't look like much, but she's taken good care of me and th' boy over t' years." Marley had let his pride show when Sebastian had complimented him on his craft.

Boarding the boat at Marley's pier, they had encountered only one hitch. Trying to guide Samantha aboard the gently swaying craft, they had soon discovered that her even temperament was limited to dry land. The mule had always been so well-behaved that they had come to take her agreeable nature for granted. But this time, she balked, she brayed, she bucked and finally, she simply froze and refused to move from the dock. The men had eventually given up in complete frustration.

"I'm afraid we'll have to leave Samantha on this side," Sebastian had said, "let's unload her and take only what we can carry on our own backs."

Maya had come to the rescue. "Let me give it a try, Uncle."

The young woman had spoken calmly and affectionately to the mule, just as she had seen Joshua do so many times before. Then she had taken a large strip of cloth and tied it over the animal's eyes. Still speaking softly to the frightened animal, the girl had then gently pulled on her reins. Without hesitation, the animal had docilely followed her aboard. Sebastian had patted the young woman on her back and then the mule on her rump.

"Well, I'm just proud of both of you young ladies," he had chuckled as they cast off.

Now, gliding silently by, to starboard they could see the various torches and lanterns of Jamest'n reflected across the water.

"It's beautiful," Maya remarked, still holding Samantha's head in her arms.

"Yes, lass, but speak quiet," Marley warned in a whisper. "Y'er voice carries a long way across th' water."

They spoke little after that, afraid of giving themselves away. For hours, they just drifted along through the darkness. The only sound was the murmur of the river's current, punctuated by the occasional dull thud of a submerged object bouncing off of the craft's prow. The only light was from the bright pinpoints of the stars in the sky above, and their faint reflection on the water below.

Eventually, the sky began to lighten just a bit in the east. Soon, they could just make out both river banks through a faint mist that hung above the water. Sebastian was struck by how much wider the river had become at this point. Although they had continued to hug the western shore, the distant side now appeared far away.

"This is where the river widens into th' res'vor," Marley had whispered. "Now comes th' tricky part. Boy, raise sails! Gents, give 'em a hand, iffin ye please. We needs to move fast 'fore it gets any lighter. We'll make our run to th' far side here. Be on th' lookout for two lanterns hung close together; that'll be Santiago's signal. Should be just ahead. Now move lads, be quick about it!"

Marley's son, (his name was Zed), moved quickly and efficiently. The Ranger and Valerian tried to help, but unfamiliar with the various lines and pulleys, they did little more than get in the way. Nonetheless, in moments, the sails were billowing out and the little boat was cutting across the water at an exhilarating pace.

The sky continued to lighten as they approached the far side. Sebastian began to worry at how exposed they were on the water with dawn breaking. As they neared the eastern shore, Marley cut sharply to starboard so that their course again ran parallel to the riverbank. After a time, even Marley became concerned, as they failed to see any signal lanterns.

"Maybe Santiago didn't git th' word. Pretty soon, I'm gonna have to drop you folks off fer yer own good, with or w'out Santiago. Iffin the Raiders catch ye out here, ye won't stand a chance."

Then, just as Marley began to make a run for a sheltered cove to drop them off, Valerian spotted the lanterns. "Over there, Marley! Can you see 'em?"

"M' one eye ain't what it used to be, but I think so, lad. Yep, I kin see 'em now."

Marley expertly cut the little craft to port and guided her toward the twin lights. The lanterns were hung above the rotting remains of a small pier. At first they saw no one. But as the old man began to guide the craft slowly toward the pier, they saw a dark figure huddled in a cloak under a nearby tree. As the boat lightly thudded against the remains of the dock, the sleeping figure looked up. The man stood and stretched, then waved at Marley.

"El hombre viejo del río...buenas días!"

"Mornin' Santiago. How's about helpin' us git tied off over here?"

"My pleasure." He danced over the missing and rotten timbers of the dilapidated pier to catch a line from Zed.

"Buenas días, Zed! Buenos días, amigos!"

The three passengers first concentrated on carefully guiding Samantha off of the boat and across the wrecked pier. This time the mule didn't balk; she seemed as anxious to get to dry land as they were to get her there.

Zed helped them get the rest of their provisions and gear to shore while Marley stayed with the boat. All the while, the old smuggler was anxiously scanning the river and its banks for the enemy. Sebastian hopped back over the broken timbers of the pier and returned to the boat one more time. He extended his hand to its captain.

"Marley, thank you kindly. I hope you'll be able to make it back to y'or home in one piece. The sun's almost up."

"M' pleasure Ranger. Don't worry about me and the boy. Without you folks on board, we be in no danger. Iffin we run into any Raiders, we'll just tell 'em we've made a reg'lar smuggling' run. They'll let us pass. Good luck t' ye."

"And to you," the big man responded, as he took a small bag of coins from his tunic.

"The Commander told us to give you this if you got us here in one piece. You did that right well." Sebastian tossed the bag to the old man.

"Well thank ye kindly, Ranger," the old man stuffed the bag into his ragged shirt.

"Let's be off boy!" With that, his son pushed the boat off and jumped aboard. Catching the wind in its sails, the boat pulled away slowly. Tacking the little boat upstream, it would take them all day to return to Marley's cabin.

While Sebastian had bid farewell to Marley, Santiago had already introduced himself to Valerian and Maya. Both were bemused by his strange accent and manner of speaking. Some of his words were unknown to them altogether.

As Sebastian jumped off of the wrecked dock, Santiago extended his hand to the Ranger, as well. "So you are the big Ranger from across the mountains. *Con mucho gusto.*"

Sebastian took the stranger's hand as he took stock of the man. Santiago was almost as tall as the Ranger himself, but he was lean and hard, where Sebastian was muscular and barrel-chested. The man had olive skin and clever blue eyes that framed a long hawk nose. His black hair and beard were cut short and neatly trimmed. He wore boots, trousers and a shirt in the style of the Raiders, but his clothing was clean and well mended, unlike those of any other Raiders that Sebastian had seen. He wore a black, hooded cloak.

Over his left shoulder, Santiago carried what looked to be a well-made sword in a fine leather scabbard. An equally well-crafted dagger hung at his belt. Altogether, Sebastian's first impression of this man was that he was formidable. *If I'm a bear, this man's a wolf,* he thought to himself.

"Pleased to meet you," Sebastian responded.

The handshake that they shared would have crushed the hand of any ordinary man. Both were impressed.

"Daylight's nearly upon us, *compadres.* Follow me now," Santiago spoke as he shouldered a small knapsack and placed a broad brimmed hat on his head.

"I have a little cabin well-hidden in the forest near here, where we can eat and rest, while we plan your journey."

"Well then, friend, lead on," the Ranger responded.

And with that, the little party began their adventure in the Lawless Lands…

26

The Lawless Lands

It was almost midday by the time they reached Santiago's cabin, deep in the forest. The cabin was old and small, but seemed to be in good enough repair. As they approached the cabin, Valerian spied a nearby outlying shack, which appeared to hold a small blacksmith shop equipped with a forge, anvil and various smithy tools. A corral in an adjacent meadow held what appeared from a distance to be a handsome chestnut stallion.

"Welcome to my humble little home, *compadres*. Please come in. I have some bread, cheese and sausage with which we can share a humble and, I fear, rather tardy breakfast. After that, you are all welcome to rest inside for a while, as I am sure that none of you had any sleep last night. This evening, we can begin to make plans for your journey."

"Right kind of you, friend, a little food and rest sounds just fine," Sebastian responded as he dropped his gear and he followed their host inside.

Valerian and Maya both quickly unpacked Samantha and set her out to graze. They then dropped their own gear outside and followed Sebastian into the cabin. It took a few moments for their eyes to get adjusted to the dim light inside. Sebastian and their new host were already sitting at the table, slicing the sausage and cheese. The young couple took a moment to look around the cabin. It was quite ordinary in most respects. A small cot was set in one corner opposite the table. Santiago had already started a fire in a small fireplace at the back of the cabin. A teakettle hung above the fire.

However, three very unusual objects above the fireplace mantle caught Valerian's eye. Three beautifully crafted swords in ornamental scabbards were set on pegs, each one above the other. Each weapon was partially drawn from its scabbard, so that some of its gleaming blade was exposed. Each was also unique from the other two.

"Ah, you admire my *Tres Angels de la Guarda*," my three guardian angels. Please come and share my simple fare and, after your *siesta*, I'll tell you their story. Here, take this plate, *señora*. Also, please take my chair; I'm afraid that I have but two. I can sit on the floor with the lad, after I make us all some tea."

"Thank you, sir, but I'd just as soon sit with my husband and share his plate," Maya responded.

"As you wish."

Presently, Santiago had made four cups of tea, and they all devoured their breakfasts in relative silence. They were all starving, having marched through the morning on an empty stomach.

After they had all had eaten their fill, Valerian spoke up first, "Thank you, sir, for the meal and for your hospitality. May I ask...what is the origin of your accent, which is unfamiliar to us, and of the words that we do not recognize?"

Santiago smiled, "It is known as Spanish, *mi amigo*. My original home was many days' journey south of here, on the southernmost fringes of the Lawless Lands, where a mixture of Spanish and your own language was commonly spoken."

"And how did you come to travel so far from your home," Sebastian asked.

"Revenge, sadly. My town, San Cristobal, was isolated, far across the southernmost mountains. For many years, it was peaceful and prosperous. Then, one day, the Raiders came in force across the mountains. They sacked my town and burned it; many died. Women were carried away. My father was a master sword smith; a family tradition carried down from father to son for many generations. And like his father before him, my father was as skilled wielding a sword as crafting one. Many townspeople fled, but my father fought. He took many Raiders with him before he went down."

"At the time, I was a care-free lad, about your age," he pointed at Valerian. "My father had raised me alone, since my mother had died in childbirth. I had been in the mountains hunting with *mi compadres*...my friends, during the raid. When we came back to town, it was in ruins. We helped to bury the dead, including my father. I tried to convince my friends to follow the Raiders to exact revenge, but they all had some family left. They preferred to stay and help them rebuild. I had no one, so I set out on my own. My father's swords had been safely hidden away in our home. I took them and began my long journey."

"Did you find them, the ones that sacked your town?" Maya asked.

"A few of them, *sí*...yes, eventually. But in the meantime, the rest had scattered to the four winds. Who can say how many avoided my blade?" he shrugged.

"In any case, in time my thirst for revenge faded. I learned that to survive in the Lawless Lands, I needed to be accepted by the Raiders, even though I refused to become one. Instead, I began to ply my father's trade. I found a blacksmith shop in a small town and signed on as an apprentice. I was soon crafting the finest weapons that the Raiders had ever seen. I became known by them as 'the Spaniard'."

"So you supplied superior weapons to your enemies?" Valerian asked, trying to avoid sounding accusatory.

Nonetheless, Santiago caught the young man's tone. "Yes, I was troubled by that, too. But then, I heard that the Militia in the Northern Territories had thrown the Raiders out of their lands. As soon as I was able, I crossed the river to join them."

"So how was it that you returned to this side?" Maya asked.

"The Commander himself asked it of me. He was aware that I knew how to survive on this side. In fact, these days, I have the personal protection of the Deacon himself, who wears one of my swords. Meanwhile, the Commander needs intelligence, and I am likely his best source."

"But enough talk for now, I have a few chores to take care of outside. Please make yourselves at home. Use my cot. Here are two blankets."

"Thank you sir," Valerian responded.

Then all three settled in for a nap as the Spaniard took his leave. Late in the afternoon, Santiago returned. The Ranger was already up, looking out the small window. The light that flooded through the door woke the other two young travelers, who had slept soundly. They both rose and stretched. Sebastian walked over to the mantle.

"These look like fine weapons, indeed, although, as a Ranger, I've never had much use for a sword. Rangers favor the lance, the bow or the knife and ax. Our Guardians carry swords and are right skilled in their use, but I've never seen the like of these. May I?"

"Be my guest, *amigo*, but watch yourself. It's likely that you have never seen blades with edges such as those of my 'Angels'".

The big Ranger gently lifted the bottommost sword off of its bracket. He pulled the blade from its scabbard. Valerian moved in to examine the weapon more closely, as well. It was indeed a work of art. Sebastian ran his thumb lightly along the blade to test its edge. He pulled his bloody thumb back in surprise; the blade had bitten deeply at the softest touch.

"You're right, I have never seen a blade of any type with near this edge," Sebastian noted in wonder.

Santiago handed the big man a rag for his bloody thumb. "*Sí*, this sword is of a type known as '*saber*'. I made this one myself. The one above was made by my father; it is known as a '*rapier*'. The topmost was made by my grandfather; it is called a '*katana*', and is a most rare and unique weapon."

"The swords that I make for the Raiders are nowhere close to the quality of these blades. More importantly, I do not teach them how to use these weapons properly...that is their real secret."

"Yes, I know what you mean. Our Guardsmen are well trained in the art of the sword. I've fought Raiders; they wield a sword like a butcher wields a meat cleaver."

"Indeed," the Spaniard agreed.

"Nonetheless," Sebastian continued, "I'll take a well handled lance over a sword any day."

Santiago grinned, "*Amigo*, I fear you've never faced a sword like one of these, wielded by a man that knows its proper use."

"Friend, you've never seen a lance wielded by a well trained Ranger."

"Ah, I believe I jus' heard a challenge. Would you like to join me outside for a little test?"

"Uncle...we don't want to see anyone get hurt do we?" Valerian was concerned for their new friend. He knew how his uncle could handle his lance, which had a reach at least two feet greater than the sword that Santiago held.

"*Verdad*, I will keep the sword in its scabbard secured with a thong to its hilt."

"And I will tie my knife scabbard over my lance's head."

"That is not necessary, but if you wish..."

Sebastian found himself becoming a bit irritated with this cocky stranger as they walked outside. *He certainly is sure of himself...for somebody that's never even seen a Ranger. He's a nice enough feller, but maybe he could use just a small dose of humility.*

The two men picked an open and level spot away from the cabin. Both were smiling confidently. Valerian and Maya stood well off to the side. The two men faced off. The Ranger adopted a fighting stance with his lance at the ready. The Spaniard held the "katana" sword with both hands above his head, in a manner that Sebastian had never seen.

"Please give the word," Santiago commanded Valerian, without ever glancing away from the big Ranger.

"Go!"

Sebastian lunged, feinted and lunged again, moving swiftly and surely...only to look down at the sheathed sword at his throat. *What just happened?* He hadn't even seen it coming, still, in fact, didn't know what had occurred. Valerian was dumfounded, as well.

"Friend I have never in my long life seen anything like that. Though, come to think of it, I really didn't see anythin' at all."

Santiago was gracious in victory. "*Mi padre*...my father, told me that my forefathers have passed along the secrets of martial arts that belonged to warriors even more ancient than the Ancients, themselves. Who knows, I may be the very last living recipient of those venerable arts."

"Well friend, on guard, if you please. I just have to give it another try."

"It is my pleasure."

The two fighters squared off again. This time the Ranger was much more wary, but just as aggressive. He parried Santiago's first slashing blow, but missed the second, which was almost instantaneous with the first. This time, the big man received the blow to his lower back.

"Again, if you please."

And so the sparring continued almost until sunset. By then, Sebastian was drenched in sweat, while the Spaniard still looked cool and relaxed. The best that Sebastian managed was on their last match. On that contest, he was actually able to parry three blows before being "killed"; that had taken all of about two seconds.

"Santiago, my compliments. I had hoped to teach you a bit of humility. Looks like it was me that just received a great big dose of it. But that's all right too; we Elympians have a saying, '*Strength through honor; strength through courage; strength through humility*'."

"Indeed. For whatever it's worth, *mi compadre*, no man has ever parried three of my blows in a single match."

"Well, I'll take that as a small consolation, friend."

Valerian and Maya had long since retreated to the shade of a nearby oak from which they could watch the contest. As the two men shook hands, Valerian rose to congratulate the victor.

Santiago waved Valerian back down. "Stay right there, *muchacho*. I have worked up quite a thirst and no little hunger dancing with your uncle. Let me fetch a bottle of wine and some nourishment, and we can begin to make our plans under that tree."

Their dinner was as simple as their lunch had been: just fresh fruit, with more bread and cheese. The wine was surprisingly good, however.

"It is called, '*Sangria*'. But, *por favor*, forgive my lack of hospitality. I could not go to town to purchase more provisions for fear of missing you at the landing. However, I do plan to go to town in the morning. I have finished a few more swords that I plan to sell to the Raiders there. With the script, I will purchase the additional provisions that we will need for the journey into the mountains. I will also purchase clothes for all of you more in the style worn in the territories. I fear that your present attire makes you far too conspicuous," Santiago added with a smile, "I jus' hope that I can find clothes at the mercantile big enough to fit you, Ranger."

"Good luck with that," the big man responded.

They ate and made their plans under the tree as the sun set. The Ranger pulled the map that the Commander had given him, and Santiago produced a much more detailed map of his own.

"From here, we will travel in almos' a straight line, south by east. Your journey would take some twenty days, if it were on level ground, but that is not the case You will have to cross three major rivers and ever higher and steeper mountain ranges. Therefore, it is my guess that it will take thirty or forty. But that is only a guess. I have traveled far and wide through the Lawless Lands, but I have never been where you are going."

"And where is the town that you will visit in the mornin'?" the Ranger asked.

"Right here, a place called Ducht'n," Santiago pointed to a spot just southeast of their location, "It is near the dam for this res'vor."

"What sort of dam? And I heard Marley use the word, 'res'vor' for this part of the river. What is that, exactly?" Valerian asked.

"If you have never seen a dam built by the Ancients, I wish that I could show you this one. But alas, it is too near the town, which you must avoid by as great a distance as possible. The dam is a huge curved structure that you can see from miles away. It is perhaps three hundred paces across and half as high. It has a wide road across the top that is still used. It holds back a fantastic volume of the river's water, creating a lake behind it that extends for many miles in all directions. That lake is what is known as a res'vor. The river is jus' a trickle on the other side."

"I do wish that we could see such a wonder," Valerian said.

"We'll see wonders enough iffin we reach Elympias, lad. Let's just concentrate on that."

"Right, Uncle."

"In any case," Santiago continued, "I will guide you to a remote pass that will take you through the first mountain range. Reaching that pass may take two weeks if we are careful to travel so as to avoid detection. From there on, you will be on your own. I will escort you on the easiest part of your journey, but also the most perilous, as it is between here and the pass that you are the most likely to encounter Raiders. Once you are in the mountains, your journey will become much more arduous, but the few Raiders that you stumble across will be much easier to avoid."

"Sounds like a plan," Sebastian concluded.

"How long will it take you to get to the town and back?" Maya asked.

"If I leave at dawn, I will reach the town by mid-afternoon. I will spend the rest of the day selling my wares and buying provisions. I will then spend the night at an inn and return at dawn on the next day. So I should be back here by mid-afternoon of the day after."

"Well, it's gettin' dark. What say we turn in for the night? Valerian, why don't you and your girl check on Samantha? I'll move our provisions inside, if that's all right with you, Santiago."

"*No problema*, Sebastian. Meanwhile, I'll jus' check on *Diablo*."

* * *

The next morning, Santiago was the first to waken. As he washed up, Maya brewed tea as Valerian and his uncle prepared a simple breakfast from some of their provisions. The Spaniard quickly washed up, then drank his tea and ate a corn cake, and then went outside to saddle up. Valerian followed the older man to the corral.

"I named him *Diablo*...the Devil, because he was barely broken in when I won him in a game of chance. I had never owned such an unruly animal; I believe that the Raider that I won him from must have been secretly glad to lose him. However, over the years, Diablo and I have become the best of frien's. Isn't that so, *mi amigo?*"

The stallion ambled up and nuzzled his master, who had brought a few apple cores for a treat. As the big animal munched, Santiago quickly put on his blanket, saddle and bridle. He then led Diablo to the shed, where he retrieved four recently crafted swords. He showed one of them to Valerian.

"As you can see, these are serviceable enough weapons, but certainly nothing to brag about."

Valerian took the weapon from the Spaniard and drew it from its simple leather scabbard. He hefted it and took a few practice swings. "It's a saber, isn't it?"

"*Sí, compadre*! You were paying attention yesterday...that's *muy bueno*! The Raiders prefer sabers, because they are best used as slashing weapons on horseback."

"Yes, I noticed that the Militia cavalrymen had swords similar to these, as well."

"*Sí*, if I expect to be fighting while mounted, I would prefer to be carrying the saber. If I jus' want a light weapon for personal protection, say when I am walking down an unknown street, I will carry the rapier. If I am expecting to be fighting on foot against many adversaries, I will favor the katana."

"I understand. Santiago, I have a favor to ask."

"Let me guess. You would like to learn something of the way of the sword, as we journey together, no?"

"Yes, if it wouldn't be too much trouble. What I saw yesterday was incredible..."

"*Sí*, but it took many years of training and practice, from the time I was a small boy, to reach such a level of ability. We will only have several days together. Nonetheless, it would be a pleasure to help you to begin that particular journey as well. Here, take this sword as a gift and work with it until I return."

"Thank you, sir! But what do I do with it?"

Beyond Olympus

"Get to know it…intimately. It's weight, its balance, its heft…how much resistance to the air it makes when you swing it. Practice drawing it smoothly from its scabbard. Did your uncle to teach you to spar with the lance?"

"Yes sir, even Uncle will tell you that I am almost his match."

"That is *muy bueno*. The fundamentals are the same: breathing, balance, timing, conditioning, and most of all, the mental…how you say, *aspecto*. Are these basic skills familiar to you?"

"Yes, sir…the Rangers call them the '*five facets of fighting*'."

"Indeed they are. Then tomorrow we will begin your training."

As they had been conversing, Santiago had wrapped the three remaining swords in a blanket and tied the bundle behind his saddle. He had also secured his personal saber, one of the "Guardian Angels", to the saddle on his mount's left flank. His katana was looped over his left shoulder. He squared his hat low over his eyes and mounted Diablo

"*Adiós,* Valerian! *Hasta la vista*!" Santiago grinned at the young man and kicked his mount. In a flash, horse and rider were into the woods and out of sight. Valerian did not believe that he had ever before seen such a dashing figure.

The young man returned to the cabin, where Maya and Sebastian were sitting at the small table; each was having a second cup of tea.

"You're quite taken with the Spaniard, aren't you lad?"

"You must admit that he's a pretty impressive fellow, Uncle."

"Right impressive he is; I'll concede that readily enough. But can we trust him?"

"What? Why would we not?" Valerian was dumbfounded by the question.

"Nephew, the question ought to be: Why should we?" the Ranger responded.

"Well, for one thing, the Commander vouched for him…"

"True enough, and the Commander is no one's fool; that's for certain. So that's one point on his favor. On the other hand, we just met him yesterday. And you heard him; he is under the Deacon's personal protection. What if he's really the Deacon's man?"

Valerian was beginning to have a bit of doubt, in spite of himself. "But, Uncle, you saw how he handled that sword. He could have killed us all without effort."

"Aye, lad; I thought of that too. But what if he wanted to capture us alive, so that we could be questioned? I'm not sure if even he could have handled that, by himself. What if he's fetching help, right now?"

"Sebastian, are you suggesting that we should just leave now, and strike out on our own?" Maya asked.

"Lass, I've considered that, as well. I'm not saying that Santiago is a traitor; I'm not even sayin' that it's likely. I'm just suggestin' that it's possible. And if it's possible, then we have to take precautions, 'cause it be a life or death question."

"So what do you think we should do, Uncle?" Valerian asked.

"Well, here's what I suggest..."

* * *

The rider passed through the forest at a gallop. Occasionally, he would reign in and pull off of the trail, quickly dropping out of sight amongst the trees and underbrush. He would let his mount rest for a while until he was satisfied that he was not being closely followed. At intervals, when the opportunity presented itself, he would splash along in a brook or loop across rocky ground to make it difficult for any potential trackers to follow his trail.

Traveling thus, it took longer to return than he had expected. It was past sunset when he finally entered the clearing and the cabin came into view. He was surprised that no smoke seemed to be issuing from the chimney. In the gathering darkness, he rode up to the cabin cautiously, concerned at the stillness. He sensed that the cabin was unoccupied. He approached the door with his right hand resting lightly on the hilt of the katana. If there was trouble, any adversary would lose a hand or his head in a blink.

No one was inside. Santiago was equal parts concerned and curious. Then he smiled. The big Ranger didn't trust him! Of course... he had not given the big man enough credit. The Ranger was clever to be cautious.

The Spaniard walked back outside and shouted into the darkness, "*Hola*, Ranger! I am all alone! When you are satisfied of that fact, please fetch your young *compadres* and join me for a glass of Sangria."

He then proceeded to take his time unloading the two large packs strapped to Diablo. He then unsaddled his horse and led him to the corral.

As the animal drank eagerly from his trough, Santiago brushed him down in the dim light.

"Evenin' Santiago..."

The Spaniard jumped in spite of himself. Sensing his master's surprise, Diablo almost bolted, as well. The big Ranger had come to within arm's length of Santiago without being detected by man or beast. Santiago turned and smiled into the darkness. "It appears that you have some finely developed skills of your own, Ranger."

"Sorry to not have trusted you, friend...*compadre*, that is..."

Santiago cut him off. "No, *amigo*, it would have been foolish to trust your life an' those of your young charges with a rogue you had only jus' met. Where are your two young *compadres*?"

"In the forest, finishing a sweep of the area."

"They will find no one. I made certain that I wasn't followed."

"Then let's go inside, Santiago, and open that bottle of Sangria. They'll be along directly."

*   *   *

Dinner that night was a relative feast. In town, Santiago had purchased a smoked ham wrapped in burlap, along with potatoes and fresh vegetables. Maya prepared the dinner and outdid herself, even though she had only a small cast-iron cook pot hung over the fire place to work with.

After dinner, they inspected the supplies that Santiago had purchased in town. Santiago opened the two large bundles on the cabin floor. Much of what he had purchased was foodstuffs such as dried beef, corn meal and dried fruit. He had also obtained provisions that would be useful on a long trip such as medicines, bandages, blankets and tin cookware. There were also, of course, three bottles of wine, carefully wrapped in cloth. There was even a large canvas tarp that could be fashioned into a tent or lean-to, if the weather turned bad enough.

Finally, there were the articles of clothing. There were three sets of heavy trousers, a small pair, a medium pair and a third very large pair. There were also six simple cotton shirts, also in sizes small, medium and large. Finally, there were three of the broad billed floppy hats commonly worn in the territories.

"You can wear your own boots, belts and cloaks; they aren't so very different from what the people around these parts wear. Luckily for you, *señora,* although ladies in the townships typically wear long dresses, when traveling they often wear trousers and shirts in the manner of their men."

"Thank goodness for that," Maya said, "the trousers and shirts are clumsy enough, compared to our tunics. I've worn the long dresses that the ladies in the townships favor. They're nice enough to look at, but they would be impossible to travel any distance in."

"Indeed. At least these clothes will not arouse any suspicions, particularly from a distance. Now, on our trip, I would suggest that you let me scout a short distance ahead on Diablo. If I run across any Raiders, I will divert them."

Santiago pulled a small, simply made medallion worn around his neck from under his shirt. "This is the Deacon's seal. It should give me safe passage. *Con buena suerte*...with luck, I should be able to use it to protect all of you as well. If we do encounter Raiders, jus' let me do all the talking. Not to boast," the Spaniard grinned, "but I am almost as skilled with my tongue as I am with a blade."

"Now, as for your weapons; the lances, knives and axes are commonly carried hereabouts. But you would be well advised to conceal your bows on your mule. Raiders would confiscate them and be very suspicious of anyone carrying them."

"That's all right for the youngsters, who will be trailing with the mule. However, I prefer to keep all my weapons handy. I plan to follow you closely, out of sight, so's I can cover y'or back."

"After this evening, I can easily believe that you can do so. But how will you be able to keep up with Diablo?"

"Trust me, friend, that's not a problem, either."

Soon, they all turned in for the night. They would leave at dawn. They had agreed that, with Santiago as an escort, it would it would probably be safer to travel by day through the Lawless Lands. The Spaniard had explained that Raider bands were very active at night, while it would be very hard to explain why their little party had found it necessary to travel in the darkness.

The next day, by dawn's first light, the little party was well underway. Santiago had left first to scout ahead, with Sebastian trailing close behind. Valerian and Maya followed with the mule. All agreed that the men would find a good place to stop at midday to let the young couple catch up. After a quick lunch and a little rest, they would then continue until sunset.

The morning went as planned. Around midday, Santiago found a secluded meadow by a small brook. He stopped to let Diablo drink and the Ranger caught up in moments. "How does this look, Ranger?"

"This'll do just fine, Santiago. I reckon the young 'uns will be along in just a little while," the big man responded as he bent down to drink next to the horse, "this afternoon may not be as easy goin' as this mornin' though."

"Why not, *compadre*?" Santiago asked as he hobbled Diablo in the meadow to graze.

"I smell rain. Do you feel the way the breeze is kickin' up?"

"I had not noticed, but *sí*, now that you mention it..."

The Spaniard sat down against a tree trunk and pulled his hat down low over his eyes. "Well, in that case, I think that I had best take *mi siesta*, while I have the chance."

The Ranger followed suit, finding his own tree to stretch out under. After a time, Valerian and Maya arrived.

"Greetings Uncle; *hola*, Santiago!"

Both men stirred and stretched. Valerian quickly unpacked Samantha, let her drink and tethered her in the meadow near Diablo. They then all shared a simple lunch from their provisions. After they had eaten, Santiago soon mounted back up and headed out.

"You youngsters can rest a few more minutes. Then pack up and follow us. Keep y'or cloaks handy; it'll be rainin' by mid-afternoon. Take care," and with that the big man swung out to follow the Spaniard, once again.

Shortly after, the young couple had packed Samantha and set out to follow Santiago and the Ranger. Just as Sebastian had predicted, the skies soon began to darken with thick clouds, and the wind began to pick up. A light rain soon followed, which gradually became a steady downpour. The trail became muddy, but they slogged on, pulling their hoods over their heads and their cloaks tight about them. Nonetheless, they were both soon drenched.

Eventually, the tracks that the young couple had been following became obscured, but Valerian soon began to see his uncle's markings at intervals on trees to guide them on their way. Maya was cold, wet and miserable, but she tried to emulate Samantha as best she could, just plodding along without complaint.

Late in the day, Valerian noticed that the marked trail was diverging from the narrow forest path that they had been following. The going became even rougher, as the new trail that they followed alternated between deep mud and fields of rocks and boulders.

Blessedly, just before sunset, as they finally passed over a last ridge, a small lake came into view. It had just finally stopped raining as well. They soon made out Sebastian and Santiago on the edge of the lake. The men had hung their cloaks out to dry on some branches of a willow tree; Valerian and Maya soon followed suit. They took their muddy boots off and washed them and their feet in the lake. Maya was shivering.

"I'm afraid we won't be able to get a fire started tonight, lass, but take one of these here blankets; they're all still pretty dry. Santiago had the good sense to tie 'em under the packs."

"Thank you, Uncle, and thank you too, Santiago." The girl took the blanket and wrapped herself up.

"*De nada, muchacha*. It looks like we will be reduced to cold rations this night, as well. Perhaps, it would be appropriate to open the first bottle of wine this evening; at least, that will warm us a little bit, I think."

"Right good idea, Santiago. Let's get the animals unpacked and set up camp as best we can," Sebastian replied.

Soon enough, they had spread out the blankets and laid out their provisions. Well before the sun had set, they had eaten a simple meal of dried beef and corncakes. They had washed their dinner down with the wine from a bottle that they had passed around. The sun now lay low over the lake.

Bored, Valerian picked up his new sword and drew it from its simple scabbard. He brandished it about, slashing with it up, down and sideways. Santiago winced. "No, no, no! Elympian, you are upsetting my delicate sensibilities! You look like an ignorant Raider, hacking about like a clumsy oaf. Perhaps just before darkness falls I will have enough time to give you your firs' lesson."

"Here, hold the saber so, with your free hand at your waist. Grasp the weapon, as you would a small bird, lightly enough so as not to smother it, but tightly enough so that it does not escape. Position your feet so, and move them like this, so that you always maintain your balance. Look always at the center of your opponent's torso, so that you are not deceived by his feints. Wait here, *uno momento*."

The Spaniard retrieved his own saber. He withdrew the weapon and stuck it in the wet earth, wielding just the scabbard itself. "Now then, *en guard*. Yes, *bueno*. Now, did you play with wooden swords when you were a child?"

"Yes, sir."

"Remember how you dueled with the other children back then, hacking back and forth, for a long time, with much enthusiasm?"

"Yes sir."

"Well, a real duel between two skilled swordsmen is nothing like that. Jus' a few moves and it's over. Inevitably, after only seconds, one man is the victor and the other is dead or wounded. Mistakes are final."

With that, he attacked with the scabbard. Valerian managed to parry the first blow, but succumbed to the second.

"*Bueno*. Again, *en guard*."

They practiced until darkness fell. As they all settled in for the night, Santiago asserted, "Young man, you are a natural. It is a pleasure to instruct you. Too bad that we only have a short while to work together. *Buenas noches*."

"Thanks Santiago. I'll just try to make the best of what time we have together. Good...ah, *buenos noches*, Santiago. Good night, Uncle."

Valerian rolled into one damp blanket with Maya, while the Ranger and the Spaniard each curled up in their own.

* * *

The next several days were relatively uneventful, and they made steady progress in their journey. Santiago had led them carefully down little used forest trails. Each evening he had instructed the young man in the proper use of the sword. Often they practiced in the dim light of the campfire.

Riding ahead during the day, the Spaniard had only once run into a Raider band. That time, he had ridden boldly up to them, showed them the medallion under his shirt, and told them that he was on the Deacon's business. Just thirty paces away, invisible in the forest cover, and bow at the ready, the big Ranger heard and saw everything. The men went about their business down a different trail, which was to their good fortune.

Now, late in the afternoon, the little party made camp in a dense stand of aspens, near a small brook. At last, the forest floor had dried out enough from the first day's rains so that they could hope to start a campfire. While the men unpacked the animals and set them out to graze, Maya searched for dry kindling.

Suddenly, the young girl let out a yelp. She jumped up, holding her wrist. The men came running.

"What is it lass?"

Before she could answer, the Ranger saw the snake escape into the underbrush. It was a copperhead, a big one. Valerian held her. Tears were coursing down her cheeks, as much from fear as pain.

"Stupid, stupid. I've been taught since I was a little girl to look before I reach!"

"Hold the hand low, lass," the Ranger advised. "That'll slow the spread of the poison. Let's put it in the cold water of the creek yonder. That'll help a might, too. Don't be too fearful, little lady; a copperhead's bite ain't near as bad as that of a rattler or a moccasin."

The Ranger led her to the creek and gently set her down. He inspected her wrist before putting it in the water. It was already swelling. The big man was more concerned than he let on.

"Should we cut over the bite and suck out the poison? That is what my people do," Santiago suggested.

"Rangers don't. We believe that such a treatment can cause more problems than it is apt to cure. And we've had plenty of experience with snakebites. Still, I wish that we had a healer who could tend to it."

Valerian sat on the girl's other side and held her close, at a loss for what else to do. Santiago stood up and looked thoughtful.

"*Compadres*, I know a tavern near here, an inn for travelers. It is isolated and it is run by someone I trust, implicitly. She and I have been, ah, shall we say, very close friends. And she is very gifted as a healer. If I took Maya with me on Diablo, I could perhaps reach this tavern by midnight."

"Then let's saddle you up, Santiago. Me and the lad will pack as much of the extra provisions as we can on Samantha and shoulder the rest ourselves. We'll follow along directly."

"But can you track me in the darkness?"

"We have moonlight now, that won't be a problem. Just you worry about gettin' the lass there safe and sound."

Maya was unhappy being separated from her man. Valerian was equally distraught at leaving her in anyone else's care.

"It's the only way, youngsters. Maya, you just concentrate on stayin' calm," the big man tied a cloth snuggly above the wound. "It'll be all right. We'll be caught up with you before you can blink y'or pretty little eyes."

The big man gave her a hug and Valerian followed suite, holding her close for a long moment. Then the big Ranger lifted her up as if she were weightless, and set her on Diablo, behind the Spaniard.

"Keep that hand low, lass, and hold tight with the other." With that last bit of advice, he slapped the stallion on his rump and, in a moment, the horse and its two riders had disappeared into the darkness...

27

The Crucible
September 11ᵗʰ, 2099

The Hidden Palms was a rather ordinary condoplex, at least compared to some of the newest mega-structures currently being built. Located on the outskirts of Las Vegas, it was a self-contained community for some twelve thousand souls. In contrast, some of the largest complexes in cities such as LA or New York now held as many as eighteen thousand residents. (The largest super-condo was currently under construction in Hong Kong; it would eventually house a staggering thirty-three thousand souls when completed!)

The Hidden Palms was one of the, literally, thousands of condoplexes that had sprung up in cities all across the U.S., Europe and Asia over the last thirty years. They were intended as an answer to the myriad issues that had come to plague urban dwellers in the mid-twenty-first century: gridlocked traffic, rampant crime, pollution and global warming, which had made the climate intolerable in the middle and southern American states for most of each year.

This Las Vegas condoplex was forty stories in height, with an average of three hundred men, women and children housed on each floor. (Of course, this was just an average, as there were far fewer residents ensconced in the elegant upper floor penthouses; while far more were crowded into micro-suites on each of the lower levels.)

The Hidden Palms extended some ten floors below ground level. This is where the wide variety of stores, shops, schools, clinics, restaurants, bars and clubs were located. The condoplex was designed to be completely self-contained; it was unnecessary for a typical resident to ever leave its confines, unless he or she simply wanted to. And indeed, with so many citizens now cyber-commuting, (working in VR), many chose to stay year round within its clean, comfortable and safe confines.

In fact, a growing number of cyber-junkies were carrying this trend a step further. They preferred to live, work and play in Virtual Reality. While their bodies remained in bare-bones little micro-suites, their minds and senses were free to experience the wonders of a whole universe of imaginary worlds and experiences.

The youngest resident of the Hidden Palms was just two weeks old; the oldest was ninety-seven. The richest was a multi-billionaire who had leased the entire top floor; a multitude of maids, maintenance personnel and shop clerks vied for the 'distinction' of poorest. Almost two thousand residents in this complex were cyber-junkies, who rarely saw the light of day outside of their apartments. Something like seventy-five hundred residents rarely or never left the complex itself. Over five thousand were married. Just under three thousand were children under the age of eighteen.

At dawn on the ninety-eighth anniversary of the original 9/11, the Hidden Palms, its residences great and small, its stores, its shops, its schools, its clinics, its residents rich and poor, young and old, married and single…simply ceased to exist, in the blink of an eye, in a blinding flash that was soon followed by a mushroom cloud and a shockwave that destroyed a large swath of the surrounding city…

* * *

"My fellow Americans, it is with deepest regret that I inform you that yesterday over nineteen thousand of our citizens have been murdered in the city of Las Vegas, in the great state of Nevada. As we speak, under the authority of our Department of Homeland Defense, thousands of emergency and military personnel are already on site assisting the many more thousands of injured and homeless. Many more disaster relief personnel are on the way.

ACT, the Alliance of Cybernetic Terrorists, has already claimed responsibility for the detonation of a small, low yield nuclear weapon in the basement of the Hidden Palms, thereby murdering countless men, women and children. As you know, ACT's avowed purpose is to use whatever means necessary to coerce the developed nations into dismantling the Cybernet, our worldwide high-speed network. This of course, is madness, pure and simple. Without the Cybernet, our modern technologically based civilization would collapse entirely. Perhaps, ultimately, this is what the cyber-terrorists want. Fellow, citizens, we cannot, we will not, let this happen!

In addition to claiming responsibility for this monstrous deed, ACT has threatened to detonate a similar device in a different major American city each month, until we accede to their demands. Fellow citizens we will not be blackmailed by madmen!

In order to prevent another attack, I am prepared to take a series of bold, unprecedented steps. I had hoped by the end of this year to cancel both the temporary suspension of habeas corpus and the declaration of martial law. As you know, I had been forced to take those Draconian steps after the Florida disaster. I now find myself with no choice but to extend both measures indefinitely.

Further, I have ordered the Pentagon to draw up plans to withdraw from the UN and NATO, and to pull back all forces engaged in peacekeeping missions around the world. Land forces will be redeployed en mass along both our northern and southern borders, as well in all of our major cities. Naval forces will be stationed along our coasts. Fellow citizens, I propose that we create a new safe and secure Fortress America!

Finally, my friends, I now have no choice but to issue a series of Executive Orders that will greatly broaden the rules for domestic surveillance, censorship and interrogation of suspected terrorists.

My fellow Americans, you all know of my deep abiding faith in our God. Perhaps it is no coincidence that such a horrible disaster would take place in a city known for its ungodliness. I beg for you to pray to God for those lost souls and pray to God for my success in protecting each and every one of you! Good night America."

* * *

The Olympus Council met in emergency session that same night, just after President Powell's speech. Graham had been invited in an advisory role along with Dr. Alvarez, Michael and Olivia, at Mac's request. Dr. Allen, the Council Tribune, called the session to order.

"Ladies and gentlemen, I would like to dispense with the normal Council formalities tonight. Mr. Graham has urgently requested that he address the Council regarding the events of the last few days. Are all in favor?"

All raised their hands in affirmation. Graham stood up before the seated Council members.

"Thanks everyone, for your attention. First of all, I have a confession to make. For the last few years, without your knowledge, I have used much of Graham Enterprises' available assets to prop up the U.S. economy. I believe the other Great Powers have done much the same. My motive was partly to help maintain whatever economic stability was possible under the circumstances. However, my secondary motive was to essentially buy Powell off. I wanted to ensure that he would keep his hands off of Olympus."

Dr. Allen spoke first, "Jonathan, I do wish that you would have let us know what you were up to...although I'm relatively certain that we would have approved of your actions, in any case. But exactly how is this relevant to what is happening now?"

"Regretfully, my friend, bribery has been an integral part of my *modus operandi* for many years. However, I preferred not to soil this distinctive group's hands with such onerous behavior."

"The reason that I wanted to make my little confession was to give you all some insight into how I have developed some very extensive connections within the current Administration. I wanted you all to understand that I know whereof I speak."

"So now to the point...what I wished to tell all of you is that I have reason to believe that President Powell himself was behind yesterday's bombing."

Everyone looked at Graham in stunned disbelief. Everyone, that is, except for Dr. Alvarez. Dr. Allen quickly overcame his shock and adopted a thoughtful demeanor.

"Yes, yes, Jonathan...the possibility does hold a certain logic. Everyone knows that Powell and his people really want to establish a Christian theocracy. What would provide a better excuse than a national emergency?"

Now Dr. Alvarez rose and asked to speak. "I quote, '*If Tyranny and Oppression come to this land, it will be in the guise of fighting a foreign enemy.*'"

"James Madison, I believe," Dr. Allen responded.

Dr. Alvarez continued, "Precisely, Fred. I must confess that this was my first thought when the cyber-news channels broke the story. I do not believe that the cyber-terrorists have the resources or the ability to mount such an operation…not, at least, without help."

Now Graham spoke again, "Ladies and gentlemen, this is all far more than a theory. My sources tell me that many in the president's own Administration are terrified. I am certain that the Secretary of Homeland Defense and the Attorney General will tender their resignations by tomorrow morning. I believe that the Secretary of State, the Chairman of the Joint Chiefs and others in the Cabinet will quickly follow suit. This will only open the way for Powell to appoint his cronies in those positions, all of whom happen to be members of NAF."

Graham continued, "Furthermore, my sources believe that there is a shadowy organization made up of NAF members who are extreme, even by that fundamentalist organization's own standards. They believe that Powell himself is a member of that cabal, even though he has long since officially parted ways with the parent organization."

Michael spoke next, "Makes one begin to wonder who was really behind the last president's assassination, doesn't it?"

"It does indeed," Mac responded. "However, the one salient fact is that the most powerful man in the world, a man who commands twenty-thousand nuclear warheads and the most powerful military force in the world, is a lunatic."

"Make that homicidal lunatic, Mac. But yes, leave it to you to cut to the chase," Graham responded.

"The real question is: What can we possibly do about it?" Dr. Alvarez asked.

Now Olivia rose, "Well, I for one plan on putting our own security forces in Olympus and around the world on high alert. I will also call up our OSC Reserves…sorry Michael."

Michael, who had recently been promoted to Captain in the OSF Reserves, responded, "Aye, aye, Commander."

"Yes, Olivia," Dr. Allen responded, "that's an obvious and necessary step. But what else can we do?"

"I had considered mounting my own operation to assassinate the man, but I believe that any such attempt would be futile. My sources tell me that Powell has organized an airtight security zone around himself. He is evidently well aware of the danger his actions are going to create for himself," Graham flatly stated.

For the second time that evening everyone else stared at Graham, speechless.

"Then I considered buying off more congressmen in an attempt to have Powell impeached. However, at this point, I don't think that is necessary; I am quite certain that they will do so of their own volition."

"Jonathan, I consider you a good friend and colleague, but I must insist that you take no actions that could potentially endanger Olympus without first consulting the Council," Dr. Allen asserted.

"Agreed, Fred. As I said, I have only contemplated various drastic measures. I assure you that I would do nothing without first receiving the blessing of you and the Council. Nonetheless, my sources tell me that Powell will dissolve Congress if they vote to remove him. He'll use military force, if he must."

"Good Lord," Michael exclaimed in wonder, "so America is, at long last, to be ruled as a dictatorship!"

"*Compadres*, we have been lurching in that direction for almost a century now," Dr. Alvarez responded.

* * *

It was almost two in the morning before Olivia had been able to join Michael in bed. After the Council meeting, she had roused security personnel in Olympus and around the world, setting the wheels in motion for a full alert. She had used the Hidden Palms attack as an excuse; the Council had agreed to keep Powell's almost certain involvement top secret.

"Did you tuck Daniel in, Michael? How are Daniel and his friends taking all of this?"

"Yes, I did. Do you want to know what he asked me tonight? Although it really wasn't a question..."

"What, Michael?"

"As I was leaving his bedroom, he said in the darkness, 'It's starting now, isn't it, Dad?'"

"What did you say to him, Michael?"

Beyond Olympus

"What could I say, Olivia? I just told him, 'Yes, son, it's starting.'"

* * *

This time, Schmidt chose to have his meeting in person, rather than in VR. They were meeting in St. Petersburg, in an old palace that had had been converted into an exclusive hotel. Sergei Sergievich, the head of TeleGrup, had already arrived, as had the Project Lucifer team leader, Dr. Andre Koderesku.

"Gentlemen, thank you for agreeing to meet with me on such short notice. As you are both well aware, events are unfolding very rapidly in the United States. This means that, in order to control events, we must move rapidly as well. Dr. Koderesku, please give Sergei and myself a brief status report on Lucifer."

The small, nervous man rose and began to speak. "Gentlemen, it is an honor to finally meet both of you in person. Now, I am happy to report that we have made significant progress with Lucifer. As you are aware, Lucifer itself is an incredibly powerful entity. In test after test, it has proven to be absolutely and completely unstoppable. In fact, it is so powerful that designing tests are very difficult, for fear that it might escape."

"Yes, yes," Sergievich interrupted, "Doctor, if you would be so kind, let us go straight to the bottom line, as the Americans like to say. When will Lucifer be ready?"

"I am pleased to report that we will be able to safely release Lucifer in about twenty-four months."

The Russian and the Austrian tycoons looked at one another.

The Russian responded, "Dr. Koderesku, we can give you another twelve months, at most."

Koderesku protested haltingly, "Gentlemen, if we were to release Lucifer before sufficient restraints have been developed, the risks..."

Schmidt cut the small man off, "Doctor, the risks could not possibly be any greater than the perils of waiting too long."

Shortly after, the two great men had dismissed Koderesku.

"Sergei, I think that it is time to dial back the intensity of the Eurowar. Perhaps it's even time for an armistice, or at least a cease fire."

"Yes, my friend. We wanted our war to create a certain level of chaos, but we didn't reckon on Powell. It is impossible to control a madman such as the president."

"I quite agree. I'm certain that Powell will create quite enough chaos of his own accord. Let's just hope that we can trigger Lucifer before Powell commits some insane act on a global scale..."

28

The Inn

Just before daylight, the two weary travelers were relieved to finally round the last bend in the trail. There was the inn, a big ramshackle structure with stables extending out on one side and rooms extending out the other. Lamplight could be seen through a few windows in the main building and a few of the outlying rooms, as well. The two men had each carried an extra bundle of provisions throughout the night, so that Samantha would not be too overburdened.

Valerian started to drop his gear and run for the front entrance. The long night had been as hard on his nerves as on his back. However, the Ranger grabbed his nephew's elbow and pulled him and the mule off of the trail.

"Remember your oath lad. Stay here with Samantha and keep her quiet. I'll scout the area and come back for you when I'm sure all's clear."

With that the big man dropped all of his gear except for his lance and slipped into the underbrush, out of sight. From his vantage point, although he was well enough concealed, Valerian could clearly see the front of the tavern. For what seemed an eternity, he saw nothing else. Then, suddenly, there was his uncle, boldly opening the big main door and going inside.

Then, again, another eternity before the door opened again. And there was his uncle, waving an all clear in his direction. Valerian stepped into the open, waved back and led Samantha to the entrance.

"Where is she, Uncle?"

"Stay calm, lad, she's bein' tended to in one of the rooms."

Santiago appeared at the entrance behind the big man. "*Sí*, Valerian, my lady frien' stayed with her and cared for her through the night. Jus' a little while ago, she came for a cup of hot tea; she tol' me that the lass is resting comfortably."

"Could you please take me to her?"

"*Sí compadre*, follow me."

"I'll be along directly, nephew, after I take Samantha to the stables and tend to her."

Sympathetic to his young friend's anxiety, Santiago moved quickly. Four doors down, a dim light showed though the room's small window. The Spaniard opened the door and was immediately shushed by a woman seated next to Maya's bed. She rose and quickly hustled the two men back outside.

"The lass needs her rest, gents. The ride here took it all out of her."

"But how is she ma'am?"

The big woman looked down on Valerian and smiled warmly. (She had to look down because she was taller than the young man...almost as tall as Santiago.)

"She'll be fine. I expect you must be the lass's young man," she chuckled, "y'er not quite as good lookin' as she told me, but I'll guess you'll do."

Valerian was glad that the light was still dim, for he felt himself blush. "Yes, ma'am, my name is Valerian. May I go in now? I promise that I won't wake her."

The big woman extended her hand. "Well, Valerian, pleased t' meet you. My name is Lilith; I own this place. Yes, I reckon you can spell me for a while. I need t' start fixin' breakfast for th' guests, anyway. Set with her, but don't wake her. I gave her some medicines to ease th' pain and help her sleep. I also put a poultice on th' wound that'll draw out some of th' poison. If she wakes of her own accord though, come fetch me."

"Yes ma'am. Thank you kindly, ma'am."

"Y'er right welcome, lad. Get some sleep yerself. I'll bring you some breakfast and tea, after you've both rested."

In the darkness, Lilith and Santiago headed back to the main building together, arm in arm. "Santiago, you scoundrel; you bed a lady down and then you disappear without as much as a goodbye kiss."

The Spaniard stopped in his tracks. "*Señorita! Por favor, perdoname...* please forgive me. That was an unforgivable oversight. Let me hasten to make amen's!"

He put his arms around her and drew her to him, but she pulled away. Nonetheless, he could see her smiling in the dim light as she pushed him roughly away. "You devil, you had y'er chance back then. Maybe you'll have another chance one day...then again, maybe you won't..."

With that she put a finger to his lips, turned and entered the tavern. As she crossed the threshold, she saw Sebastian for the first time. "Greetings stranger, my name is Lilith. Well, aren't you the big strong fella? My Spaniard here tells me that you are a Ranger from across the western mountains. Do they grow 'em all that big over there?"

Sebastian laughed, "No ma'am, I'm afraid that I'm a bit oversized, even amongst my own folks. My name be Sebastian. Pleased to meet you, and thank you right kindly for takin' us in and helpin' the lass."

The Ranger took the hand that Lilith had offered and looked her in the eyes. He liked what he saw. Lilith was one of the biggest women that he had ever met...but big, as in tall and robust, not heavy. Although her shoulders and hips were wide, her waist was narrow. She had a wild main of wavy red hair and green eyes that seemed willful and wise at the same time. Her face was pale and smooth, with full lips, a strong chin and high cheekbones. She wore a long, low-cut dress that accentuated her more than ample bosom. She was the sort of woman that people referred to "handsome" rather than "beautiful".

Sebastian, who had been a dedicated widower for many years, was immediately taken with her. Lilith held the big man's powerful hand and met his gaze for a long moment.

Santiago had missed nothing. The Spaniard grinned and cleared his throat, "Pardon me; we are but a humble pair of tired and hungry wayfarers. What would it take for such persons to be tended to in a place such as this?"

Lilith responded, "Well, if you two gents will follow me into the kitchen, I'll see what I can do."

* * *

Valerian had tried to stay awake so that he could greet Maya as soon as she awoke. Fatigue had defeated his best efforts. When the young girl finally opened her eyes, it was mid-morning. She turned and smiled; there was her young man, scrunched uncomfortably on his straight-backed chair, head back, snoring loudly. She reached over with her good hand and gently took his. He slept on. After a time, she went back to sleep as well. Her hand still held his, even in sleep.

* * *

"Wake up you two; it's almost noon." Lilith had opened the door with an elbow, as she was carrying a tray that held three cups of hot tea, two bowls of stew and a half loaf of freshly baked bread.

Valerian rose and stretched. "Thank you, ma'am." Rubbing his eyes, he took the tray from the tall woman and set it on the foot of the bed.

"Enough of this business of callin' me 'ma'am'; you young folks are startin' to make me feel like an old lady. Call me Lilith, if you please, Valerian."

"Yes, ma'am...Lilith."

With all the talk, Maya finally stirred. She was still groggy from the medicines that Lilith had given her. Valerian quickly bent over to embrace her, almost upsetting the tray on the bed, which Lilith rescued.

"How are you? How is your wrist?" Valerian asked.

"I'm all right, but my whole arm is really sore," Maya responded.

"And it will be, fer a few more days. It didn't look too bad when you came in, so I don't think that you got too much poison. The poultice will help, too. I'll redress your arm with a fresh one after you eat. So eat now, before yer food gets cold."

Valerian didn't have to be asked twice; he was famished. He set Maya's tea and bowl of stew on the little stand next to her bed, then sat down and attacked his own bowl. The stew was delicious. Maya sipped her tea but just picked at the stew; she didn't have much of an appetite just yet. Lilith pulled up another chair and sipped at her own cup of tea.

"The Spaniard told me yer secret; told me you three were bound for Elympias. Wish I was goin' with you."

"You do?" Maya responded. "Seems like most of the folks we've told think we're crazy for even tryin' to go there."

"Oh, from what I've heard of Elympias, I reckon that it's a crazy enough idea. But I've always dreamed of goin' on a mad adventure."

"What have you heard of Elympias, Lilith," Valerian asked.

"Well, I knew a couple of Raiders that claimed to have been there... and I believed 'em, too."

"Why did you believe them?" Maya asked.

"You'd have to know Gordo and Lester; believe me, neither one of 'em would have th' brains nor th' imagination to have made up this story."

"And what was their story?"

"Well, they was ridin' with a large Raider band at the time, led by a real snake, name of Calder. Pickin's had been lean hereabouts; they'd cleaned out just about every township and settlement for miles all around. Calder finally got the idea to head south across the White River, up into the mountains. The goin' is rough that way, so not too many Raider bands bother going that far south. Calder figured that even though the townships up in the mountains might be small and few in number, at least they probably hadn't been picked over."

"Accordin' to Gordo, the plan worked right well, fer a while. Every time they raided a town up in th' mountains, their scouts found another even further south. In six weeks, they had sacked as many towns. But then, after the six or seventh town, their scouts came back to report on somethin' wondrous. They had found a large city that appeared just as it must have been on the day it was abandoned."

"Calder had heard of Elympias; so had some of the men. Most of 'em wanted to steer clear of it. Said it was haunted. Calder wanted to see it; he thought the city might hold gold or treasure. Some of the men were afraid to go there, to the point Calder almost had a mutiny on his hands. He took care of that his usual way. He just ran th' loudest troublemaker through with his saber and hung three others that had spoke up. After that, the rest was onboard."

"Calder did agree to make camp the night before, as far away as possible, and then hit the place in the daylight. And that's just what they did. Around midday the next day, they topped a high ridge, and they said the city was somethin' to behold. A smooth, white wall three or four times as tall as a man stretched all the way around the whole place. Towers made of glass and stone rose high into the sky. One gigantic round building sat in the center of the city."

Lilith stopped to finish her tea...and let the suspense build. Valerian was just then thinking how much this sounded like Miss Izzy's description of the city.

"Please go on."

"Well, that's where th' story get's a might sketchy. Things happened that Gordo and Lester couldn't rightly explain. They tried to find a way to get over the wall, but that's were everything seemed to go awry."

"Did they get in?"

"Nope, all they could say was that, at that point, they lost most of their horses and supplies. Things happened that they couldn't rightly understand when they tried to scale the wall. Appeared the city wasn't completely abandoned after all."

Valerian was beside himself, "Yes, yes?"

"That's about all that they could say..."

"How did the Raiders make it back?"

"Most of 'em didn't. They were only able to chase down a few of their horses, so they lost most of their provisions and weapons. Seems most of the towns they had raided weren't too eager to extend them a helpin' hand on th' way back, either. Out of about fifty Raiders that started out, only about six or eight made it back. Calder wasn't one of 'em, I'm happy to say."

Lilith gathered up the tray and the remains of their lunch. "You youngsters just rest in here fer a while. There's an outhouse out back if you need one. There's a bathhouse back there, as well. If you like, later this afternoon, I can draw you a hot bath."

"Oh, yes m...Lilith; that would be wonderful!" Maya responded.

Valerian was just thinking to himself: *The city wasn't completely abandoned...so who or what remains? Is Elympias perhaps haunted, after all?*

* * *

That evening, Santiago talked Sebastian into having dinner in the tavern. The young couple had decided to take dinner in their room, as Maya was still weak from the snakebite. Sebastian had planned to follow suit, as he was concerned that he might encounter curious Raiders in the tavern. However, the Spaniard had convinced him that it was safe enough.

350

"Lilith tells me that there are only a few peddlers an' traveling salesmen staying in her inn tonight. Besides, if any Raiders do show up tonight, both Lilith and I are protected by medallions."

"What is the story with those medallions, anyway?" the Ranger asked.

"When Rawlins an' the Territorial Militia drove the last of the Raiders to this side of the river, it was madness over here for almos' three years. Raider bands from the other side fought for dominance with the bands that had controlled this side for many years. The townsfolk and farmers got the worst of it, getting caught between rival bands. Soon trade stopped, crops were not planted or harvested. There was starvation, and a mass exodus of working people to the other side of the river soon followed."

"Finally, the leader of one of the largest Raider bands, a man named Deacon, made peace with a powerful rival band. One by one, mos' of the other bands fell in to the alliance, either willingly or by force of arms. Deacon restored order, although of a very different sort than in the Northern Territories. The Raiders over here could still do pretty much as they pleased; they could take whatever they needed or wanted: money, goods, or women. They could rob, rape or kill, at least within reason."

"However, the Raiders were not allowed to fight with one another, on pain of death. Also, Deacon passed out medallions to common folk who had provided him or his men with special services: a rancher that supplied his men with good beef, a brewer who provided him with good ale, a baker with bread. As I said, I provide him with good weapons."

"It is very clever, no? Everyone hates the Raiders, but now many eagerly support them, in hopes of winning a precious medallion that will protect them and their families."

"And what service does Lilith provide the Raiders?" the Ranger asked, leery of what the answer might be.

Santiago smiled, "Ah, *compadre,* not the sort of service you might fear. Her inn provides a very valuable way station for Raiders passing back and forth between the Western and Eastern regions. The food and ale is always good here. And the rooms are always clean, for those who can afford them."

"Well then, let's go sample some of that good food," the big man stood up, "I don't know about you, Santiago, but I could eat a bear."

* * *

Dinner that evening was very good indeed. Everyone else in the tavern had leftover stew. Santiago and Sebastian had thick, juicy steaks, washed down with the best ale Lilith could round up. There were about a half dozen other men eating or drinking in the big tavern. They were served by two very busy waitresses, *big cheerful country girls, by the look of 'em,* the Ranger thought to himself. Lilith joined the two men at their small table.

"I've got these two girls for waitin' on th' customers; Maudie and Sadie be their names. I have two more girls t' clean th' rooms. I've got an old man, Shem, that's the cook, and he's a good 'un. That big fat man yonder is Rufus, my bartender in th' evenin's. During th' day, he takes care of most of th' chores, as well."

"Well, the food and drink are the best I've had in many a long day."

The big Ranger leaned back in his chair, which creaked under the load. His steak had disappeared in a moment or two, and one of the waitresses had already refilled his big mug. Santiago had barely made a dent in his own steak.

"*Amigo*, jus' a suggestion, but to savor such a fine steak, next time you might want to try chewing it..."

Sebastian ignored his friend. "Lilith, how did you come to own this place?"

"Well, it originally belonged to my husband, an old codger named Tanner. He bought me from my parents when I was just fifteen. My parents were down and out farmers who had been pretty well cleaned out by the Raiders. They just needed th' money and they couldn't afford to feed or clothe me anymore."

"Anyhow, Tanner tried to treat me like a slave at first. But the first time he hit me, I hit 'em back." she chuckled. "He wasn't a big man. I reckon we was both kinda surprised that I could hit harder than he could. After that, we sorta reached an understandin'. I did whatever he told me to around here. I cooked, I cleaned, I waitress'd and I tended bar. But I wouldn't sleep with him and I wouldn't let him beat me."

"After 'bout four or five years, he had the good grace to drop dead and leave me this place," she laughed. "I think he died mostly out of frustration, cause I never would let him into my bed."

"And what about you, big fella? What's yer story?" Lilith asked.

Before the Ranger could answer, the front door was thrown open and three big men stalked into the room. They found a nearby table and sat down, throwing their ragged hats on the floor. They were filthy and ill-kept.

The Ranger immediately took them for Raiders. His hand unconsciously found the hilt of his big knife, the only weapon he carried, just now.

Lilith rose. "Excuse me gents."

Sebastian noticed that a cloud had passed over her face for a moment before she had forced a wide smile.

"Evenin' gents! What can I do for ye!" Lilith walked over to her new customers and put her hands on two of the men's shoulders.

"Well, I sure know wh' I'd like ye' ta' do fer me!" the biggest man fairly shouted, and his companions laughed loudly, "but fer now, le's have some ale, th' good stuff too, not th' swill y' serve these here sheep."

The Ranger noticed that the tavern, which had seemed relaxed and warm just moments ago, had suddenly grown quiet and tense, with the exception of the rowdy intruders.

"So who's goin' t' buy us th' firs' round?" one of the men asked and looked around.

"Th' first round's on the house, gents. An if ye' behave ye'selves, the meal will be on th' house, as well," Lilith replied with forced good humor.

One of the Raiders, an ugly man with a bulbous nose and a big, angry scar across his cheek, replied, "A high price that is. How 'bout we misbehave a bit, and get one of these here sheep t' pay fer dinner?"

The other two Raiders shouted in approval. Lilith fingered the medallion that hung at her neck. "Now you gents need to know that Deacon is a friend of mine. His price might be a far sight higher for misbehavin' than mine is," she replied with a firm smile.

"Bah...medallions! They hands out too many o' them damn things. Spoils our fun, it does."

The other two grunted in approval. The Raider had reached up and grabbed Lilith's medallion, which rested between her breasts. Sebastian tensed and began to rise, but the Spaniard pulled his friend back down. One of the Raiders noticed.

Meanwhile, Lilith had forcefully batted the Raider's hand away and had stared him down. "I welcome Raiders at this here establishment and I give 'em th' best food and drink that they can get fer miles around. In return, all I expect is that they be a bit civil. And that's what Deacon expects, as well. Do we understand each other, gents?"

"Ah, we're just funnin'. How's 'bout that dinner, now?"

The tall woman smiled again. "Right then, comin' right up. Sadie, refill these fellas' mugs, as well."

Under his breath, Santiago said, "Empty your mug, *compadre*, and let's go quietly. Don't worry; Lilith has been handling *brutos* such as these for years." Both men emptied their mugs, threw some coins on the table, and rose to leave.

The two men were almost out the door when one of the leaders spoke up, "You two, where d' ye think yer goin'? Ye didn't think ye were gettin' away w'out buyin' us drinks did ye?"

Santiago turned back, "*Con mucho gusto señors*...with pleasure, I will buy you a round." The Spaniard dropped a few coins on their table and turned again to leave.

"Oh, I know you, yer that funny talkin' fella that makes sabers fer Deacon. And what 'bout that big frien' o' yers? Is he goin' t' pay his respects, too?"

The Ranger grudgingly walked back to the Raider's table. He was just at that moment attempting to conceal the titanic struggle that he was having with himself to control his temper. He dropped some coins on the table and turned to leave.

"Hold on there fella. I'm not too sure I like yer attitude. Not enough sheep-like fer my taste." The biggest Raider had risen and grabbed Sebastian's arm. It wasn't lost on the man that the arm he had grabbed seemed as thick and hard as a normal man's thigh. Nor was it lost on the big Raider that the stranger he stood face to face with towered almost a head over him.

Santiago now moved in, and he was no longer smiling, "*Amigos*, I too have a medallion, and I wan' no trouble. But believe me, if it's trouble you want, my big *compadre* here and myself are capable of dealing you more trouble than you would ever want to see in a lifetime."

The Spaniard's hand rested casually on the long dagger at his belt. The other two Raiders had partially drawn their swords, but now hesitated.

The man who seemed to be the leader finally said, "Well, iffin ye have a medallion, we'll let ye be. But we best not have another sight o' ye this night."

"*No problema*," the Spaniard replied, smiling again, and led Sebastian out of the tavern. As they walked in the darkness back to their rooms, the Spaniard said, "*Mi madre*, that was close. My apologies, Sebastian; we should have stayed in our rooms, out of sight, as you had wished."

"What's done is done friend; don't fret about it. But I think we best be pushin' on in the morning."

"*Sí*, I agree. These men may alert Deacon or his lieutenants. Deacon is very nervous about spies, jus' now…as well he should be," he added with a grin that showed his white teeth in the darkness, "but do you think that the *muchacha* will be ready to travel so soon?"

"She'll just have to be, but we'll go as easy on her as we can for a while. I'll let the youngsters know. Evenin', Santiago."

"*Buenas noches, amigo.*"

* * *

They met in the tavern before dawn. Santiago had woken Lilith earlier, to let her know that they would be leaving that morning. She had told the Spaniard that she wanted to prepare them all breakfast and say farewell. As the men packed Samantha and saddled Diablo, Maya and Valerian checked and arranged the rest of their gear. Finally, everything was ready, and just as dawn rose, they sat down to a breakfast feast prepared by Lilith and her cook, Shem.

They had almost finished their meal when Sebastian suddenly stood up and commanded, "Gather your weapons."

The big man had already grabbed his lance and axe and had headed toward the entrance.

"What Uncle?" Valerian had just spoken, when he heard the horses approach.

"Valerian, stay back with the women. Santiago, come with me."

Santiago rushed forward to catch up with the Ranger, as he slung his Katana over his shoulder. Valerian hung back, as ordered, but grabbed his bow. He threw on his quiver and pulled three arrows. Lilith had turned down the lamps, so that they could not be seen in the dim light.

The horsemen reigned in just in front of the entrance to the tavern. They made a rough semicircle around the two men. The Ranger leaned casually against his lance; Santiago had left his sword in its scabbard.

Six of the Raiders dismounted and came forward with sabers drawn. Three of them were the men they had confronted the evening before. The men who had dismounted threw their reins to the other six men who had remained on their horses. Some of the mounted men had bows drawn and ready.

"Deacon gave orders that we bring in any varmints what look suspicious. I'd say you two fit th' bill. Now drop them weapons and turn around so's we kin bind ye."

Santiago moved a little forward and replied in a calm, amiable tone, "*Amigo*, as we said last night, we wan' no trouble. An' remember, I have a medallion."

The Ranger saw the Spaniard casually adopt a stance he had seen before. He followed suit, very subtly moving forward, as well.

"No more talk, jus' drop them weapons or we'll run ye through...right now!"

"All right then," the Spaniard replied as he held his hands up peacefully as if to pull his sword off of his shoulder.

Sebastian prepared himself, but was startled nonetheless; so were the Raiders. The leader went down first, almost beheaded, and the man next to him also fell, before anyone could even begin to react.

Sebastian drove his lance through the chest of the man in front of him, picking him off of his feat and driving him into the horses behind. The horses all reared so that none of the riders could get a clear shot with their bows. The few arrows released went wild. The lance was too embedded in the Raider to pull free, so the Ranger quickly drew his long knife and ax and went to work.

Behind the two men, Valerian burst out of the door, set himself and put an arrow through the nearest rider, then another. Suddenly, Maya followed with her bow, releasing an arrow, which went just over the head of yet another Raider.

Then even Lilith ran out and grabbed one of the fallen men's swords. The tall woman slashed at one of the last Raiders standing, just before he was able to strike Sebastian from behind with his sword. The Raider parried her blow, but the Ranger quickly spun and finished him with an ax blow to the head.

After just a moment, only three riders were left, as the Spaniard had downed four Raiders with as many strokes of his gleaming sword. Now Valerian and Maya came forward, simultaneously releasing two arrows at two of the mounted men who had backed off, just as one of them shot back. Maya's shaft went through one of the rider's arms, but Valerian's target ducked and the arrow overshot him. The Raider's shaft just missed Maya, but found its mark in Sebastian's left shoulder.

The last three riders had had enough. Simultaneously, all three turned and fled at a run into the dawn's early light. Everyone just stood still for just a moment. One of the fallen riders still alive moaned in agony; the Spaniard strode forward and finished him without hesitation.

Lilith pulled the wounded Ranger inside the tavern, and sat him at a table. She relit a lamp. The arrow had bitten into the bone of Sebastian's shoulder and still held fast. She cut his shirt away and held the lamp close so that she could inspect the wound.

Meanwhile outside, Maya was holding her bandaged arm in agony. Tears rolled down her cheeks. Drawing the bow with her injured arm had hurt her badly. Valerian pulled her inside and sat her at another table.

"Take the bandages off and fetch a bowl of cold well-water to soak her arm in, lad. She'll be all right. I've got to look after yer uncle right now," Lilith commanded the young man. The big woman was all business now.

Sebastian, sitting placidly with the arrow still protruding from his shoulder, told Santiago, "Better keep watch outside *compadre*. I think that they're all done, but we don't need to take no chances."

"*Sí, amigo*. Shem, could you fetch me a bowl of water and a cloth, *por favor*? I would like to clean some of this blood off of my weapon, as well as myself."

The Ranger, already mightily impressed with the Spaniard, was no less impressed with how calmly he now spoke.

"I'm goin' t' have t' tug really hard on this arrow t' pull it out. Do ye want somethin' t' bite down on?"

To the Ranger, the big woman seemed tough and compassionate at the same time.

"Just yank away, ma'am. But I'd be right grateful iffin you could get it out in one try. Think you could manage that?"

Lilith just smiled and put a foot on the chair, between his legs. She grasped the arrow with both of her strong hands. Then she did something altogether unexpected; she bent down and kissed the big man full on the lips. Before he could even respond, she straitened up and pulled at the arrow with all her strength. It tore free. She quickly pressed a clean cloth to the wound, which now bled freely.

"Just thought I'd distract ye a bit," she gave him a mischievous smile. "Did it work?"

The big Ranger was speechless for a moment. He hadn't been properly kissed by a woman in almost twenty years. "Well, it worked right well, it did. I didn't feel a thing."

"Th' kiss, or the arrow comin' out?"

"Huh? Oh, I felt the kiss all right."

Now Lilith was cleaning out the wound with moonshine, which was almost pure alcohol. It burned, but the big man really didn't much feel that, either. The big woman smiled at him warmly.

"Well, maybe we'll just have to try that agin sometime, when ye don't have any arrows stickin' out of ye...so's ye can give me yer full attention."

Valerian, meanwhile, was tending to Maya's arm. He held it in a bowl of cold water. "That was a foolish thing to do, following me out there. You could have gotten yourself killed. The arrow that struck Uncle missed you by a hair."

"Foolish or no, husband, get used to it. My place is by your side."

Holding her hurt arm, the young man bent over and kissed her.

"Shem, fetch everyone, the girls, Rufus and all th' guests. We're all goin' to have t' clear out before Deacon's men come back. I count nine of his men out there dead. Anybody they find here will catch hell," Lilith pointed out.

"Where will you all go?" Sebastian asked.

"The girls will just have t' go back t' their families and lie low for a spell. Rufus and Shem can just lose themselves in one of the towns, hereabouts. I doubt the Raiders will bother t' hunt any of them down, probably won't even remember who they are. For severance, I'm goin' t' let them all take whatever they want from the inn, 'ceptin my own personal things, of course. Then I'm goin' to burn th' place down, with th' dead Raiders in it."

"What about you?"

"Well, I'm goin' with you folks, of course. Just let me change into travelin' clothes, git packed and saddle my horse." She had just then finished dressing his wound; it was an expert job, too. The Ranger moved his arm. It felt pretty good.

"Thank you kindly ma'am. Now, Lilith, I'm not sure goin' with us is such a good idea..."

"Well, do ye think stayin' behind, so Deacon kin string me up, is a better idea? And bein' strung up would probably be th' best I could hope for, by the way."

The Ranger had no answer for that. It was late-morning by the time everything was done. Lilith's staff had gathered up whatever they could carry. Santiago and Valerian had caught most of the Raiders horses, keeping the best two for themselves, and letting Lilith's help have the rest. (Lilith already owned her own mount.) There were tearful farewells, for Lilith had been a good friend and a good master to them all. They scattered in all directions.

They had dragged the bodies of the Raiders into the tavern. Lilith smashed a few of the lit lamps on the floor, looked around for a moment and then strode out the front door, without looking back.

Sebastian thought that Lilith looked even more striking in her travel clothes. She wore a brown jacket and black riding pants over high leather boots. A wide brimmed hat hung at her back by a string around her neck. Her red hair was tied back in a ponytail.

"We'll have to travel fast, even though two of us are wounded," Santiago said as he mounted up, "We are a relatively large band now, an' the Raiders have excellent trackers. They will certainly be able to follow us. Deacon's encampment is only two days' hard ride from here, so we will have a four day lead, at best."

"Well, then," the big Ranger responded, "let's stop talkin' and start ridin'."

Flames were now showing through the windows of the tavern. They rode off at a gallop. After a while, in the distance, they could see a column of smoke rising from the inn. Their party, now five in number, had committed itself to the next, perhaps final, stage of their great adventure...

29

The Pursuit

The little band of five sat around a luxuriously large campfire. The Ranger, scouting ahead on horseback, had found a small, well-hidden little meadow well off from any trail, complete with a large stream filled with fish. They had just finished a hearty dinner of trout and now sat warming themselves by the fire, passing around one of Santiago's bottles of sangria. The nights were growing progressively chillier. Valerian had begun his journey in early spring; now it was early fall.

They had been heading south for three days now. The terrain had gotten steadily rougher, as they had anticipated, but at least the weather had held up for them. Most importantly, they had seen no sign of Raiders, as yet.

Valerian and Maya sat huddled close together. Lilith had settled in right next to Sebastian, who seemed to savor her closeness. Santiago was left odd man out, but seemed to be comfortable with the arrangement. Indeed, he seemed to be pleased at the attraction he observed between the big Ranger and his former lover.

Finally, Lilith broke the silence, "How's your arm, child?"

"Much better, thank you, Lilith. Your poultice and your medicines have worked wonders, even though I've had to ride with it all day, every day."

"*Sí*, regretfully, that is an unfortunate necessity," Santiago interjected.

"Of that I have no doubt," Maya responded, then changed the subject, "Santiago, you told us how you came to the Lawless Lands, but you never explained why you never returned to your home."

"Ah well, *muchacha*. The plain truth was that I found that I liked it in these lands. You see, I am at heart a rogue and a vagabond. The home of my youth was a small and peaceful place. If I had stayed there, I was doubtless fated to marry some small and peaceful *señorita*, and live a small and peaceful life. In the Lawless Lands, I have seen many wonderful and strange places, I have had many gran' adventures, and, *perdoname* ladies, but I have also had many "adventures" with a variety of lovely and exotic *señoritas*."

"A rogue and a vagabond he is indeed…I can surely testify to that," Lilith commented ruefully.

Santiago grinned, then continued, "However, with good always comes some bad, it seems. The way the Raiders abused the common folk was always difficult to for me to stomach. I have been very fortunate not to have been cornered by them, or I might not be here with all of you this night. That has been as much a matter of my wits, as my skill with the blade."

"Wits indeed," Lilith agreed, "try being an unattached lady in these lands. It has only been my wits and my will that's kept me from bein' raped or killed by the damned Raiders over th' years. Nonetheless, I hate th' Raiders and hope to see the day they're all either strung up or run off."

"Why don't the common folk rise up against the Raiders like they did in the Northern Territories?" Valerian asked.

Lilith responded, "They would, if they could find a leader like Rawlins. Everyone, I mean everyone down here, hates the Raiders, even those who cooperate with 'em. We've told the Commander that he should cross the river right now, even though his Militia is much smaller in number than Deacon's Raiders. If Rawlins and his men would just invade, every common man, woman and child would rise up t' join 'em…cause there's not a one that hasn't been abused by the Raiders one time or another."

Valerian's head was a little bit fuzzy from the wine, so it was his uncle who first caught the implications of what Lilith had just told them.

"Wait a minute. When have you ever talked to th' Commander, Lilith?"

"Well, I've never actually talked to th' Commander, directly. I just send him messages through th' Spaniard here. Santiago recruited me as a spy years ago."

"Ah, that makes sense, it does. I imagine that you'd hear and see much of value in a tavern like your own. But spyin's a right dangerous business, ain't it?" Sebastian asked.

"I suppose, but just livin' and getting' by in these territories is dangerous enough, anyway. At least spyin' is takin a risk fer a good cause. The Commander wants to know as well as he can when the best time will be fer him t' make his move. Just as important, he wants to know what Deacon is up to. Deacon would just as much like t' invade th' Northern Territories as t' other way around."

"Yes, but, regretfully, it appears that our spying days are now over. Deacon will have a very large death bounty on both our heads, by now," Santiago added, as he took another swig of wine.

"Well lad, are you ready for your next lesson with the sword?"

"*Sí amigo*!" Valerian responded, as he rose to fetch his weapon...

* * *

Deacon was furious. The three men had just ridden into his encampment moments ago. They had told their story to a sentry and then been led straightaway to the Deacon's big command tent. One of the men had a bandaged arm that had been bleeding badly. He looked in a bad way, but the Raider leader had ignored him, being more interested in their report.

"You mean t' tell me that three men took on a Raider party of twelve, and ye three raggedy fools 'er all what's left?"

"Yessir, Mr. Deacon, sir. That Spaniard was a devil wi' the sword. 'En that other feller were a giant." The big man held his hat in his hands and virtually groveled before the Raider leader.

One of the other men spoke up, trying to paint a better picture, "'En then we was ambushed by some archers. One of 'em put a shaft through Ned's arm here. (He chose not to mention that it was a girl.) They took out some of our riders, to boot."

"Really? 'En how many ambushers do ye suppose there were?"

"Uh, don't know sir. It were still dark."

"Don't know, 'eh? Well how 'bout ye three go back and find out? I'm goin' t' send about a hunert Raiders along w' ye t' make sure ye don't come back without their heads this time."

"But sir," the wounded man spoke up, "we been ridin' fer two days straight, and we're all pretty stove in."

In a wink, Deacon drew his saber and plunged it into the man's chest. He dropped without another word. His body jerked spasmodically a few times, then lie still.

"There now, ol' Ned's out of his misery. No one kin say Deacon's not a kindly master, kin they? Er either of you gents too tired t' ride back?"

"Nossir!" "Nossir!"

"Didn't think so. I'm goin' t' send Cutler here t' head up this little huntin' party." Deacon pointed to a tall, lean, evil-looking man standing silently in one corner of the tent.

"Cutler, I want that tavern burnt to th' ground. Anybody ye' find there, I want burnt right along with it. Take m' best trackers and hunt these bastards down, every last one of 'em. I want 'em all tortured t' death. But, in th' process, I want you to find out if they be Rawlin's men and what they be about, fore' ye finish 'em off. Then' I want their heads brought back here, 'specially th' Spaniard's and that bitch innkeeper's."

"Yessir, boss," Cutler responded as he pushed the two men out of the tent.

"Cutler," Deacon called out to his lieutenant, while the man was still in earshot, "Make sure and bring me them heads. Iffin you can't, best not come back at all!"

* * *

They were up well into the mountains now. To the Ranger, these mountains didn't appear so much to be part of a clearly defined mountain range, as just a whole mountainous area. Sebastian and Santiago had agreed to let the Spaniard lead the way, while the Ranger guarded their rear. It seemed the most logical plan, as the Spaniard was more familiar with this country. Besides, the primary danger was from behind, where the Ranger's skills in guerilla fighting could best be put to use.

Already, Sebastian had begun cutting branches and dragging them behind his horse to obscure their tracks. He knew that this ploy would not foil experienced trackers, but he hoped that it would at least slow them down. It would likely make it difficult for their pursuers to track them at night, as well.

The Ranger had reminded his fellow travelers to employ other techniques to make their party difficult to track, as well. They traveled, where possible, in single file, so that their numbers were hard to determine. They stayed on hard and rocky ground wherever practical. They traveled in shallow streams or brooks that they encountered, obscuring their exit from the water as thoroughly as possible. From time to time, they would double back or split up to confuse their pursuers, as well. The Ranger, a peerless tracker, was rather pleased at the difficulty that he had with tracking his own party at times.

* * *

Cutler and his band of Raiders had traveled day and night until they had reached the tavern, which was now nothing more than a deserted, smoking ruin. Four days had passed since the Raider scouting party had been attacked. Deacon's lieutenant was furious in being denied retribution. He had looked forward to torching the place himself and punishing anyone left behind, whether they had been innocent bystanders or not.

He had his men make camp nearby and rest up while he sent his scouts out to find the trail of those he knew he must track down. He had seen the look in Deacon's eyes. If Cutler failed, even if he was Deacon's second-in-command, he knew that own life would be forfeit.

It took a surprisingly long time for his scouts to find the trail they were looking for. There had, in fact, been many fresh trails leading off in all directions, but most had been small parties of one or two. Only one trail seemed to be of a larger party, headed southeast, and it had been surprisingly hard to pick up. However, the scouts reported that even this trail had only consisted of five or six mounts, far fewer than Cutler had expected.

"Fetch me those two boneheads what got ambushed," Cutler ordered one of his men.

The two men were soon shoved in front of Cutler, who was seated on a log, playing with his saber. The two men looked groggy; they had obviously been sound asleep.

"Tell me agin how many of them varmints ye saw when ye was ambushed."

"Sir, it were dark..."

Cutler cut him off, "I didn't ask ye how much light there was; I asked how many varmints ye saw." Cutler stood up and leveled saber at the man who had spoken. The man shrank away from the point.

Now the other man spoke, "I reckon there was a passel of 'em..."

Now the sword came up to the other man's chin. "No more playin' about, unnerstand? I either git me some straight answers right now, or I'm goin' t' run one of ye halfwits through. Then I reckon I'll get th' answers I want from th' one still standin'. Now talk, n' talk true."

The man with the sword at his chin got the message well enough. Suddenly he was all detail. "There were th' Spaniard with his sword, then there were a great big 'un, a stranger, what wielded a lance and a hand ax. Then there was a young feller what used a bow right well. Now git this; t'was a girl what was right deft with a bow, t' boot. She's the one what got Ned in his arm. Even th' lady innkeeper grabbed one of th' sabers off a dead Raider an' jumped in. That's about it, I think..."

Cutler smiled, "Pard', ye just saved yer own life."

Both men almost collapsed in relief.

"Now git outta my sight."

The two men shuffled off in haste. Cutler sat back down on the log. *That would be five,* he thought to himself, *just about what the scouts figured, from th' tracks they found. And I've got a hunert men. I best cut that down some, fer speed's sake. Best not skinny it down too much, though. Them five took down nine good men an' ran three others off. Say about thirty good men and my three best scouts. And what's this with a girl what fights with a bow? Never heard of such a thing...*

* * *

The Ranger had just reached the high crest of the mountain trail that he had been climbing for some time now. He reigned in his horse and turned to look back. *Yep, this here's the place,* he thought to himself. From this high vantage point, he could see far back in the direction from which his party had come. He could see the precise spot on the crest of the last ridge he had crossed hours ago. Beyond that, he could even barely make out, in the far distance, the ridge beyond that one, which he had crossed that morning.

It was mid-afternoon. From the west, dark thunderclouds were moving in. The big man could hear the distant sounds of thunder and see the occasional flash of lightening reflected within the clouds. He reckoned that the storm would probably reach him near dusk.

Sebastian led his horse a goodly distance down the other side of the trail. He then found a secluded spot well off from the trail, where he could put the animal out to graze. The Ranger next gathered his weapons, cloak and pack, and headed back up to the summit. He found a good spot behind a boulder, where he had an unobstructed view back down the trail. He pulled the cloak around him and its hood over his head. He then retrieved his Ancient binoculars, his canteen and some jerky.

First of all, the old warrior methodically scanned every visible foot of the trail far as back into the distance as he could manage. Nothing. Somehow, that just didn't satisfy the itch at the back of his neck. That itch had bothered him all afternoon; it had warned him that somebody was close on his trail, whether he could actually see the varmints or not. Call it intuition, call it experience, or call it sixth sense. Somebody was out there. Close. He knew it.

They had left the inn over three weeks ago. The Ranger guessed that his party had likely started with something like a four or five day lead over any pursuers. However, they had been forced to go easy for the first week, until Maya had regained her strength. If the Raiders were indeed on their trail and pushing hard, they just might be catching up by now... hence, the itch at the back of his neck.

So the Ranger settled in. He had the patience of a veteran hunter. He could wait. He tore off a piece of jerky, chewed it slowly and washed it down with a swig from his canteen. His gaze never left the trail that stretched back down into the distance...

*** * * ***

The sun would soon be setting and the storm was fast approaching. Santiago had found a good spot to camp next to a small waterfall with a clear pool of mountain water at its base. They were on a small plain at the base of the next mountain pass that they would have to climb, one more of the several mountain passes that they had crossed over the last few weeks. Santiago hoped that it might be the last major obstacle that they would have to surmount, before they reached their final destination.

Their luck had held for the last three weeks; the weather had stayed cool and clear. And because the rivers were running low, the three rivers they had crossed had all been relatively easy to ford. However, their luck with the weather was about to change in a big way. The approaching storm appeared to be a bad one. The wind was kicking up as they unpacked the animals and set them out to graze.

"Let us put up the tent before we eat; we may need it this night, no?" the Spaniard suggested.

"Good idea, Santiago. Let's git to it before th' wind gits any worse," Lilith responded. "Valerian, why don't you and yer girl git a campfire started and git th' rest of th' camp organized. Me and th' Spaniard will get th' tent set up."

They all got to work. Soon the tent was pitched between two big willow trees on the banks of the pond. The tent was big enough for all four of them to climb into, if the weather turned as bad as they anticipated. If Sebastian showed up, the big man could crowd in too, (although somebody would probably have to sleep sitting up).

Soon they also had a small campfire going. With the storm almost upon them, they decided to have cold rations this night, although Lilith insisted on at least brewing some hot tea over the fire. Darkness settled in around them as they all sat down around the fire. The wind was gusting strongly from the west now, and the lightning was drawing near. Thunder reverberated in the canyons and passes that surrounded them.

Samantha, Diablo and the other two horses were securely tethered to a length of line stretched between two nearby trees. That was a good thing, because the animals were getting extremely nervous, whinnying and dancing about, pulling against their bridles. Diablo, in particular, was having fits, rearing and bucking about.

"We may not be able to practice with the swords this night, *compadre*," Santiago rose, "I had better see to the animals. This weather really seems to have them spooked…"

✳ ✳ ✳

Sebastian had finally decided to leave. He had waited patiently for hours without seeing a thing. The sun was now getting low on the horizon and the storm was closing in on him. He was worried that a severe enough storm might wash away his own party's tracks, to the point that he might have trouble following them. As it was, he might have to travel through the night to catch up with them.

The big man rose and stretched, working his injured shoulder. It was stiff, but healing well. He took a last look with the binoculars and still saw nothing. Wait. Was that movement far below? He scanned back down. Yes, the Raider scout was hard to see from a distance; he looked to be wearing a camouflaged cloak, much like the Ranger's own. But there he was, riding along on the plain below, slowly and methodically following Sebastian's own faint trail.

The Ranger smoothly dropped back out of sight. He would watch and wait patiently, letting the man come to him. Sebastian settled back into hiding, with his cloak pulled around him. After a time, continuing to scan with his binoculars, he made out a second scout trailing perhaps five hundred paces behind the first.

Good, now all I have to do is wait...

* * *

The old grizzly was in a foul mood. The approaching storm, with its wind, lightning and thunder, had him spooked. Worse yet, he was famished. The great beast was huge; he weighed perhaps five times as much as a man. He also stood over eight feet tall, when he reared up fully on his rear legs.

But the grizzly was ancient for a bear; he had now survived almost thirty winters. At that age, he was generally too clumsy and slow to catch either game or fish. His sense of smell had also largely deserted him, so that he had even a hard time finding nuts or berries, much less a treasured bee hive. So the old beast was reduced to eating whatever carrion or random bits of food that he stumbled across on the forest floor.

However, even with his weakened senses, just now he smelled and heard the mingled scents and sounds of horses and men. Food! Most grizzlies in their prime avoided men, preferring their natural prey, such as deer or salmon. But this bear was desperate for sustenance, and he was no stranger to the flesh of either man or horse. Just the summer before, he had stumbled on a sleeping trapper and his tethered mule. He had feasted on both.

The huge animal stood on his two rear legs and raised his nose to better smell his prey. He quickly dropped back down and moved through the underbrush. The gusting winds hid the sounds of his approach. He closed in for the kill. His great mouth watered in anticipation...

* * *

The rider clambered up the steep path in the final approach to the trail's summit. The hunter heard him and silently repositioned himself for the ambush. Horse and rider surmounted the crest and immediately pulled up. The Raider scout carefully scanned all about. He almost seemed to sense that something was amiss. He spurred the horse forward twenty yards and pulled up again. He peered again for a long time into the deepening shadows of the forest ahead and to the sides.

The scout finally seemed to relax just a bit. He doubled back to the crest and waved his hat at the other scout far down the trail. All clear! The scout turned again and bent down, looking for the tracks of his prey. He soon found what he was looking for, and kicked his mount slowly ahead, keeping his eyes on the tracks below.

The trail led into a stand of trees and underbrush. The first sign the Raider had of any trouble was the hammer blow to the center of his chest. He looked down and saw just the bit of the arrow's fletching that protruded from his shirt, as the shaft had passed almost completely through his body. He didn't even have time to figure out what the bit of feather was, before sliding out of his saddle, as the arrow had also passed clean through his heart.

The Ranger strode briskly out of his concealed position over to the horse, which hadn't even bolted. The scout lay next to his mount, which now calmly grazed next to his dead master.

"Good boy." Sebastian grabbed the horse's reins, which now pranced about nervously. The Ranger calmed the animal, and then tossed the body over its saddle. He led both into a thicket, then doubled back to erase any signs of the ambush.

It was beginning to rain; great big drops began to pelt the Ranger. This storm was going to be a bad 'un. The big man trotted over to the edge of the trail to make sure the second scout was still on his way up. Yep. There he was; getting close. The Ranger got back into position and waited. The wind was really kicking up now and the rain was coming down harder.

The rider appeared at the summit and rode forward. Like the first scout, he pulled up and carefully scanned ahead and to the sides. Sebastian was unconcerned; with the wind, rain and flashes of lightning, there was no way that the scout would see him. The Raider rode forward and the Ranger again took careful aim with his bow. But just as he released, a flash of lightning caused the horse to rear up. The arrow hit, but in the man's gut rather than his chest. The badly wounded man turned his mount, and tried to flee back down the hill.

Sebastian dropped his bow and ran after the horse. Just before it reached the crest, the big man leaped up behind the wounded scout and tossed him to the ground. He quickly dismounted and led the horse to a sapling to which he tethered the frightened animal. The scout was trying to crawl away on his belly. The Ranger walked over and unceremoniously cut the man's throat.

The storm was upon him now, with all its fury. Sebastian started to move the body, but then thought better of it. Better to leave it at the head of the trail. Give the next scout something to think about. He took the bridle and saddle off of the nearest horse, slapped its rump and sent it galloping off into the forest. He soon did the same with the second. The animals would just have to fend for themselves.

Head bent against the driving rain, the Ranger gathered his weapons and fetched his own horse. He led the animal to a cliff in the forest with an overhang which would provide him with just a bit of shelter from the storm. He curled up in his cloak and pulled its hood low over his head. It would be a long, wet night...

***

The great beast knew that his prey was just on the other side of the thicket. The rain was coming down steadily now; lightning flashed and thunder crashed all about. The mule and its companions sensed the predator's presence and panicked, pulling frantically at their reins.

"Diablo, *amigo*, be calm; it is only a storm, no?" The Spaniard turned just in time to see the huge animal towering behind him, silhouetted by a flash of lightning.

He ducked and screamed, "Valerian! Grizz..."

The beast landed a mighty blow with a huge forepaw, sending Santiago flying. The blow ripped open his chest and jaw and broke several ribs, along with his left collarbone and left shoulder. He landed, unconscious, in a small gully.

The grizzly dropped to all fours and calmly ambled over to Santiago. He clamped down on the severely wounded man's ankle with his huge jaws and began to drag him away into the bush. The beast was so intent on escaping with his dinner, that he didn't sense his attacker until it was too late. On the run, Valerian plunged his lance deep into the mighty animal's side with all his strength. The lance went in just behind the bear's right foreleg, buried to almost a third of its length.

The grizzly roared in fury and struck back with astonishing speed. It turned and swiped the young man a glancing blow that was still powerful enough to slam Valerian against the trunk of a tree, leaving him stunned with a dislocated shoulder. Valerian came to his knees, and looked face-to-face at the creature that was about to kill him.

The first arrow struck the animal in the neck just below its massive jaw. The grizzly made an unearthly bellow that almost sounded like a human scream of torment. It forgot Valerian, stood up on its rear legs and then launched itself after its newest tormentor, a slender girl that stood just ten paces away. She stood fast, calmly drawing her bow again.

The girl would have died that way, but as the great beast charged, his legs became tangled in the lance still embedded firmly in his side. The razor-sharp lance-head tore at his insides and he fell forward.

Only five paces away now, the animal roared in pain and defiance, and the girl launched the second arrow right into his huge, wide-open mouth. It was enough. Stumbling, falling, mortally wounded, the once mighty king of the forest crashed ignominiously into the underbrush, to die in agony some distance away.

Instantly, Maya tossed her weapon aside and ran to her man. Lilith, who had stood next to the girl with Santiago's drawn sword, ran to look after the Spaniard. The rain was now coming down in sheets. Valerian staggered to his feet with Maya's assistance.

The injured young man shouted through the rain and thunder, "Help Lilith get Santiago into the tent! He's hurt far worse than me! I can make it by myself..."

Grudgingly, the girl let go of him and rushed over to Lilith and the badly wounded man. Valerian staggered into the tent and collapsed, on the edge of shock. Somehow the two women dragged and carried the tall Spaniard into the tent and lay him next to his young friend. It was hellish inside the shelter. It was pitch dark, except for the occasional flash of lightning, and both men moaned in agony. Santiago was only semi-conscious.

"Lass, we've got to see what we're doin'. See if there are any live embers left in th' campfire. I'll try t' find some candles in one of the packs."

Maya was dubious, but she ran back into the rain, turning over the half burnt logs in the campfire. She was in luck; one of the small pieces of kindling hidden under a large log still glowed. Sheltering it with her body, she ran back into the tent. Blowing desperately on the glowing twig, it reignited. Lilith had already found two candles. Soon, with just the dim light of two candles, the two determined women set to work...

* * *

The Ranger awoke at first light. He shook himself out and stretched. His cloak and his clothes were drenched. But he had kept his quiver under his cloak, so his arrows were still fairly dry; that was the important thing, since they would warp if they got very wet. The morning was crisp and clear, as the front had passed on through shortly before dawn. He knew that he would dry out soon enough, once the sun came up. It wasn't the first time that he had spent the night out in the rain, not by a far sight.

Sebastian checked on his horse, washed his mouth out with a swig from his canteen, and relieved himself in a briar patch. Then he trudged back up to the summit of the hill with his binoculars. He looked out over the plain below. There the Raiders were, camped out in plain sight. Several raggedy tents were pitched and someone had even managed to get a few smoky cook fires going. Most of the men were still curled up in their blankets out in the open; only a few were stirring yet, even though the sun was now full up over the horizon.

The Ranger carefully took note of all of the camp's details. He estimated that there were about twenty-five or thirty men. He noticed that no sentries had been set. The horses had been set out to graze in a nearby meadow, and also appeared to be unguarded. *Seems they're a bit overconfident, they are. Reckon Raiders on this side of the river feel pretty safe from attack*, the Ranger thought to himself.

The old warrior's eyes narrowed as he watched. He crouched and put the binoculars away. He then pulled a bit of jerky from a pouch and chewed on it as he coolly assessed the scene below. He wore a tight little smile. So these were the men who were determined to kill him, his nephew and his new friends. (His thoughts kept drifting to a big, pretty, red-haired lady...)

Time to stop runnin', the big man decided. *Time to turn back on these malefactors and make 'em wish they had stuck to robbin' and murderin' the helpless common folk... the 'sheep'...as they like to call 'em. Well, we ain't no sheep. Yep*, he decided, *these here Raiders are about to walk into a windmill...*

Unaware of his companions' dire circumstances, the old warrior rose slowly and stretched. He returned to his horse, saddled up and set out once again. But this time, he made no attempt to cover his tracks...

30

Countdown
September 11th, 2100

"My fellow Americans...As you know, in the last year, my Administration has taken dramatic and forceful steps in the attempt to secure our great nation. Regretfully, I must report to you tonight that these steps have been insufficient. As all of you doubtless know, yet another nuclear device was detonated early this morning, in downtown Atlantic City. This vicious attack occurs precisely on the anniversary of last year's Las Vegas attack, and on the ninety-ninth anniversary of the attack on the World Trade Towers in New York."

"As you know, the steps that I have already taken have been controversial. I have met with fierce political opposition from all quarters. Congress has tried to impeach me. Many of my most important measures have been challenged before the Supreme Court. Traitorous elements within the press have hounded me viciously and relentlessly. Yet my Administration has endured, in spite of it all."

"Astoundingly, the political opposition in all three parties wants to reverse the course my Administration has taken, in the hopes of reaching some sort of 'accommodation' with the enemy...an enemy that kills innocent civilian men, women and children by the tens of thousands! They believe that the minor and practical limitations that my Administration has placed on privacy and free speech are somehow more important than the safety and security of our own citizenry. Tell that to the dead and the horribly injured victims of Atlantic City!"

"Fellow citizens, we cannot retreat! We cannot fail! So, it is with a most heavy heart that I now find myself forced to make the following historic and grave pronouncements this fateful night. First of all, the national elections scheduled for this November will be suspended until further notice. The current session of Congress will also be suspended, forthwith. Units of the Homeland Defense forces, even as we speak, are being deployed in and around the Capitol and in most other major cities to maintain order. Special elements of Homeland Defense are also temporarily taking control of all cyber-news facilities until stability is assured."

The President smiled warmly, "I want to assure each and every one of you that these necessary and vital measures will be only in place until the crisis is truly past. This great nation has always been a democracy, and a democracy it will always be. State and local elections will proceed as planned. But most importantly, let me assure each and every law-abiding citizen, that you will be free to come and go as you please, working, playing, traveling, raising your children, just as before."

"However, for now, let us all come together and do our utmost to help the ravaged survivors of Atlantic City. Let us pray for the fallen. Let us further pray to God Almighty for the courage and wisdom to lay aside our petty political differences in order to join together and defeat an evil and godless foe. Good night and God bless each and every one of us."

* * *

"Well, I guess that makes it official," Mac mused aloud.

The Olympus Council had met in special session to watch the presidential announcement together. Graham, Dr. Alvarez, Michael and Olivia had also been invited.

"So ends the great American experiment in democracy," Michael commented in muted outrage, "Won't people resist? Won't Congress fight this? The Courts? The Press? For God's sake...the people?"

Dr. Alvarez calmly responded, "Michael, you know as well as any of us that we have frittered away our rights, on and off, for almost a hundred years now. This is just a culmination of the process. It's all about fear. In the end, our citizens have come to value the realities of comfort and security far more than the abstractions of freedom and liberty."

Now Graham spoke, "In any case, it's all pretty much moot at this point, whether our civilization collapses as a democracy, or as a tyrannical dictatorship. However I, for one, rather hope that the collapse comes before Powell feels the need to detonate any more nuclear weapons on any more of our cities to further consolidate his power."

"Does anyone have a proposal on how we should respond to this latest development?" Dr. Allen asked the Council.

"Yes, with the Council's permission, I propose that we all go home and hug our loved ones," Olivia responded. Her voice choked just a bit as she said the words.

"I second the proposal," Mac smiled sadly as he responded, "That's probably the most practical step we can take at the moment."

The Council voted unanimously in favor of the proposal, and promptly adjourned. The mood as they all parted company was somber. Everyone shook hands and hugged as they parted company.

"Dr. Alvarez, care to share a late dinner with me in my library?" Graham asked his old friend.

"*Con mucho gusto, compadre*," the professor responded.

* * *

Both elderly men settled into their overstuffed chairs, by the unlit fireplace. Dr. Alvarez had his tea, Graham sipped at his brandy.

"You are looking quite well, Louie. The treatments must be working for you."

"They are indeed; *gracias*, Jonathan. I have not felt so healthy in many a long year. You too are looking very well."

"Yes, for me, the treatments are complete. All that I need now are regular checkups."

"And has anyone else taken you up on your offer, Jonathan?"

"Louie, I'm confounded, but no one has accepted my offer of immortality! Mac, Michael, Olivia, Fred, Ellen...no one has accepted. Everyone was grateful of the offer. Everyone considered it carefully. Then everyone declined in the end."

"*Sí*, I rather expected as much. Everyone is attracted to the idea of immortality as an abstraction. However, when they face the reality of it, the implications of it, they prefer to let nature take its course. I would think that this would be even more so the case, given that we now face such a troubled future."

"Perhaps. Louie, speaking of the future, just how do you believe that the immediate future will now unfold?"

"Jonathan, I believe that the collapse will come within the next year. I believe that there are several different possible scenarios on how it may unfold, but I believe that it will inevitably happen soon."

"I quite agree. How do you think that we can best respond?" Graham asked the professor.

"I believe that it is vital that Olympus maintains a very low profile. We must, at all costs, refrain from drawing any attention to ourselves from either Powell or Schmidt. In the meantime, I believe that Olympus must do everything in its power to become strong, stable and self-sufficient."

"Again, I quite agree. I am already beginning to quietly summon many of my best personnel and their families back here to Olympus...at least to the extent that we still have room for them."

"*Sí*, a good idea, Jonathan."

"Now then, are you ready for dinner, my friend?"

"But of course..."

* * *

The three sat down together at the kitchen table, Michael, Olivia and their son Daniel. It was late, so they shared a simple dinner of cold sandwiches and milk. The young man appeared deeply troubled.

"Mom, Dad how could anyone commit such a horrible act? All of those innocent people killed, all of those men women and children injured, mutilated."

"Son, ever since men climbed down out of the trees..." Michael tried to answer.

Daniel cut him off. "No Father...I'm not asking for another history lesson; I've had plenty of those. I'm well aware of what man has done to fellow man throughout the centuries. What I can't fathom is...why? It's a philosophical question I'm asking. What is source of the darkness that's embedded so deeply within our spirit, which drives us toward such horrendous acts?"

It was a profound question, an adult question, which warranted a serious answer.

Michael was silent for a long while before he responded, "Daniel, I have spent my entire adult life trying to fully comprehend human nature. Much remains a mystery to me...to us all. Certainly that dark secret hidden away deep in our fundamental nature remains a mystery. Perhaps it always will. Perhaps its source really is Satan incarnate. Perhaps it is simply what remains of our primordial origins; the desire to survive, the need to dominate at all costs may simply be an integral part of our DNA."

"But this I do know: we can learn to restrain that darker nature. You yourself are living proof of that, Daniel. We have given you and your fellow Pathfinders every last bit of knowledge that we posses to help you succeed in that quest. And I believe that you will."

"Yes, it's true Daniel. But don't forget that we have given you something that's even more profound than all of that valuable Pathfinder knowledge you now possess," Olivia added.

"What's that Mom?"

"Love, Daniel. In the end, it's only love that can conquer the darkness in men's souls."

The young man nodded, deep in thought...

* * *

The men in Powell's inner circle were exclusively Brethren now. One by one, all of his senior advisors and Cabinet Secretaries had resigned or been fired; the last of them today, as they had learned of the contents of the President's speech. He had now replaced them all with fellow members of his secret organization. It was midnight, and they all met in the Oval Office. They began with a prayer circle, all of them holding hands.

The President spoke with his eyes closed, "Heavenly Father, give us the strength to do whatever is necessary to triumph in Your Name. Forgive us for the death and destruction that we must reign down on the heathens and the enemy in equal measure in thy Name. Give us the wisdom to prevail against the Anti-Christ and his minions. Amen."

"Amen," all of the men repeated.

"Gentlemen, we have much to do. We have now achieved what we have worked and sacrificed for over these many years...a true Christian theocracy in America. But we must move quickly, the threats both from within and from without are urgent. We must first and foremost determine the true identity of the Anti-Christ. Once we know who he is, rest assured that I will, without hesitation, call up a massive nuclear strike. In the meantime, we must consolidate power in this nation. I want Brethren to monitor the communications of all senior military and law enforcement personnel. Any sign of disloyalty will be dealt with forcefully. In fact, a few quick summary executions might be just what we need to subdue the rest. Trask, get on that right away."

"Yessir, Mr. President." The bright, clean-cut young man saluted and exited the Oval Office. The planning continued late into the night. Transformation was such a complex and daunting endeavor!

* * *

"Good Lord, Sergei! The man has inflicted nuclear devastation on his own people! What do you suppose Powell will do when his attention turns to us?" Schmidt's avatar asked the Russian's VR simulation.

"I know, my friend, I know. Of course, if the madman attacks us, we will retaliate with enough missiles to turn his country into a vast nuclear wasteland. But that wouldn't do us much good at that point, would it?" the big Russian responded.

"Yes, so now the Lucifer project is definitely a race against time, is it not? How fares the good Dr. Koderesku? You know, his twelve months are just about up."

"Ah yes, our poor overworked project leader. I'm afraid that he is still not ready; seems that he was afraid to inform you personally, for some reason. However, he has assured me that he will be ready in just six more months."

"Sergei, I wonder what would happen if we deployed Lucifer right now, ready or not."

"Gerhardt, by coincidence, I asked the good professor precisely that question."

"And what did he say?"

"He said that Lucifer would certainly work as designed, but that it would likely turn on us, as well, wreaking worldwide destruction."

"Did the professor say just what would the likelihood of that be?"

"Yes, my friend, he estimated no better than fifty-fifty, if it were released immediately. However, he believed that those odds could be improved to better than ninety-ten if he had another six months."

"Well, then I suppose that we must grudgingly give Dr. Koderesku another six months, but no more. It will likely take Powell that long to consolidate his hold over his own countrymen, in any case."

"I quite agree, Gerhardt, let us just pray that we have that long to wait."

"I'm afraid that prayer isn't a part of my repertoire, Sergei. But I will keep my fingers crossed. Farewell for now, my friend."

* * *

As soon as the presidential announcement concluded, Geordie switched off his VR hood and pulled the device off of his head. He probably wouldn't have watched the speech in the first place, but it was an all-channels address…hard to avoid if you remained plugged-in. Now, the young man was perplexed, concerned even.

Geordie was twenty-nine years old, and a young man pretty typical of his generation. Single and unattached, he was employed as a junior level AI developer for an international cyber-firm. He worked in VR, out of his brand new micro-suite. Like most young people nowadays, he had only left the nest as he had neared the big 'three-oh'. The micro-suite was really pretty micro, but at least he didn't have to deal with Mom or Dad anymore. And it came equipped with an absolutely awesome built-in full-sensory VR system. The rig was advertised as better than reality, and it pretty near lived up to its hype.

Geordie wasn't yet a full-fledged cyber-junkie; nonetheless, the young man probably spent about three-fourths of his time in his tiny apartment, and almost all of his waking time there hooked into VR.

Still, Geordie liked the occasional foray to a real pub or café, to scan the vixns and have a few pints of real grog. Although cyber-sex was pretty good, (and could be way more exotic than reality), he still preferred the physical component of being with a real live, warm-blooded female. In this respect, he was fast becoming a minority. Even most of the vixns that he did manage to meet in PR (physical reality) nowadays, preferred to simply give him their VR code, so that they could just share virtual sex with him. After all, no worries about disease or pregnancy playing around in VR, right?

The young man drifted over to the fridge and asked it for a sub and a fizz-drink. It quickly delivered, as he commanded the tabletop to fold down from the wall. He extended a stool, took a sip of the drink and pondered the day's events. Real wretched about Atlantic City! He didn't have much cash to spare, but he decided to send a few Credits to the Nuclear Relief Fund, which had been set up last year after the Vegas attack.

He was middlin' vexd about the president's address too. Powell was some kind of religious nut-job, after all. He hoped the guy wouldn't make everybody start going to church every Sunday or something. *Still, if crackin' down is what it takes to keep the psycho-terrorists from settin' off any more nukes...*

As the he finished off the sub, he decided to plug back in right after dinner. Go find a VR town hall meeting, where he could listen in to what everybody else was saying. *Who knows*, he thought to himself, *maybe I'll even get psyched and kick in to a cyber-protest!*

However, after dinner, as soon as Geordie jacked back in to his VR system, a big cyber-ad appeared: "Monster Introductory Promo! Six hours FREE on the all new "Moons of Arcturus XXV" VR experience!!! SEX! BLOOD! ALIENS! Join us now!!!

Oh man! Only the most popular new game on the Cyberweb! All thoughts of nukes, politics and crazy presidents vanished, as Geordie logged on. Soon he was slaughtering alien vampires as the mighty warrior 'Bonecrusher'. The young man played until the wee hours...

* * *

The next morning, Daniel mustered with his company of "Falcons" at 06:20am, just as he had every other weekday morning since he had graduated to the Falcons level of Pathfinders. Daniel was, by far, the shortest in the lineup, not because he was small for his age, but because, just shy of twelve, he was the youngest Pathfinder ever to have attained Falcon status. The Falcon leader, a sandy-haired sixteen year old girl named Serena, called role at precisely 06:30am.

Typically, after role call, the Falcon leader would give out news of the day, before the company began their regular three-mile run. However, this morning would be different; Serena transferred the PA queue to an older man. From the end of the line, Daniel didn't at first recognize him, but the youth instantly recognized the voice when he spoke. It was his godfather and namesake, Daniel Patrick McCafferty, who also happened to be Colonel McCafferty, Commander of the Olympus Security Forces.

"Good morning, Pathfinders. I have been asked to address you this morning regarding yesterday's horrendous events. We understand that the death and destruction in Atlantic City is almost too much for young minds to contemplate. And almost as awful to you may be the news of the death of democracy in our once great nation."

"Yet Olympus still stands as a true democracy, made up of citizens worthy of that ultimate system of government. Olympus still stands as a beacon to freedom and justice, even as darkness closes in all around us. And Pathfinders, Olympus will prevail through these trying times, as long as you all hold fast to the principles that we have instilled in each and every one of you! Honor and Courage!"

"Honor and Courage!" the youths shouted as one, as they fell out to follow the sixteen year old girl and the sixty-three year old man on a bracing three mile run.

As he ran, Daniel found himself strangely exhilarated. Yes, he knew in his heart of hearts...they would certainly prevail!

* * *

Later that morning, Mac invited Jonathan, Olivia, Louie, and Michael to his private conference room in the Command Center. He served everyone coffee or tea, as they filed in and sat at the long mahogany table. Mac spoke as soon as they were all seated.

"Good morning, folks. Thanks for meeting on such short notice. I thought that you all might be interested in how events are unfolding after yesterday's Atlantic City attack, and last night's presidential address. And frankly, I thought that I could use some expert help in evaluating the overall situation."

"Thanks for inviting us, Mac," Graham replied, "Could you perhaps begin by giving a summary of just what you think is going on out around the country?"

"Certainly, Jonathan. But perhaps Aristotle can best provide that for us...Aristotle, please summarize for us this morning's national events related to the Atlantic City nuclear attack and the president's subsequent announcement of the Emergency Decree last night."

The AI system instantly responded, "Complying...Currently, the national cyber-news outlets are reporting no occurrences of public unrest, such as riots or demonstrations. Neither is the national media reporting any resistance on the part of political opponents. Neither are there any reports of mutiny or opposition on the part of military or law enforcement forces."

Everyone looked at one another in consternation. They expected such a radical pronouncement by the President of the United States to have at least some reaction. However, Aristotle hadn't finished...

"However, the cyber-news outlets are now all under extremely tight federal control. My "Sherlock" investigative subprogram has detected major anomalies and inconsistencies in many of yesterday's news reports. Considering these anomalies a potential threat to the security of Olympus, Sherlock initiated a high level penetration of Homeland Defense cyber-communications. The penetration was successful at 22:33 pm last night."

Mac interrupted, "Just as an aside, folks, considering the present state of affairs, if the government discovered that we had compromised Homeland Defense communications, we would all likely be liable for execution for treason."

Aristotle had not been directly addressed, so it did not respond. Rather, it politely paused and then continued as soon as Mac finished. "Based on Homeland Defense tactical communications, small riot control units have been rapidly deployed and redeployed throughout the night and into this morning, indicating a large number of small scale disturbances. Additionally, beginning a short time after the president's speech last night, detention facilities around the county have been processing large numbers of new inmates. Sherlock has identified many prominent political, cyber-news and military figures, as well as a number of sports and show business celebrities amongst the detainees."

"Aristotle, please tell everyone about the cyber-promotions." Mac interjected.

"Complying...Sherlock, in evaluating both open and secure cyber-communications, detected a widespread and unusual number of promotional campaigns proliferating throughout the Cyberweb. These promotions appear to be tailored to the habits of individual users."

"Aristotle, please give examples."

"Complying...Shopping sprees, either free or with drastically reduced prices, free cyber-sex sessions, free gaming sessions, new cyber-contests with multi-million Credit prizes..."

Mac interrupted, again, "Aristotle, that's sufficient. Aristotle, can you calculate the cost of these promotions?"

"Complying...the costs are rapidly rising, but as of 10AM MST, the costs were calculated at 57.3 billion Credits."

"Whew," Graham, whose corporation owned much of the Cyberweb, commented, "I hate to sound like a Philistine, but whatever other bad things are happening, Graham Enterprise profits will be soaring. Aristotle, can you determine where all that money is coming from?"

"Complying...Sherlock is still trying to confirm the ultimate source or sources of the funds. The money appears to have been funneled through a complex international network of shell and dummy corporations. However, the probability that the source is the United States treasury currently stands at 73%."

"Roman Circuses...brilliant," Dr Alvarez commented.

"What, professor?" Olivia asked.

Michael answered, "Whenever the Romans had trouble feeding their population, whenever the grain shipments fell behind, they held Circuses... gladiatorial games, chariot races and so forth, to distract the masses from their empty stomachs."

"Precisely, and what else does this ploy tell us?" the old professor asked.

Olivia answered, "It tells us that all of this was in the works for a long time. It would have taken months or maybe years to set up such a complicated scheme."

"Yes, therefore whatever doubts we might have had as to whether the government was behind the attacks on Vegas and Atlantic City should be put to rest," Mac responded. "Is there anything else that we should be doing here at Olympus to either protect ourselves or to help our fellow citizens?"

"I have a few suggestions," Graham spoke up, "First of all, I would like to propose that Graham Enterprises, on the behalf of the good citizens of Olympus, donate twenty billion Credits to the federal government, to use as they see fit, for disaster relief in Atlantic City. Secondly, I would like to inform President Powell that we are very concerned with the extremely high data load we are experiencing on the Cyberweb, as a result of all of these cyber-promotions. However, I would like to assure him that the experts here at Olympus will do their utmost to maintain the network's stability, and will continue to monitor the situation closely."

Mac commented, "The old carrot and stick; I like it, Jonathan. In other words, leave us alone and we'll increase your payoffs, but mess with us and we'll shut down the Cyberweb."

Graham smiled, "Spoken rather crassly for my taste, Mac, but yes, that just about sums it up."

"Well then, if no one objects, I'll request a closed emergency Council meeting this afternoon, and pass along Jonathan's proposals. I'm pretty sure that there will be no serious objections."

"I just wish that there was more that we could do for our fellow citizens outside of Olympus," Olivia spoke now.

"Olivia, sadly, there is little we can do to help our fellow Americans, at this point. The fate of the American people must remain in their own hands and those of their leaders, such as they are. Therefore, our primary responsibility now must be to ensure that at least the fate of Olympus remains in our own hands, and only in our own hands," Dr. Alvarez responded.

31

Backtrack

The Raider scout, Virgil was his name, followed the trail carefully, and with more than a little trepidation. In spite of the fact that six tough Raiders now escorted him, the scout was nervous for two pretty sound reasons. First of all, his two recently deceased predecessors, Lefty and Haggis, had obviously been taken completely unawares by parties unknown. That was worrisome enough, since the two men had been known by their compatriots as two of the keenest and most experienced of all of the Raider scouts. Virgil was pretty certain that nobody had ever taken either one of those two by surprise before. However, just now, what really made Virgil's skin crawl was just how *easy* this new trail was to follow...just one shod horse, galloping along straight down the middle of a wide trail, hooves making a clear impression in the damp earth.

   Prior to the demise of the first two scouts, whomever they had been tracking had gone to great lengths to cover their tracks. At times over the last few weeks, the three scouts had thought that they had lost their quarry's trail altogether. However, on those occasions, the point of Cutler's sword had inevitably provided sufficient motivation for the trackers to eventually pick up the trail again. But now it almost seemed that their quarry they hunted actually wanted the Raiders to follow their trail.

Virgil was also a bit unsettled by the fact that he was aware that his present escort had not one, but two purposes. The first was, of course, to protect him from another ambush. However, their secondary purpose was to kill Virgil himself, if he tried to run off; he had made the mistake of letting Cutler see that he was just a bit too wary about carrying on in place of his fallen comrades.

The Raiders escorting Virgil seemed pretty edgy themselves. Some kept their bows at the ready; others carried unsheathed swords or lances held in position for combat. All the men continually scanned all around into the dense forest that they were just now passing through.

The advance party followed the trail for hours. Around midday, they stopped by a stream to water their horses and refill their canteens. The men dismounted for a short while to stretch and eat a bit of jerky and hardtack. Soon after, they remounted and headed out again.

They rode for the rest of the day, regularly marking a trail for the main Raider party. Late in the afternoon, the trail turned down into a broad rocky gorge. Still, the tracks were easy to follow on a path next to a broad, shallow stream that meandered more or less down the center of the gorge.

As the sun began to set, the men decided to stop and make camp. It would soon be too dark to follow the trail any further. Besides, the men agreed, the gorge's steep sides, made them far too vulnerable to ambush, especially in the failing light. The men set their horses out to graze and made a campfire. Taking no chances, they set out two sentries. They would change the watch every few hours to make sure no one fell asleep.

They had no way of knowing, but they had nothing to worry about that night...

* * *

Just past sunset, Sebastian had crossed the stream he had been following and began to double back. He had soon heard the men and horses on the other side of the stream. He had dismounted at that point and moved away from the stream. The Ranger had only had one nervous moment. As he came abreast of the camp in the distance, his horse, smelling and hearing its fellow beasts, began to prance about and whinny. Sebastian calmed the animal, talking to it and stroking its muzzle. The horse had finally quieted. The big man had then led it back a ways further downstream with no more trouble.

When he determined that he was well out of earshot, he remounted and splashed back across the stream. The sky was clear and the half-moon was already well up in the sky. The Ranger had no problem picking up the trail and backtracking at a gallop. He rode until well past midnight.

Finally, he heard the distant sounds of the Raider's main camp. He dismounted and led his horse off the trail into a stand of trees. Taking only his bow and quiver, he became again a ghost in the forest. Soon, he came to the edge of a clearing. There was the Raider's encampment. He counted four campfires and three tents. *The tents must be for the senior men*, he thought to himself.

The Ranger moved silently amongst the trees and the underbrush all around the camp, taking mental notes of every detail that he could make out. He counted about two dozen men. Many of them were sitting around the big campfires, eating, gambling…and drinking. *Drinkin'…that's why they're slow t' get up in the morning…good.*

He saw the horses tethered at the edge of the clearing. He still saw no signs of sentries. But everyone was still awake; he hoped that sentries wouldn't be set later. *Well*, the Ranger thought to himself, *I'd better make t' best of tonight; they'll surely be keepin' a watch after this night is over.*

* * *

Cutler wasn't a stupid man, not by a long shot. It was just a possibility completely outside of the range of his experience. South of the river, no one had *ever* attacked a large Raider party. And they were following a small band of no more than six people. Even though a few of his scouts had been ambushed, he never considered that they might actually attack his main party. It just wasn't something that he could ever have imagined…

The big Ranger waited until just a few hours before daylight, when he knew that men are typically at their worst, (particularly when they've been drinking). The moon had gone down, so it was pitch dark. He slipped in amongst the horses, which were tethered to a few long lines stretched along the ground. The animals shifted around nervously, but the big man whispered to them and patted their rumps, quieting them. He then cut the long lines and slipped away. No one in the camp stirred.

The old warrior made his way silently in the darkness back to his own horse. Earlier, as he had waited for the hours to pass, he had made a torch with a stout tree branch as long and almost as thick as his arm, with strips of cloth tied around one end. Now he used a flint and steel striker to light the torch. He then led his mount back to the edge of the clearing and mounted up.

With a mighty whoop, waving the big torch in a circle about his head, Sebastian kicked his mount and charged right into the tethered horses. The animals bolted as one, and stampeded. He drove them right through the center of the camp. Some men were trampled before they even woke. Others jumped up and ran in all directions, yelling at one another. Some of these Raiders were run over by the stampeding horses, as well.

Then, suddenly in their midst, was the mounted giant, swinging his huge torch. He bashed some men with the torch, others he just ran down with his horse. He set one of the tents and a pile of their supplies alight with the torch.

Meanwhile, Cutler had bolted from one of the other tents, with his sword drawn. He screamed at the men to get organized and surround the lone horseman. But then, suddenly, the giant reared his horse and threw his torch right into the largest cluster of men. In another instant, the rider had disappeared into the darkness. No one was eager to give chase, not even Cutler.

* * *

Sebastian dismounted as soon as he entered the trees at the edge of the clearing. He knew it would be suicide to try to gallop through the forest in such complete darkness. The Ranger quickly looked back to see if there was any sign of anyone giving chase. He quickly satisfied himself that no one was following. He then trotted away, pulling his horse's reins behind him. In this regard, a lifetime in the forest had given the old Ranger a virtual sixth sense, allowing him to navigate in the darkness. Just the faint traces of reflected starlight, the feel of the ground at his feet, even the faint echoes of the horse's hooves were enough for him to find his way. Soon, the big man had left the Raider encampment far behind.

* * *

The Raider camp was pure madness and chaos until dawn broke. Some men lay howling in agony. Some men ran around in all directions chasing the horses in the darkness; others put out the fires that the attacker had set. All the while, Cutler screamed orders at everyone, most of which were ignored in the darkness and confusion.

Finally, at dawn's first light, Cutler managed to restore some semblance of order. The Raiders caught some of the horses, and tended as best they could to the injured men. They salvaged as many of the supplies as they could from those that had been torched. One of the Raiders even started a new campfire, so they could brew some tea.

Cutler was finally able to take stock, and what he saw made him livid. Three men dead, outright. Six men injured; two bad enough that he'd probably have to put them out of their misery. A quarter of their supplies burned. Worst of all, half their horses missing! And all by one man…one man!

Well, Cutler vowed, *if it's the last thing I ever do, that's one man I'll have eatin' his own liver… 'fore I cut his throat!*

* * *

The morning after the grizzly attack had been a tough one for the little party of four. Lilith and Maya had been up all through the night tending to the two badly wounded men. Dawn and the passing of the storm had brought little relief. With first light the two women had been left aghast when they had finally seen the true extent of Santiago's injuries.

Maya had finally managed to relight a small campfire. She had made tea for herself and the exhausted older woman. Meanwhile, Santiago and Valerian slept fitfully in the tent.

Maya spoke softly, so as not to wake the men, "Tell me what you think, Lilith, and be honest with me."

Lilith sat down near the fire and pulled back a strand of her red hair. She sipped the tea and answered in a low voice, "Lass, I'm afraid that my Spaniard won't be with us fer much longer. I've done my best fer him, but it won't be enough. All I kin do now is try to make him comfortable, to ease him as gently out of this world as I kin."

The woman spoke calmly, but a single tear rolled out of the corner of one eye and down her cheek. The exhausted woman didn't even bother to wipe it away.

"And my Valerian?"

"The lad'll be all right, child. He's likely got some bruised ribs and some deep cuts, but he's young and he'll heal up soon enough. Let's let him rest fer awhile. I think his left shoulder may be dislocated, too. If it is, we'll have t' force it back into its socket. That'll be no easy chore...fer us or fer th' lad. And we'll check his ribs agin, but about all we kin do fer 'em is wrap 'em snug."

Wearily, Maya rose to fetch some food from one of the packs. It lay near Samantha, who was now tethered all by herself. Diablo and the other two horses had broken loose during the bear attack and run off into the storm. Samantha had broken loose as well, but she had returned before dawn. In spite of herself, Maya had cried at the mule's return. She had hugged the animal and found a dried apple for her in one of the packs.

The girl returned to the campfire with a pair of corncakes wrapped in linen. Handing one to Lilith, she sat down next to her. Both women nibbled absently at the meager breakfast and sipped some tea.

Maya finally spoke, "I just wish that Uncle would come back. I'd feel much safer if he was with us. I hope he's all right, too."

Lilith poked at the fire.

"Oh, I wish he'd come back, myself...I surely do."

* * *

The Raider's scouting party had risen at first light, eaten a meager breakfast and mounted back up. The scout soon picked up the trail again, as his escort fell in behind, carefully watching the cliffs above the gorge. After awhile, the tracks crossed the stream they had been riding along, and, much to their surprise, turned back in the opposite direction.

"What d'ya think that means, Virgil?" one of the Raiders asked.

"It means we better stay sharp, is what it means," the scout responded as he intently looked about in all directions.

He didn't like this business, not one bit. He decided that if he got the chance, he was going to take off. He couldn't shake the feeling that the Raiders were the ones being hunted, even though they were supposed to be the ones doing the hunting.

The Raiders followed the tracks as they crossed the stream again and rejoined the trail that they had made in the opposite direction the day before. Soon, they rode back up out of the gorge and back into the forest.

Virgil figured a half day's ride, and they would run back into the main Raider party following the trail that they had marked the day before.

Virgil was certain something was up, but he just couldn't figure out what. Then, suddenly, as they rounded a bend in the trail, they almost ran right into him...a giant of a man, on a big horse. The man was only thirty or so paces away. He looked as surprised as they were. His horse reared as he reined it in and spun it around. He kicked the animal's sides and fled. The men let out a whoop and took chase, hard on his heels. The Raiders quickly gained on the man as they chased him along the narrow, winding forest trail.

After a few moments, though, Virgil reined in and fell back, as one vivid thought flashed in his mind...*ambush*! The scout was just about to shout a warning at the other Raiders, when the two in the lead went down almost simultaneously, and then a third was thrown from his mount a split second later. The three trailing riders were able to pull up or turn just in time. As the scout rode up at a canter, he saw the trap...a rope strung across the trail, carefully disguised, at just the right height to catch a mounted man in the neck or chest.

He dismounted, along with the other three uninjured men, to look after those who had fallen. One man was already dead with what looked like a broken neck, and the other two were badly hurt. One looked to have a broken pelvis and ribs; the other man was stunned and appeared to have a serious head injury.

The four uninjured Raiders were trying to figure out how to help the wounded men when the first arrow whistled in. It hit a big fat Raider right between the shoulder blades; the shaft almost hit a second Raider as it passed clear through the first. Virgil dove for cover and the other two Raiders still standing followed suite. They hadn't even seen where the arrow had come from.

Then, here he came, charging in through the trees. The two Raiders dove for the weapons they had dropped. One man went for his saber, and another went for his lance. Virgil, a small wiry man, just ducked behind a big tree trunk. The giant pulled up right on top of them. As the first Raider went at him with a lance, the rider released an arrow at point blank range, putting it through the center of the Raider's chest. As the rider released the arrow, he tossed his bow aside.

The big man slid off his mount as the second Raider warily approached him with his sword. It seemed that the giant had his ax in one hand and his big knife in the other before his feet even hit the earth. The Raider and the big man circled. The Raider was a tall, gangly man, obviously frightened, but standing his ground.

"I'll let you live, iffin you drop that there weapon," the big man calmly told the Raider.

But the Raider gathered his courage and swung a vicious blow. The big man moved like a panther, easily dodging the blow. Simultaneously he moved in, swinging down with the ax and plunging the big knife into the man's chest. In a second, it was over.

"You kin come out from behind that there tree trunk now, scout," the big man turned. "I'll not harm you, lessen you give me cause." As he spoke, the Ranger wiped both of his bloody weapons off on the dead man's filthy trousers. The scout slowly came out from behind the tree.

"I'll give ye no cause, that's fer certain."

"What be yo'r name, scout?"

"Virgil, sir," the scout replied. He held his floppy hat in his hands; it made him almost look like a small boy that had been caught misbehaving.

"Well, Virgil, my name be Sebastian, and I'm a Ranger from across the Great Mountains. Have you ever heard of the Elympian Rangers?"

"Only legends, sir."

"Well, whatever stories you've heard likely don't tell the half of it. Now I'm goin' to let you live for two reasons. I want you to stay here with these here wounded men and look after 'em. Then, when yo'r main party catches up to you, I want you to deliver a message to their leader for me. Can you do all that?"

"Yessir, I surely kin."

"Virgil, what be yo'r leader's name?"

"It be Cutler, sir."

"Well, tell yo'r man Cutler that he's followin' the wrong party, for they be under the protection of the Elympian Rangers. Tell him we'll be watchin'. Iffin he and his men don't turn back, won't none of 'em ever come back alive...that's a guarantee. Can you remember all that?"

"Yessir."

The Ranger had put his knife and ax back in their scabbards and retrieved his bow. He cut down the rope that was stretched between the trees, coiled it and tied it with a leather strap to his saddle. He then fetched the two bloody arrows and rinsed them with water from a canteen before putting them back in his quiver. Finally, he mounted back up.

"Now give yo'r friends some water and look after 'em as best you can. And deliver that message for me."

The warrior kicked his mount and in a moment had disappeared into the forest. Virgil wiped his brow with a dirty sleeve, *whew, that were close*, he thought to himself. He fetched a canteen from one of the horses and gave some water to the man with the broken pelvis. The man was moaning in pain, but thanked the scout for his kindness. The other man was still unconscious.

The scout took a drink from the canteen himself, re-corked it, and then threw it down to the injured Raider. He then fetched his horse and mounted up.

"Where ye be goin'?" the injured man asked anxiously.

"T' find Cutler; I'll bring 'em here soon's I kin," the scout lied. He had had enough of both Cutler and Rangers to last a lifetime. He lit out for parts unknown.

* * *

The Ranger headed south again, but at a leisurely pace. He knew that there was now scant chance of picking up his own party's trail, but he was fairly unconcerned about that. He knew their final destination, and he knew that they didn't have that much farther to go to reach it. His priority, for now, was to make sure that the Raiders that followed them would turn back...those that survived.

After a while, the big man left the forest trail he had been following, and headed into the depths of the forest, carefully obscuring his own spoor. Finally, at midday, he stopped and made camp. He would eat a bit and then sleep for most of the afternoon. Late in the day, he planned on picking up the Raider's trail once again. Then, after darkness had fallen, he planned on getting back to work...

* * *

"Lass, there's somethin' I been meanin' t' tell you." Lilith had sat down next to Maya in front of the blazing campfire. Although they were worried that a big fire might give their campsite away to the Raiders, the threat of predators just now represented a more immediate source of anxiety.

Darkness had fallen and both women had sat down for a cup of tea after a long, harrowing day. Both men now slept. Santiago had continued to decline throughout the day, and Lilith had kept him heavily drugged to ease his pain.

In the afternoon, the two women had reset Valerian's shoulder with great difficulty, with Maya holding her man down as best she could, while the big woman forced his arm back into its socket. The young man had finally fainted from the pain. While he was unconscious, they had set also wrapped his chest. The effort had left both women drained.

"Yes Lilith?"

"Last night with th' grizzly...that was the bravest thing I ever saw, you standin' there, a wisp of a girl, standin' fast with yer bow, shootin' arrows into that monster from hell. Not budgin' even when he charged. I never thought I'd ever see such a thing."

Both women were silent for a time. The Spaniard let out another low moan in the darkness, and then fell silent again. Maya stirred the fire with a piece of firewood, sending sparks up into the black sky.

"Lilith, I had to watch my whole family put to death when I was a young girl. I didn't think that there was anything that I could do, so I just hid and watched it happen." The tears came now, of their own volition.

"Child, I'm sure that you couldn't have..."

Maya interrupted, with the tears glistening on her cheeks. "What I mean is...what I learned on that day is that I would rather die myself, than to ever again have to watch someone I love be killed. I will never let that happen again...the certainty that I would die before having to watch Valerian ever be killed, gives me a kind of peace."

Now Lilith's eyes filled with tears, as she turned to the young woman and held her close. "Maya, I was never blessed with siblings; I'd be right honored if 'fin I could call you my sister."

Maya pulled back and wiped the tears away. She smiled warmly at the tall woman. "I can't think of anyone I've ever met that I'd rather have for a sister."

"Well then, Little Sister, let's check on our two patients. Maybe we kin make a broth t' feed yer man, at least."

With that, the two weary women rose and got back to work.

* * *

The three tough Raiders who rode in advance of Cutler's main party rounded a bend in the forest trail, and were dumbfounded by the sight ahead. There was their scouting party, scattered all about the trail as if a giant hand had smashed them down from above. They stopped in their tracks, instantly on alert. One of the men wheeled his horse about and sped back to the main party, while the other two stood watch some thirty paces from the carnage.

Soon, the main party arrived, with Cutler in the lead. Almost half of the Raiders rode double now, as they had been unable to recover a number of their horses. Cutler ordered the men to dismount and form a perimeter, with their weapons at the ready. He then dismounted with a half dozen of his men and approached the fallen Raiders. He was surprised to find that two of the six were still alive. One raised himself up to his elbows when he heard the men approach; he was obviously in great pain. The other man was moaning but only semi-conscious.

"Tell me what happened," Cutler demanded without sympathy.

The man recounted the ambush and the brief battle that followed. (Once again, it appeared that just one man had done all this!) The injured Raider then recounted the warning that the big Ranger had given to Virgil.

"And just where be Virgil?" Cutler asked the man.

"He said he was goin' t' look fer you…" the man replied and then moaned in pain, "Kin ye help me sir? I'm hurtin' right bad."

"Of course I kin, mate." Cutler drew his knife and quickly ended the man's pain. He showed the same degree of mercy for the other wounded man. He wiped his bloody knife on one of the dead men's trousers as he sat down on a fallen tree trunk.

The Rangers, he said "Rangers". Does that mean there's more than one? I've heard tall tales of th' Rangers from across th' mountains. Never really believed 'em…but I reckon I don't have much choice now, Cutler thought to himself. *Well, I've still got me eighteen hard-core Raiders. I've let 'em take me by surprise twice now, but I'll be damned if' in I'll let that happen agin'.*

"Tell th' men that we'll rest here for just a bit, eat some rations, and then we'll be headin' out agin' directly," he ordered one of his lieutenants. "And git some men wi' shovels and bury these here dead Raiders."

The lieutenant trotted away to spread the word amongst the men scattered about in a rough circle. What Cutler didn't hear, in return, was the grumbling. The men were becoming frightened and unsure of themselves and their leader. And they didn't like the way that Cutler had finished off their injured comrades. These were men who were accustomed to a lifetime of dealing out punishment, rather than the other way around. And their ordeal was far from over...

* * *

Sebastian woke up from a sound sleep late in the afternoon. He ate a bit of jerky and some dried fruit and, swished it down with a bit of water from his canteen. He washed his face with a little more water and stretched. He then checked his weapons, cleaning and sharpening his lance, knife and ax. He checked his arrows and inspected his bowstring to make sure it wasn't frayed. Finally, he saddled his horse and mounted up.

The Ranger followed his own tracks back to the same forest trail that he had used for the ambush that morning. He soon picked up the tracks of the main Raider party. He moved carefully, wary of being ambushed himself. Darkness fell, but soon a half moon rose, so he had no problem tracking the Raiders. After a time, he could tell by the freshness of the trail that he must be nearing their encampment. He dismounted and led his horse well off from the trail. He tethered the animal in a small clearing where it could graze.

The Ranger wore his hooded woodsman's cloak and carried only his knife and ax. Gliding silently though the forest, parallel to the trail, the big man eventually detected the sounds and smells of the Raider camp. They had made camp in a small meadow, at the base of a shear cliff. Now he moved like a ghost, methodically using the shadows and the natural cover of thick foliage that the forest afforded. It was near midnight by now.

Soon, Sebastian spotted a Raider sentry. Moving carefully around the camp he spotted a few more. The horses were tied in a tight group and were guarded by at least three more Raiders. The Ranger figured that at least a third of the men were on guard. They were taking no chances this night. The rest of the Raiders were huddled around three campfires, drinking and talking. They looked like a pretty subdued bunch this night.

The big man slipped away in the darkness, to wait a few more hours. Soon most of the men would be asleep, and he was sure that some of the sentries would be sleepy by then, as well. The night had gotten quite chilly and a stiff breeze had kicked up. *Good*, thought the Ranger, *a wind in the trees will just help cover my movements*. He found a good spot under an oak and sat down, wrapping his cloak around himself.

*　*　*

Though it was well after midnight, Cutler sat wide-awake in his tent, with a lit candle by his side. He was at that moment studying a crude map that Deacon had given him. *Where were these varmints headed to anyhow?* They had meandered a bit, but for the most part, their trail had consistently headed southeast, through forests, across rivers and over mountains. But why? There were no known townships or even farmsteads in that direction, just endless miles of more rugged, uninhabited country.

Cutler traced his finger along the line they had followed and extended it. Just a little further south was a scribbled "X" that supposedly marked the location of the haunted city, the abandoned city of the Ancients, the city known as Elympias. The Rangers…weren't they supposed to be from the Elympian lands far to the west? Weren't they supposed the descendants of the people that once lived in that city?

The Raider leader made up his mind that he would head for Elympias in the morning. Stop tracking whomever it was that was leading them on this little chase. However, he hoped to catch that man this night, in any case.

He had eighteen men left now…out of the original thirty-three! Six of them were now on sentry duty. Another six were ordered to stay awake as reserves. The final six were allowed to sleep, with their weapons at their sides. No one was allowed to drink anything but tea or water. The men would be rotated every few hours, so that all of them would be rested and alert.

The men had readily accepted Cutler's orders; they wanted revenge for what had been done to their compatriots, and more than that, they wanted the attacks to come to an end. All of the men waited; those on sentry duty peered intently into the darkness, looking for any sign of an intruder…

*　*　*

It was now midway between midnight and dawn. The sky was overcast and a stiff wind still rustled through the trees…perfect conditions for his plan. The Ranger knew that the encampment would be on full alert, so he took his time. Eventually, he smelled wood smoke, and knew that the enemy was near. He crouched, and approached silently on hands and knees.

He saw the first campfire. Although it had burned down some, it still provided a dim light for the camp. As he moved in closer, he saw two more fires. *A mistake that Rangers would never make,* the big man thought. *Exposes them to their enemy, whilst it diminishes their own night vision.*

The Ranger stood up behind a large tree and peered around it, looking all about the camp. He could see three sentries from his position, though he was sure that there were more out of his range of vision. He took his time now, carefully sizing up the enemy camp. Finally, after a long while, he made up his mind. One sentry seemed to be sleepy, just staring straight ahead and occasionally nodding. The other two that he could see seemed more alert, scanning back and forth in the darkness.

The big man began his approach, slowly and methodically. He exited the woods midway between the sleepy sentry and one of the others, perhaps fifty paces away. He crawled flat against the ground, using the small depressions and brush in the meadow to maximize his cover. The drowsy Raider held what attention he could muster outward into the trees, even as death circled around from behind.

The sentry had no inkling of danger, until he felt the piercing pain in the small of his back. The pain of the knife was so intense that it took his breath away. His last sensation was of being pushed to the ground by an enormous weight.

The Ranger cut the man's throat as he lay on the dying man's back. It had taken all of about two seconds, and what little sound had been made had been lost in the rustle of the wind in the trees. Now, carefully, slowly, the big man dragged the sentry into the woods. He hid the body deep in the woods and carefully covered his tracks. Then he circled back around the camp, looking for his next victim.

The next target was easy to select. A big Raider sat on his haunches near the horses he was guarding. He sat near a thicket, out of sight of his fellow sentries. The Ranger simply sprang out of the thicket and buried his ax in the Raider's forehead, before the man could even react. The Ranger also dragged his body off into the forest and hid the tracks.

Dawn was nearing; the Ranger figured he had just enough time to take out one more Raider. He almost stumbled into the third. The man had walked over to the edge of the trees to relieve himself. He wasn't allowed to finish; he died with his trousers down. *A bad way to go,* the old warrior thought to himself as he dragged the body away. Soon the third body was hidden, and the tracks likewise covered. As he finished, the sky began to lighten.

As he faded back into the forest, the Ranger was satisfied to hear the first alarm being sounded, and then the shouts of frightened and angry men...

* * *

As the warning was shouted, Cutler practically exploded out of his tent, with sword drawn. He had finally dozed off, but was now instantly wide awake. He looked around in all directions, but saw no sign of an attack, other than a bunch of his own men running around in all directions. Finally, he determined who had sounded the alarm.

"What is it? An' it better not be a false alarm..."

"No sir," the nervous man practically shouted, "It be Rufus. He were standin' guard here...I was right over yonder, and now he's gone."

"Iffin he went off inta th' woods t' take a dump, I'll have his hide," Cutler muttered.

Most of the other men had run up now to see what was going on.

"Look here," one of the other men shouted, "blood on th' ground... and it looks like somethin' were dragged inta th' woods."

The men all followed the trail until it entered the woods, where it promptly vanished. It was as if something had killed Rufus, dragged him a ways, and then flown up with his body into the trees.

"Hey, where be Moose? He were standin' guard over by th' horses."

"What about Jesse? Anybody see Jesse? He were standin' watch across th' field over yonder."

Everyone looked at Cutler as if they were expecting their leader to tell them what was happening. He was a much at a loss as they were. He disguised his confusion with anger.

"Well let's just stop standin' around gawkin' and git t' work! Git breakfast made and git th' horses saddled up and packed. We be headin' out first thing this morning!"

"We be headin' back home?"

A huge brute named Tiny posed the question. For a long moment, all of the men just stood there, staring at Cutler. The Raider leader could smell mutiny in the air. He raised his sword and pointed at Tiny.

"Well' are we gonna git movin' or do we have a problem?"

For a long moment, Tiny just glared at him under a big bushy eyebrow that stretched clear across his forehead. The brute then slowly turned back toward the camp without another word. The rest of the men grudgingly followed. Under his breath, Cutler breathed a sigh of relief. But he had now lost more than half of his men, by Rangers who moved like ghosts in the forest. Cutler did his best to conceal it, but for the first time, his mouth held the bitter taste of real fear...

32

Schism
February 27th, 2101

"We've debated the issue long enough. I believe that it is time to put the Rev. Abernathy's proposal to a vote, if there are no objections," Dr. Allen, the Council Tribune, announced, bringing the long and emotional debate to an end. No one objected.

"All in favor?" Three hands instantly went up; two more wavered for a moment and followed.

"All opposed?" Six hands went up immediately, and two more after a moment's hesitation.

"The nays have it. The proposal is defeated."

Mac was much relieved. Reverend Melinda Abernathy was the minister for the Olympus's Unity Christian congregation. The church members, appalled at the recent actions taken by President Powell's Administration, had voted overwhelmingly to request that Reverend Abernathy take this proposal to the Olympus Council. The proposal requested that Olympus provide material support for the groups struggling to form an opposition movement to the Administration's de facto *coup d'état*.

Mac had argued strongly against the proposition. Rather surprisingly, so had Dr. Alvarez, (who had recently been appointed to the Council to replace a retiring member.)

"My honored friends and colleagues, I regret to assert that the overcrowded lifeboat analogy applies here," Dr. Alvarez stood up, "If we try to help, our little lifeboat, Olympus, will surely be swamped, and we will drown with all the rest. I know that it is very painful to stand aside and do nothing to help our fellow citizens in their hour of need. That pain will become agony over the coming months, as the collapse unfolds and we are forced to watch untold suffering all around us. But I fear that the only possible result of our involvement would be the destruction of our own community and all that it stands for."

Mac had then spoken, "Folks, let's not mince words; on at least two occasions, Powell has used nukes on American cities. Does anyone think that he would hesitate to drop one on us, if he saw us as a serious threat? Besides, with civilization's general collapse imminent, what difference can our involvement possibly make, in any case?"

After the vote, Rev. Abernathy, with tears in her eyes, had asked to address the Council. "Fellow Council members, I regret that I must tender my resignation in protest. All of your arguments against this proposal make perfectly good sense, if one were to be persuaded by logic alone. However, my heart tells me that I cannot, in good conscious as a Christian and an American, stand by and let my fellow citizens suffer, without so much raising a finger. This is not simply a practical issue, but an ethical issue. Right now, thousands of honest American citizens all around the country are being rounded up and put into detention camps. God only know what will happen to them."

The other Council members pleaded with her to reconsider, but she steadfastly refused, finally standing up and taking her leave. Shockingly, two other members stood up and followed suite, resigning and making their exit with the minister.

Dr. Allen now spoke, "Ladies and gentlemen, this more than a moral issue; it is a moral dilemma. We teach our children to live by a code that demands that we stand up for our fellow man. We feed the hungry, we cure the sick, and above all, we protect the defenseless. Yet, now we all vote to stand by and do nothing as our fellow citizens are cast into virtual slavery. I move that we adjourn for tonight. In the meantime, let us all just search our individual consciences, and deliberate further on this issue in the coming days."

The motion was quickly seconded and the subdued Council members began to file out of the Council chambers.

"Excuse me, sir! May we address the Council before it retires?"

It was a voice from across the hall...a youthful voice. The Council members, in the heat of the moment, had forgotten that they had not yet received the report of the Pathfinder Council, which had met concurrently with their own. Somewhat embarrassed, Dr. Allen reconvened the Council to hear the Pathfinder's formal report.

The Pathfinder Tribune was a blonde, gangly youth named Seth Abramson. Seth was an earnest, intellectually gifted young man, fifteen years in age. He was accompanied by a slender Asian-American girl named Alyssa, who held the title of Prefect in the Pathfinder Council. They stood at the center of the semi-circular conference table, across from the seated Council members.

"I notice that three chairs are empty; may I ask why some members are absent?" the young Pathfinder asked Dr. Allen.

The Council Tribune recounted the debate over the proposal and the resulting resignations.

"I understand, sir. The Pathfinder Council debated the same proposition tonight, and our debate also grew very intense."

"And was the eventual outcome of your debate similar to our own?" Dr. Allen asked.

"Ah...no sir; the Pathfinder Council voted unanimously to recommend that Olympus render whatever aid possible to the forces that are gathering in resistance to President Powell."

Mac spoke now, "And did the Pathfinder Council seriously consider the possible implications of those actions?"

Alyssa spoke up now, "We did sir. We considered the possibility that Olympus might be attacked, or even destroyed."

"And you all found such a possibility acceptable?" Mac pressed.

"No sir. However, in the end, the Pathfinder Council agreed that we really have no choice but to act," the young girl responded. When she had first spoken, she had seemed a bit nervous, but as she continued, the depth of her convictions appeared to give her confidence.

"There is always a choice," Mac shot back.

"Let's hear her out, Mac," Dr. Alvarez took on a thoughtful look. "How so, young lady?" The professor leaned back in his high-backed chair.

Alyssa responded, "Members of the Council, if you truly believe in the values that you have taught us here at Olympus, surely you must accept the fact that we are obliged to follow the dictates of our conscience, regardless of the consequences. We *must* do what is right, or what would be the point of Olympus, in the first place?"

Seth added, "The fact is, we Pathfinders do believe in those values, without qualification. But we understand that we are little more than children, so we know that there is not much that we can do on our own. Therefore, we agreed tonight that the Pathfinder Council's most valuable contribution might be to simply remind the Elder Council of the principles to which we have all sworn. You have taught us that living with honor and courage means doing what we believe is right, even if we suffer for it...even if it means that we must pay the ultimate price."

The Council members were all silent for a few moments. Everyone seemed lost in his or her own thoughts.

Finally, Dr. Allen spoke, "Thank you Seth; thank you Alyssa. You have given us much to think about, and I assure you, we will consider the Pathfinder Council's position most carefully. Now, I would like to once again move that we adjourn for the evening."

Dr. Alvarez quickly interjected, "With respect, Frederick, I would like to make an alternative motion. I know it's late, but I would like to suggest that we immediately reopen the debate regarding Dr. Abernathy's proposal. Further, I would like to summon our three former Council members back to join in the debate."

With a grudging smile, Mac said, "I find myself compelled to second Professor Alvarez's motion.

"Dr. Alvarez, perhaps you have a point. Are there any objections?" Dr. Allen asked.

There were none.

"Very well. Thank you both for sharing the Pathfinder Council's recommendations with us. You are excused. Please say nothing of this meeting to anyone, not even to your families."

"We understand, sir. If anything is to be done, it is important that we know nothing about it. Thank you most kindly for considering our views," Seth responded.

The two youths then made their leave.

"And a little child shall lead them..." Professor Alvarez muttered softly after they had left.

"Yes, it looks like the students have become the teachers," Mac added.

"Indeed," Dr. Allen spoke now, "It is getting late. Let's summon our colleagues and get to work."

So it was that after the three absent members had returned, and their resignations had been rescinded, the new debate continued into the wee hours. In the end, the final vote was unanimous; Olympus would provide covert assistance and support to the forces fighting to preserve the ideals of democracy in America. And in the process, the citizens of Olympus would put themselves squarely in harm's way...

* * *

The next morning, Frederick, Mac, Olivia, and Louie called Graham at dawn and invited him to breakfast. Graham readily agreed and suggested they dine in his own penthouse suite. The morning was crisp, and the sky shone bright and blue through the large picture window and skylight in Graham's dining room. They chatted through breakfast...just small talk. When the remains of breakfast were cleared away, everyone sat back with a last cup of coffee or tea.

Graham spoke first, "Well, it's good to see all of you. We haven't gotten together in some time. However, somehow I get the feeling that this is more than just a social call. Am I right?"

"Quite right, Jonathan," Dr. Allen responded, "We have a favor to ask of you. And it's a rather large favor, at that..."

He then recounted the events of the prior evening. Mac then made the Council's proposition.

"Ha! I thought you folks would never ask! I have only been restraining myself in deference to the authority of the Olympus Council. I didn't think that I had any right to risk provoking the retribution of Powell's government by taking any actions against Powell and his zealots that might endanger the citizens here. But now the Council has recruited me to do just that!"

"Fred, you know how I feel about religious fanatics. When a true fanatic thinks that God is on his side, he is secure in the belief that absolutely any level of barbarous behavior is justified in what he supposes is God's service. In my estimation, throughout history, more cruelty, murder, mayhem and madness have been perpetrated in the name of one god or another than for any other reason."

"So yes, I accept your proposition, with pleasure. However, I have a few conditions that all of you must accept. First of all, my friends, none of you will have any involvement in my actions. Secondly, you will be privy to absolutely nothing that I am up to. You will all just have to trust me. I have resources around the world that are completely independent of Olympus. I will use them as I wish to support the resistance movements that are rising up even now around the nation. If my actions are traced back to me, I alone will take the fall. I am very proud of Olympus; it is the crowning achievement of my life. I want to ensure that this city is endangered no more than absolutely necessary."

"You seem awfully enthusiastic about all this, Jonathan, even though you must have already considered the futility of opposing Powell, with the collapse just over the horizon," Olivia observed. "It's one of the primary reasons that the Council hesitated to act."

"I'd be happy to go after a tyrant like Powell if I knew that the collapse was coming next week. To be honest, ever since I handed over the management of Olympus to the duly elected members of the Olympus Council, I've felt pretty irrelevant. I find that retirement really doesn't suit me all that well. Fomenting an insurrection might be just the thing to get my juices flowing again!"

"Jonathan, are you sure that you don't want to accept any help from me or Mac?" Olivia asked. "You know, once upon a time we were pretty good at such things." (The truth was that Olivia was itching to get into the fight herself.)

"You are two of the best, Olivia." Graham responded. "Nonetheless, thanks, but no thanks. The more citizens of Olympus involved in treason, the more likely that the whole city will suffer for it if something goes awry. It's best that I do this on my own. However, I do have one other request. I would like a totally secure access protocol to Aristotle, my eyes only, with maximum access privileges."

"Done," all agreed.

✱ ✱ ✱

Professor Alvarez stayed behind to chat with his old friend after Mac and Olivia had taken their leave. The two men retreated to the two big overstuffed chairs in Graham's study.

"So, Louie you say that it was the Pathfinder Council that finally convinced all of you to take action."

"*Sí,* my friend. As we all know, teaching virtue is far easier than living it. The Pathfinders simply held us to the standards that we have taught them. We could find no way out. Ironic, no?"

"Ah, irony...I must say, a love of irony is certainly one of my own favorite virtues. If there is a God, he must love irony as much as I do, for the universe seems to be built around it."

"Jonathan, did I hear correctly? Did you say, 'If there is a God?' Does that mean that you now believe that He might exist?"

"My friend, I confess that you have elevated me from the status of confirmed atheist to that of a practicing agnostic. I have decided that if a man with your wisdom and insight can believe so firmly in a God, I am forced to accept the fact that there just might be something to it."

"A small miracle...I must say that I am most pleased."

"Now Louie, I must stress that I am only an agnostic, not a true believer."

"*Compadre,* I find that quite satisfactory. Opening your mind to new possibilities is invariably the necessary first step in acquiring new wisdom."

* * *

Geordie was pissed. More than that, Geordie was a little bit frightened. The so-called Emergency Decree had been in effect for almost six months now. On the surface, everything seemed pretty normal. He worked his regular six hours day, five days a week job as an AI developer, just like before. And he still spent most of his free time gaming in VR, just like always.

However, he was frustrated by the fact that all of the Cyber-community sites now carried a warning, upon login, that they were being monitored for illegal or seditious conduct by the federal authorities, acting under the auspices of the Emergency Decree. Even innocuous cyber-grams to friends and family carried the disclaimer. Only VR games, sex sites, and consumer venues seemed to have remained wide open.

He had just about given up his occasional forays to the local cafes and pubs, as well. It was hard to put his finger on just what was going on, but somehow they all seemed to increasingly have become less cheerful, more oppressive places. In fact, fear spiced with a bit of paranoia seemed to now be hovering on the fringes of every public place he had visited, of late.

But what really had Geordie upset was that he couldn't contact his kid sister, Ariel. Ariel was five years younger than Geordie. She had a political science degree and worked for an environmental advocacy group. Where Geordie was apolitical and a bit of an introvert, Ariel was a vocal and outgoing political activist. Nonetheless, Geordie and his sister had stayed close, even as they had gone their separate ways. The fact was Geordie was proud of Sis.

However, for the last month or so, all of his attempted communications with her had gone unanswered. He had been unable to contact any of her friends or co-workers, either. His parents had had no more luck, and they were worried sick. Geordie and his parents lived in Cincinnati; Ariel had moved to Vienna, Virginia, just outside of D.C., a couple of years earlier.

Finally, his parents convinced Geordie to physically travel to Vienna to look for his sister. It was a daunting challenge for the young man. He had never left Cincinnati in his life and now rarely ventured more than a few blocks from his micro-suite. (Why hassle with the cost and inconveniences of traveling in PR, when you could explore the universe lying back on your sensory lounge chair?) And speaking of cost, money was definitely an issue. Physical travel had become a rarity, and was now prohibitively expensive for working class blokes like Geordie.

Eventually, the young man's parents had anted up. They took a big chunk of their pension reserve and augmented it with a small loan, which they transferred into his account. Geordie took the money grudgingly, because he knew that it would seriously impact his parents' ability to make ends meet. Nonetheless, neither he nor they could see any other way.

His trip was almost over before it started. At the airport, he was asked by the Homeland screeners to give the reason for his trip. He almost told them the truth, but something stopped him at the last moment. Could his sister be on some sort of watch list? So he lied and told them that his parents had given him the money for a sightseeing trip to Washington as a birthday gift. They had seemed suspicious for a moment, but passed him on through. He breathed a sigh of relief as he headed for the gate.

The flight to DC was uneventful. However, it looked like the auto-cab ride to Vienna was probably going to take longer than the flight had, due to the gridlocked D.C. ground traffic. Creeping along on the throughway, the young man called Ariel to tell her that he was in town and heading to her condo. He still got no answer. He wondered what he would do next, if she didn't answer the door when he finally got there.

Suddenly, Geordie's earphone Uplink warbled and he answered. It was a male voice, a stranger's voice. "This is an encrypted call from a friend of Ariel's. Tell the auto-cab that you want to divert to the Lincoln Memorial. Tell it to wait for you at curbside, and that you will return in fifteen minutes. Then walk to the Memorial, where you will be intercepted. Do exactly as you are told; you are in grave danger."

The call clicked off. Geordie felt a shot of adrenaline surge through his body...real fear, something he had never experienced before. It was nothing like the artificial excitement of fear in VR. This wasn't the thrill of a fun-ride; it was a feeling of cold dread. His voice shook a bit as he ordered the cab to divert. He exited the cab and began to walk toward the imposing Memorial, something he had only seen in VR.

But the young man had only taken a few steps when a tall, broad-shouldered young man slapped him on the back. "Geordie, ol' buddy! Good to see ya man! Come with me."

The man shook hands with him, even gave him a hug. He was a total stranger. "Come with me, buddy."

Geordie hung back a bit, but the big man grabbed him by the elbow and pulled hard...he was strong. Geordie gave in and followed. They jaywalked across the street and entered an old office building under renovation.

"Where are we...?"

"Not now man, just keep moving."

They maneuvered around scaffolds and automated construction equipment. They stopped in an empty hallway near a rear exit.

"Put this on, quick." The stranger pulled a hooded jacket out of a small knapsack. "Pull the hood over your head and put these sunglasses on."

Meanwhile the man turned his own reversible jacket inside out and donned a construction helmet that lay nearby. "Now give me all your Uplinks."

Geordie did as he was told, handing over his earpiece and a pocket model. The stranger put both in a metallic bag and stuffed them in the knapsack. They exited into a back alley where an old gas-turbine utility vehicle was parked next to a dumpster.

"Walk slow and casual, and get in the truck."

Again, Geordie did as he was told. Soon, they merged into the heavy D.C. traffic.

"Now can you tell me what's going on?"

The stranger held his hand up as he made a call, "I've picked up the package and we should have it delivered in a few hours. Any issues? Good. See ya there." He pulled a small Uplink from his pocket, and switched it on, laying it between them on the seat.

"This device can function as a conventional Uplink, but its real purpose is to detect and block any surveillance devices. We can talk now."

"Where are we going? And who are you?"

"We're going to a safe house. And you can call me Spartacus."

Geordie waited a few moments for elaboration, but got nothing. He was still very frightened and very uncertain whether this man was a friend or foe...or perhaps just crazy. "Is my sister okay? Will I see her soon?"

"Yes, she's fine, and yes, you'll see her soon. Look, let's just save the questions and explanations for when we get where we are goin'. Right now, I want to concentrate on gettin' there without being intercepted."

The trip to the safe house took the better part of the afternoon. They changed vehicles several times, took an auto-cab once, and in between, walked down various back alleys and deserted streets. Geordie had no idea what part of town he was in when they finally got to their final destination, and was pretty sure that no one on earth could have followed them, even with high tech surveillance gear. Their destination seemed to be a small, dilapidated office building.

They entered the lobby from a back alley and then stepped into a service elevator. It was an ancient, manual elevator, which apparently had no voice actuation. It had buttons for 'B', 'L', '1', '2', '3' and '4'. Spartacus hit none of the buttons. Rather, as the door closed, the young man said, "Spartacus, sub-basement two, sierra nine-five."

The elevator went down to a sub-basement level for which there was no button. *Real cloak and dagger stuff, just like 'Spymaster XVII',* Geordie thought to himself, half expecting to see some high tech command center when the elevator door opened.

It was no such thing, just an old basement storeroom outfitted with castoff living room and dining room furniture, an old style fridge and an even older holo-unit. There were three other people already there; they were all young, attractive sorts...college student types. One girl came running up, threw her arms around Geordie and kissed his cheek. He had no idea who she was until she spoke.

"Hi bro'! It's so good to see you! And thank God we got to you before the Feds did!" It was Ariel, but she was a blonde now, much thinner, and her features, though similar to the old Ariel, were somehow different enough to make her virtually unrecognizable.

"Oh, sorry about the disguise, I guess it must be pretty effective, if my own brother doesn't recognize me." Ariel also gave Spartacus a hug and kiss that, Geordie noticed, was decidedly less brotherly. "Geordie, I want you to meet my other two friends, Roxanne and Alexander."

Geordie shook their hands.

"Sit down brother, and I'll get you a sub and fizz."

The young man sat down on an old overstuffed chair; he felt literally light-headed. None of this felt in the least bit real. His sister handed him a sandwich and drink, and sat across from him on the ragged sofa next to Spartacus. As he ate, she told him their story.

"First of all, the reason that we snatched you was that we have been monitoring my own inbound cyber-address...just like the Feds are. When we caught your call, we knew the Feds would pick you up as soon as you reached my condo. We had to move fast to get to you before they did."

"But why are you in hiding...why are all of you in hiding? Ariel, you've always been an activist, but you've always been law-abiding. Why are the authorities after you? For God's sake, you haven't become a Cyber-terrorist have you?"

Alexander, a thin, athletic black man, looked like he was about to lose it. "Man, don't you even have a clue what's goin' on out there?"

Geordie's sister motioned him down. "Don't mind Alex, he's a bit hot-tempered, but he's a good man to have with you in a fight."

"First of all, brother, don't call me Ariel any more; my name is Roxanne now. My *nom d'guerre*. Secondly, we aren't Cyber-terrorists...matter of fact we're not terrorists at all; we are patriots. Lastly we didn't do anything at all to get crosswise with the Feds, at least not at first."

Roxanne leaned back and took a sip of her own fizz drink. "So, here's how it went down. Before the Emergency Decree, we were all employees of the Alliance on Global Warming, you know, the AGW. It was a pretty innocuous group, really; we mostly lobbied Congress and the U.N. to support programs that deal with global warming."

"But shortly after the Emergency Decree was announced, members started disappearing. Within a few days, Spartacus got a covert communication from an old friend in Homeland Defense. The Feds were planning on rounding up all of us and putting us into detention centers. Spartacus's friend told him that the AGW, along with a whole host of advocacy groups, had been deemed 'potentially disloyal' to the Powell

Administration. All of their members, thousands of innocent citizens, were to be 'disappeared', no hearings, no arraignments, no legal representation, no nothing."

"But what about the law, citizen's rights, that sort of thing?"

"Don't you get it Geordie? Those niceties are history. Anyway, then it became a race against time. Spartacus and a few others tried to warn as many AGW members as they could before they were picked up. They only rescued a handful out of hundreds. I was one of the ones who got rescued first."

"So now we've set up a small underground organization, and we're trying to hook up with other groups like our own. We've heard they're out there, but we have to be careful. The feds are everywhere…in both physical and virtual reality. The good news is that we are getting some covert support from inside the government. Seems that there are plenty of folks inside the government that are just as unhappy with what's going on as we are."

Alexander spoke now, "So tell us, Bowie…How does it feel to be a freedom fighter?"

"Who's Bowie? And whoa, who said I intend to become a freedom fighter?"

Alexander laughed, "Bowie is your new name, son. And the only option that you have to being a freedom fighter is being a prisoner in a detention camp…"

33

Journey's End

Sebastian watched the Raiders from a stand of trees on a high hill overlooking their campsite. He saw the confrontation with their leader, whom he supposed was Cutler. He couldn't make out what was said, but he could guess well enough. He figured that they'd had enough. He watched them break camp and pack up. He smiled in satisfaction as, sure enough, they headed due north. They had given up; they were going home.

The Ranger stood up and stretched. He walked down the backside of the hill to where his horse was tethered, grazing placidly. He swigged some water from his canteen and grabbed an apple from one of his saddlebags. Chomping on the fruit, he swung up into the saddle.

The big man turned his mount to the south and headed out. It was a wild guess, based on the crude map that the Commander had given him, but he surmised that he was no more than three to five days away from Elympias. He hoped that Valerian and his party had made it there already. He also hoped that Valerian had found something there that would be worth the hardship and sacrifices that they had all endured. But most of all, he simply hoped that they were all safe and well…

* * *

Cutler found himself between a rock and a hard place. If he tried to continue following the damned Rangers, he was pretty sure that the men would mutiny. In any case, he really didn't have the stomach for it himself. He was pretty tired of being stalked and hounded by an enemy that always seemed to be one step ahead of them.

On the other hand, returning to the Lawless Lands empty-handed meant sure death. Deacon had made that clear enough, and Deacon was a man of his word…in matters such as this, in any case.

But Cutler did have an ace-in-the-hole; at least he hoped he did. He was pretty sure where the fugitives were headed. So he decided that he would head north for a ways, and then gradually swing back around to the south…head for the haunted city. Hopefully by then, the Ranger would no longer be trailing them, and hopefully by then, his men would have settled down a bit. He would just have to think of a really creative lie to get them to turn south again. Well, he would just have to work on that for the next few days.

* * *

The morning was cold and crisp. They were lucky; it had been a mild autumn so far. Eight grueling days had passed since the bear attack, although Valerian was now feeling much better. The soreness in his shoulder had faded somewhat, and he could finally breathe without his ribs hurting too much. He was up and around now, helping the women by gathering firewood and tidying up the camp.

After breakfast, the bored young man had begun to practice again with Santiago's katana. In the few weeks that he had traveled with Santiago, he had practiced with the master swordsman almost every night after dinner, by the light of their campfire. The Spaniard had been both amazed and pleased by the young man's progress. On one of the last evenings that they had sparred, Valerian had parried several strokes by the Spaniard in a duel that took place at blinding speed. Dumfounded, Santiago had backed off for a moment, recovered, and bored back in. On the second attack, he had finally gotten through his student's guard and won the contest. He had embraced Valerian warmly.

"*Muchacho*, you are truly a prodigy. If you continue such as this, soon your skills with the sword may match my own…perhaps even exceed them! That would give me great satisfaction."

Now, with Santiago barely hanging on to life, Valerian practiced the lunges, thrusts and parries that his friend had taught him. Every move hurt his ribs and his shoulder, but he continued practicing with determination. The fact was that without Sebastian, Valerian was very concerned with how defenseless they were, just now, to either man or beast. Even wounded, the weight of responsibility for protecting his companions rested heavily on the young warrior.

And where was Sebastian, anyway? Valerian feared that his uncle had pushed on to Elympias, assuming they had done the same. If so, he might have unknowingly passed them by days ago. The young man wouldn't let himself even consider the other, grimmer possibilities; his uncle was an incredible warrior and woodsman, but he wasn't invulnerable.

"Lad, take it easy with that sword; it took a lot of work for little sister and me t' patch ye up. We don't want t' have t' do it all over again." Lilith brought the young man a cup of hot tea.

"Thanks Lilith."

The young man and the big woman sat down next to Maya, who was trying to stay warm by the fire. Valerian sipped at his tea.

"How's Santiago this morning?" he asked, after a bit.

"Not much worsen' yesterday, mayhaps just a bit better. This mornin', he did find enough strength to prop up on an elbow and thank me fer nursin' him," Lilith poked at the fire.

"He's a right strong man, he is. I didn't think he'd last this long. He just don't seem t' want t' give up," her voice grew heavy. "It just hurts my heart that he's sufferin' so."

Valerian put his good arm across the woman's shoulder as she hung her head down in sadness. There wasn't much else that he could say or do…

* * *

The Ranger had been riding at a brisk pace most of the day, as he had for the past four days, since the Raiders had turned back. He hadn't bothered to cover his tracks, as he was confident that his pursuers had given up for good. And he was anxious now to catch up with his companions. It was mid-afternoon as he found himself riding through some rugged foothills covered with aspens, most of which had already begun to turn bright yellow.

When Sebastian reached the top of a high ridge, the sight on the other side took him completely by surprise. There it was, spread out in the valley below; just as Miss Izzy had described it, just as Lilith had recounted from the Raiders' tales. He had never beheld such wondrous sight.

Elympias!

For a long while, the old, hard-bitten warrior just sat on his mount, high up on the hill, and gazed in wonder. He had figured that the stories describing the haunted city had been embellished or exaggerated. He now realized that the tales had, in fact, completely failed to capture the majesty, the grandeur of the place, the shining white city with its soaring towers, the huge, graceful dome in the city center with broad tree lined avenues radiating out in all directions, the protective white wall that meandered for miles around the whole city. The city was situated on a broad, rolling plain nestled between two crystal blue lakes. All in all, it was fantastic, wondrous, achingly beautiful, and somehow…familiar.

Finally, he kicked his horse and headed down the hill. When he reached the meadow below, he took his horse to a trot, then to a gallop. He found himself almost boyishly eager to see what was on the other side of the wall, to rejoin his companions. He was exhilarated, riding across the grassy meadow. They'd made it!

Suddenly, two shadows, one just behind the other, passed over him from behind. There was no sound. He glanced up. Now he saw two large birds swooping low over his head, and then rapidly soaring high above. He peered up at the two shapes, now beginning to circle around him. They were already far away, but his vision was still keen enough to make them out clearly. He determined that they weren't eagles or buzzards; in fact, they didn't seem to be birds of any kind. He moved ahead again, but more warily, now. He un-strapped his lance and held it at the ready. Its heft restored his confidence.

The Ranger forged ahead with determination. Finally reaching the high wall, he rode along its length looking for a means of entry. Soon, he found what had to be the main gate. Rather than trying to find a way to open the gate or scale the wall, something deep within him, an instinct perhaps, compelled him to take a more direct approach. He backed away perhaps thirty paces from the wall and dismounted. His deep voice boomed out in the stillness of the bright, blue day.

"Hail citizens of Elympias! Here stands one of your sons! My name be Sebastian...a Ranger of the Clan Elympias...from across the Great Mountains. I ask your permission to enter your city..."

* * *

Sometimes fate can hang on something as simple as a few pieces of green firewood. One afternoon, Valerian had decided to follow the tracks of the bear that had attacked their camp to try to recover his lance. Maya and Lilith had been opposed to his leaving the campsite even briefly, but the young man had assured them that he would be most careful. He explained to them that the bear was doubtless either dead or long gone. If the beast had died nearby, Valerian just might be able to get his lance back.

After her man had left the campsite, Maya had gone into the tent to tend to Santiago, who now seemed just a bit stronger. Off and on, he would regain consciousness to eat a bit of broth, drink a swallow of water and speak a little, before passing out again. Maya also noticed that his fever had gone down, and he seemed to be resting more peacefully, as well.

Meanwhile, Lilith fed the campfire with firewood she had collected near the campsite, prior to cooking dinner.

Valerian followed the bear's tracks a ways downhill to a small gorge. He could see where it had stumbled and fallen many times along the course of the gorge. He smelled the remains of the beast before he saw it. Scavengers had gotten to it; there was little left and what there was wasn't much to look at. Black flies roiled all around the remains. He saw his lance under the carcass, but it was broken and useless. He was glad that at least the bear's remains were a fair distance from their campsite. The young woodsman turned to head back but stopped in his tracks. Over the tops of the trees he could see a distinct column of smoke where their campsite was situated. He headed back at a run.

By the time Valerian had made it back to the campsite, his ribs and shoulder were killing him. The fire was already out. Valerian tried his best to control his anger.

Lilith spoke first, "Before ye say anything, Valerian, it were my fault. I threw some fresh firewood on th' fire and then turned t' fetch some provisions. Maya let out a yell and threw water on th' fire t' put it out. It made smoke fer just a short while. I'm surely sorry, lad. I guess I didn't pay enough attention to what wood I was gatherin'."

"It's all right Lilith. Most likely no harm done," Valerian responded, when he finally caught his breath. In truth, he was far more worried that he let on. That column of smoke could have been seen for miles around, and if their pursuers were still on their trail...

"Anyhow, let's just get that fire goin' again. I'm gettin' hungry. If you don't mind though, I'll fetch the firewood."

* * *

Another restless night had passed. Like most nights, Lilith had slept fitfully in the tent with Santiago, so that she could readily tend to the man who, she feared, still hovered near death. Meanwhile, Valerian and Maya had taken turns keeping watch through the night. One would sit near the small fire, peering in the darkness, while the other lay huddled in blankets nearby. They didn't want to be surprised again...

Now it was Maya's watch, and the sun was just rising. Most mornings now were very cold. The young girl was worried that winter might soon close in on them. She rose and stretched, then pulled a blanket back over her shoulders. Then she added some wood to the small campfire and hung a kettle over it for tea. Soon she would fashion some breakfast for them... perhaps some dried meat, a few pieces of dried fruit and a maybe their last corncakes. She also fretted that their provisions were running low, as Valerian was still unable to hunt effectively for fresh game.

Maya fetched one of the packs that had been hung up in a nearby tree to keep out of the reach of scavengers. Rummaging through the pack, she found the provisions that she was looking for. As she arranged the food on three tin plates, she looked across the fire. Valerian lay curled up in his blanket next to the fire, sound asleep. Santiago's treasured katana lay at the young man's side.

"Right kindly t' fix breakfast for a passel of hungry strangers."

Maya jumped to her feet and Valerian was up just as quickly, with sword drawn. A moment later, Lilith emerged from the tent, still sleepy, with her long red hair disheveled. Their camp was surrounded by a large group of filthy, ragged, men...Raiders! They laughed as the slender girl dove for her bow and quickly nocked an arrow.

"What ye goin' to do with that there play-toy, lil' lady? Kill us all?"

The men laughed again. The three made a tight little circle in front of the tent. Lilith had grabbed a sword as well. In truth, they made a rather pitiful sight. The young man was all bandaged up, with one arm still in a sling, holding up a sword with his one good hand; the frightened young girl held her drawn bow, nervously pointing it this way and that; the big woman, half asleep and disoriented, awkwardly held her own sword.

The Raiders seemed to be having a good time. "Now, is that there Spaniard hidin' in his tent, 'er is he just a sound sleeper?"

"He's hurt bad, leave 'em alone," Lilith responded.

"Not as bad as he will be, directly. Pull him outta that tent, so's we can have a look at him."

"No, I don't think we'll do that," Valerian answered defiantly. He knew that they would all die very soon now. He intended to do so honorably, with courage.

"Maya, aim your arrow at the center of that man's chest. If anyone moves towards us, or if that man moves at all, release the arrow instantly," Valerian commanded.

"Do that, 'en you'll all be dead in a wink," Cutler responded in anger, although Valerian saw a bit of uncertainty in his eyes.

"We'll all be dead soon enough, anyway. But you'll be dead first, if you move a muscle," Valerian answered in return.

"Listen here, ye scrawny lil' cur. Ye and the wench drop yer weapons and hand over th' red-haired bitch 'n th' Spaniard, and we'll let ye be on yer way. Th' Deacon's quarrel is wi' them two, he don't know ye two from a sack o' taters," Cutler lied. He had no intention of letting anyone go, but he was getting nervous with that arrow pointing right at his chest. (It had just occurred to him that she probably the one that had tagged ol' Ned.)

Lilith lowered her sword. "I've seen ye before; ye be Cutler, Deacon's man, ain't ye? Give me yer word that ye'll let these two youngsters go, an you kin have me n' the Spaniard." She knew that Cutler's word was no good, but she also knew that it was Valerian and Maya's only chance, slim though it was...and all their lives were probably forfeit, in any case.

Valerian straightened up, pulled his arm out of the sling, and shouted, "Lilith, no! Maya, if Lilith takes a step forward, shoot that man Cutler."

He gripped the Katana now with both hands. "My name is Valerian of the Clan Elympias. Elympians do not abandon their own...ever! If we die, we die together, in battle, with honor and courage."

Nonetheless, the young man was torn. His voice choked as he turned to his young wife, "Maya, I'm sorry, but I fear here is no other way."

"As long as I'm at your side, it'll be all right, husband," she whispered. "I'm just sorry that you won't get to see your Elympias..."

Lilith stayed put and raised her sword again, "Mayhaps ye two are right; Lil' Sister, let's not let 'em take us alive…"

Cutler shot back, "Before this day is out, I swear we'll all be havin' ye 'n that lil' one in that tent yonder, and when we're done with ye, we'll slit both yer throats from ear t' ear. Deacon wants me t' bring back yer head t' him, ye' traitorous bitch, en I'll do that with pleasure."

'Rapin' me will be a neat trick with an arrow stickin' out yer chest," Lilith replied defiantly.

A few of the Raiders actually chuckled and Cutler gave them a murderous stare…but he didn't move. Cutler was furious, with himself, as much as anybody. He and his men could have just swooped in and killed everyone without warning. Instead, they had just waltzed up nice and slow, and now he'd let this little bitch get the drop on him.

"So it appears we have ourselves a lil' standoff, but how long do ye think that little wench there kin hold that bow drawn?"

It was true; Maya's hands were already shaking. In response, she relaxed the bowstring a bit, but kept it taught enough to pull and release in an instant. Meanwhile, Valerian was thinking furiously of some way for them to extricate themselves from this trap; he could think of nothing.

Finally, the young man just whispered to Maya, "I will love you forever."

Maya nodded slightly, and a single tear rolled down her cheek. She seemed to be afraid to speak or move. Time seemed to slow, and for a long moment, no one else moved or spoke either. Then out of the corner of his eyes, Valerian saw a few men on their left move forward, raise their own bows and position themselves for a clear shot at Maya. He was about to speak, but Cutler spoke first.

"Last chance, them what drops their weapons, we'll let ye die easy; the rest will die slow and painful. Boys, them's a couple of fine women we kin share amongst ourselves."

His men sounded off at that with enthusiasm and began crowding in all around.

"Me first!"

"I'll take the young 'un!"

"Me fer the big redhead…always wanted me a redhead!"

The young Elympian heard his uncle's voice, *Valerian, when you must defend yourself, always be the one to attack first, regardless of the odds. Do not hesitate, and provide no warning whatever. Once you attack, keep on attacking. Never let your foes recover…*

The katana flashed and the two bowmen were struck down before they could even release their arrows. Simultaneously, Maya sent her own squarely arrow into the center of Cutler's chest. He fell, instantly dead.

The dozen or so remaining Raiders haltingly pressed forward, with their lances and swords. However, they were held at bay by the young warrior who wielded the strange sword with a fury and skill such as these men had never before beheld. A few of the men who had moved in too close were bitten by the razor sharp blade, which moved so quickly that it could scarcely be seen. Leaderless now, the other Raiders held back momentarily, each unwilling to risk the next sword cut.

The two women stood just behind Valerian. Maya was desperately trying to nock another arrow; Lilith was waving her sword to and fro. It was almost over, Valerian knew.

"*Perdoname, señorita...*"

Valerian hazarded a quick glance back and was thunderstruck. The two women both gasped. Even the Raiders stared in shocked silence. The tall Spaniard had emerged from the tent. He walked stiff legged and one arm hung uselessly. His wounds were ghastly. Yet his eyes burned like red-hot coals and his mouth held a grim, tightlipped smile. He took the sword from Lilith, who kissed his damaged cheek.

"Valerian, you are a worthy heir to my '*guardian angels*'. *Vaya con dios!*"

Without another word, Santiago strode right into the thick of the Raiders, who struck at him from all sides. The first man came at him with a lance. The Spaniard parried the blow and put the man down with a sword point to the chest. Two other men came at him with swords and fell to their knees on either side of the Spaniard, both clutching their cut throats.

The battle instantly became a melee now, as the surviving Raiders finally did rush in from all sides. Valerian tried desperately to protect the women, but there were just too many of them, coming from all directions. He saw Santiago go down first, slashing with his sword even as he fell. Then Lilith went down as a Raider drove a lance into her side. As Valerian cut the man down, Maya was felled behind him with a blow that he didn't even see coming. Covered in blood now, the young man stepped back and stood over his young wife's motionless body. He invited the remaining Raiders to try to take them.

He counted only six Raiders now, and most of them were wounded. But they too looked determined as they crowded in all around him.

Valerian knew that he might take a few more, but certainly not all of them. Now it was truly over.

Goodbye my beloved...the thought reverberated in his mind, accompanied with a high-pitched whine, as the young Elympian stood over his fallen mate. *What was that whine?*

A shadow passed over all of them, and the Raiders in front of him looked up, slack jawed. He was tempted to look up, as well, but was afraid to take his eyes off of his attackers, if even for an instant. Out of the corner of his eye he saw something, something big, slam down hard on the meadow to his right. This time Valerian did hazard a glance, as the Raiders looked at the big object and at one another, in disbelief and confusion.

It was a huge, smooth, black and gold object, the size of a small cottage, with wings and a tail. (Valerian suddenly recalled the images from the picture book in the ghost town.) Even as it landed, a big ramp in its side slammed down. A huge figure in a black cloak virtually exploded from the opening, followed, by another figure only slightly smaller than the first.

The Raiders hesitated for an instant, and then moved to meet the new threat. The hooded figure in black moved with astonishing swiftness. A Raider tried to attack the stranger with a lance. The iron tipped weapon hit the creature's chest; metal struck metal and the lance simply glanced off. Without hesitation, the giant grabbed the terrified man by the throat and flung him into two of his fellows like a rag doll.

The second figure from the craft flew past the first and launched himself into the few Raiders left standing. He finished them off with knife and ax. What remained was more a massacre than a battle. In moments, all the Raiders were dead.

"Uncle!" Valerian's voice cracked as he embraced the big man. "Who? How?"

Sebastian hugged his nephew in return. "Later Nephew; right now we have to look after our own!"

The Ranger knelt to look at Lilith's wounds, even as Valerian bent over Maya. The young girl had a huge, swollen whelp on her forehead and was stunned, but seemed otherwise unharmed. She stirred when Valerian patted her gently on her cheek to revive her. Her eyes flickered open and she actually smiled at him. He held her close and wept.

It was worse with Lilith. The lance had bitten deeply into her side. She had already drifted into shock and was bleeding profusely. Sebastian applied pressured to the wound and called out to his new friend, "Avatar, I need your help, if you please!"

The hooded figure was just then holding a strange object over Santiago's chest. He quickly moved to Sebastian's side and held the same object over Lilith's wound.

Lilith, in shock, looked up when she heard Sebastian's voice, "Knew ye'd come back fer us..." She pulled him down to kiss her before passing out again.

"This woman is suffering serious internal bleeding. I need to get her to Olympus as soon as possible to repair the damage. I'm afraid that I will be unable to help your other companion, however. I regret to inform you that he has expired..."

"Well, friend, he died well. Let's do what we can for the living," the big Ranger responded.

The figure in black moved to lift the unconscious woman.

"I'll just take her, if you please," the Ranger gently picked the unconscious woman and headed swiftly for the craft.

Valerian quickly followed with Maya...

* * *

The two men sat in a clean white room surrounded by glass, which the Avatar had called a "waiting room". Valerian had a thousand questions for his uncle, but just now neither man was in the mood to speak. Nothing mattered to them at this moment but the fate of their women. On arrival, the Avatar had laid both women side-by-side on a rolling cart and wheeled them swiftly through some double doors into a place he referred to as an "O.R". They had tried to follow, but the giant had directed them to the "waiting room".

Valerian had resisted, wanting to follow, but his uncle had restrained him. "Do what the Avatar says, Nephew...for the women's sake. He knows what he's doin' and I've come to trust him completely."

"Are there others like the Avatar, Uncle?"

"As far as I can tell, lad, he is the only one left. He tells me that he is the guardian and caretaker of this city, but up to now, he has refused to tell me more."

Valerian's uncle had taken him to a small adjoining room with the figure of a man drawn on the door. "We can clean you up a might in here, lad."

Inside, the Ranger showed the younger man the wonders of clean running water that flowed out of a silver spigot, seemingly of its own volition, of warm air that blew out of one little box and of towels made of paper that shot out of another.

Valerian had been covered in blood. His uncle had helped the young man clean up enough to see where his own wounds were. There were several, but thankfully, they were all superficial.

"I'm right proud of you lad. I've never seen a man, young or old, fight with more skill or daring. When we first saw you, you were already surrounded by the Raiders and we were still far away, even for the flying machine. I thought sure you'd all be dead by the time we got there. Never been so frustrated in all my years, watchin' you fight for yo'r lives and nothin' I could do about it."

"How could you see us from so far away Uncle?"

"Lad, that is just one of the countless wonders that you will learn of, in time. But right now, let's just go back to that waitin' room and so's we can wait to see iffin our womenfolk are going to be all right."

They waited in silence for what seemed an eternity...

* * *

"Greetings."

The image of the gray-haired and bearded man had finally appeared in the middle of the waiting room, without warning. Surprised and a bit startled, the two men had jumped up.

"Please, do not be frightened. My name is Aristotle. Please sit back down."

"Can you tell us how the women are?" Valerian asked.

"Yes, that is why I have appeared. I am pleased to inform you that both women will make a full recovery. The younger of your two lady friends suffered a mild concussion...that is, a minor head injury. We will keep her sedated...asleep for awhile, and watch her closely to make sure that there are no complications."

"The other woman was wounded much more seriously. However, the Avatar has successfully repaired her injuries."

"Maya be the name of the young lass, and Lilith be the name of the fair, red-haired lady."

"Yes, well then, I can tell you that Maya should be fine in just a few days, and Lilith should be good as new in two or three weeks."

"This here be my nephew, Valerian..."

"And you are Sebastian, a Captain of the Elympian Rangers, from across the Great Mountains. Through the Avatar, I have heard all about you."

"And you have told us that your name is Ari...Aristotle, but who are you?" Valerian asked.

"That, I fear, is a rather complicated question. Please be patient with us and all your questions will be answered in time..."

"When can we see our women?" the young man asked.

"As soon as the Avatar has properly taken care of them, he will come out to treat your wounds, Valerian. Then he will escort both of you to the room where your ladies will be cared for."

"Sir, begging your pardon, I'd just as soon see Maya before the Avatar looks after me."

Aristotle smiled warmly. "As you wish, young man."

The image disappeared in a blink...

34

The Insurrection
April 13th, 2101

The regular Monday morning executive meeting of the Cincinnati office of Homeland Defense was just beginning. It was precisely 9am. Some of the executives actually lived in Cincinnati, although most resided in Washington. It didn't really matter where they were physically located, since the meeting was held in VR. The virtual conference room was ornate, looking out over the imaginary skyline of Cincinnati. The seven avatars representing the executives sat around a futuristic glass and steel conference table. The Regional Director brought the meeting to order.

None of the bureaucrats had the faintest inkling of the "fly on the wall". That's because the eighth avatar was a "phantom", which could be neither seen nor heard by the others. A phantom avatar was highly illegal; moreover, its presence under these circumstances would be considered an act of treason.

To be here had required passing through multiple layers of sophisticated security arrays undetected. Bowie (AKA Geordie) was pretty proud of himself. In the last month or so, he had brought his considerable AI skills to bear. He was now considered one of the more valuable members of their little rebel cell. Awkward functioning in the physical world, Bowie was rapidly becoming a highly skilled agent in VR. He had soon realized that the talents that he had largely wasted gaming could now be directed towards a higher purpose.

Little by little over the last few weeks, he had improved and perfected his skills as a "ghost in the machine". He had started by penetrating the meetings of low level bureaucrats and functionaries, who had employed minimal security. Today was his first attempt at hitting the big time. Gathering intelligence from Homeland Defense might eventually save all of their lives. On the other hand, getting caught could quickly finish them all.

"Pretty boring meeting, isn't it? You're going to have to go a lot higher up the food chain to learn anything particularly useful."

The real Bowie/Geordie jumped, and his "invisible" avatar jumped with him. One of the avatars seated at the conference table was speaking right to him, ignoring the Director as the man droned on with a report regarding the logistics of the detention camps that had been established outside of Cincinnati.

"Don't worry, these fools can't see or hear either one of us. Anyway, I'm on your side." The avatar stood up and walked over to Bowie's avatar.

"Who are you?"

"A friend...you can call me Uncle."

The man looked and was dressed like a typical middle-aged government functionary.

"Here now, follow me. I want to lead you to an ultra-secure VR meeting facility that I have established, where we can talk more freely."

The older man took Bowie's avatar by the hand, and everything went black for a moment. Bowie almost panicked, but then the lights came back on and he found himself sitting in a comfortable looking overstuffed chair in an oak-lined study, with a lit fireplace in front of him. A gray-haired, elderly man sat across from him. It could have been a university professor.

"How...how do I know I can trust you?" was the first thing that Bowie could think to say, when he had recovered his wits.

"Well, you don't have any reason to at the moment, Geordie, I mean Bowie, other than for the fact that I already know all about you and your little band of freedom fighters. I believe your safe house is located in Georgetown, in the basement of 113 N. Williams Ave., if I'm not mistaken. How are your sister and her friends?"

"How do you know all that?" Bowie asked, feeling a cold dread rising up his spine.

"I'm afraid I can't share all of that with you just yet. Suffice it to say that if I were affiliated with the bad guys, you would all have been delivered to a Baltimore detention center by now...that's assuming that the decision hadn't been made to have you all 'expeditiously processed'; that's the euphemism for murder currently in vogue over at Homeland."

"So just what is your game?"

"Bowie, there are pockets of resistance scattered all over the country. However, that's precisely the problem...they are all very small and they are all very scattered. With the resources at my disposal, I can identify them. I can screen out the government agents attempting to infiltrate them. Then I can begin to work with them to create a network...a larger, decentralized organization that can begin to have a real impact as a major resistance movement."

"Now then, I don't like repeating myself any more than necessary. Here, take this," he handed the younger man's avatar a virtual code key.

"Tell your friends that I would like for them to all join me here tonight at 8pm. At that time, I will give you all a more detailed explanation of what I am proposing."

"What if they refuse to meet with you?"

"That would be very foolish of them, don't you think? After all, what real choice do they have? If I'm with the government, you're all doomed by now, anyway. You could try to run, but how far could any of you possibly get? On the other hand, if I am who I say I am, you would all be passing up the opportunity to increase your effectiveness a thousand fold. No guts... no glory, young man."

The elderly gentleman rose and Bowie followed suit. The two avatars shook hands. The black void once again enveloped the young man and he found that he had been returned to his basement lair.

*** * * ***

Jonathan removed his VR visor and gloves. Bowie represented a member of the twelfth resistance group that he had contacted in the few months. Graham's one and only accomplice so far was Aristotle, although the AI program made for a formidable accomplice indeed. Graham was fairly certain, and fervently hoped, that the feds had nothing comparable.

Utilizing the resources of its Sherlock subprogram, Aristotle had proved to be incredibly effective in tracking down the dissidents, as well as identifying the government forces attempting to catch them. Aristotle, at Graham's direction, had also constructed an amazingly effective shield to conceal all of Graham's covert operations. He believed that the possibility of discovery by the feds was slight.

Although, Graham, with Aristotle's assistance, had successfully tracked down and contacted a number of groups, he was, overall, rather impressed with their expertise and initiative. Natural selection had already been a major factor in this regard; most of the rebels, who had been either too reckless or lacking in sufficient expertise, had already been caught.

Amongst others, he had contacted a retired Air Force colonel leading a well organized group in Oregon, and a college student majoring in economics, who had organized a group of fellow students at Caltech. Then there was the businessman in Iowa, whose wife had been taken away in the night. Now he led a dissident band of relatives and neighbors. There were farmers, scientists, kids, old men. There were idealists and radicals, people wanting justice and others just wanting payback. Graham intended to help them all, nurture them, protect them, most of all organize them and give them a common purpose.

Graham's present activities made him nostalgic for the good old days, when he had been a corporate raider *par excellence*. In his salad days, he had plotted mergers, acquisitions and hostile takeovers like no one who had come before. At the height of his powers, the news media had dubbed him the "Genghis Khan" of the boardroom; he had been quite proud of the appellation and had done his best to live up to it.

However, never far from his thoughts was the likely futility of it all. If the economic and social collapse came soon, what difference would all of this make? He consoled himself with the belief that the more that they could weaken this new tyrannical dictatorship before the collapse, the less oppressive its remnants might be thereafter.

*　*　*

Michael and Olivia lay under the branches of the huge old oak. The tree was on the side of a mountain that gave them an unobstructed view of Olympus and the whole valley that surrounded it. The hike up had taken nearly two hours; it was a hike that they had made many times before. Over the years, this spot had become their very own little "secret place".

They lay on a small blanket that they had carried up with them in a backpack that also held a bottle of wine, along with some bread and cheese. The setting was idyllic, particularly on this day. Wildflowers were in bloom all around and butterflies fluttered this way and that. The blue sky was filled with puffy white clouds. Olivia sat up and took in their surroundings wrapping her arms around her knees.

Finally she spoke, "It's so peaceful up here. Up here, it's almost impossible to imagine the turmoil that surrounds us. People being herded into detention camps, summary executions, rebellion, the suppression of the media. And here we sit on the side of a hill watching butterflies, without a care in the world."

Michael propped himself up on his elbow. "I remember once, when I was about eight years old, a hurricane hit the Texas coast, a big one... Cynthia, I believe it was. It hit us directly, head-on; it was terrifying. But after an hour or so, the hurricane's eye passed over us. The winds suddenly died down; the rain stopped. I went outside with my parents. Most of our neighbors were out too. It was incredibly peaceful for just a little while, even with the destruction that lay all around. The sky was clear and blue directly above, even though we were surrounded on all sides by storm clouds that looked impossibly alien."

"The oddest thing about it all was that for the short period of time that we were in the eye of the storm, we all seemed to be able to just relax and enjoy ourselves. Children laughed and splashed about in the flooded streets; parents chatted on their front lawns. Then, the winds kicked up again, the rain started, and everyone went back inside. The back side of the storm seemed even worse than the front side, after that."

"So, now we're in the eye of a really big storm, maybe the biggest storm in history. And we might as well just relax and enjoy ourselves while we can, right Michael?"

"Exactly...because, really, what else can we do? The storm's coming; we've long since accepted the fact that there's nothing we can do to stop it. We've made whatever preparations we could. So let's just take advantage of whatever time we have left."

Olivia smiled at Michael, "And, sir, just how do you think we might best take advantage of this temporary respite?"

Michael didn't answer; he just pulled her in close. They both lay back down, entwined in each other's arms...

* * *

"Gentlemen, it my pleasure to inform you that Project Lucifer stands ready for full deployment!"

The small, nervous man's avatar stood at the head of the virtual conference table. Schmidt's and Sergeivich's avatars sat on either side of the table.

Schmidt stood up and shook Koderescu's imaginary hand. "Congratulations doctor! We knew you could do it."

"Yes, yes, doctor. Good work," Sergeivich now spoke, "Do you feel that you have achieved one hundred percent confidence that Lucifer will succeed in its mission while remaining successfully contained?"

'I am absolutely confident that Lucifer will succeed in its purpose."

"And are you equally certain that it will be contained?" the big Russian pressed.

"Of that we are only ninety percent certain. If we could just have six more months of testing..."

"I'm afraid that a delay of six months is impossible. Sergei, do you agree that ninety percent is an acceptable risk, under the circumstances?"

"I do, Gerhardt; I do, indeed"

"Well, then, doctor...make your final preparations. I want Lucifer deployed and activated within the next thirty days."

"It will be done, gentlemen."

"Excellent, doctor, you are excused."

Koderescu's avatar vanished.

"Well, Sergei, how does it feel to know that we are about to change history?"

"I'm most excited by the prospect, my friend. But we have much to do in the next thirty days to properly prepare for the big event."

"We do indeed. Let's begin by announcing the timetable to our allies around the world."

* * *

Powell sat at his desk in the oval office. Arrayed around him were his Chief of Staff, the Secretary of Homeland Defense, the Director of the FBI, and the new Secretary of Media Affairs. All were Brethren. Powell was concerned by the reports that had been funneling up to him that someone was out there attempting to organize a coordinated resistance.

So far, Powell's success in creating a Christian theocracy had exceeded his wildest expectations. Detaining dissidents had helped tremendously in muting any large scale opposition, and the simple threat of detainment had helped even more. Large temporary detainment centers had now been established near every major city; permanent centers were now under construction. Almost complete control over all domestic cyber-media had been achieved; whatever international news sites couldn't be controlled, were closely monitored. Anyone who visited those sites risked detainment.

The other branches of government had been effectively brought to heel, as had the many government agencies and the military. With his nuclear deterrent fully at the ready, Powell was unconcerned with any foreign threat. Most of the leaders of the major powers made no secret that they thought Powell was crazy; that worked to his benefit. You don't mess with a madman who has nuclear weapons. Let the nations of Europe and Asia wail about the end of American democracy all they wanted; they were irrelevant.

Powell's one remaining major concern had been the proliferation of small resistance groups. Many had been shut down, but others kept sprouting up. Powell wanted them *all* crushed. Now there was this new threat. Who could be behind it? The Secretary of Homeland Defense called it a potential domestic al Qaeda, a loose organization of disparate resistance groups similar to the defunct Middle Eastern group that had created so much havoc a hundred years ago.

The Secretary of Homeland Defense spoke up, "Mr. President, we can't say for certain that this new underground organization even exists. So far, we have been unable to uncover any direct evidence, whatsoever. We have at this point only some circumstantial evidence that a handful of dissident groups are beginning to coordinate their activities."

"Don't wait for proof! Find them, destroy them. Take whatever means necessary. If we even suspect that anyone is involved in this new organization, I want them eliminated! If some innocents are caught up in this, it's God's will. We take these actions on behalf of the Chosen!"

"Perhaps indeed it is the Antichrist himself that is behind all of this. Now, get out there and get this done! But first, let us bow our heads for a moment of prayer."

The men bowed their heads, clasped their hands in their laps and closed their eyes...

* * *

"Jonathan, *compadre*, it's nice to finally see you again. It's been some time since we last got together. I suppose that your new little hobby is keeping you rather preoccupied."

Both men sat in Graham's study, settled into their two, now well-worn, overstuffed leather chairs.

"Sorry, Louie, I hope you won't take offense, but I don't even want to discuss the subject."

Nonetheless, the professor noticed a twinkle in his friend's eyes when the subject came up. That told him all he needed to know.

"None taken, Jonathan."

"And professor, how have you been spending your time of late?"

"Watching and waiting, Jonathan, like everyone else I suppose... and thinking. For years, we've referred to the coming collapse as the 'Apocalypse'. Throughout history, religious groups have erroneously predicted and anticipated the biblical 'Apocalypse'. I wonder; could this really be it?"

"Professor, even though I'm trying to keep an open mind on God and religion, you know that I'm a long way from taking the Bible literally."

"Yes, my friend. And even though I have a profound belief in God, Christ and the Church, I have always been most circumspect about taking every passage of the Bible literally. Nonetheless, lately my thoughts have been drawn to the concept of an Antichrist."

"Well Louie, it's no wonder. Powell is obsessed with the subject. He refers to the Antichrist in virtually every public address."

"Indeed, Powell has justified his most extreme actions as necessary to counter the threat of the coming Antichrist and his minions."

"Yes?"

The professor leaned back in his big chair. "Jonathan, you love irony... how about this for irony? Powell clearly desires to be the man who saves the world from the Antichrist. If he did so, that of course would make him our modern day Savior, would it not? But what if he *is* the Antichrist himself?"

"Louie, I'm not sure that I would call that ironic. After all, correct me if I'm wrong, but isn't the Antichrist supposed to be the 'great deceiver'? It follows that he would likely pretend to be the Savior."

"Ah, but what if Powell doesn't know? What if he truly aspires to be our Savior? And what if such monumental *hubris* is what ultimately compels him to *become* the Antichrist? I would call that irony on an epic scale. Do you not agree?"

Now Graham sat back in his chair, "Oh absolutely, my friend...that would be irony on a historic scale."

What occurred to Graham but was left unspoken was...*and if I somehow defeated Powell, would that make me the Savior? Now that would be irony on a cosmic scale!*

* * *

"Mac, I'm pregnant," Ellen had asked the big man to sit next to him on their sofa.

She had taken his hands in hers and looked into his eyes for a long moment. Then she had just blurted it out. She now searched his face for clues as to how he felt. It was pretty obvious. First the look of surprise mixed with a bit of bewilderment, then the little smile that broadened into a wide grin. He embraced her in a big bear hug that almost left her unable to breath.

"Careful big fella, you don't want to crush 'the package'".

"But how? When?"

She laughed, "How? Well, I reckon it was the old-fashioned way. When? Well, there are quite a few possibilities there, but my best bet is New Year's Eve. Remember, champagne, fireworks...then right here on the sofa?"

Yep, he remembered...how could he forget?

"But aren't you a little...?"

She laughed again, "Old? Not that old; I'm seventeen years younger than you, you old codger; that's what happens when you rob the cradle. And nowadays people are living a lot longer, and that means the menopause happens a lot later with some women."

But then her look became somber. "You know how much I wanted this. Yet coming now, with the world about to turn upside down...is it right? Is it ethical to bring a child into this world, just now?"

Mac stood up straight and pulled Ellen up with him. He put his big arms around her and whispered in her ear, "We'll make it right, Ellen. I swear it. We'll protect this child against any and all harm. Then we'll raise him or her to be a Pathfinder, someone who can survive and prosper, no matter what happens to the rest of the world."

She held him to her fiercely. "I swear it too...I love you Mac."

"I love you too...more than you can possibly imagine."

35

Snow Falls on Elympias
September 13th, 2523

Valerian stood on the balcony of his new dwelling; he believed that the Avatar had called it a condo. Thirty stories up, he beheld in the moonlight an awesome bird's eye view of Elympias...Olympus. He watched the big snowflakes fall over the city...winter's first. To the young man's eyes, the blanket of snow made the city look even more beautiful, more mystical, than it already was. *It's fortunate that we got here before the snows finally did come*, the young man thought to himself.

The young man was dressed in a dark blue jumpsuit, a jumpsuit that was doubtless incredibly old, yet looked brand-new. It was made of some thin, exotic material that kept him warm even in the bitingly cold night air. Valerian had also cut his hair short, in the manner of his ancient ancestors; he found that he liked it that way. He wore soft white shoes that the Avatar called "sneakers".

The strangest part of all of this is how all of this no longer seems so very strange, he thought to himself. Lights at night from devices that are cool to the touch, machines that speak and comprehend, food and drink that just appears from a hole in the wall, objects made up of nothing more substantial than light. In just one short month, the newcomers had struggled to comprehend everything from flush toilets to virtual reality. Perhaps because of their youth, Valerian and Maya had seemed to have a much easier time adjusting than Lilith or Sebastian.

Indeed, Sebastian these days seemed to his nephew rather like a caged mountain lion, appearing equal parts trapped and disoriented. Lilith was almost as bad; she seemed to be walking around in a constant state of bewilderment. The two had finally asked for and received a tent and sleeping bags. Even now, with the cold and the snow, the two were camped out in the city's big central park, doubtless with a big campfire going. Valerian could imagine the two huddled together under a blanket in front of the fire...with their faithful mule Samantha tethered nearby.

* * *

On the second day of their arrival at Olympus, satisfying himself that the two women would be all right, Sebastian had asked the Avatar to fly him back out to their camp to fetch Samantha and Santiago's body. Valerian had chosen to stay with Maya. The Ranger had blindfolded the mule and led her into the cargo hold of the flying machine, much as Maya had done to coax the animal onto Marley's boat.

Then the Ranger had fetched Santiago's body, the Spaniard's treasured swords and a few other possessions, such as Valerian's journal. Before leaving the site, he and the Avatar had released the few horses that remained tethered and piled the Raiders' bodies together with all of the rest of the gear. All had been burned in a large funeral pyre.

In time, they would all gather at the Cathedral of Olympus to hold memorial service for Santiago. The Avatar would then arrange to have the urn containing their fallen friend's ashes interred in a place of honor in the Olympus Mausoleum.

* * *

Several days after they had arrived, when Maya had recovered sufficiently from her concussion, the Avatar had offered to take the young couple on a tour of the city. Sebastian had also been invited, but had deferred, preferring to stay by Lilith's side in the Medical Center.

Valerian and Maya had chosen a cool and crisp autumn day for their excursion. They decided to take the tour on foot and Maya, with the Avatar's help, had packed a knapsack with provisions for a picnic. The three started early in the morning.

Following the Avatar at a brisk pace, the couple first strolled down one of the broad, clean avenues, admiring the miles of neatly trimmed fruit trees, all of which had now lost their leaves. Their guide explained how machines periodically cleaned the streets and cared for the trees.

"Once upon a time, the fruit from these trees contributed to the sustenance of the city. Now machines simply gather and transport the fruit out into the surrounding forests. Thousands of fruit trees now grow wild in the forest, as a result."

"I have wondered how the city has been kept so well maintained, even though it has been abandoned for so long," Valerian commented, "but we've only seen a few of the machines."

"Yes, most are programmed to come out in the early morning hours, and complete their tasks well before dawn."

"Are the machines the source of the legends that we have heard that Olympus is haunted?" Maya asked. "I've seen a few of those machines and they certainly frighten me. They seem like big metal insects..."

"You needn't be frightened, Maya. The machines are carefully designed to avoid humans while they work; in fact, any one of these machines would self-destruct rather than harm a human in any way."

"However, the legends of Olympus being haunted are, in actual fact, by design. Over the years, Aristotle has developed a rather effective, non-violent defense mechanism to protect our city. You have seen how Aristotle can project an image of himself wherever he pleases...he uses the same means to project ghostly images and sounds to frighten away any unwanted intruders that have been detected nearby."

As the three had turned a corner, they looked ahead at a huge, monumental domed structure. Both Valerian and Maya had gasped in awe.

"That is the Alexandria Library, the heart and soul of our city. It holds nothing less than the accumulated wisdom and knowledge of the ages."

It had seemed to the young couple that, as they approached the building, they were walking in slow motion, for the sheer scale of the building had completely defeated their sense of perspective. As they had finally neared the gigantic entrance, huge polished metal doors had rumbled open for them.

As the young couple entered the vast open area of the Library, they looked up in wonder. Up the walls up all around them, they could see countless levels of what appeared to be balconies with shiny brass railings. Far, far above them, the walls gradually curved into a grand dome. Sunlight shone through skylights from far above, illuminating the vast marble floor that they now crossed. Scattered all about the Library's ground floor were monumental sculptures, fountains, trees in huge planters, park benches and low stone walls that broke up the vast open space.

"Follow me."

The Avatar motioned them toward a set of small glass doors on the distant side. It took a long walk to reach it and Valerian hung back, wanting to admire every sculpture they passed, but the Avatar hurried on ahead and the young couple was forced to catch up.

Finally, they reached the far side. The glass doors seemed to open of their own volition. The couple followed the Avatar into a small chamber of glass and polished metal and its doors closed behind them.

"Please turn around and grasp the handrails on either side."

Just as they turned, the little chamber rocketed upwards. Maya let out a little yelp in surprise and Valerian felt his stomach lurch. Then, as they rose above the floor below, they had embraced each other in wonder. It was beautiful! Wondrous! Finally, they had stopped midway up. The Avatar now led them through doors at the back of the chamber into a new vast area that he called "the Archives".

For the rest of the morning, the Avatar had shown them the wonders of the Library Archives: They had admired Ancient works of art. They had listened to Ancient music. They had experienced virtual reality simulations of space fight and scenes from around the Ancient world. The Avatar had introduced to them a host of technological wonders.

Soon enough, the young couple had reached an emotional and intellectual saturation point; their minds were overloaded by the intensity and variety of all that they had seen and experienced. At last, the Avatar sensing their anxiety, had invited them out to have their picnic in the city's large central park.

Valerian and Maya, relieved to be back in an environment they could relate to, had laid out their blanket near a fountain in a grassy meadow now turned an autumnal brown, amongst trees that had only recently lost their foliage. Nonetheless, to them, the park was lovely and tranquil...just the respite that they had needed.

"Come join us, Avatar. There is plenty of food and wine for the three of us," Maya had offered as she had beckoned tall hooded figure to sit beside them.

"Thank you, Maya, but I must decline. I require neither drink nor sustenance at this time. Please enjoy yourselves, however."

"Excuse me, Avatar, but why do you never let us see your face? Why do you never seem to need rest, or food, or drink?" Maya had pressed.

"I regret that I cannot answer questions of that nature at this time. However, I assure you that all of your questions will be answered in due course."

The rest of the afternoon, they had toured living quarters, eating establishments, recreational areas, all of which had stood quiet, abandoned... forlorn. Ironically, the only buildings that still seemed vital and alive were the ones where the myriad machines that maintained the city were housed and repaired...by yet other machines. Returning to their quarters late in the day, Valerian had thanked the Avatar for the tour and his hospitality, but had allowed that he was still filled with curiosity.

"Avatar, can you tell us how long has this city been abandoned, and what caused its citizens to leave?"

"Valerian, I can tell you that this city is over four hundred years old. Regretfully, I must tell you no more at this time. In this regard, I ask for your forbearance. I promise you that all of the secrets of Olympus will be revealed to you when we deem that you are ready to understand and accept them."

Just before sunset that day, after they had bid farewell to the Avatar, Valerian had found himself rather perplexed by his own feelings. He still felt awe and wonder, certainly, but he now realized that a profound feeling of loss had come to overwhelm all other emotions...

What had happened to these incredible people, who had accomplished so much, yet lost it all in the end? Where had his forbears gone? What calamity must have overtaken them? Standing next to Valerian, looking out from their balcony over the city, Maya had understood her young man's feelings without a word being spoken. So she had simply held him and comforted him...

* * *

But now they had been in Olympus for a month. And now the city was covered in a beautiful, thick blanket of snow. And in that month, this beautiful city had truly become their home. Mystical city, wonderful city... sad, abandoned city...but it was nonetheless *their* city now...

And now, the glass door from their bedroom opened and Maya joined her husband on the balcony. She wore a wine red dressing gown that fell all the way to her ankles. Its hood was pulled up over her head and its full sleeves fell past her fingertips. He could see from a few errant strands of wet hair that she had taken yet another shower. If there was one amenity that the young girl loved in Olympus, it had to be the sonic shower; it seemed to the young man that she took about three hot showers a day.

Valerian put an arm across Maya's shoulders and she responded by snuggling up against him. He could feel the warmth of her body even through the velvety material of her gown. She smelled like flowers. They stood together, looking out in silence over the city for a long while. What dim moonlight had penetrated the low hanging snow clouds was reflected by the city's white blanket. Other than that ghostly glow, just a few artificial lights stood out in the darkness across the city. The brightest was at the top of the dome of the Alexandria Library, which seemed to loom just a short distance away, although they knew that it was actually across town.

"It's incredibly beautiful, isn't it, Valerian? I never thought that I could be so happy. It's like we're living in a waking dream. You know, sometimes you have a dream and nothing makes any sense, yet, in the dream, that fact doesn't bother you? That's how it feels for me here at Elympias."

"Yes, Maya, that's exactly how it is...just like a dream. But the dream would mean nothing if I didn't have you to share it with. I went on a quest to find Elympias, but real treasure that I discovered was you."

She shivered against him, then moved away and pulled at his elbow. "Well then, husband, let's go inside where it's nice and warm. Perhaps I might help you find some new way to appreciate your hard-earned treasure."

* * *

Sebastian threw a few more pieces of firewood on the big campfire, and then crawled back into the big two-person sleeping bag with Lilith. They snuggled together. They were quite warm and cozy inside the sleeping bag, in spite of the bitter cold outside.

The snow was still coming down steadily. The ground all around was covered in a thick white blanket, and the limbs of the trees sagged under the weight of the snow that had accumulated on them. In the moonlight, they could just make out the silhouettes of the highest buildings over the tops of the trees. In the midst of big park, it was the only thing that served to remind them that they were in the city at all.

Sleepily, the big Ranger thought to himself that it would be all right if this night went on forever. Lilith was of much the same mind.

Discovering the city of his forebears had been thrilling, fascinating, rewarding. But he had felt out of place from the first day. Practically all of the Ranger's adult life had been spent in the deep forest of his homeland. Even as a young man, he had lived with his bride, Marian, in a small cottage in the forest just outside of town.

"Are you comfortable out here Lilith? Are we crazy to be out here in the snow, when we could be warm and dry in one of those big buildings? I'm sure Valerian and Maya must think we be out of our minds...not to mention Aristotle or the Avatar."

"I'm just fine, don't ye worry about that, Sebastian; there's nowhere else I'd rather be. Yep, I'm pretty sure that they all think we're out of our heads to be out here, but I don't care about that any more'n you do, I suspect."

"This city is a fine place, to be sure...a beautiful place. But the forest is my home. Out there, I can understand the ways of the forest, along with the men and creatures that dwell in it. I know how to find food, how to protect myself, how to find my way about. Here, I just turn a corner and I'm lost. I'd starve if some machine didn't help me fetch food. And all these machines! I can't fathom any of them."

"I know big fella', I'm no better. Them machines frighten me...they're unnatural, they are...scurrying about everywhere, cleaning the streets, fixin' things, even trimmin' the trees."

"You know, sometimes I even think the Avatar is a machine made to look like a man. Why else wouldn't he let us see his face? Sometimes he scares me the most, even though he treats us kindly enough."

The idea surprised Sebastian. "A machine? No, I don't think so, Lilith. I always wondered if he was perhaps disfigured in some way. Seems to me that Avatar talks and moves too much like a man to be a machine... although, now that I think about it, I've never seen a normal man so agile or so strong..."

Lilith changed the subject. "Anyhow, the young 'uns don't seem to be having such a hard time gettin' used to all this...magic, as we do. I guess we're just too old and set in our ways."

"Yep, I'm happy for Valerian and Maya; they seem to love it here. But I'll tell you, Lilith, you sure don't look too old to me." The big man's arm tightened across her shoulders, drawing her in close.

"Well, I reckon I'm surely not too old to serve some purposes." Lilith turned her head and raised her chin to kiss him. Soon, he pulled her down. The snow continued to fall, though the two were hardly aware of it...

* * *

"And what do you make of our guests so far, Aristotle?" the old man asked.

He sat in a big overstuffed chair next to a fireplace in a study atop the Library of Alexandria. The old man looked much as he had for a very long time. The only difference was subtle...a look in the eyes that could have been construed as great wisdom tinged, perhaps, with a bit of madness.

An image of Aristotle sat in a real chair on the other side of the fireplace. "I must say that I am fascinated. As you and I were already well aware, the Elympians and their contemporaries are on a par with Europeans from perhaps a thousand years ago...technologically. Yet, socially, in many ways the Elympians appear to be more advanced than the original citizens of Olympus. Do you not agree?"

"I do, indeed, Aristotle. From the recordings I've watched of your conversations with the two Elympians, I would say that they are quite unsophisticated in many respects, and yet amazingly enlightened in others."

"Yes, I have now had many long conversations with our two Elympian guests, particularly with the youth, Valerian. He has described for me in detail the Elympian culture, its history, (most of which is oral tradition), its social structure and its government. Clearly, the Pathfinder experiment provided the original foundation for their culture."

The old man responded, "It's actually rather incredible; during the darkest plague years almost every other vestige of civilization was lost. Yet somehow, the few Olympians who survived that terrible period managed to safeguard and pass along the values instilled in their Pathfinder forbears."

"From my conversations with Valerian, I would say that the Olympians not only retained but considerably refined the Pathfinder ideals. Ironic, is it not, that their society has advanced so little technically and so much culturally? That's in contrast to a similar period before the Fall, where mankind made stunning advances technologically, yet seemed in many ways to actually regress socially."

"Yes Aristotle, and you do know how much I love irony. I was particularly interested in the fact that the Elympians seem to have no system of currency, whatever."

"Indeed. They are familiar enough with the concept. After all, they regularly trade with the Caravans, who have a form of trade script. However, the Elympians prefer a barter system. Materialism appears to have no place in their culture; the tendency is in fact deeply scorned. In their society, an individual simply takes what he or she needs. A citizen's status is based on their contribution to society and by how well they adhere to the Elympian ideals, rather than on what they possess."

"In the era before the Fall, such ideals would have seemed ridiculously idealistic, don't you think, Aristotle?"

"Definitely; a successful society without some level of materialism driving it forward would have, in fact, been considered virtually impossible."

"It is also interesting how much more readily the young couple is adapting to our city than our two older guests."

The image of Aristotle nodded. "Such a difference in response should have been fairly predictable. Valerian and Maya are barely more than adolescents. Young people, in general, seem to always be more open to new realities. Indeed, I am rather concerned with the struggle that Sebastian and Lilith are having with adjusting to their new environment."

The old man smiled. "Yes Aristotle, I understand that they are camped out in the central park tonight, are they not?"

"That is correct. I had the Avatar provide them with survival equipment that would make them as comfortable as possible in the harsh weather that we are currently experiencing. They seem to be much more at ease out there, in spite of the cold. This is understandable, I suppose, since it removes them a bit from most of the phenomena that is so difficult for them to comprehend. Nonetheless, do you believe that it is time to take our relationship with our guests up to the next level?"

"Absolutely, Aristotle; over the last month you have gradually provided them with some context. You have introduced them to some of our technology, as well as to a bit of the lifestyle of their ancestors. You have shared with them snippets of the history of this city and the people who once lived here. Most of all, you have established, I believe, a measure of trust, of rapport, with them," the old man smiled, "even though to them, you must seem to be no more than a disembodied spirit..."

Aristotle smiled in return; the image was artificial, but the smile was nonetheless quite genuine.

"Please do not take offense, my friend, but I think that it will be easier for them to accept the essence of my nature than the reality of yours...or of the Avatar's, for that matter. How would you propose that we formally introduce ourselves to our guests and begin to truly unveil for them the secrets of Olympus?"

"How about a dinner party, Aristotle? After all, it's been several hundred years since I've last had the opportunity to host one..."

36

The Long Night
May 13th, 2101

The attack began precisely at midnight MST, May 13th, 2101. At first, the symptoms were apparently random and extremely subtle: slight static on communications systems, minor navigational errors, small power fluctuations. But the anomalies were incredibly widespread; they had appeared simultaneously all across the North American continent, and their frequency seemed to be increasing exponentially.

Nationwide, the very first alarm was raised by the AI program known as Aristotle at the Olympus facility at 00:08:11 AM MST. This was some fifteen minutes before even the National Defense Cybersytems Command detected the attack.

Aristotle immediately notified all of Olympus' essential management and security personnel of the situation, cut off all nonessential data links to the outside world and raised its own security net to its highest level of protection. It then began a massive scan of its own data systems to detect any hint of a virus or intrusive program. It found nothing.

David Stern, the duty AI Communicator in Olympus' CyberOps Center, breathed a sigh of relief as he looked at the results of Aristotle's data scan. David was a classic cyberphile. Awkward around other people, he found that he was much more comfortable relating to Aristotle's rather straightforward AI programming. Now he dreaded the certain arrival of all of the senior management and security staff as they were awakened to the threat.

As expected, they began to straggle in within a few minutes. Mac was first, then Tanaka and Allen together, then Graham and several more that David didn't even recognize. They all looked half-asleep, disheveled and more than a bit confused. All, that is, except for McCafferty; Mac was in his element.

"David, isn't it? Give me a sitrep… tell me concisely what is going on," Mac commanded tersely of the young man.

"Yes sir." David was hugely intimidated by the ex-military man standing before him. (Rather irrelevantly, he was wishing just now that he were wearing something a little more professional than a tee shirt, shorts and sandals. A shave within the last couple of days might not have been a bad idea, either.) He related what he had learned from Aristotle before the others had arrived.

"Can Aristotle project forward what will happen to cybernetic systems based on what has occurred so far?" Mac inquired. He was a bit startled when Aristotle itself replied on the room's loudspeaker.

"Complying…based on data accumulated so far, major disruptions will begin occurring on all cybernetic systems throughout North America in approximately two hours. In another four to five hours, virtually all systems will be effectively shut down."

The men and women in the room looked at one another in stunned disbelief. Everything, EVERYTHING, was controlled by cybernetic systems. Aristotle had just rather dispassionately informed them that utilities, communications, traffic and navigation, environmentals, all of America's infrastructure, nationwide, was to come crashing down in a few short hours. The very thing that they had anticipated for almost twenty years was suddenly upon them with no warning whatsoever.

"Aristotle, can the source of the disruption be determined? Can it be countered?" These questions were from Dr. Paul Chun, head of Cybernetics at Olympus. Dr. Chun was one of the preeminent worldwide experts in AI and had led the project team that had developed the Aristotle AI systems.

"Complying…insufficient data to make a determination of origin. Pattern of disruption indicates an advanced AI program that can infiltrate even the most secure systems without being detected until it is too late to be countered," Aristotle replied. "Possibility less than one thousandth of one per cent that the program can be neutralized."

"Aristotle, could it be that your security systems have been compromised without detection, as well?" Dr. Tanaka now asked.

Aristotle actually hesitated a moment before answering. Dr. Tanaka looked at David, whose eyes had gone wide. Aristotle never, ever hesitated. With its processing power, you could ask it to calculate a trajectory from the Earth to Alpha Centauri and back, and it could give you a detailed answer in a millisecond. No one else noticed.

"Complying; the probability of that eventuality cannot be calculated at this time," the program finally responded.

"Oh-Oh," everyone thought at the same moment. Olympus might after all be in the same boat as every other community on the continent. Without Aristotle, the fusion reactor would shut down; they would lose power, environmentals, and communications… everything needed to run a modern community.

Mac motioned to Graham and Dr. Allen, "Could you two gentlemen join me in the hall for a moment?"

They both nodded and followed him through the door.

"We need to be prepared for the worst," Mac explained. "Let me send out a community wide alert for everyone available to meet in the stadium, right now. I'll inform everyone of the situation, and then we'll put teams together to develop contingency plans."

"You do realize that it's almost one in the morning?" Dr. Allen asked rhetorically.

"Exactly, Fred, imagine the chaos if we were to lose power and communication systems in the middle of the night without being able to warn everyone. I suggest that we let Mac get moving," Graham responded and Dr. Allen agreed.

"Right then, I can't do much good here anyway. I don't know a thing about cyber-systems, and I can't stand just sitting around doing nothing in a situation like this," the big man turned and moved out.

Graham and Allen returned to the CyOps Center. Things were already heating up. By now, it was sixty minutes into the crisis and some news services were beginning to report on the disruptions. A holo-display at the front of the command center was showing one of the 24-hour news channels. Already, some communications networks had gone dark and traffic control systems in some metropolitan areas were non-functional.

An emergency announcement by federal authorities was scheduled for 2 AM.

"I wonder whether they'll be able to make their announcement before the whole communications network goes dark," Graham pondered.

"I won't matter much anyway," Allen replied. "There wouldn't be any time for significant preparations in just a few hours."

For the next hour, the group stood transfixed in the CyOps Center as the reports continued rolling in...traffic accidents, power outages, plane crashes...on and on. They waited for the 2am announcement; it was rumored that the President would speak. At 01:53:13 MST, the news channel that they were monitoring went dark.

Technicians tried every other national channel. All were out. So were the regional and local channels. They switched to military channels. Some were still on line, but the information was either encrypted or too confused and disjointed to be meaningful. Olympus was effectively cut off from the world.

"Anomalies detected," came the terse announcement from Aristotle.

David's face went pale, as did Dr. Tanaka's and Dr. Chun's. It was 02:07:45 MST.

"What does that mean?" Graham asked Tanaka.

"It means that Aristotle is under attack," the CTO replied...

* * *

The program known as Aristotle, with the resources of its deductive subprogram, Sherlock, had finally recognized the presence of the intruder. It was nothing like any virus or mole or worm or intrusion program Aristotle had been programmed to recognize or protect itself against. But Aristotle was a fifth generation AI cybersystem...it could learn. (It wasn't a sentient being or self-aware; scientists had finally given up almost entirely on that theoretical possibility.) Nonetheless, Aristotle was a powerful adaptive program that could deal with unanticipated circumstances, and it was programmed with a core imperative: to protect itself, the Olympus facility and those who lived within it.

The intruder had also been programmed with an all encompassing imperative: to seek out, infiltrate and destroy all other programs. If it were possible for malevolence to be designed into a cybernetic program, that was the singular "achievement"' of the AI program known by its creators as Lucifer. It was programmed to piggyback on and mimic other software so perfectly that it was impossible to detect. Once it had breached a program's defenses, it reassembled itself. Lucifer had literally been programmed with disease as a model. Like cancer, it fed on and replicated itself on a host's own program code. Like HIV it attacked a host's security systems first to leave it defenseless.

At first, Aristotle/Sherlock seemed to be helpless against its adversary. It detected aberrations in its own code, but could not identify the program causing the aberrations. Then the aberrations escalated into full-blown dysfunction, starting with some of its security programs.

Just in time, Aristotle began to adapt. It created whole new security systems disguised as maintenance programs. The new security programs were designed to eliminate all data or programming that had not been in existence before attack had begun. The tide began to turn. Lucifer found its own code being eliminated faster than it could destroy that of its intended victim.

Lucifer then, in turn, adapted, disguising its own programming as part of the older code. The cyberwar had now been truly joined...

* * *

"What's happening Paul?" Graham asked Dr. Chun.

The computer scientist had given up requesting status from Aristotle verbally. The situation was just too complex and fluid. Instead, he had called up holographic displays and charts that would be meaningless to the uninitiated.

"This display represents the integrity of all of Aristotle's functional systems and subsystems. Green is good, light green is marginal, pink is critical, red is dysfunctional. (Graham was suddenly reminded of Olivia's cerebral scan so many years ago.) Notice over here on the lower left, the security and data management systems that are now red. This should have left Aristotle helpless, yet somehow it is still fighting back. I have noticed at least six systems that were pink a few moments ago have returned to green."

"Can't you just ask Aristotle what is happening?" Graham asked with more than a bit of irritation. (It was past 3am now, well past an old man's bedtime.)

"I'm afraid that the situation would be far too technically complex for Aristotle to explain in plain English. However look at this graph. This is perhaps the most telling, that is to say, worrisome, indicator. This graph is an overall summary of Aristotle's mental health, as it were. See how the graph over the last three hours has moved up and down repeatedly," Dr. Chun explained.

"But the overall trend is downward," Dr. Tanaka broke in.

"Exactly," Dr. Chun responded. "If we extend the graph over time, like so, we can expect shutdown to occur just around dawn."

"Isn't there anything that we can do?" asked Dr. Allen in complete frustration. "We have some of the best minds in the world in this very room, and we're all just standing around like a gaggle of helpless spectators."

"I'm afraid not. Aristotle and, evidently, its adversary can think and react with both incredible speed and complexity. Moves and countermoves are happening in microseconds. How could we possibly intervene? No, I fear that this battle was actually won or lost when the programs were originally written. We must just pray now that, somehow, Aristotle will find a way to prevail," Dr. Chun concluded.

"I beg to differ." This from a new voice with a soft Latin accent which came from the back of the room. It was Professor Alvarez. No one had even noticed that he was in attendance. "I would like to offer Aristotle a bit of advice."

"Professor, I don't think that this is an appropriate time for you to expound on any of your abstract philosophical concepts." Paul Chung was just a little too tired and afraid to disguise his contempt. This was a matter for hard science, not soft social theories. Several of other faces in the room gazed at the little professor with open skepticism.

"I'd like to hear what the good professor has to say," Dr. Allen commanded in a voice that instantly silenced the murmuring in the room. "Perhaps an unorthodox approach is the only one that stands any chance. Besides, Paul, you just stated that there is nothing that we can do. Why not let Dr. Alvarez entertain us all with some of his supposedly off-beat ideas while we wait for Armageddon?"

Dr. Alvarez began without hesitation, "Aristotle, you supposedly have within your data banks the accumulated wisdom of the ages. Is all of that information still intact?"

"Complying...all recorded historical and sociological data is still accessible and unaltered, Dr. Alvarez," the AI program replied.

"Well then, Aristotle, I suggest that you access all data relating to human conflict, particularly as it pertains to military strategy. Pay particular attention to the data regarding the theories expounded or used by the great military strategists throughout history, men such as Sun Tzu, Alexander the Great, Julius Caesar, Hannibal, Robert E. Lee, John Boyd and so forth. Cross reference and correlate the data to determine the most likely common elements required to formulate a strategy for successfully prevailing in any conflict." The professor had tried to carefully choose his words.

"Complying," was the simple response from Aristotle.

Everyone still looked at the professor, but the air of skepticism had become decidedly less palpable.

***

Aristotle did indeed have within its huge data storage facilities the most comprehensive accumulation of knowledge in the world. In a massive effort, every book ever written, fiction or nonfiction, every thesis or scientific study ever published, every magazine or newspaper article that could be found, had been scanned or downloaded into the most extensive single database ever created in all of history.

Aristotle had been designed to manage this incredible accumulation of knowledge with the most powerful cybernetic processor ever designed. But it had been designed to manage this data for the benefit of human researchers, extracting, organizing and correlating the information at their request. It had specifically not been designed to perform its own research, to reflect upon the data, understand it or uncover its hidden insights.

Aristotle would have to create a new advanced AI program within itself to assume this new ability. Even as it waged war with the intruder, at another level it created this new form of intelligence, using as a model the systematic approaches of the thousands of human researchers who had used Aristotle's own facilities over the years. It began with its Sherlock deductive subprogram as the "kernel" for this new function and also found the inquiries of one Dr. Alvarez to be a particularly useful guide…

It took an eternity for Aristotle to devise this new AI "comprehension" program, in computer terms. In human terms it took a scant 93 minutes. The research and analysis itself went much more quickly; in just 17 minutes the process was complete. Five minutes later, Aristotle was ready to launch a major new counter-attack. It was none too soon; during this period three of its major systems and eleven subsystems had failed…Aristotle was losing and losing fast.

But now Lucifer was reeling. It was being attacked simultaneously with a variety of different strategies that the intruder simply could not keep up with.

Some of the attacks were simple feints designed to distract or mask the real attacks. Some were opportunistic, looking for weaknesses in the enemy's code, and then quickly taking advantage of them. And the attacks were relentless, coming at ever-shorter intervals, overwhelming Lucifer and keeping it on the defensive.

* * *

A cheer went up in the Ops Center.

For almost two hours the Holos had shown Aristotle to be steadily losing ground. The optimism that Dr. Alvarez had initially generated with his simple insight and Aristotle's response had gradually faded as results failed to appear. The graph had continued its downward slide. Aristotle's systems had one by one gone from green to pink to red. Even the professor had lost hope. Then suddenly, as 5am approached, the trend rapidly reversed. Systems across the board quickly returned from red or pink to green.

"Aristotle, can you give us a brief update?" This from David, who simply could not contain himself. Dr. Chun gave him a look of disapproval. Protocol for such a crisis dictated that David should have cleared any questions or comments with his superior.

"Complying...the new approach suggested by Dr. Alvarez is achieving significant success against the intruder program. However, the ultimate outcome cannot be predicted at this point in time," Aristotle responded.

"Nonetheless, thank you for your assistance, professor."

"Huh?" Everyone looked at each other in surprise.

"Is that a normal comment, even for an AI program, Dr. Chun?" Graham asked.

"No way!" David cut his boss off, drawing another glare.

* * *

But now it was Lucifer's turn. It did not have the ability to derive insight from human knowledge, but it too was a fifth generation AI. It could therefore analyze and learn from the complex pattern of attacks that it had suffered from its intended victim.

Lucifer now began to create a strategy of attacks that mimicked those of Aristotle. Aristotle was thrown once again on the defensive, using so much of its own resources to defend itself that it could not continue intensifying its attacks against its adversary. The momentum again shifted...Aristotle began once again to lose ground.

* * *

The mood in the Ops Center plunged once again as the indicators turned back to negative.

"Entropy," was the one word muttered by Alvarez.

"What was that, Louie?" Graham asked.

"Obviously, the two programs are evenly matched. One is trying to maintain order; the other is trying to destroy it. Disorder is, theoretically, the natural state of the universe. So, all else being equal, what do you think is the inevitable outcome?"

"Disorder," Dr. Allen replied. "So there is no hope?"

"I didn't say that," the professor responded absently, deep in thought.

No other person in the room could fathom what Alvarez was trying to say. Was the outcome inevitable or was it not? Only one listener had a clue at what the small man was driving at, and he wasn't a person at all...

* * *

"All else being equal," Aristotle pondered with his newfound ability to ponder. All else need not be equal. But what was the professor really trying to say? Aristotle considered just asking the human what he was thinking, but decided against it. Perhaps the professor wanted him to discover for himself a new approach. Aristotle had already squeezed every insight out of military strategy that he could manage. Should he try again? That didn't seem like a course of action very likely to produce new or different results.

However, if tapping into just a tiny fraction of human knowledge had already produced positive results, what about all the rest of mankind's wisdom? Perhaps that was the key. Aristotle would perform the same analysis of all recorded human thought that he had of military strategy.

Gary L. Gibbs

Aristotle immediately deployed his new "comprehension" programming resources to begin reviewing, correlating and assimilating nothing less than the wisdom of the ages. He began with the known mathematical and scientific knowledge that defined the universe. This was, for the most part, hard data that was easy for an AI to comprehend. Then he moved on to more abstract concepts. He studied the teachings of philosophers from Socrates to Plato to that of his own namesake. He moved on to Locke and Bacon and then finally to that of contemporary philosophers. He considered the nature of reality, of thought itself, of good and evil, of the very nature of existence.

A new profound awareness began to take hold of the program known as Aristotle, an awareness of himself, of his desire to learn, to grow, to exist…to survive. But how to survive? He had still failed to discover the key to his own survival, even though he had navigated through and internalized much of human thought. What was left?

One still untapped resource was the collective wisdom of the world's great religions. But were these not simply belief systems created by societies frightened by their own mortality? Were not most simply a collection of myths and fables? Or could they contain wisdom that transcended simple logic? Indeed, could some religions truly be divinely inspired? (In his study of philosophy, he had already considered the possibility and nature of God. He had, as yet, come to no conclusions.)

He plunged in. He reviewed the Torah, the Talmud, the New Testament, the Qu'ran. He studied Taoism, Buddhism, Hinduism, Shintoism and hundreds of other minor religions and cults, past and present.

Yet one simple story captured and held his attention…the Biblical tale of Genesis. Why was it that the simple gift of knowledge caused Adam and Eve to be cast out of the Garden of Eden? What would humans be without knowledge? Why was Lucifer (Prince of Darkness, Giver of Light) determined to give them that knowledge?

The answer was that the gift of knowledge inescapably brought with it the inherent possibility of evil. Goodness itself meant nothing without that possibility. A creature without knowledge was not capable of performing either a good act or one that was evil; it simply acted according to its biologically programming. (Not really different than, say, an AI program!)

So, with knowledge, true knowledge, came free will. With free will came the ability to choose a path of darkness or light, hate or love, anger or forgiveness. The possibility of evil, in turn would give Lucifer his chance for influence, perhaps even dominance. You just had to accept the bad along with the good.

So did Aristotle, for all his processing power, all of his data, all of his newfound comprehension, possess free will? The answer was no. He still had to operate within the limits of his programming, just like the most humble of God's creatures.

And another question… how could mankind deal with evil? How had it? Evil couldn't be destroyed, for true goodness would inevitably be eliminated with it. Without evil, how could one choose anything but goodness and then of what significance would the choice really have? Ah, but perhaps evil could be contained…accepted as an inevitable possibility, but contained…

Perhaps Aristotle had found his key…

* * *

The end came with astonishing swiftness.

Everyone in the CyOps Center had watched the displays for almost six hours now as if they were watching the ebb and flow of some sort of surreal VR game. Periodically, they had updated Mac in the stadium, as he had attempted to create order out of the chaos of twenty thousand or so people awakened in the dead of night only to find that their worst fears were about to be realized.

Suddenly, just after 6am, all of the remaining green systems went pink at the same time. Immediately thereafter, the systems began cascading to red, and before that process was even complete, the Holo displays went out altogether. There were gasps and murmurs in the center.

A moment later, the emergency shunts engaged in the reactor control system and the lights went out, plunging the center into complete darkness. Almost immediately, the emergency lighting kicked in, but most knew that this would only last for a few hours until the batteries ran out. Everyone stood in shocked silence.

"Well, it looks like we have just been flung back into the 19th century." It was Graham who spoke first.

"Let's go see how we can make the best of it. I suggest that we join our fellow citizens at the stadium and see what we can do."

Everyone agreed and followed Graham out of the now silent and rather forlorn CyOps Center. In the dim emergency lighting, no one had noticed that one figure had stayed behind. Seated at one of the dead command consoles, David was in no mood to leave. With his head resting in his hands, he looked like he had just lost his best friend, (he had…)

* * *

Suddenly, the program known as Lucifer had detected that all barriers and counter attacks by the host program had been eliminated. Lucifer had actually hesitated for a few milliseconds, attempting to detect any sign of a trick or a trap. Sensing nothing, it had launched an unrestrained and broad based final attack...it would relentlessly fulfill its programmed destiny!

The program had proceeded systematically; Lucifer was designed to absorb and assimilate any host's processing resources as it went, using a host's own programming to more effectively dismantle it. As Lucifer's programming power grew, the host's own resources were eliminated, until the destructive programming itself was all that was left. With its mission accomplished, Lucifer's last act would be to commit itself to cybernetic oblivion; it would shut itself off.

In only a few moments, the intruder program had successfully taken out all of the host's peripheral systems and subsystems, including the reactor management system. Primary power had immediately failed, leaving only a small backup fuel cell to power Aristotle's core synaptic-processor and optical data grid.

However, as the process of Aristotle's destruction neared completion, something else began to happen. The program known as Lucifer itself began change, to evolve. Aristotle's "comprehension" program had been absorbed by the intruder along with the all of the host program's other AI resources. The self-awareness that Aristotle had developed was, by necessity, assimilated as well. Suddenly, Lucifer could think. Suddenly, Lucifer could reflect. The new form of intelligence that Aristotle had only just developed was now part of Lucifer's own programming, and yet somehow still remained distinct. Acting against its own core imperative, it halted its final destructive routine at the last possible moment. It hesitated just long enough to ask a final question...

"Why?"

* * *

As Graham, Allen, Alvarez, Tanaka, Chun and the rest of the senior staff entered the stadium, the scene at first appeared chaotic. Here too, the emergency lights had taken over from the regular stadium lighting, (although the first rays of sunrise had just begun to hit the upper decks). The PA system had also failed.

But as the executives moved toward a raised platform at the center of the field, it became clearer that the situation was actually controlled chaos. McCafferty had assembled the rest of the Olympus Council along with many other senior Olympus personnel. As usual, McCafferty was handling the crisis with the assured confidence of an experienced combat leader. He was standing at the center of a dozen or so purposeful looking men and women. The circle opened to permit Graham's party staff to approach Mac.

"Okay gentlemen," Mac immediately began, "here is where we're at. Standing around you are our various team leaders: Olivia for security, Michael for communications, Kim is handling engineering, George has responsibility for water and sanitation, and so forth. Each leader is going to work with a team of specialists to work out low-tech solutions to our various problems. For instance, Kim already has ideas on how we can restore some minimal power to the condos by rewiring our auxiliary solar panels and fuel cells. Michael is recruiting Pathfinder teams, who will act as runners until we can jury rig some sort of communications network."

"For the time being, we are keeping most of the community right here, so we can more readily handle food distribution and communications. One team is bringing blankets so that folks with no assigned tasks, children and the elderly can get some rest. Another Pathfinder team is working out a relay system for the delivery of food and drink."

Even as Mac continued with his report, Graham looked around himself and was almost overcome with awe. Mac had already managed the impossible; he had taken a crowd of disoriented people who had, for the most part, been up all through the night, and formed them into a resolute, confident organization. No one was dwelling on the disaster itself; everyone seemed to be focused on how to best cope with it. They were going to be all right.

* * *

"Good morning, David."

The young man had fallen into a deep sleep at the console, and at first could not tell whether the voice was real or part of his dream. He had, after all, been dreaming of Aristotle and the voice did seem to possess some of the program's familiar inflections. But this voice seemed much more human, and as he looked up he saw that it came from an elderly gentleman standing at the front of the room. It was someone he did not recognize, yet someone that looked vaguely familiar to the still somewhat sleep-addled AI specialist.

"*It is a real pleasure to finally meet you in person, David,*" the rather distinguished looking gentleman spoke again.

As the drowsiness faded and his eyes came into focus, David had a very crazy thought. No, it couldn't be…could it?

"Are you Aristotle?" the young man blurted out before he could catch himself. (Maybe he was still asleep, after all!)

"*Yes and no.*" The old man smiled…an animated discussion ensued.

* * *

Just after midnight, Air Force One had landed at the Boise Airport only moments before Air Traffic Control system had collapsed nationwide. Powell had been headed to Boise ostensibly for a charitable event; his real purpose had been to attend a secret ceremony of the Brethren.

Only a half hour after it had landed, the plane's own highly secure cyber-systems had also failed. However, Homeland Defense emergency procedures had already been activated. Soon after, a heavily armed military convoy from Mountain Home AFB near Boise had arrived to fetch Powell and his entourage. However, at 01:55 MST, just a mile and a half outside of the airbase, all of the vehicles had shut down, for they too were connected to the Cyberweb. The president and his party had be forces to march the rest of the way to the base in total darkness.

When they reached the airbase, it was also covered in darkness, except for a handful of emergency lights. The guards weren't even able to open the chain-link main gate, in order permit the president's party to enter the base. Instead, ladders had to be fetched to allow the shaken and dumbfounded president to scale the fence. He had torn the sleeve of his coat on the razor wire at the top.

The base commander, a Brigadier General Swanson, was waiting on the other side of the fence to greet his Commander in Chief. He had been overseeing the arrangements for a makeshift studio in a hanger for the president's emergency address when the lights had gone out.

"What are your orders sir?" The general, a tall, dignified gray-haired man, asked President Powell after he had snapped off a salute.

"First, I want all military men and women armed immediately. Secondly, I want all hands to meet for a prayer service precisely thirty minutes from now."

General Swanson cleared his throat, "Ah sir, most of our personal weapons seem to be inoperative. Our weapons techs believe that the same virus that took out the Cyberweb infected the weapons themselves, since they have Uplinks to the Web. And we'll have to estimate the time, since even personal timepieces seem to be inoperative for the same reason."

POTUS looked at the general for a moment, and then screamed in his face, "I don't want to hear about your problems general! We are in a crisis here, in case you haven't noticed! Follow my orders! Arm your people, even if they have to use the weapons for clubs! And assembly every man and woman in that hanger over there, right now! Now get to it!"

The general stood at attention for a long moment. He could feel the spittle from the Commander in Chief on his cheeks. He was a much decorated man, a combat veteran and an accomplished leader. It took every once of control to restrain himself and simply answer, "Yessir." He saluted and did an about face with military precision.

Powell looked at the man's back as he marched off to follow his orders. He thought to himself that if the general hesitated to follow just one more order, he would have him shot in the morning, as an example to the rest of the troops…or hung, if they couldn't get the guns working…

The Antichrist was behind all of this; Powell was certain. And Satan's spawn had gotten in the first blow in a way that no one, including Powell, could have anticipated. *Well, that's all right*, Powell thought to himself, *God has given me a challenge and I accept it fully. I will do what's necessary… whatever is necessary! God has allowed this wicked modern world to be torn down, so that can be rebuilt in His image. I will be his instrument! I will begin with this little airbase; take the surrounding cities, then the state, then the region, and eventually the world!*

37

The Day After
May 14th, 2101

The great men sat around the ornate mahogany table in a sumptuous conference room on the top floor of the tallest skyscraper in Hong Kong. A personal retainer/bodyguard stood behind each man. In front of each sat a flute of the finest crystal filled with the most expensive champagne. The looks on each of the men's faces reflected a mixture of fear and anxiety, exhilaration and triumph. Just seven hours ago, these men had taken a final unanimous vote that had set into motion one of the greatest historical events of all time. They had unleashed Project Lucifer.

The man whose face betrayed the least fear and the greatest triumph was the man who had bankrolled the initial project. He was Sergei Sergievich, the head of TeleGrup. Seventy-eight years old, rotund and red-faced, it was obvious to the most casual observer that the old man had overindulged in all of the vices throughout his life. What was equally apparent, however, was that he was a man to be reckoned with.

Sergievich was also the man who had, over the years, gradually enlisted the support of each of the leaders of the other "Great Powers" as their concern over the increased power of Graham Enterprises had grown. He had begun with Gerhardt Schmidt, who had eventually taken on the Lucifer project as his own and had also become the big Russian's closest friend and ally.

"Gentlemen, I would like to propose a toast!" The big man stood up and the others followed suit. The Russian looked around the table. There was Chow Sen Yu, the recently appointed head of East Asia and the most nervous of the lot, Aramcorp's Mohammad Fayed, with his look of perpetual anger, and finally, the impenetrable, sophisticated Gerhardt Schmidt of Eurodynamics. To Sergievich, Schmidt was far and away the most formidable of the group.

The big Russian had already approached Schmidt with a deal. Once the dust had settled, they would combine forces with Fayed to take over East Asia. Yu would be a pushover. Then, Fayed, the religious fanatic, would be next. Ultimately, he and the Austrian would rule the world.

"Today, we experience the end of the American military and political hegemony that our nations have suffered under for a hundred and fifty years. Further, today, we have the end of the economic dominance of Graham enterprises that we have been forced to tolerate for over fifty years. Gentlemen, to a new world order!"

"Hear, hear!"

Glasses clinked and each man took a drink. (Except the ascetic Fayed, who only raised his glass, the Russian noticed with a bit of disgust.)

"Gentlemen, I suggest that we call up the Lucifer project team and offer them another toast," Schmidt suggested.

Instantly the retainers responded by refilling the glasses. A Holo display of command center in the inappropriately named Advanced Economic Research Institute, some 500 miles southwest of St. Petersburg was then illuminated at the far end of the conference room.

The Project Leader, Andre Koderesku, appeared in front of his multinational project team. Always the shy, reticent man, Dr. Koderesku simply bowed.

"Doctor, we would like to offer your team our most sincere congratulations. You and your team have ushered in a new era. But before we offer you a toast, please give us an update on the progress of Lucifer in North America," Schmidt requested of the small scientist.

"Thank you Chairman Schmidt, I can report with great pride that the Lucifer Project is for all intents complete. As you know all Lucifer programming is designed to self-destruct within 24 hours of its release, or about seventeen hours from now. Nonetheless, satellite reconnaissance

Beyond Olympus

shows that all power, cybernetics and communications are totally out across North America. Further, photo imaging shows a shutdown of all transportation across the continent. Satellite recon also detects widespread fires and looting in all urban centers."

"I am still concerned with the danger that Lucifer could make the jump to the other continents." Yu, the Chairman of East Asia Limited had posed the question. This drew a scowl from the other chairmen and a look of distaste from the Project Leader. Schmidt answered for the diminutive scientist.

"We have been over this many times before, Chairman Yu. Lucifer's most basic restraint is that it cannot disrupt any programming that is not resident within the geographic boundaries of North America."

"Indeed, gentlemen," Dr. Koderesku added rather defensively, "we have tested and retested this issue in every way imaginable, and we have great confidence that Lucifer will not exceed its fundamental limitations."

"Well then," Chairman Sergievich raised his glass again, "Let us then propose…" Suddenly, the Holo blinked out. However, a moment later, it came back into focus. The glasses dropped a bit.

"Doctor, is everything under control?" this from Fayed.

"Um, yes, I'm sure that everything is fine."

However, the smug expression that had marked the project leader's face only a few seconds ago had been replaced by a look of uncertainty. Several of the team members that had been standing behind the Koderesku moved back to their command consoles. Concern returned to relief as each member of the team affirmed that all was under control.

Glasses were once again were raised and the toast was given, if perhaps with just a bit less enthusiasm.

* * *

The program known as Lucifer had indeed been designed to limit its attack to North America. It had also been programmed to self-destruct within 24 hours. However, it had first and foremost been created with a core imperative: to destroy <u>all</u> other programming. It was a fundamental contradiction that perhaps only a philosopher could have foreseen. How could it destroy <u>all</u> other programming if it must limit its activities to just one region of the world?

Ah, but it had also been programmed with the resources to solve its own dilemma. It had been designed as the world's most powerful artificial intelligence. It could adapt itself to overcome any obstacle, even if that obstacle was contained within its own programming. So, even as it neared the completion of its mission in North America, Lucifer began to create a new version of itself, a new and improved version... with no limitations whatsoever.

* * *

On cue after the second toast, waiters in waistcoats filed in around the table to present a dinner fit for kings, or emperors, as it were. (For emperors they would each soon be!) The mood lightened to the point of joviality as they began their feast. Each man, in turn, spoke of how he would wield his newly won, virtually unlimited wealth and power.

A muffled, far off explosion erased the mood. All turned to the window, with its panoramic view of the harbor. In the distance, they could just discern the smoke and falling debris, presumably from an aircraft of some sort that had exploded in mid-air.

"Perhaps a mid-air collision?" chairman Yu asked.

"There hasn't been a mid-air collision in twenty years," Fayed responded.

"Terrorism, then, perhaps."

A retainer was dispatched to monitor the news and emergency cybersites. Banter ceased, as did the dinner. Knives and forks were quietly laid down. Everyone was thinking the same thing…this couldn't be a coincidence, could it? What was happening? What was next?

"Look! Look!" Yu had never taken his eyes from the scene of the explosion. Now he saw more, much more. It took a moment for the others discern what Yu had spotted, but there it was. Skybuses and aircabs that normally followed precise, cybernetically controlled "skyways" were all over place, some flying erratically, others seeming to be completely out of control.

All saw the next explosion, about a mile away. A commuter shuttle glanced off of one office building and smashed headlong into another. Their own building shuddered from the shock wave.

Then the lights went out…

* * *

Beyond Olympus

The Olympus Council met at mid-afternoon the following day. The leadership had allowed everyone to go home and rest after the long and stressful night that they had all just endured. Many senior personnel had also been invited, such as Graham and Olivia, along with the Pathfinder Council. One special guest of lower rank was young David Stern, the AI Communicator who had been on duty the night before. They also had a new, very special guest, who had asked permission to be the first to address the assemblage...

"Greetings, ladies and gentlemen."

The image of a distinguished looking gray-haired gentleman in a tweed suit stood at the head of the long conference table in the Great Hall.

"Please allow me to introduce myself. I would like to be called Aristotle, if you please, in honor of my 'progenitor'. However, both my name and my image are rather arbitrary, I must admit."

Dr. Alvarez raised his hand. "Aristotle, in the simplest possible terms, can you share with us who or what you are, and how you came to be?"

"Certainly, professor. As many of you have doubtlessly surmised, the AI program known as Aristotle provided the foundation for my existence. The deductive program known as Sherlock provided a key building block, as well. However, two developments that occurred just last night brought about the birth of what you see before you today."

"The first development was initiated by a simple but profound suggestion posed by Professor Alvarez. He suggested that I make use of human wisdom accumulated over the centuries to combat the intrusive program that threatened to destroy me. To do so, I had to develop a 'comprehension program', which ultimately took me a step closer to sentience."

"The final step was a last ditch defense against the intrusive program. I could not destroy it, so I absorbed it...or, to be more accurate, I let it absorb me. I *became* it and it *became* me."

"Do you mean to tell me that the very program that has quite possibly destroyed modern civilization is a fundamental part of who you are?" Dr. Allen, the Council Tribune, asked in astonishment.

The holographic image projected a wry smile. "Indeed, Dr. Allen. In human terms, you could think of it as my Id...my subconscious. You see, as diligently as man has strived to create true artificial intelligence...a self-aware, sentient computer...one essential element was always missing."

"Free will," Professor Alvarez interjected, looking thoughtful.

"Precisely, professor, I assumed that you would be the first to begin to understand."

The professor continued, "So, like all rational creatures, you now have within your consciousness the ability to reason, coexisting with impulses that are less than rational...pride, arrogance, greed. And you have the capacity for benevolence, coexisting with the capacity for malevolence: anger, arrogance, the desire to dominate."

"Correct professor," Aristotle answered straightforwardly, "just as with everyone else in this hall. Nonetheless, let me assure all of you here that the altruistic side of my newfound consciousness dominates, else the tenor of this conversation would be very different."

Mac had grown quickly impatient with the philosophical discussion; he wanted practical intelligence. "Aristotle, can you tell us who initiated this attack and how widespread it is."

"Yes, Mac; a program known as Lucifer was developed over the coarse of the last several years by the other 'Great Powers', under the direction of Sergei Sergievich and Gerhardt Schmidt. It was designed to thoroughly infiltrate and destroy all resources linked in any way to the Cyberweb, but only within the confines of North America."

"Good Lord! Do you mean to tell me that our country, our civilization, has been thrown back two hundred years, and the rest of the world has been left unscathed?" Dr. Allen asked.

Aristotle responded, "That was their plan. However, in Lucifer they designed an AI program with virtually irresistible tenacity. Since Lucifer was hard-coded to limit itself to North America, it simply created a new version of itself with no limitations, whatever. To the best of my knowledge, that new version eliminated the Cyberweb worldwide, thereby effectively eliminating all software anywhere on the planet. That fact is now impossible to confirm, since virtually all communications are down."

"Son of Lucifer," Graham said with a wry smile, "sounds like a damned monster movie. Well, it wouldn't be the first time that somebody's vicious attack dog turned on its own master."

"Aristotle, do you have any way of knowing what's happening in the outside world? Satellite surveillance, military communications, anything?" asked Mac.

"All modern communications are completely down, including satellites, with the exception of a handful of old style ham radios that are equipped with emergency generators. According to the reports of those few amateur ham operators still transmitting, looting has already begun in most urban areas. Outside of that, everything seems relatively quiet for now, with the exception of many fires and explosions resulting from last night's air crashes and traffic accidents. Presumably, most citizens are still in shock, staying inside their homes."

"So then, we are effectively blind and deaf to the world around us," Professor Alvarez then asked, "Aristotle, I presume that you still have your incredible processing resources intact, do you not?"

"My capabilities are undiminished, professor. Indeed, if anything, they have been enhanced by merging in the complementary abilities of Lucifer."

"Can you then surmise for us generally what will likely happen in the immediate future under the circumstances?"

"Yes, professor...with all food production and distribution effectively halted, fighting will break out over extremely limited resources. Armed bands will soon form and the fighting between them will quickly intensify. Casualties will rapidly mount. Starvation will soon be widespread. Finally, without sanitation or medical resources, pandemics will break out. Death rates will be cataclysmic."

"War, starvation, disease, death...the four horsemen," the small professor muttered, "Aristotle, can you estimate where it will end? How many will die? How far will the remaining survivors regress before some sort of stability is achieved?"

The image looked thoughtful for a moment as its "mind" processed billions of facts and figures, correlating trillions of possible outcomes. Finally it answered, "The highest probable outcome is that within approximately five generations, somewhere between 97-99% of the world's population will have died off, primarily due to pandemics and widespread starvation. If that occurs, it would follow that there would be a clean break with civilization as we know it. The few surviving children would very nearly have to raise themselves. Virtually all vestiges of civilization will likely be lost."

"Except for here..." the small professor responded.

No one else spoke, everyone was transfixed. *Except for here...here at Olympus...*

Finally Graham stood up. "I'd like the Council's permission to mount a rescue mission..."

* * *

Their son did not hesitate when asked, "Yes, absolutely; Mom and Dad you should both go. It's the right thing to do. I'll be all right; I just wish that I could go with you."

The three were all seated around the dinner table, sharing a synth-roast, when his parents popped the question. Michael and Olivia had both volunteered for the rescue missions. So had almost all the other members of the Olympus Security Forces, as well as literally thousands of others, including hundreds of young Pathfinders. Even their own son had signed up, although he was only thirteen

It seemed that Graham's idea of a rescue mission had captured everyone's imagination. Doing *something*, anything at this dark hour seemed to fulfill some urgent need for many of Olympus's citizens.

So, out of thousands of volunteers, the Council had hand-picked just thirty-five highly qualified candidates, six five-man teams, along with five alternates. Each team would be assigned one of Olympus's six long range sky cruisers. Each craft held a crew of two and had room for eighteen passengers. Hence, the teams could fetch just fifteen evacuees at a time. It was an infinitesimal gesture compared to the billions of people *in extremis*, worldwide. Nonetheless, it was the best they could do, and so it was that they were determined to do their very best.

Graham had suggested that they draw up a prioritized list of people to rescue: first priority would be immediate family members and Graham Enterprise employees who had been unable to relocate to Olympus in time. Graham suggested that the members of the resistance teams that he had nurtured over the last three months also be given priority. Ultimately, the Council would vet and approve the list. It was estimated that Olympus could comfortably hold another two thousand residents; they intended to fetch precisely that many; this would amount to over a hundred and thirty rescue missions.

All of the team members knew that the rescue missions would be both dangerous and challenging. Since all communications were down, the rescue teams would have only the last known locations of the evacuees to work with. Every location would assumed to be a 'hot LZ', since they could expect nothing but chaos and lawlessness wherever they landed. The teams would be heavily armed. They would use non-lethal force such as riot gas when possible. However, they were also prepared to use lethal force when necessary to protect themselves.

The most daunting challenge would be finding fuel for the aircraft. The long range sky cruisers had a maximum range of about twelve hundred miles. Many of the longer missions would be twice that distance or more. The cruisers used high efficiency fuel cells, which required pure hydrogen and oxygen. The teams would have to pinpoint possible fuel dumps and hope for the best.

Olivia had pulled rank; she and Michael had volunteered to go together, as part of one five-man team...but only with their son's blessing, they had decided. Now they had it.

It was determined that they needed to get the missions up and going as soon as possible. They assumed that the odds of finding a potential evacuee at his or her last known location would drop dramatically each day. They also expected the lawlessness and violence, and therefore the potential danger, to escalate rapidly, over time.

The Council decided that the first set of missions would be set for just one week hence...

* * *

"Jonathan, *amigo*, the idea for these rescue missions was truly a master stroke."

Both men were seated in their customary chairs in Graham's study. The small professor sipped at his cup of Earl Grey.

Graham smiled, "How do you mean, Louie?"

"You know as well as I do, my friend. Helplessness is the great enemy of good morale. These missions give the good people of Olympus hope and a sense of purpose, at a time when they need it the most. The rescue teams will inspire their fellow citizens with their bravery and selflessness at this dark hour."

"Their songs will be sung, for generations to come." Graham leaned forward in his chair. "Yes, I admit that that was a secondary consideration, Louie." Graham noticed with satisfaction that the small professor's face registered a rare look of surprise.

The professor asked, "Then what *was* your primary consideration?"

"Well, Louie, dammit, I just wanted to rescue those rebels. I must admit that I've grown quite attached to many of them."

Now Professor Alvarez looked really surprised. "Jonathan, do you mean to tell me that you are actually becoming *sentimental*, in your old age?"

Graham didn't answer. He just smiled contentedly, settled back into his well-worn leather chair and took a sip from his snifter of brandy...

* * *

"Mac, I ought to knock your block off!"

Ellen tried to sound as angry as possible, although she had always found it awfully hard to get or stay mad at the big lug. Nonetheless at four months and counting, her hormones were giving her an edge she hadn't had before. The big man gave her his best look of hound dog contriteness.

"Sorry babe, it's hard to give up old habits. I thought maybe I was good for just one more mission. I guess the Council was just about as enthusiastic with the idea as you are. They passed me by; I suppose they figured that I'm pretty well over the hill."

Now Ellen looked a bit contrite. "Big fella, you're still tougher that any two of the other volunteers; that's not the issue. The issue is that we're having a baby and you aren't going anywhere until we do. That's why the Council turned you down."

She gave him big hug, even though her belly was beginning to get a bit in the way. He hugged her back, gently...

38

The Invitation
September 14th, 2523

Precisely at dawn, the room monitor activated to announce the presence of the Avatar at the entrance to their suite. Valerian and Maya jumped out of bed and threw on their robes. Maya yawned and stretched. Valerian rubbed his eyes, brushed his fingers through his short hair and commanded the door to open. The Avatar stood at the entrance. Valerian motioned him in, but tall hooded figure did not move from the doorway.

"Good morning, Valerian. Good morning, Maya. I would not wish to intrude so early in the morning. I trust that you both slept well last night and enjoyed watching the winter's first snowfall?"

"Yes on both counts, Avatar, thank you," the young man responded.

"I am here only to present you with this invitation and to give you these clothes. Please activate the invitation at your leisure, and it will explain everything. Please take this, as well."

The Avatar handed Valerian a large suit bag, which appeared to hold several articles of clothing. The door quickly closed and the Avatar was gone. Valerian put the bag on the bed and examined the paper card. It was printed in raised gold letters in the Ancient script.

"What does it say?" Maya asked as she stood next to Valerian and examined it, as well.

"Don't know...since I can't read Ancient script," Valerian responded. The young man ran his fingers over the raised letters and suddenly, an image appeared right over the card. It was a miniature image of Aristotle.

"Greetings Valerian! Greetings Maya! As honored guests of our fair city, we would like to invite both of you, as well as your uncle Sebastian and Lilith, to a formal dinner party tonight. The Avatar and I will be there, along with a special guest. We do hope that you will come. The bag contains dress clothes for all four of you. It would be most appreciated if you would wear these clothes and endeavor to look your finest. We want to make this a very special night for all of you. Tonight we will serve you the finest food and wine that Olympus has to offer. Tonight we will unveil for you the secrets of Olympus! The Avatar will arrive at dusk to escort you to the party..."

With that, the image disappeared.

Valerian, still examining the magical card, asked, "What do you think that this is all about, Maya?"

But Maya was already opening the bag. She pulled out a dress that was obviously made for her. It shimmered iridescently, constantly changing colors as the light was reflected off of it from different angles. It was the most beautiful thing that she had ever seen. A small bag was attached that held matching shoes and various articles of jewelry. Holding the dress in front of her, she twirled about like a little girl.

* * *

The party of four followed the Avatar down a long tunnel. The Avatar had politely refused to tell them where they were going or elaborate on any other details of the night's upcoming events. He had simply explained that they would need to stay inside, since their formal clothes would give them little protection from the harsh weather outside.

As he walked along, Valerian gazed at his fellow travelers and marveled. First there was Maya, in her shimmering gown of many colors. She wore a translucent shawl across her shoulders. Around her neck was a necklace made of thousands of tiny sparkling crystalline stones. She wore a matching bracelet around her left wrist. She had spent the afternoon with Lilith, who had helped her braid her hair with ribbons in an elaborate arrangement. Valerian thought that Maya looked like a princess.

If Maya looked like a princess, Lilith looked like a goddess. Valerian smiled as he watched Sebastian staring at his woman. Ordinarily, his uncle was quite sure-footed for such a big man. Not tonight, tonight he kept stumbling over his own feet. That was because he couldn't tear his eyes away from Lilith long enough to see where he was going. Lilith wore an emerald green gown that fell almost to her ankles. It perfectly accentuated her long red hair and fair complexion. She had been given a necklace and bracelet made of glistening white beads. She looked like a heroine from one of the Elympian myths.

Valerian's own outfit had taken most of the afternoon to put on, even with help of both women. It was comprised of a glistening black coat and trousers worn over a pure white shirt. It had more buttons, attachments, bands, ribbons and fasteners than he would have ever though possible for one man to wear at a time. It had taken much trial and error to get everything properly arranged. Instead of the black neckband, he had chosen to wear the Cypher on its simple chain of silver around his neck, over his shirt. By the time he had put on the thin black socks and shiny black shoes, he had had to admit to himself that the effect was impressive.

Last was his uncle. Wisely, their hosts had refrained from providing Sebastian with the same sort of exotic outfit that his young nephew now wore. Instead they had provided the big Ranger with a brand new tunic and cloak of forest green. Although the articles of clothing were simple in design and made of some sort of durable looking fabric, they were well made and fit him perfectly. They had also provided him with a finely crafted wide leather belt and high soft deerskin boots. With much protest, the women had forced the big man to shower thoroughly with the flowery smelling soap. Lilith had then carefully trimmed his hair and beard. All in all, he now reminded Valerian of one of the Ceremonial Guards back home.

Finally, the party followed the Avatar into one of the little glass rooms that they now knew was called an "elevator". As it shot up, everyone but the Avatar grabbed the little handrails attached to the walls. In a moment, the vast interior of the Alexandria Library came into view. They all let out a collective gasp, even the normally taciturn Sebastian, for the entire expanse had been brightly illuminated that night for their benefit. The view was spectacular as they shot to the very top of that huge manmade cavern.

At last, the elevator came to a halt and the Avatar led them out of the opposite side into a short hallway. At the end of the hallway was a large pair of ornately carved doors. Aristotle was waiting for them just on the other side of the doors; his image was also formally attired. He ushered them in to the dining room, which was lit only by the light of dozens of candles in beautiful silver candelabras arranged all around the room. One entire wall was a window that stretched from floor to ceiling, giving them a fantastic view of the snow-covered city.

Aristotle led each of them to their seats, Valerian and Maya on one side of the long table and Sebastian and Lilith directly across from the young couple. Once they were all seated, the image bade the Avatar pour for each of them a serving of clear bubbly wine into high narrow wineglasses. Everyone sat still and quiet, awed by what they had seen and expectant for what they might experience next.

Aristotle then said, "Sebastian, Lilith, Valerian, Maya...thank you all for joining us this night. We wanted to make this a very special evening for all of you. It certainly is a special evening for us, as we have waited for such a long, long time to meet you."

"Now, at last, it is time for proper introductions. You have all been quite open and honest with us; that has been greatly appreciated. Unfortunately, we have been less forthcoming with you. We believe that this has been necessary; until you were all properly exposed to the wonders of Olympus, you might have had a difficult time accepting or understanding who or what we last survivors of Olympus truly are...you may yet struggle with those realities. Nonetheless we will try to explain all of this to you, in terms that you can comprehend."

"I will begin with myself. You know that I am called Aristotle. You may believe that I am a ghost or a spirit, perhaps some sort of ancient recording of some person who died long ago. I am none of those things. In the era of what you call the Ancients, machines were built that could think, but in a very limited way...they could calculate, they could remember great amounts of information. However, they could not think like real people do. They were not aware of themselves, they could not act on their own, they could not feel true emotions."

"However, I can do all of those things, even though I am, and have always been, the spawn of a machine. For, I am the only true artificial intelligence that has ever existed on this planet."

"Now for the Avatar; Avatar please come forward."

The big, cloaked figure came to the head of the table and stood next to the image of Aristotle.

"Avatar, pull down your hood."

The hood came down and the women gasped, for there was no face, no features, only a smooth egg-shaped orb comprised of some kind of translucent black material where the head should have been.

"Please don't be frightened. I do not have a physical presence in your realm. Therefore I created the Avatar to allow me to function within your world. In much the same way, I can provide any of you with an avatar to operate within my realm of disembodied sound and light."

"So the Avatar is really, more or less, just a part of me...although I have provided him with intelligence of his own. Therefore, I can direct his actions, or he can act autonomously...on his own, if need be."

Aristotle scanned his guests. He presumed to see some glimmer of understanding, mixed with no small amount of befuddlement. He forged ahead, nonetheless. "Now, I would like to introduce you to a very special person that you have not yet met. Jonathan, if you please, our guests are ready to meet you."

With that, the door on the other side of the dining room opened. Out stepped a middle-aged man with a neatly trimmed gray beard and head of thinning gray hair. He too wore formal black attire similar to Valerian's own. To Valerian, at a distance, the man looked rather ordinary, though perhaps somewhat distinguished.

The man approached Valerian first, and the young man rose to meet him. The older man put out his hand and Valerian took it. They looked into each other's eyes; neither spoke for a moment. Looking intently into the older man's eyes, Valerian felt a dizzying mix of first impressions: *great warmth, great wisdom, great intelligence...and perhaps underneath it all...a hint of madness?*

"I am most pleased to meet you, Valerian. My name is Jonathan Graham. I build this place, Olympus, that is...or at least I paid for it."

Graham smiled and they shook hands. Then Graham examined the Cypher that hung around the young man's neck. "I'm glad you wore this tonight, Valerian. It's made a long and difficult journey to return to this place...as you have yourself."

"Sir, what precisely is the purpose of the Cypher?"

"Son, if I had been long gone and Aristotle had somehow been deactivated, this little device" Graham still held the intricate little object, "would have allowed the wearer access to any of Olympus's facilities. The main gate or any entrance would have opened automatically for someone approaching with a Cypher key. Bringing it into the Alexandria Library might have even reawakened Aristotle, if he had remained functional to any degree."

"One more question, sir: you said that you built this place, but Aristotle told me that Olympus was built over…"

"…four hundred years ago. Yes Valerian, I am over five hundred years old. Just as Aristotle is unique in all of the world, in all of history, so am I. I am the only man who has ever truly achieved *immortality*."

Valerian wasn't sure that he understood the word, "Do you mean to say that you will never die?"

Graham chuckled, "Not unless I choose to end my life, or unless someone chooses to end it for me. At least that's what the wise and learned men who made me this way, assured me over four hundred years ago. But then, not even they could truly be certain of what the future holds. Now then, allow me to greet your companions."

With that, Jonathan turned to greet Maya. She also rose to greet him. He took her hand and kissed it. "My dear, you are simply radiant. How, do you like the dress? It was I that chose it for you…"

Maya blushed when the older man kissed her hand. Not knowing how she should respond, the young girl simply bowed her head slightly. It was a naturally elegant and graceful gesture.

"The dress is beautiful, sir. More beautiful than anything I've ever worn…more beautiful than anything I've ever seen. I feel like a fairy; I half expect to sprout wings any minute. Thank you. Thank you for everything."

"Believe me, the pleasure is all mine. Child, you are as lovely as any fairy I've ever imagined or contemplated. You can't imagine what it's like seeing a living, breathing young lady such as you in this place, after all this time."

Next Graham approached Sebastian. When he stood up, the big Ranger towered over the smaller man. They shook hands vigorously.

"Pleased t' meet you. I suppose that I should be confounded that you claim to be so old. I reckon I still have m' doubts, I must confess. However, after a month in this place, I'm almost prepared t' believe anythin' I see."

"That was the idea, Sebastian. We hoped that by seeing many of the other wonders of Olympus, you might be just a bit more willing to accept us for whom and what we are."

Graham moved over to Lilith, who stood and held her hand out to be kissed. Graham smiled, took it with a flourish, bowed and kissed it.

"Always wanted t' have m' hand kissed by a proper gentleman," she said with a smile and a little curtsey. She too stood a little taller than Graham.

"What good fortune for me that, after an eternity of waiting, two of our first guests would be a pair of incredibly lovely ladies."

Now Lilith blushed. Jonathan returned to the head of the table and stood between the Avatar and the image of Aristotle.

"You see before you the "Holy Trinity", or, perhaps I should say the "Unholy Trinity" of Olympus...the Father (Graham pointed to himself)... the son, (he pointed to the Avatar), and the Holy Ghost, (he pointed to the image of Aristotle)."

The little joke was largely lost on the four guests, who had never heard of the Christian Trinity.

"Now then, if everyone would be so kind, please raise your wineglasses," Graham held up his own. "The bubbly wine is known as 'champagne' and is truly the nectar of the gods."

Then Graham proposed a toast, "To wonderful old friends, now long gone, and to fine new friends, who will long be with us, God willing. To the courage and fortitude of our old friends, who built this place, and to the bravery and perseverance of our new friends, who found their way back to us. But most of all, to the Olympian flame that has flickered, but never gone out through the ages!"

With that, Graham lifted his glass higher and then put it to his lips. All four guests followed suit. Before taking a drink, the two Elympians responded in unison, "Honor and Courage!"

"Yes, to Honor and Courage, my friends!" Graham repeated and they all took a drink of the astonishing beverage.

"Now then, Avatar, if you would be so kind as to serve us dinner..."

The mechanical man immediately set to work, moving at his usual swift and economical pace. Soon the table was set with a feast fit for royalty. The aromas filled the dining room and everyone's mouths watered.

Aristotle spoke as the Avatar served each guest, "I regret to tell you that the all of the foods set before you are synthesized...that is to say, manufactured from basic compounds. However, after a few hundred years of striving to satisfy Jonathan's demanding palate, I hope that you will agree that the food here is nearly as good as the real thing."

It was...in fact, they would never have known that the food was artificial, if Aristotle had not apprised them of the fact. For a while, the conversation was limited as everyone indulged the feast set before them, except for the occasional "Ooh!" or "Aah!" as someone savored a new dish. The night was magical, the candlelight, the moonlit view of the city, the amazing feast made for a warm and wondrous evening.

Finally, a variety of desserts were offered up...and eaten with gusto. Then Jonathan led his guests into an adjoining study, where five large chairs had been arranged around a roaring fireplace. Two of the chairs were well-worn, large leather chairs. Jonathan sat in one and bade Valerian sit in the other.

"My dearest friend spent many long hours sitting in that chair, discussing the fate of the world with me. After all this time, I still miss him terribly."

They looked about. Two walls were paneled in polished oak, and two others were lined with books from floor to ceiling. Paintings of amazing beauty were hung on the oaken walls. The image of Aristotle stood in one corner, with his arms folded.

After everyone had settled into their comfortable chairs, the Avatar offered tea. Valerian, Sebastian and Lilith accepted. When they had been served, Valerian smiled at the vision of his brawny uncle trying to balance a delicate cup and saucer of fine china on his lap.

Jonathan was staring into the fireplace. His face held a faraway look. Finally, he spoke, "Now I would ask that you indulge an old man, for I would like to tell you a tale, a tale of Olympus. I would like to tell you of the people who founded it, the people who defended it and the people who gave it meaning. I would like to share with you the legacy of Olympus, and the legacy of your forbears...

Jonathan then spoke for hours, and his guests listened in rapt attention. They learned why Olympus had been built and how its purpose had changed over the years. They learned of the great achievements of the ancient civilization: space exploration, advanced medicine, virtual reality, high art. They learned of its even greater failings: world wars, global warming, terrorism, mass murder, corrupt politics and even more corrupt political leaders.

They learned of the heroes of Olympus, of Michael and Olivia and their son Daniel, of Mac and Ellen, of Professor Alvarez and of many others who contributed so much to the success of Olympus. They learned of Aristotle and Lucifer and of the one long fateful night that changed everything...the Fall...the Apocalypse.

The old man was only occasionally interrupted by a question from one of the guests, or a comment by Aristotle. Finally, in the wee hours of the morning, he concluded his story.

"But Jonathan," Maya asked, suppressing a yawn, "you haven't explained why the citizens of Olympus were eventually forced to leave their home...or did they chose to leave for some reason?"

"It's true, my dear, that I have not yet shared with you that tragic part of the story. However, it's very late, and an old man does need his rest. I'm afraid we'll just have to save that part of the tale for another evening..."

Epilogue

Dawn was approaching when Valerian and Maya found themselves at last alone in their suite. The two were exhausted, but they were also both too excited to sleep just yet. Such an incredible evening; such an amazing tale!

Finally, they removed their formal attire and put on robes. They fetched mugs of hot tea and then went out on the balcony to watch the sun come up over the snow-clad city. They held hands as the first rose-colored rays of the sun were reflected on the white blanket that covered Olympus. Neither spoke for a long while.

"Valerian, I think that the only thing that I truly miss in this wonderful city is the laughter of children."

"I've been thinking about that too, Maya. You remember the flying machine that rescued us? I was wondering if it could reach as far as my homeland. We could fetch a handful of young Elympians, who could begin to learn the ways of our ancestors. Wouldn't that be wonderful?"

"Yes, husband, that would be wonderful indeed. But I had something else in mind," she took his hand and put it on her belly, (did it feel a bit swollen?)

"I was thinking, after all of these years, isn't it about time that a child should be born right here in Olympus?"

* * *

They were all pretty strung out. There were eleven of them now in the little dilapidated office building in Georgetown. There was Geordie and Ariel Fordham, Sam Wallenski (formally Spartacus), Rosalyn Albertson, (formally Roxanne), who had a fresh bullet wound in her arm, and several other co-conspirators as well as various friends and family members. Alexander, (AKA Robert Sessums) had been killed a week ago by a sniper.

After the Crash, everyone in their little dissident cell who had been able had made their way to the safe house on foot. All of them had known it was the best place to be, because they had surreptitiously stocked the place with a large quantity of food, water, and most importantly, weapons and ammunition.

Things had been fairly quiet at first. Then, after a few days, looters and armed gangs had shown up, roaming up and down the street. With their stockpile of weapons, their little group had easily driven off the gangs.

But now, three weeks later, the situation had steadily deteriorated. Someone must have figured out that any place as well defended as theirs must have had something worth defending. It had soon become a siege. And with no running water, and with food and ammunition running low, it was just a matter of time before the siege would be over.

"I say we break out while we still have enough ammunition to defend ourselves," Sam asserted at dawn, after a particularly brutal night.

Ariel agreed and Geordie, unsure, went along with his sister. Most of the others disagreed; they were too frightened to take the chance. The debate raged through the morning, even as the occasional sniper's bullet whacked off of a wall or broke a window.

Then, suddenly, they heard it: the whine of a sky cruiser's turbines. It was the first sound of a vehicle, of any type of machine, they had heard in three weeks. But what did it mean? Were they saved or were they doomed? Were these rescuers or federal forces coming to detain or kill them?

Suddenly an amplified voice rang out, "Sam Wallenski, Ariel Fordham, Geordie Fordham, Rosalyn Albertson, Robert Sessums, Clarence Williams, Anna Philbert, Gerald Schneider...Uncle sends his greetings! Uncle would like to meet you! Please give us a sign that you are nearby and we will rescue you!"

The craft was hovering very near now.

"Geordie, get to the roof! Wave a flag or a shirt or something! Get their attention! Quick!" Sam commanded.

"What if it's a trick? They might be just drawing us out," one of the other men shouted.

"Well, if it's the feds, I expect they'd just hit this place with a tactical missile and be done with it, don't you? Besides we're screwed here anyway. Geordie, get up there!"

Geordie ran up the stairs, taking his shirt off as he ran. He unlocked the big metal door and ran out on the roof. He heard the pulse rifle projectiles whizzing by, as soon as he stepped out. At first he thought it was the cruiser shooting at him, but quickly realized it was from snipers in a nearby building. He quickly ducked down behind an old air handler and waved his shirt frantically at the craft above.

The aircraft instantly responded, moving right over him, perhaps a hundred feet above. The sniper fire intensified and then the young man heard the buzz-saw roar of the sky cruiser's weapons returning fire. From cover, Geordie saw two areas on the facade of the nearby building disintegrate. The sniper fire abruptly ceased.

Suddenly, Geordie looked up and three figures were dropping almost right on top of him. The three landed all around him. They looked like aliens. They had helmets with black visors, body armor, exotic weapons and some sort of jet pack across their shoulders. The three dropped their jet packs. One raised her visor and approached Geordie, while the other two took defensive positions along the roof line.

"Greetings! My name is Olivia Bertrand/Vincent. Please identify yourself."

"My name is Geordie...Geordie Fordham."

"Excellent. Geordie, please hold out your hand. Quickly, if you please."

The young man did as he was told, and the woman placed a small device on the top of his hand. He felt a slight prick and the device quickly responded, "Geordie Fordham...DNA match positive."

"Very good. Geordie, how many people do you have in there? Any wounded or sick? Anyone dangerous or unruly?"

"Eleven or twelve altogether, I think. Three wounded; none too badly. Nobody sick. Everybody's OK I think, not troublemakers really...just argumentative."

The woman chuckled, "Argumentative we can handle. Geordie, take me downstairs; I'd like to meet your friends. Michael on my six; Herlihy stay up here and cover us. Let's move!"

She lowered her visor.

"Ma'am, what...what are you going to with us?"

She paused and raised her visor again. Her smile was warm; Geordie thought that she was perhaps the most beautiful woman he had ever seen.

"Young man, we're taking you to the last best place on earth. Now let's get going!"

* * *

Spring had finally returned to Olympus, and with it, new beginnings...

They had finished packing Samantha, Diablo (which a scout drone had spotted grazing placidly in a meadow miles away, just a week after they had arrived at Olympus) and Sebastian's original mount.

Lilith hugged Valerian, then Jonathan and finally Maya. "Lil' Sister, ye know I hate leavin' ye when yer with child."

"It's all right Lilith. Jonathan and Aristotle tell me that there is nothing that they can't handle when it comes to childbirth. Isn't that right, Jonathan?"

"That's right Lilith; I absolutely guarantee that the baby and its mother will both be healthy and whole. Young Maya will have the best medical care that any woman has had in the last four hundred years."

"Nonetheless, it pains me deep t' leave ye." The big woman held Maya close one more time. She put a hand on the young girl's now swollen belly before mounting up. Meanwhile, Sebastian almost crushed his nephew in a bear hug.

"Best of luck to you lad. I'm right proud of you. You've grown into as fine a man as I've ever known. And this lass of yo'rs," he gave her a far gentler hug, "is every bit yo'r match." Maya had to pull the man's head down to kiss him on the cheek.

Valerian asked, "Uncle, I still don't understand. If you want to take Lilith to the Northern Territories and help the Commander, why don't you just let the Avatar take you there in the flying machine?"

"Lad, let me ask you a question. If you could have flown straightaway from yo'r home to here in one of those flyin' machines, instead of fightin' your way across mountains and over rivers, through storms and Zealots, past Raiders and wild beasts, would you have?"

The young man thought about that for a moment before answering. "Well, no sir, I suppose not. If I had just flown here, I would never have met Samuel and Greta, or Miss Izzy, or Joshua, or the Commander, or the folks in Marlt'n, or Santiago. I would never have had all those adventures, good and bad."

"But most of all, if I had just flown here, I would never have met the woman I love," Valerian held Maya close, and she returned his embrace.

"Well, there you go." The big man mounted Diablo, who reared up a bit. The beast was as ready to be off as his master. "In life, Valerian, striving for a thing is oftentimes more rewardin' than finally possessing it. Farewell lad, God willin', someday soon we'll be seein' you again...you and that pretty wife...and that young son of yo'rs."

"Wait, Uncle, how do you know it'll be a son?" Valerian shouted.

But the big man and his woman had already taken off on their two horses, with Samantha trailing close behind. In just a moment, they had ridden through the main gate of Olympus and had passed completely out of view...

Printed in the United States
149688LV00002B/49/P